BROKEN
HERO

ALSO AVAILABLE FROM JONATHAN WOOD AND TITAN BOOKS

No Hero
Yesterday's Hero
Anti-Hero

BROKEN HERO

JONATHAN WOOD

TITAN BOOKS

BROKEN HERO
Print edition ISBN: 9781783294527
E-book edition ISBN: 9781783294534

Published by Titan Books
A division of Titan Publishing Group Ltd
144 Southwark Street, London SE1 0UP

First edition: January 2016

10 9 8 7 6 5 4 3 2 1

Did you enjoy this book? We love to hear from our readers.
Please email us at readerfeedback@titanemail.com or write to us at
Reader Feedback at the above address.

To receive advance information, news, competitions, and exclusive offers online, please sign up for the Titan newsletter on our website
TITANBOOKS.COM

1

You can always be fairly certain that the agency retreat has gone awry when your co-worker ends up pointing a sword at her step-daughter's throat.

The co-worker in question is Kayla MacDoyle. On a day-to-day basis she's fairly easy-going for a superpowered, psychosis-ridden swordswoman. Sure, we've had our differences—like the time when we'd known each other for eight seconds and she stabbed me in the lung—but over the past year we've developed a fairly reliable working groove where she keeps her abuse verbal rather than physical.

This, however, cannot be categorized as one of her better days.

"Jesus, this is so fucking typical!"

That's Ephemera, or Ephie, Kayla's step-daughter, the one at the sword's more offensive end. I can't help but think that it's a sad day for modern parenting when a child gets to say that.

She's decked out in unseasonably sparse clothing. A T-shirt exposes one narrow shoulder, and it looks like someone got bored halfway through weaving her shorts. Skinny knees look red in the cold of the room. Large hoop earrings sway as she shouts.

Compared to Ephie, a swordswoman with super-powers and issues is fairly simple. Ephie is… OK, let me see if I can get this right.

My aforementioned stabbing at Kayla's hands led me to discover the existence of MI37, the British government's department for dealing with threats to the nation's sovereign borders that are supernatural, extraterrestrial, or generally batshit weird. And that in turn led to them recruiting me. And once I joined MI37, I discovered that reality wasn't quite what I thought it was.

It turns out there are, in fact, multiple realities. They all vary in some small but important way. Say, for example, in one mayonnaise is awesome and the most amazing thing to happen to sandwiches ever. On another it is a slimy plague on one's tastebuds. That sort of thing.

Except—and here's where I go cross-eyed and have to sit down in a dark room for half an hour with a very strong Scotch—it turns out that multiple individual realities is actually the kiddy-school version. In fact, the reality I know and occasionally love is actually a composite made up of a very large number of realities piled one atop the other like cheap balsa wood.

Now, multiple realities coming together is like multiple members of my family coming together—they don't always agree. The mayonnaise-is-great and the mayonnaise-is-awful realities have trouble coexisting. Again, just like in my family. But on the reality side of this metaphor, sometimes serious paradoxical things happen that just can't coexist. Like people living in one reality and dying in another. So there needs to be something that makes sure that only one of the paradoxical things really happens in the composite. To prevent us from all getting a headache or disappearing into the heat-death of the universe. And that something is the Dreamers.

I don't really understand the Dreamers. I don't think anyone really does. I guess the main point is that they are the arbiters of reality. They decide what's real and what's not. The rest of us live with their decisions.

They are, essentially, gods.

And that's where I get to Ephie. Because Ephie is a Dreamer. She's had the power to literally turn my head into a cabbage for about a year now. And Kayla seems to think pointing a sword at her and shouting is a really good idea.

"Maybe we should all calm down a little."

That's Felicity. My boss. Kayla's boss. The boss of everyone who works at MI37 actually. She's also my girlfriend. Just me. Arthur Wallace's girlfriend. Everyone else at MI37 can make their own arrangements.

Felicity is also the voice of reason, which is a handy thing to have around at times like this. Especially, say, when you're in a moderately busy pub and people are starting to stare.

Felicity tries to wedge herself between Kayla and Ephie, but the sword has only left an inch or two of room, and Felicity, who is of a lovely figure, and who looks wonderful in her pants suit, is not capable of fitting into that narrow a gap.

"You shut your feckin' trap, you wee shite," Kayla shouts at Ephie. Kayla is less the voice of reason and more the voice of Scottish belligerence.

"That's probably not a helpful suggestion, Kayla," Felicity says.

The interest at the bar is growing. And it turns out that this pub's primary clientele are very large men with very large fists.

In some ways, my being here is really all Felicity's fault. She and Kayla have known each other for years. Since shortly after Kayla adopted Ephie in fact. While Kayla seems to regard me, at best, as a human-shaped pin-cushion, she actually seems to respect Felicity.

We were having a debrief last week, when Kayla brought up the issues she was having in her relationship with Ephie. As she explained it, the whole hormonal teenager thing was causing some friction.

"She's turned herself into a whiny feckin' whore who won't listen to good feckin' sense," were her exact words, I think.

Which is marvelous, of course. Because not only do I have to deal with a deity, I have to deal with her when her hormones resemble the cocktails I used to make at the end of college parties and just wanted to use up all the left over booze.

It had been a good debrief up until then. We'd just gotten back from dealing with two enthusiastic gardeners who had stumbled across a grimoire and subsequently grown semi-sentient broccoli that had formed a primitive religion and were threatening to overthrow the local village council. I'd gotten to use a flamethrower. Not very sporting, but once you've been stabbed in the leg with a plastic fork wielded by an overly aggressive broccoli stalk, then those sorts of things stop being a major concern.

And then Kayla was talking about parenting advice, and authority figures, and wanting to re-establish relationships, and showing Ephie where she grew up in the Highlands. And then Felicity was agreeing to go. And that was fine, I suppose, but then Felicity asked me to go because she wanted to discuss some Things. The capitalization was definitely audible. But once I was coming, suddenly everyone wanted in on the trip, and as things had been so quiet we were having to deal with tribes of semi-sentient broccoli, Felicity seemed all right with the idea.

And now, I'm in a pub in the middle of the Scottish Highlands, with a pint halfway between table and mouth, overly aware of the five large men at the bar looking at a group of adults threaten a small teenage girl with a sword.

"Is there a problem here?" says one of them, with an even thicker accent than Kayla, and with the distinct suggestion in his tone that he's already made up his mind.

"Sit down. Shut up. Don't be a clever bastard. You're not one."

And that's Tabitha. Tabitha is… Well, maybe the nicest way to put it is to say she's good with computers. Very good in fact. She can eviscerate a firewall as quickly as Kayla can eviscerate the average-sized co-worker. And when you need an obscure thaumaturgical fact found, she makes Google look like a doddering old man troubled by excessive drool.

It's just other stuff that Tabitha has trouble with. Other stuff like people, and the real world, and sentences that don't contain insults. Things like that.

"You know," says one of the peanut gallery from the bar, "that does sound a lot like a problem." He cracks his knuckles.

There's a chance Tabitha's appearance is making things worse. Not many people seem prepared for a small Pakistani goth covered in white ink tattoos, and whose close-cropped hair has been carefully gelled into two small devil horns. I'm only guessing though.

"See," Ephie spits at Kayla, "you're bloody mental. You can't even come for a nice meal without it becoming World War bloody Three. You're like a fucking Nazi!"

"Language!" Kayla barks, and the sword blade shudders forward an inch.

"Actually comparing her to a Nazi is not really... You know. Well, one doesn't want to make generalizations about what people do and don't say, but for the sake of this argument I think what I'm voicing is a fair assumption... Because, well, I don't think that's really a fair thing to say."

And that's Clyde.

Clyde is... well, the long story is complicated, involves reincarnation, artificial intelligence, and the zombpocalyse, but the short version is that he's a very nice, slightly nerdy man who happens to be able to do magic.

"I mean," he continues, "I know Nazis have become the bogey man of the twenty-first century. Sort of comic-book, computer-game, default villain types. Standard bad person type X. Or not type X. But, you know, stereotyped. Which, and this is again, opinion, editorial, not strict facts, but a defensible argument I think—which rather takes away from how truly evil they were. I mean I don't think, from what I know at least, that we can really say what Kayla has done here, say behavior A, is really comparable with, say, well, let's call it behavior B—persecuting an entire religious group and mass exterminations in concentration camps."

I often assume that to gain his magical aptitude, Clyde made some Faustian bargain that involved him giving up the ability to end sentences. Nothing in my experience working for MI37 has really made that seem unlikely.

"Oh piss off, Clyde," says Ephie. Which is a touch uncalled for.

"Hey," Tabitha and I both say at the same time.

Tabitha shoots me an annoyed look. Whether it's because I stole her line or because I drew attention to her demonstrating mild compassion for another human being is difficult to say.

"You know," says the bartender, possibly the biggest of all the men in the pub, "I don't honestly give a fuck for your troubles. All I know is you have plenty, and I don't want any of them in my pub. And you'll all be leaving now, and not taking the girl with you, and then I'll be calling the police on you all."

I would have thought he would have been more intimidated by

the sword. The folk north of the border seem to be made from pretty sturdy stuff.

That said, I have been in fights with people and things far scarier than the bartender. All of MI37 has. Hell, we're in a verbal fight with one now. The problem is it's harder to justify the violence when it's a man trying to defend a small girl.

"Oh," snaps Kayla, who I sense is not really taking the time to think through all the possible outcomes, "she's perfectly feckin' capable of taking care of her wee self if she feckin' wants. Can't help but tell me all the time, can she?" This last bit is spat back at Ephie.

Three of the men rumble off their stools.

"Jimmy there told you to get out," says the one on the left. "I suggest you do as you're told."

I think it is the politest invitation to a beating I've ever received.

"Look," I say, as this is becoming what could be categorized as a field expedition, and my role at MI37 is to be in charge of those, "I think there's a lot of misunderstandings going on here." The men look doubtful. I can't really blame them. "Kayla is clearly not going to stab her *daughter*." I put emphasis on the last word, hoping it will help bring a certain level of sanity to the discussion.

"I feckin' am."

Kayla and I are not really on the same page at all, I think.

"That fucking does it," says a fourth man at the end of the bar. He heaves himself to his feet. "I'm going to knock some heads."

Oh crap.

"That really isn't necessary," Felicity starts.

And then the man throws his glass at her.

And then a lot of things happen at once.

Felicity darts to the side, stabs out with a flat palm, and sends the glass spinning away through the air to smash against a framed vintage print of several racehorses.

Kayla becomes something of a blur and slams into the glass thrower. She's a short woman, with a lean narrow frame largely hidden in the billowing folds of a red flannel shirt, a few shades off her hair. She comes up to the glass thrower's nipples. The palm she throws up under his chin lifts him off the floor and sends him flying backwards over the bar.

Tabitha sweeps her laptop off the table and starts to shove it into a waterproof bag. Priorities and all.

Clyde pulls two AA batteries from his pocket. It's the whole magic thing. When Clyde violates reality he does it by pulling something out of another parallel reality. To reach between realities he needs electricity. Apparently it acts as some sort of inter-reality lubricant. Without electricity there is inter-reality friction, which tends to result in the person reaching into realities being transfigured into a detonating pile of organic matter.

I go for shouting. "Stop!" seems like a good place to start.

We are, for better or worse, considerably more lethal than we look. And, as the evidence clearly states right now, we are not good at restraint. The last bloody thing I need is for us to accidentally murder a good Samaritan. Well, a Samaritan. I'm not so sure about the good thing. One of them did just try to bottle my girlfriend.

Anyway, that's around the time when one of the men gets across the room and lands his fist in my stomach.

I sit down with an "Ooph," try to inhale, fail, and for good measure, stab my heels into the man's knee caps.

While he sits down hard, I get my breath back long enough to clamber to my feet.

Kayla has the bartender's hair clenched in her fist and is repeatedly bouncing his head off the bar. Felicity is tracing an invisible circle with a man who looks like he's carrying twice her weight, mostly across the shoulders and chest. I don't feel good for his odds.

Tabitha, however, is in a headlock. Her assailant is attempting to drag her to the door. Clyde is starting to mutter the nonsense gibberish that will help him shape his thoughts so he can punch into the correct reality to pull out a six-pack of whoopass.

"No!" I snap at him, with as much breath as I can get into my body. "We are not doing this. We are a government department. We are paid for by taxpayers like this. We do not savage them with spells!"

"What Arthur said," Felicity snaps as the man opposite her stops circling and lunges. She side-steps his charge neatly, and does something complicated looking with her body that results in him plowing headfirst into the floor. "Except that guy," I hear her mutter.

She is not the only one subvocalizing. I can see Clyde still working his jaw. Tabitha is still in a headlock. "He's not going to hurt her, Clyde."

"Well," says a thick Scottish voice from behind me. "I'm certainly going to fuck you up."

Ah. The man whose knee caps I savaged has recovered. I was rather hoping he wouldn't. He grabs my shirt with a meaty fist, cocks the other.

Without warning, a massive crash reverberates throughout the pub.

The fist that is about to beat the literal snot out of me hesitates. Despite the imminent danger of my situation I twist around as best as I am able, trying to determine who was responsible. Was it Ephie? I have rather lost track of her in the fight. I still can't see her.

I look for Clyde. Did he unleash his spell, send someone spinning across the floor? But there is Tabitha still with her head locked between torso and elbow. But she's not moving either.

Another crash. The walls visibly vibrate. Dust erupts from between the floorboards in narrow plumes. Several pictures fall from the walls. A pint glass tumbles from a table edge, shatters.

Kayla is holding onto the bartender's rather bloody head. She shrugs at me, then smacks him into the bar again. He groans, but the thud is nowhere near the gravity of whatever just shook the pub.

Still clenched in my attacker's large fist, I reach out a hand toward her. "Stop th—" I start.

I don't finish.

The floor of the bar erupts. A monumental explosion of wood and cement and steel. Pipes and wires, unmoored, slam around the room. I am thrown from my attacker's grasp, over a table, crash backwards, as *something* emerges.

At first I can't really make it out. My vision is shaky, and I'm half upside down, and whatever is at the explosion's heart is obscured by billowing dust and dirt. One of the men from the bar is yelling, deep baritone bellows of fear. A bare wire is snapping and crackling across the floor. I can hear water gushing out of a pipe, down into the basement.

And there, beneath that, another sound. Something mechanical.

An irregular ticking, a grinding like rusty metal on rusty metal. An angry whir. It makes me think of a thousand grandfather clocks all quietly breaking down at the same time.

And then the dust clears.

The man bellowing stops so short, it's like his legs have been taken off at the knees.

It is massive, hulking, vaguely humanoid but hewn in shades of copper and bronze. Vast curving sheets of metal define its hunched shoulders, its barrel-thick arms. Fists the size of arm chairs but with little of the implied comfort, press dented steel fingers into the floor. Its chest is a massive mesh of exposed gears, all twitching and whirling.

It stands. The gears scream. A piercing metallic cry for help. Perched between the massive shoulders, a vaguely insectile head swings back and forth. It is all round glassy eyes and broad chattering mouth. Key-like teeth piston up and down and it emits an odd string of harsh syllables. "*Da va ga sca, shna, gick.*"

It shudders, then with abrupt and terrifying speed slams its fist into a wall that looks like it probably enjoys the responsibility of some important weight-bearing duties. Bricks turn to dust.

"*Da sha va!*" it howls.

The man starts bellowing in terror again, twice as loud and twice as fast, whimpering hyperventilations making an odd backbeat.

And you know how you can be fairly certain that the agency retreat has gone awry? When the giant mechanical robot smashes through the floor and starts to destroy everything in sight. That is exactly when.

2

All in all, it seems to me like a good moment to be upright. I heave myself back over the table, find my feet. I even go the whole hog and pull my gun.

The man who was, moments ago, considering a little light reconstructive surgery to my face via the medium of his fist, backs into me hard.

"Would you mind?" I ask.

He spins, fists up, sees the gun, and decides to cower instead.

"Thanks," I say.

Then I start shooting.

I'm not even the first one to that party. Felicity has assumed a shooter's stance, feet squared, gun held out in front of her in both hands. She empties a magazine into the mechanical robot's churning guts. Things ping and whine, metal screams.

I have a worse angle. My shots smash against its massive shoulder, denting metal. They achieve little else.

"*Ma da ga ma!*" the robot yells, and it starts to move.

Its first step leaves a crater in the floor. The second almost punches a new hole into the basement. By the third it's starting to accelerate beyond human speeds.

It's heading for Felicity.

She flings herself aside, rolls over the shrapnel-laden floor, ripping her suit, hair whipping around her face. The robot's massive foot plows into the floor inches from her, then she is gone from its path. It crashes into a wall, sends plasterboard spraying across the room.

"*Damak ma shnek!*" it bellows as it turns.

"Clyde!" is my response.

Magic is a subtle and nuanced tool. With near infinite realities to reach into, magicians have a near infinite array of tools with which they can carefully manipulate the situation to their advantage. Typically Clyde goes for something that resembles hitting things with a large invisible hammer.

"*Meshrat al kaltak*," Clyde gibbers as nonsensically as the robot. Then he flings his arms forward. One of the robot's vast, round shoulders abruptly becomes its vast, crumpled, and vaguely rectangular shoulder.

Technically, I believe, Clyde is summoning the kinetic energy from a reality where a lot of things are traveling very fast all the time, but it still definitely looks like he's hitting things with a large invisible hammer.

"*Da ga ba!*" the robot howls and starts to accelerate again. The arm below its injured shoulder hangs limp. The other one whirls around in perfect circles, for all the world like a toddler throwing a tantrum. Assuming, of course, that the toddler in question is ten feet tall and made of metal.

I keep firing. My bullets keep cracking off the metal plates down the robot's flanks. The ricochets are barely audible over the destruction wrought by its titanic footsteps.

Kayla flings herself over the pub's bar, slides across the floor toward the robot's wildly flying legs. She ducks smoothly beneath its dangling arm. Her sword lances out, smashes into a seam between two metal plates on its leg. She leaps, heaves on the sword. The blade bends violently. Then with an enormous crack, two rivets fly across the room like bullets. They smash through the bar, shred bottles, embed themselves in the wall. A metal plate catapults out from the leg at a forty-five degree angle to the rivets. It skims past the nose of one of the men from the bar, embeds itself in the ceiling with a concussive blast of plaster dust.

Kayla flies free, curled up on herself, an angry Scottish pinball. She smashes into a wall, but somehow has her feet beneath her, even if beneath her is at a distinct right angle to its usual position. Her legs bunch, and she springs back into the fray, executing another perfect tumble in midair, landing with a grace that would make Olympic gymnasts proud.

For all this finesse, the robot continues to blunder on in much the same way a steam roller would if someone hit it with a pea shooter. Another important-looking column is turned to matchsticks. Men dive left and right. The robot buries itself into a second wall with a scream of *"Shna ka vich!"*

I pivot around, try to angle a shot at the exposed mechanics of its foot. I find myself abruptly shoulder to shoulder with Felicity. Our guns point out in parallel.

"I'm going to go with: what the fuck?" I tell her.

She shrugs and lets off five shots in rapid succession. They ping off the metal plating.

"No clue," she says. "Shoot first. Questions later."

As much as that is the tactic of movie villains since 1945, it does seem like sound advice. I keep firing while the robot extracts its head from the wall and shakes it free of debris. Above it the ceiling creaks ominously. I do a quick tally of beams and internal walls.

"We've got to get it outside!" I shout.

"Yeah," Kayla says. She's holding her sword like a javelin. "You feckin' do that."

She launches her sword. It sails across the room, a steel lightning bolt, smashes into the mechanics she exposed in the robot's leg.

The robot goes to take a step. There is a hideous grinding sound. It strains. And then the sword flies free with a burst of bronze cogs, tumbling end over end, until it too is buried in the bar. It lands about an inch from the head of the dazed bartender.

"We've got to clear the civilians!" That thought probably should have occurred to me before one of them was almost forced into doing a unicorn impression.

"Would you shut the feck up and start killing that feckin' thing!"

The robot takes a grinding step forward. Its damaged foot

digs a trench through the floorboards. Its injured arm dangles. Its uninjured one smashes another important-looking support column. I could swear the ceiling is starting to sag.

"Everybody out!" I yell.

"Did I not just say—" Kayla starts, but this latest suggestion is a popular one. She is half-bowled over by a fleeing man, somehow still hanging onto his pint.

Across the room another man lets out a loud, "Ooph!" and drops to the floor with his hands buried between his thighs. It's the man who had Tabitha in a headlock. He seems to have recovered enough of his senses to let her go. Her knee is still raised after delivering a powerful blow to his genitals.

"I said save them!" I snap. "Not engage in family planning!"

I try to move toward the man but there's a careening robot screaming "*Da shek! Da shnek!*" between me and him so that plan has to be put on hold.

"Kayla," Felicity snaps, "listen to Arthur and get that idiot out of here!"

"Oh, because you totally don't feckin' need me." Kayla, I think, is still out of sorts after her conversation with Ephie.

"Clyde," I say. "Hit the robot again."

Clyde mutters. His arms fly outward. The robot staggers back, good arm pinwheeling afresh as it tries to stay on its one working foot.

"Feckin' point taken," Kayla grumbles, then blurs into motion, darting between staggering feet, and snatching up both the man and Tabitha.

"Hands! Remove!" Tabitha yells. Kayla ignores her as she bodily drags her toward the door.

The robot recovers itself, props its head against a thick wooden beam. "*Nell vick shnigh!*" Now it's not worrying about the whole balance thing, it seems to be taking stock of its surroundings more. The insectile eyes flicker back and forth across the room. It lowers its head, hunches its shoulders, stalks one stumbling step forward.

"Again, Clyde!"

"Right on it." Clyde is edging around the quivering walls of the pub, one hand wafting away clouds of plaster dust. "Totally hearing you and about to make my move. Never worry. It's just I'm trying to get line of sight on his foot. Sort of want to make every spell count. Want to do that always, of course. Not suggesting frivolous spellcasting is my usual modus operandi. Very focused at all times. Professional at work. It's just Elkman's Push is hell on battery life."

"*Nar bin gest!*" The robot snatches a length of fallen timber from the floor and starts swishing it back and forth. A table sails toward a wall, lands minus three of its legs. Pint glasses become well-batted grenades.

"How many batteries do you have left?" I duck under a tangle of fallen wiring. I want to get close enough so that I have a decent chance of shooting the robot in an eye, but not so close that I get turned into a cricket ball by that stick it's wielding.

"There's a slim chance that I'm down to three AAs and a nine volt."

I pause in my approach to allow my incredulity to have its full moment. "That's it?" That is less of a magical armament and more of a massive blow to my chances of surviving long enough to watch the six o'clock news.

"Well, in my, you know, defense… And well, hindsight benefitting from the acuity of vision that it does, in retrospect this may resemble a phrase my mother was always fond of saying: assumptions make an ass out of both you and me. Though, mostly I think she meant me. As you probably will. Not an unfair call, I suspect. But as I was saying, I was rather assuming that the afternoon would involve more of a quiet pint and less of a battle to the death, and that affected my packing plans."

Which is about as catty as Clyde gets. What's more he has a point. I peer back at the exposed electrical wiring I just ducked beneath. "Can that help you?"

Clyde's eyebrows pop up and he grins.

"See," Felicity says between potshots at the robot's head, "that's why I made you field lead."

If I wasn't busy avoiding being beaten to death it would be quite a cool moment. As it is, the robot's bat smashes into the ground one foot to my left. Splinters stitch a path up my leg as the beam's end impacts on the floorboards.

I snap off a shot, see it raise sparks off the robot's bronze skull, and then I'm ducking and rolling as the robot sweeps the beam sideways, slamming it into my shoulder and making the world explode in pain.

Somewhere distant, I hear Felicity yell. The pings of ricochets. A few dull clunks as other shots land home, bury themselves in gearwork.

My shoulder feels like it took a bullet. I stumble to my feet. My hands are shaking. The white blaze of adrenaline stumbling over the abrupt agony. I can see the robot raising the beam above my head.

I kick forward, propel myself toward its legs. I haven't much momentum, but it's enough to dodge the blow. I fly between its splayed feet, crash to the ground, land on my injured shoulder, and bellow in pain. I roll over, staring up at the robot's back, trying to clutch at the injury.

From beyond the robot, a roar from Clyde. A sound like a generator blowing.

"—al kaltak!"

And then a great rending of metal.

Clyde has hit the exposed wires. Has hit a bigger power source. So he can tear a bigger hole into another reality. The robot scrabbles to stay upright, fighting its injured foot. The sound of gears crunching, metal ripping and twisting fills the world. It's the sound of victory. Except I'm lying beneath the thing. Or, as some might describe it, right in the spot where it will land and squash me like a particularly juicy, human-shaped grape.

I try to get my limbs all working together, try to scramble on all fours, but it's difficult when one of the four is out of commission, and another is preoccupied with trying to keep that one safe. It is ungainly, and decidedly ineffective. The robot stumbles back a step. I feel its thigh strike my back, propel me forward. I half trip, half sprawl over a fallen chair. And then I'm down, on my back, staring as the massive machine teeters over me.

I empty a clip at it. Anything I can do to tip its balance away from me. My bullets slam into its midriff.

Maybe that's what makes the machine take a step to the side. Maybe it's capricious chance. I don't particularly give a shit. The fact is, it steps back, past me, and I don't become pâté.

Instead yet another column takes the hit. I feel like we're running out of them. From the ceiling's groan, it seems to agree with me.

I get my breath back long enough to expel it. "We *have* to get out of here."

"Noted!" Felicity is hustling. Clyde is on the move too, heading to the far wall, circling around toward the door.

I scan the devastation. Wood fragments and glass shards. Exposed wiring and pipes. Plaster dust and broken picture frames. But everyone's out. No one's dead yet.

Oh shit.

At the bar, the one part of the pub still mostly intact: the bartender. Goddamn, Kayla. I knew she was hitting him too hard. He's still slumped there, staring at where her sword landed near his head. His eyes aren't focused.

"One civilian still in the building!"

I lunge forward, away from Felicity and Clyde, away from the pub's door, and the safety of the sky not falling on my head. The ceiling groans again. Then it screams. The opposite corner of the room gives way. A great tearing crash as the contents of the room above deposit themselves on the floor. Wooden beams and brickwork spill loose. A glimpse of the sun shines through the torn-down wall, diffuse through the dust.

"Arthur!" Felicity yells.

"Almost there! Go!" I yell without looking. I make it to the bartender, grab him, heave.

He doesn't move.

I heave again. He slides six inches down the bar, his head knocks into the flat of Kayla's blade, still embedded there. He's dead weight at the end of my arm. And apparently, when he's dead, he's going to weigh a shit-ton.

"Come on, you bastard!" Bizarrely, yelling that doesn't make him weigh less.

To my left, there is the sound of metal doing something it shouldn't.

I turn, look, wish I hadn't. The robot is up. Or mostly up. The leg Kayla injured is now an ugly twisted mess. The shoulder Clyde injured now ends in a ragged stump of broken metal, hemorrhaging black oil and something blue that could be antifreeze. Its chest is horribly ravaged—the bronze sheet that covered it contorted, half buried in the gears. I hear them scraping against the tattered metal, the grinding of axles bent well out of true. Half of its bronze skull cap has been torn away exposing chittering gears behind the wide insectile eyes.

In its remaining hand, it still holds the wooden beam. And its eyes are fixed on me.

"Oh crap."

Over the protests of my injured shoulder, I grab the bartender with both hands.

The robot lurches forward, an ugly half-hop.

I heave on the bartender. My shoulder screams. To keep it company, I do too.

The robot hops again. It raises its fist, its wooden beam.

Behind it more of the ceiling gives way. A creeping roar of descending debris, slowly filling the room.

With a bellow, I stop hauling the bartender toward the door and reverse direction. I slam into him, putting my good shoulder into his midriff. It's like running into a cow. At least, I assume it is. I've done some weird stuff because of this job but never that.

My face is buried in the bartender's side. The world around me is just noise. It doesn't sound good.

Then the bartender starts to move, sliding. Then his shoulders and head are off the bar, and he's falling down, collapsing onto the floor. I sit down hard. I look up.

I stare into the robot's glass eyes.

It stands directly above me. It holds the beam up high.

And then it brings it down.

3

This is far from the first time I've been in a life-threatening position. My whole job description at MI37 seems to largely involve being more carefree with my will to live than most people consider healthy.

Actually, one time I really did die. Well, I might not have done. I got a do-over. Maybe. I'm not really sure how parallel timelines work. But it didn't stick. Hence my being here, watching my life expectancy shorten dramatically.

And the thing about repeatedly exposing yourself to terrifying, life-threatening danger—you sort of get used to it. Once you've crash-landed one mangled aircraft in an irradiated ghost town, you've crash-landed a hundred mangled aircraft in a hundred irradiated ghost towns. I don't think it's really a healthy adaptation—in a very literal sense, actually—but I suppose it's a natural one. There's probably even a biochemical reason for it involving the desensitization of adrenaline receptors in the body, or something similar. I imagine Clyde could go on about it at great length.

So, at this point, when death is more proximal than I'd like it to be, I do sort of expect to find myself shrugging, saying "Oh bollocks, not again," and fighting my way free.

So I fight. My legs scramble for purchase on the floor. My arms scramble for anything to hang onto, to drag myself away.

And I don't find anything.

I'm caught completely flat-footed. My weight is wrong, and I am too slow, and the club is coming down just too fast.

I am helpless.

And sitting on my arse on the bar floor I am suddenly, horribly struck by the inevitability of my own death.

It will not be in an attempt to save the world. It will not be sacrificing myself for a noble goal. It will not have great philosophical meaning that will resonate through the lives of friends and strangers alike. It will simply be short, blunt, and very, very messy.

The club descends, adrenaline dragging the moment out in slow motion. I can see the grain of the wood, the jagged splinters. I can see the oil in the knuckles of the robot's hand. I can see each individual lens of glass on its large eyes.

My stomach is a knot. I think I'd vomit if I had the time, but there isn't. Maybe that's a good thing. No one wants to be found dead in a pile of his own yak.

They say your life is meant to flash before your eyes at times like these. I wish it did. I could really use the distraction.

Instead I am acutely aware of the club. Of my fingers scrabbling at the smooth floorboards, my feet drumming up and down in a panicked, senseless frenzy. I can feel the wind of the club descending. A foot away. Six inches. Five. Four.

I am going to die.

Three.

Really, genuinely going to die.

Two.

And it's probably going to hurt very badly.

One.

4

There is a sound like trains colliding. Like the world ending. And I don't remember it being this noisy last time I died. And then I think, well, if Descartes was right... I am thinking, so I must be being. Or to put it another way, I am not being dead.

I realize I have closed my eyes. I could not quite stare death in the face. I open them.

The robot is not there. The club is not there. Not quite.

Adrenaline still has me clenched in its crushing grip. Time is ducking under the usual rules. The robot is in midair. The club is whipping sideways, sliding away from me, from the side of my ear, the distance increasing. Its ruined leg is spinning free from its body. There is a long, protracted, "*Naaaaaaa!*" echoing out of its chittering mouth.

I sit. I watch it fly away, collapse. There is an enormous, ruinous boom of sound. It slaps me like I'm a misbehaving child.

Clyde. Clyde at the very last possible moment. Pulling power out of some other reality's proverbial arse. Clyde saving me.

And then I vomit. All over the bartender, unfortunately. He's still not really together enough to object. And he is a bartender. This can't be the first time it's happened to him.

From the tangled ball of metal comes a jerking, clicking voice. "*Gooten ma ma ma.*"

And suddenly all my fear, all my terror, is sublimated. It is rage, pure and blinding. I am dragging myself to my feet, heaving myself up on the bar, with arms that feel stiff and useless, with hands and fingers that are shaking, with a shoulder that screams in pain, and goddamn this fucking piece of scrap metal. Fuck it straight to hell.

My pistol is still in my hand. I advance, through billowing clouds of dust, stumbling over rubble. I hold the gun out in front of me, clenched in a death grip, my knuckles white. Behind me I can hear Felicity calling my name, but it's dim, something heard through water. I have something to take care of before I fully come back to the world.

The shadow of the robot resolves through the cloud of devastation. It is tattered and twitching. Its arm stump jerks through a repeating cycle of movements. Its eyes snap back and forth.

"*Ma. Ma. Ma. Ma*," it repeats over and over, hard and guttural. The exposed gears in its head stop and start.

I point my pistol.

"Fuck you."

I empty what's left of the magazine into its head. Its eyes shatter. Gears spin away. Metal mangles. It stops jerking, lies still.

And just for good measure I vomit again, all over the bloody thing. Bloody deserves it.

I stand there for a moment, staring at the metal corpse. Trying to work out where my head's at. Trying to find my way back to baseline. But all I can see is that club descending over and over. All I can think about is that feeling of powerlessness. It's all I can do to stop myself from loading a new magazine and shooting the thing some more.

"Arthur!" A hand grabs my arm. Felicity's. She breaks through my fog. She fixes me with a stare, looks deep, searching to see if I'm OK. I don't think I am.

"We have to get out of here," she says.

To emphasize her point, half the ceiling collapses.

I hack and cough as dust swallows us. I try to get my bearings. I want to run. I want to scream. I want to fight. I don't know what I want. I try to hang onto the last scraps of my professionalism.

"The bartender," I manage when I stop hacking. "We have to—"

"Together."

It's hard to find the bar in the fog, but the moaning ceiling adds urgency. "Here!" Felicity yells. We both grab an arm. It takes a lot, but he moves.

And I want to say something, to explain how wrong this all feels, how I can't seem to get my breathing under control, and how I just want to stop and curl up, and have this all go away, but I can't. I have to save this man. I have to not die. I have to not die. God, I can't, I can't…

Sunlight, bright and sharp. Abruptly we are out of the nightmare of the pub, out on a street in a little Highland village, with the wind cutting through, and the sound of cattle lowing to each other somewhere in the distance. We are in reality. We are safe.

Behind me, the pub gives one final groan, and caves to the ground.

5

"My feckin' sword!" Kayla stands and stares at the pile of rubble that used to be a drinking establishment. "Someone please tell me you got my feckin' sword out of there."

Nobody answers. Felicity is too busy coughing up a lungful of plaster dust. Clyde and Tabitha are knelt beside each other, each repeatedly checking to ensure the other is OK. The crowd of innocent... well, mostly innocent bystanders stares and tries to find words for their bewilderment.

And I... I just... God, I don't know. I can't look behind me. I can't look back at that place. The robot's club didn't make contact with my skull but it still feels like something has been knocked seriously out of alignment. I'm having trouble catching my breathing—

The club falling. Coming to kill me. And there's nothing I can do.

I shake my head, try to snap out of this, slow the rise and fall of my chest. We're still in the field. I'm still in charge. And that really is a crowd of bystanders for once.

I get enough air in to shout, "Someone call 999!" I'm sure we got everyone out, but this has to follow the script of confusion. Generally the British government is of the opinion that people shouldn't know that the world is actually terrifyingly strange, and we try to keep things like this hushed up.

"Did you see that?" I hear someone say. Not a good start.

I walk toward Felicity, as steadily as I am able—

—the club, falling, inevitable—

—take a breath and say loudly, "Must have been a gas leak. I was seeing the weirdest stuff before it blew." It's a horrible lie, but sometimes a horrible lie is all it really takes. Something for people to cling to as reality fractures.

I reach Felicity, put a hand on her shoulder. She's wiping at the dust caked beneath her nostrils. Her suit is torn, her hair matted. It basically makes her look like a badass.

"You OK?" I ask.

"I think so." She nods. "You?"

I don't want to lie to Felicity so I ignore that question. "We still have to get out of here," I say instead. "Before local law enforcement shows up and we have to explain things."

She nods again. "Good thought. Go get Kayla. I'll handle Tabitha and Clyde."

I steel myself, then look back at the building. For a moment the world seems to quaver.

I could be in there. I could be under that.

My breathing pattern threatens to slip away from me again. I yank hard on my own reins and muscle the rising bubble of panic back down again.

Kayla is waist deep in rubble, flinging massive chunks of masonry left and right, and shouting curses at the world.

As casually as I'm able I ask, "Can I do Clyde and Tabitha?"

"You really want to step in sexual tension so thick you'll have to wash it off your clothes later?"

I glance over at the pair. They kneel close to each other. Their hands seem to move without conscious will, tentatively reaching out and then pulling back. Both look deathly worried for the other, but then casually feign indifference whenever their own health is inquired after.

Tabitha and Clyde's relationship has more history than some small European countries. In the game of on-again/off-again, they've been off for about eleven months, but that looks likely to change soon.

I do the mental math. Post traumatic stress disorder or watch

Clyde and Tabitha end their dry spell right in front of me.

"OK," I say, "I'll take Kayla."

I approach her, dodging the occasional flung bricks. They whistle past my head, threatening the sound barrier, then detonate against buildings on the far side of the road.

"Erm—" I clear my throat. "Kayla?"

She pauses from her work, looks up at me. I try to work out if I could dodge a rock if she chose to fling it directly at me. I suspect not.

"We were thinking that—" I pause, swallow. I am field lead, damnit. Just because Kayla could break me like a twig...

Except it's not really her death stare that's making my palms sweat. It's the spar of wood jutting out of the rubble next to her.

Whistling down. Five. Four. Three—

I swallow again. "We're leaving," I say.

Kayla turns away from me, grabs something deep in the pit she's excavated.

"Kayla," I say, trying to sound as if I've lost my patience and not as if I'm desperate to get away.

She heaves, muscles bunch. The rubble shifts, some deep tectonic movement. Then with a grunt, she straightens, arms wrenching, and something like half the pub's front wall comes up with her. She flips it away. It comes down with a crash that makes me jump despite myself.

So much for keeping a low bloody profile.

Kayla stoops again, plucks something out of the cloud of dust. It gleams silver. She examines her sword's blade.

"Just so you know," she says conversationally, "if the blade's nicked, I'm going to sharpen it on your feckin' spine."

That, at least, is a threat I can deal with without the fear overcoming me. "Oh," I say, "just come on."

LATER, ON A TRAIN HEADING BACK TO OXFORD

I focus on the steady clack of the train wheels on the track. The shuddering rhythms of the train car. I'm actually grateful for the post-adrenaline exhaustion. It's stopping me from going too deep into the task of mentally cataloging all the times this job has almost killed me.

My hands are still shaking, and my mind cannot stop poking the wound in my psyche, the sudden introduction of fear. The words "The Future" hang in my mind and suddenly feel elusive. This train has a destination but where the hell am I heading?

I turn to Felicity. "You know," I say as conversationally as I can manage, "no one ever discussed MI37's retirement policy with me."

"Mmm?" She rolls her head toward mine, shrugs.

"I mean," I plow on, "how many people actually retire from MI37?" I can't think of one story I know that involves a grizzled MI37 veteran. I'd ask her where they all went, except I'm suddenly sure the answer is a graveyard.

Felicity gives me another shrug, and accompanies it with a puzzled look. "Arthur, I'm the oldest member of MI37, and I'm forty-three, I don't think you have to worry about your state pension yet."

Not a completely reassuring answer all told.

Across the aisle from us, Clyde is deep in conversation with Tabitha. Kayla sits at the far end of the car, ignoring us all. Besides MI37, the car's only other occupants are a few tired-looking men in suits, and the one requisite twenty-something with a beard, backpack, and inability to wear clothes that have been washed any time this month.

"But," Felicity rolls on, oblivious to my internal floundering, "if we're on the topic of the future, there is something I've been meaning to ask you."

The future. Something in my gut curls up defensively. I can poke the wound, but the last thing I want is someone else jamming their fist in it.

I turn away, then force myself to turn back. This is Felicity. The woman I'm sharing my life with. Plus, clambering up my own arse has never proven itself to be that useful a tactic.

"What?" I manage.

"Well," she says, "I mean, I'm not one to usually put much emphasis on these sorts of things. And, you know, it's really just a coincidence of calendars. Really, putting a date on it is silly. But, there is this coincidence, or confluence, or whatever you want to call it—"

She's stopped looking at me, while she talks. I put my hand on her elbow.

"Felicity," I ask, "why do you sound like Clyde?"

She looks at me. Her cheeks flush slightly. "Our one year anniversary is coming up," she says as quickly as she can.

My gut twists again, unbidden. That stab of panic that I can't somehow get a lid on. The image of the club, crashing down on my reason. Jesus. The idea of "now" has suddenly become fragile. I can't deal with this future stuff. Why the hell did I bring it up?

"And," Felicity continues, smoothing her pants legs, "it has occurred to me—" She hesitates, composes herself. "You spend a lot of time at my place these days."

I smile at her. It feels like a rictus. I feel trapped. I want off this ride for a moment to catch my breath. And the fact that I know this is all irrational is not helping at all.

I try to focus on the facts. She's right. I don't think I've seen my apartment in about two weeks.

Felicity waits for a reaction I'm not giving her, then closes her eyes.

"God," she says, "I've got a meeting with the Prime Minister tonight, and this is the conversation I'm having trouble with."

The meeting with the Prime Minister is a Big Deal complete with capitalization and many, many late night talks about dress code, appropriate phrasing, and general web research about the man's favorite football team. Turns out he's a Cambridge United man, the poor bastard.

I'd love to have that conversation actually. That's the sort of future I can deal with right now. It's short-term and definitely not happening to me.

But we're not having that conversation. I attempt to get a grip on myself. "I stay at your place a lot," I say. It sounds like bad movie dialog.

"Yes." Felicity nods, steeples her fingers, lets them collapse into her lap. "So, I think, and, well if…" She cuts herself off again, mumbles something that could possibly be, but surely isn't,

"Fucking Clyde," and then turns to look me in the eye. "I think you should move into my place, Arthur," she says. Then she looks sharply away.

Moving in. Moving in. That's all. No need for all this panic. Because the answer is obvious. I love Felicity Shaw. I open my mouth.

Nothing comes out.

The club descending.

No. Not now. Not pissing now. But my hands are starting to shake.

"I mean," Felicity continues, not looking at me, "you've basically been living at my apartment for eleven months now, and it really doesn't make sense for us to be paying for two places. We could rent your place out, or, well, I don't know how you feel about selling it. I don't want to push anything. But that makes a certain amount of financial sense. I mean, that could set us up with a good nest egg for later in life, if, well, I don't want to get ahead of myself, but down payments on houses can be a significant barrier, and that would definitely put us ahead. When the time comes, of course. If the time comes. But, well, what I'm saying is that this is a good first step, that—"

I've got lost somewhere in the blur of words and eminently sensible logic. I'm stuck in my own head. There's an image of a house, and a white fence, and there are rose bushes, and a rather picturesque path, and perhaps a thatched roof, I can't quite tell, and Felicity is there, and she's wearing a summer dress, and really looks very fetching. But I'm not there. I'm somewhere else. I'm in a bar, having my head caved in by a robot with a club.

Who retires from MI37? Nobody. This job kills us. We don't get houses and fences and thatched roofs. We get tombstones.

"—do you think?"

I come back to the world and Felicity has just stopped talking. She is still staring straight ahead, then her gaze snaps to me, holds for a few seconds. She searches me, eyes questioning.

My mouth is still noiselessly open. I try to force out a sound, a word. Nothing comes. I am trapped in that moment. The word locked behind the thunder of my pulse.

Felicity looks away.

Oh God…

"Sure," I croak, forcing it out. And I want this. I want this, damnit. "Yes," I repeat, going for something more forceful, and failing to achieve it.

Felicity looks at me, eyes narrow, suspicious. I barf up the smile again.

And then she smiles too.

"Excellent!" She claps her hands. Two of the business men look up from their newspapers, wearing vaguely irritated expressions. Felicity leans forward and kisses me on my lips.

I close my eyes, kiss her back. I wish it was a romantic moment, but mostly I'm just focusing on trying to ensure the snakes stay in my stomach and don't rise to the surface.

Felicity pulls back, squeezes my hand. "This is great," she says. Then she checks my face, concern crossing her brow. "You're sure?" she asks. "I don't want to feel like I'm pushing you into anything."

"Of course," I squeak.

She smiles again, though there is a slightly puzzled look on her face. I wish I could respond the way this moment deserves. I wish I could throw my arms around her and tell her she's a genius. I wish I could be myself, but… Jesus. I need to change the subject, to get out of here, so I can get my head straight and be myself again.

"You're all set for tonight?" I ask, grasping for a conversational straw.

Felicity blinks, shudders slightly. "Yes. I suppose." She regards her torn suit. "Change of clothes, and… well, how scary can the leader of our country really be?"

It's a rhetorical question but I answer anyway. "He's not going to shut MI37 down." I find an element of certainty in reassuring her. Concentrating on her worries instead of mine. "We've been over this," I tell her. "We've done good this year."

And it's true. We saved the world from imminent destruction three times last October alone. And it's not got anywhere near that close to disaster since. Felicity has been politicking like a mad woman. We're in a good place.

"It's going to be a pat on the back," I tell her. "And it'll be nice enough even if you do have to laugh at his rather ridiculous jokes."

Felicity sighs. "Yes. I know. You're right." The mantra of a woman reassuring herself. "But it's been a year, and our budget still blows. We're still understaffed. I can't move Tabitha up into a full-time field role until we find a replacement researcher, and it's not like we couldn't use an extra hand in the field. Hell, it's not like we couldn't use an extra fifteen hands in the field."

It's a familiar litany of complaints. And perhaps if we were at home, and the TV was rumbling in the background, I would groan a little inside, but it's nice here and now. Familiar territory. It's safe to look back, to live just in the here and now. I lean my head against Felicity's shoulder, letting the fug of fading adrenaline take over.

If nothing could change—that would be perfect. Yes, that's what I want. For everything to just stay the same forever.

6

BACK AMONG THE DREAMING SPIRES

Evening has set in by the time we step off the train in Oxford. The autumn chills the air, but compared to the bite of the Highlands, it's positively balmy.

Kayla still looks like someone took a piss in her Bovril. Tabitha and Clyde still have their heads bent together. Felicity stretches, shoulders cracking, then glances at her watch.

"OK," she says turning to me, "I've got a few hours to get to Downing Street. Which means I had to go and straighten up about twenty minutes ago." She turns and looks at Tabitha. "Any chance you can start the search on what the hell that robot was? We must have something in the paper archives."

Tabitha grimaces. "Analog data. Fuck."

I think she means yes. Felicity nods as if she does. "The rest of you…" She shrugs.

"Pub?" I suggest. I think I've earned it.

"Feck yes." I think that's the most vehemently Kayla has ever agreed with me.

"That sounds lovely," Clyde adds.

Tabitha shoots Clyde a look. "Help? Waiting for your offer here."

Clyde shrugs uncomfortably five or six times. "Well, you see, the thing is—and I do apologize for this—but I sort of, rather had a question that I wanted to ask Arthur. And you know, if it was a multiple choice issue, just pick a, b, or c, then I'd just ask him here, get it all done with and—as I'm sure you can appreciate—be more than happy to go off with you and get really stuck in to some obscure texts. But this is more of a discussion question, show your working kind of deal, and actually a public house offers an excellent forum for the topic, and so, therefore, hitherto, whatever, I was sort of *carpe*-ing the *diem*. If that makes sense."

Tabitha grunts, though whether it's acknowledgment or dismissal, I can't really tell.

"All right then," Felicity says. She leans forward and pecks me on the cheek. "Try not to get in a fight with any robots this time," she says, and turns to go before she has a chance to see me blanch.

LATER, WITH PINTS UPON THE TABLE

The Turf is a bit of a trek from the station, and usually clogged with students, but it's still got the best atmosphere anywhere in the city, and it's not too hard to drag Clyde and Kayla over there. We order, grab a recently vacated table, and set our pints down.

"So," Clyde says, with a surprising lack of preamble, "as mentioned in my earlier discussion with Tabby—"

I cut him off by picking my pint back up, pointing it to the ceiling's wooden beams, and downing half its contents.

"All feckin' right," says Kayla. "Felicity's away and we can do this feckin' properly." Her pint vanishes down her throat.

"Oh," says Clyde, contemplating his glass. "I, erm…" This, it seems, is not his kind of party.

I wave him to keep talking. "No, I say. I just needed… Near-death experience today and everything."

Kayla scoffs. "Feckin' pussy."

Clyde seems unsure how to proceed after this particular piece of color commentary. I try to smile encouragingly. Around us the press of students negotiating the narrow aisles between tables adds a sort of anonymity to the discussion.

"OK." Clyde licks his lips, takes a small sip, and looks at us both. "So. Rather glad Tabby isn't here actually. That was really the *diem* I was *carpe*-ing earlier actually. Bit of a white lie to her about that, but I don't think any harm done. At least, well, only minor twangs of the conscience. Not that this is anything nefarious, or, you know, underhand. Quite the opposite really. Just seeking some advice from knowledgeable parties, really. And, well—"

Kayla cuts him off. "Feck her."

Clyde blinks then fires off three quick shrugs. "I'm sorry?"

Kayla rolls her eyes. "You're going to ask if we think you should start dipping your wee magic wand in her bubbling cauldron again, or some feckin' variant of the same, and I'm saying feckin' go for it, and feck her."

I always knew dating advice from Kayla would be horrible, but I never realized it would be so vile as to contain the phrase, "bubbling cauldron."

"Oh God," Clyde says, burying his face in his hands. "Is it that obvious?"

"Well—" I start.

"Yes," says Kayla, for whom tact is more of a foreign concept.

"Look," I start again, "what seems obvious to an outsider can seem far from obvious to someone stuck in the middle of a situation."

Clyde peers up from his fingertips. "It's just there's so much... stuff. I mean, we weren't together, then we got together, but I was really an alien. Then I was resurrected as a wooden mask, and we were together. Then she thought I died, but actually I'd turned into a super-villain. And then there were copies of me that she hated. And then she killed super-villain me while working with one of the copies of me. And then you put me back in a proper body, and we were just... God, here. And it's been good, you know, rediscovering trust, friendship, all that stuff, but there's also, well, it's difficult for a man to use the word 'frisson' and to be taken seriously, but that's the word I'm going to use, and I wouldn't say sexual tension exactly, but maybe I'll say 'frisson of sexual tension,' just for the lack of a superior thesaurus, and I think that gets the rough basics of the idea across. At least, I hope it does. But maybe, and this really is the rub, to paraphrase the old suicidal Danish prince, maybe it's just me, and not her at all, and I'm a colossal fool." He shrugs once more, and takes a more substantial gulp of his pint. "That's sort of the problem I have," he says.

History. Yes. Tabitha and Clyde have history. Except really, it's not a question about the past. It's one about the future. About the best path to chart, to… to what?

My hands are getting sweaty again. I take another gulp of my pint and hope no one notices I've finished three-quarters of it in two sips.

"Just feck her already," Kayla suggests.

"I was," Clyde says, shrugging furiously, "sort of, and I don't mean this to come across as dismissive, or as unappreciative in anyway, because I really do value your input, but I was sort of hoping for something a little more nuanced, perhaps."

I look at my pint, try to ground myself. Clyde and Tabitha. Tabitha and Clyde. Their future.

—a club descending—

"Look," I say, staring into the depths of my remaining beer, "you said it yourself, things are good right now. Why mess with that? Just, you know, steady hand on the tiller, sustain the now."

Kayla looks at me like I just told Clyde to get naked and start dancing for twenties on the table. "Sustain the now? The feck? What morning-TV, pop-psych, bollocks, propaganda feck-shite is that?" She turns to Clyde, stabs a finger at him like a sword. "Feck her or I'll feck you up, you feckin' got that?"

Clyde swallows. "Well, that is a fairly convincing line of reasoning, yes. I will concede that."

I am abruptly, unreasonably angry with Clyde. It feels like something from outside of me momentarily grabbing control. Maybe it's the beer, but I don't think it's had time. But there's not time to figure out what the impulse is, because suddenly I'm leaning across the table at him. "You're bloody mad," I tell him. "Don't listen to her. Nothing is certain, everything is up in the air. What you have now is all you have. Hold onto it. Keep it right. That's all you can count on."

My hand is shaking so hard, I'm spilling my drink, which is

quite the achievement considering how empty the glass is. I force my hand back down to still it, but it just seems like I'm trying to emphasize my point by slamming my glass down.

There is a moment of silence. Clyde and Tabitha are both staring at me. I think if I could stare at myself, I might do it too.

"The feck is wrong with you, you weird feck?" Kayla asks with her usual level of diplomacy.

"Are you all right?" Clyde looks genuinely concerned.

I shake my head, try to work out where that came from. "I'm sorry," I say. "I don't…" What I don't have is an explanation. The sentence withers and dies. They keep on staring at me. I need to say something.

"Felicity asked me to move in with her today."

Why the bloody hell did I say that? That doesn't even make sense.

Clyde and Kayla go from staring at me to staring at each other. Clyde looks back to me first. "That's a good thing, right?" He looks uncertain.

"Yes," I say. It comes out sounding reedy and thin.

"'Cos you feckin' love the shit out of her, right?" Kayla adds.

While my actual attitude to Felicity's fecal matter is possibly a little more ambiguous than that, I go with nodding.

"So," Kayla double checks, "your relationship is going really feckin' well, so Clyde should not have his own one? That's your feckin' point?"

Which I suppose it is. Why the hell did I tell them that? Moving in isn't even that big a change in the existing situation. Though I suppose then the next step will be, well I guess, I mean, Felicity's over forty…

"Moving in," I say, "it's sort of a big step, though, right? I mean, it's sort of making a pretty major commitment to what is, let's face it, a fairly uncertain future."

Kayla leans forward. "If you say 'sustain the now' again, I will feckin' glass you."

"No," I shake my head. "I want to move in. I do." I try to convince myself that's true. It should be true. I am, to correct Kayla a little bit, more fond of Felicity's shit than I am of anybody else's in the world. It's just… I don't know what it is.

—*a club descending*—

Goddamn it. I need to get that out of my head. I grab the pint off the table and finish it off. I need to get blisteringly, blindingly drunk. That seems as good a reset button as any.

"Sod it," I say. "Let's get another round in."

"All feckin' right."

MANY ROUNDS LATER

Oxford has become oddly blurry as we stumble out of the Turf. I have to lean against a building as we make our way back toward the city center and cabs that may direct us to our various abodes.

"I'm jus'… I'm jus'… feckin' saying," Kayla mumbles. "Kids, right?"

"Not kids!" I try to put my hands over my ears but miss somehow.

"Shut up or I'll stab you." Kayla's words carry conviction. "I'm saying, kids. If I could do it all over again, I'd do it different." She wheels on me, jabs me with a finger almost hard enough to snap a rib. I grunt. "When you and Felicity finally do it, man. When you…" She proceeds to describe the entire process of making and birthing a baby with a few fairly graphic movements of her fingers. "Don't do it like I did it with feckin' Ephie, and shit."

"Now," says Clyde, who is somehow a lot less worse for wear than Kayla and I, "look here. I don't think you should beat yourself up about that at all. You did a fine job with Ephie."

Then he stops talking. Which is staggeringly blunt and direct for Clyde. So in retrospect, maybe he's the one who's really blasted. Also he is trying to use his wallet as a phone to call a cab right now. The jury's out on this one.

"You know," says Kayla, "I should do it all again. Do it right. I like being a mum. I'd be a feckin' great mum now. Now I know how to do shit. Feckin' hindsight and all that bullshit. Just find someone, make him put a baby in my belly." She nods to herself and falls over the curb.

She lies sprawled in the gutter. I look down at her.

"That's a shit idea," I tell her. "Genuinely and utterly shit."

"You know," Clyde adds, "I do actually agree with Arthur on that one. You have a teenage daughter who needs your love and support."

I don't think I can handle drunk Clyde. It's too much. Then I lose focus on the street for a moment. When I get it back, I look down at Kayla. "Sustain the now," I tell her, and then I have to sit down in the street myself because I'm laughing so hard.

When I recover Clyde is standing over us. "So," he says, "just to recap. Tabby. I should…"

"Stick your dick in her before I stick my sword in you," Kayla says.

"Don't do it!" I shout as loud as I can. "Everything is good! Everything is perfect! Hold onto it! Don't throw it away! You're a fool to yourself!"

Kayla reaches up from where she lies in the street and pushes me over. "Shut up, Arthur," she says. "You're feckin' drunk."

She's right. I am. And it's glorious.

7

MORNING

Oh God. Being drunk is awful.

At some point I thought there was a certain entertaining irony in programming my cell to ring like a horrible office phone. The sort of electronic bleating that would emerge were an electronic sheep being brutally murdered in an electronic slaughterhouse. In retrospect, I probably should have given more thought to how it would sound when I was epically hungover.

My phone slices through sleep and violently kicks me into consciousness. A moment's disorientation. Eventually I realize I am in my apartment, face down on my bed, and still wearing my clothes from the night before. My tongue appears to have doubled in size.

My phone lets loose another barrage of electronic murder. I try to grab the thing from my bedside table, fail. After two more attempts, I realize my phone is still in my pocket. I fumble it out, try to focus on the name there, fail, and just accept the call.

"Urghn?"

"Hello?" It's Felicity's voice. She sounds concerned. "Arthur?"

"Urnugh," I confirm.

"What?" There's silence. Then, "I think this is a bad connection."

The morning light is dim and heavy in the room, tumbling in around the edges of dark green curtains. Stacks of vinyl records propped on a bookshelf at the foot of my bed cast reassuringly familiar shadows. I attempt to rally a little. Enough to at least master the basics of the English language.

"Sno-kay," is the best I can come up with. "Just woke up. Head... ouch."

"Head ouch?"

I nod gently, then remember how telephones work. "Close enough," I mumble.

There is silence on the end of the phone. Then, "I rather expected you to be home when I got in last night."

It's not exactly an accusation. Not yet anyway. We're still at the statement-of-fact stage. I attempt to dredge up my decision-making process from the previous evening. It is like putting my arm in sewage up to the elbow.

"I went out for drinks with Kayla and, erm, Clyde," I manage. "And it went on, erm, a little longer than expected. And I suspect I probably thought something along the lines of you not wanting a heinous drunk in your apartment."

If pursed lips made a sound, then I would hear it right now. Then, "OK, I mean, yes, of course. That makes sense. I just, well, I don't know, I just thought after yesterday's conversation about the whole living arrangements thing, that you'd be here, I suppose."

Oh crap. I wrack my sodden memory a second time. Bits of the previous night tumble back. I sort of wish they hadn't. I think I was a bit of an ass.

"You weren't worried, were you?" I ask. That's the last thing I would want to make her. She has enough on her plate without worrying that I stumbled into the path of some oncoming car.

"No, no. Just... surprised, like I said." Another pause that I am in no fit state to interpret yet. "Look Arthur, just, when you get in this morning, if you could come straight to my office, OK?"

"Erm, yeah, sure," I say. "Yes, boss." A little joke, and not enough to really cover up the fact that I got wasted last night and reneged on a fairly major life promise. And if wincing made a sound, Felicity would probably hear that now.

HALF OF A MONUMENTAL CUP OF COFFEE LATER

Despite its subterranean location, Felicity's office is full of daylight. Clutching a Starbucks coffee large enough to drown a child in, I blink owlishly at the myriad of bulbs clipped in place along the shelves that line one office wall. Under their watchful gazes, orchids slowly, delicately bloom.

Along the office's facing wall, there are filing cabinets. They're easier on my headache.

Between the opposing walls stand two women. Felicity—dressed efficiently in a practical pants suit and sensible shoes—and a younger black woman I don't recognize. The latter is dressed… well in many ways it mirrors what Felicity's wearing. It is a pants suit. Sensible, flat-soled shoes are involved. And yet, something is somehow subtly altered. While Felicity's suit is perhaps a little severe, the other woman's is more relaxed, and gives off the vague sense of asymmetry. Where Felicity's shirt is white, the other woman's is a defiantly bright purple. Felicity's hair is shoulder length and pulled back in a loose bun. The other woman has cut it short, tight curls cropped close to the skin. Felicity eschews jewelry. The other woman has series of jade studs stitching their way up her right ear.

"Ah," Felicity says, as I push open the door, "Arthur, excellent. Come in. I want you to meet Hannah Bearings."

Grossly hungover is not usually how I like to meet people. Or do anything except curl up and wait for tomorrow. But we don't get a huge number of visitors at MI37, and when they do come, they rarely bear good news.

I try to kick the withered stump of the detective I used to be into action despite the soupy slur of my hangover. Hannah Bearings is in her late twenties. From her clothes, I'd guess she's ambitious but holding onto her individuality. So not necessarily someone who will play well with others, but possibly someone who's good enough that they don't have to. It's just what she's good at that I don't know.

I step up to her, my hand extended, trying to cover up how much I'm assessing her.

"Hi," I say, "Arthur Wallace, nice to meet you."

"All right," she says, with a light cockney accent it seems she's decided to not lose entirely. She shakes my hand. A firm grip.

"Arthur's our field lead," Felicity says.

Which means Ms. Bearings is aware of who we are and what we do. Which means government.

Felicity keeps talking. "You'll be reporting directly to him," she says to Hannah.

Which means...

"Say what?"

In terms of welcoming someone to the family fold of MI37, it is possibly not the best way to handle things. But the best way to handle things probably doesn't also involve me being blindsided while horribly hungover.

"Hannah," Felicity says with a degree of force that I suspect is meant to reach back in time and erase my faux pas, "is coming to us *on transfer* from *MI6*, where she has garnered the *very highest praise* from her *superiors*. She is the *bright young thing* over there and we are *very lucky* to have her."

MI6. The last time I had a serious encounter with MI6, I was running through their offices while their agents tried to shoot me. We haven't really been on speaking terms since.

Hannah feigns being oblivious to all this subtext, examining Felicity's office plants.

"Orchids, right?" she says, looking up from the shelves.

"Yes." Felicity is all smiles again.

"Nice," Hannah says. "They're tricky, though, right? I fancy spider plants myself. Little buggers spread all over the place and take over everything, but you only have to water them once a week and you're golden."

It's said in a friendly way. There's a smile behind it. But still I flick a glance at Felicity, try to use the telepathy of a year-long relationship. *Really?* I want to ask her. *You went to 10 Downing Street and all you brought me back was this lousy MI6 agent?*

Felicity arches her eyebrows meaningfully, but the exact message is probably about as obvious as mine is. Which means I'm none the wiser.

"So," I say, trying to affect a tone that's more jaunty than suspicious, "what's your background?"

She turns to me, another big friendly grin. "You know," she says, "standard drill." She shrugs. "I could tell you, but then I'd have to kill you."

I laugh. It's a little laugh. Because I'm waiting for the actual answer.

It doesn't come.

"Wait," I say. "Seriously?"

"Well," Hannah shrugs, "you know, not trying to be a dick about any of it, and, you know, I've seen your file and you've done some really stellar stuff, I must say, but I reckon if it came down to a square standoff, I could probably murder you, yeah."

I look up at Felicity just to make sure this is still reality I'm in.

"She's part of MI37, Arthur," Felicity says with patience that seems more than a little feigned. "You're not part of MI6. Your need-to-know is not her need-to-know. If you ever go and join MI6, I'm sure you can find out lots about what they do."

I shake my head. It throbs back at me. This is reality. It's just shittier this morning than it usually is.

"All right," I say, "so you're an MI6 badass. That about cover it?"

"Well," Hannah gives me a look that's as assessing as any I've given her. I'm not the only one trying to work out where the land lies. "I'm trained in small arms, rifles, machine guns, a smattering of heavy artillery pieces. I'm proficient in jujitsu, tae kwon do, capoeira, krav maga, and a few other martial arts. I'm also a pretty decent friend to have in a knife fight. I've been a field operative in deep cover for three years, and I speak eight languages. Is that enough for you?"

There is a challenge at the end of the sentence. Whether it's there consciously or not, I'm unsure.

In the end of course, it is impressive. And we do need more hands in the field.

Except...

Except every time we've introduced a new element to the mix somebody has died. Often, to be perfectly honest, it's been Clyde. But others have fallen along the way. And capable though she may be, Hannah Bearings has not seen what we have seen, has not been prepared for what we deal with. There's throwing someone in at the deep end and there's tying concrete blocks to their feet and hurling them into the Marianas Trench.

And I could be the person who pays the price for that...

I shut that line of thinking down. I've had enough of that. Today is a new day. I hit the reset button. Everything is OK. I shove my hands deep into my pockets.

"Of *course* it's enough," Felicity says. "Arthur isn't challenging you. You'll just find that this job breeds a certain amount of curiosity." It's a smooth recovery.

"Of course," I manage. "Good to have you on board."

Hannah Bearings is still weighing me. "Yeah," she says. "Totally." Her nod is slight, her smile slighter.

"Now," Felicity says clapping her hands in a business-like fashion, "I believe Tabitha wanted to talk to us about something she found in the files last night. Arthur, show Hannah to conference room B, would you?"

I hold the door for the newcomer. She slips through. Just as I'm about to follow, Felicity catches my elbow. "That coffee," she says, "drink it faster."

CONFERENCE ROOM B

All eyes fall on Hannah as we enter the room. Kayla sits with her back to the white board, feet up on the table, holding a small tub of yogurt, spoon jammed in her mouth. Tabitha and Clyde huddle together at the far end of the table, papers spread out before them, muttering and pointing. They look up, fingers still on the page, tips pressed together.

I buy a second with the last dregs of the coffee then meet the gazes. But Kayla's mouth is already off and running.

"The feck are you?" she asks Hannah.

"Hannah fucking Bearings," Hannah replies without missing a beat.

Kayla nods. "All right then."

I do my best to ignore this preamble. "This is Hannah," I say to the room, "formerly with MI6 and now a field agent of MI37." I nod in Kayla's direction. "That's Kayla MacDoyle, another of our field agents. She..." I struggle for a job description.

"I feck things up," Kayla offers. "Professionally."

Which seems accurate. So I move on, pointing to Clyde. "That's Clyde Bradley, our magician." I glance at Hannah to see if that knocks her off her stride, but she just nods.

"Nice one," she says.

Clyde looks up, leans forward, eyes bright. "Completely charmed to meet you," he says, "and very excited to have someone new on board. Really looking forward to working with you, which, well I don't want to put you under any undue pressure, or make you feel as if you'll be judged excessively, but I just wanted to say that I really think working in the field with you is going to be excellent. Very good feeling. Not a scientific assessment of course, can't put too much stock in feelings. Well, some mediums with a low reality-barrier threshold can. But I'm not one of them, so I can't. But still, confident. Totally confident."

"Rrright." Hannah drags out the word. And that might have thrown her off her stride a little.

Finally I point at Tabitha. "And that's Tabitha Mulvani, our researcher."

Tabitha eyeballs Hannah. "New field agent?" she says.

"Yeah," Hannah and I both say at the same time. Out of the corner of my eye I see Kayla arch an eyebrow.

"So, I'm not going to be a field agent?" she asks.

Kayla's other eyebrow pops up.

"No," I say. This isn't my mess, it's Felicity's. And I realize that I should be being more charitable, but... Well, I'm still hungover, goddamn it.

Tabitha fist pumps. "You," she says to Hannah, "don't screw up. I want my library and my laptops. You want balls on the line and threats of death. Keep it that way."

Hannah just gives Tabitha a thumbs up and swings into a seat.

And it's not as if she could know that it's the seat I usually take. And I'm not one of those petty idiots who's going to force the newbie to take a worse seat, but I am overly aware of Kayla's raised eyebrow following me as I squeeze past Hannah to take a seat between her and Clyde.

There is a protracted moment of silence.

"So," says Clyde, "I guess this means you're not the new guy anymore, Arthur."

I almost double take. "New guy?" I ask him. "I've been here a year now."

"Well, yes." He nods. "Totally valid point. Time marches on. Waits for no man. Lot of proverbial stuff. Very busy chap, Time. Or chapess. Don't mean to be sexist. Though the image is Old Father Time. Though he was probably called that by sexists. Though, nice of them to show support for the seniors. Not ageist of them at least. Old Person Time, perhaps. Though that leads to all sorts of pronoun confusion. Anyway, I am now far from the garden path, in the bushes, floundering in cliché, trying to find my way back to pointing out, though, that you were—up until about a minute ago—technically speaking of course, the newest member of MI37. Now you're not. Now you're the old hand. Though not as old as Old Person Time, of course. Not that there would be anything wrong with you being that old. Except, well, I mean even the most pro-senior-citizen advocate couldn't help but acknowledge that being an old man probably would make this job a lot harder. Difficult to perform acts of derring-do when your hip replacement is acting up, I suspect. Can't speak from experience, but, well, I think you know what I'm saying."

At least that makes one of us.

Hannah looks at me. "He always talk like that?"

Something defensive flares up in me. "We don't judge here," I say. I'm shocked to hear something close to a snap in my voice.

Hannah doesn't react though. "Wasn't, mate," she says. "It's just, you know, I've been hazed before. Though that did seem like a really bloody weird way to do it."

"Well…" I flounder a bit, unsure of what direction I'm taking the conversation in. My emotions seem to have gone a little rogue of late. "You'll find a lot of things are weird at MI37," I say. Which I think confuses me as much as it does Hannah.

I am saved from digging myself out of this particular hole by Felicity's arrival. She pushes into the cramped conference room, wedges herself in at the head of the table.

"Hello then," she says, "I trust you've all had time to meet Hannah, so down to business. Tabitha, if you'd take us through your findings."

Tabitha stands. She's wearing a featureless gray tube of a dress, her neck and upper torso wreathed in loose gray scarves. It gives her an oddly top-heavy appearance.

"Right," she says. "Recap: yesterday, in a pub, in the Highlands. Great big robot comes through the floor, attacks everything. We kill it. It knocks over the pub. We all wonder, 'what the hell?'"

She looks for any signs of dissent. Hannah looks slightly dubious, but keeps her peace for now.

"Nothing in the digital databases," Tabitha continues, "but we suck at scanning, so not the end of the world. Hit the analog data." She points at the papers on the data. "Found something."

She pushes a piece of blue-gray paper across the table, the edges brittle and flaking. Faded schematics recorded in a tight neat hand. Front view, side view. Detailed sketches of cogs meshing together. Tiny, indecipherable notes with arrows pointing to shoulder joints, to plates of armor.

It is not our robot, not exactly, but it is a pretty close cousin, if not a direct relation.

"Prototype schematic," Tabitha says, "for an Uhrwerkmänn."

"That means clockwork man in German," Clyde throws in. "Not really a very imaginative name, but it sounds fantastic."

Tabitha rolls her eyes at the interruption. "Whatever. Interesting bit: schematics drawn by Professor Joseph Lang."

She leaves a pause for the reaction that doesn't come. She hangs her head. "Fucking philistines."

Clyde looks around the room. "Joseph Lang? Anybody? Seriously?" We all fail to spontaneously know things. "Oh, this is great stuff. Goes right back to the founding of MI37 itself in 1935. The whole discovery of The Book at the peak of Mount Everest, its revelations about the existence of multiple realities, plus bonus details how to access them. It's the book that triggered the whole magical arms race of the seventies and eighties. Big deal. But the expedition to Everest—"

"Wait," Hannah interrupts. "Everest weren't climbed until Edmund Hillary in the fifties."

"Exactly," Clyde nods.

Hannah gives Clyde the perplexed stare that I thought I owned the copyright on.

"You see," Clyde says, "the actual first expedition was in 1933, but because of the discovery of The Book, it was all hushed up. Stymied Himalayan exploration for years actually. A not much talked about consequence in the annals of magical history in fact. I considered writing a treatise on it once, but the problem with magical treatises is that they're usually only read after you've died by the people ransacking your tomb. In fact, the whole publishing track in thaumaturgy is disastrous, but I suppose that's neither here nor there, really. The point is that Joseph Lang was part of that original 1933 expedition."

And that actually gets my attention. "Joseph Lang was involved in the founding of MI37?" I glance over at Felicity. This looks like it's news to her as well.

"Oh yes, very much so. The Germans at that time were hugely into the whole occult thing."

"Wait—" It's Hannah again, apparently unable to let Clyde's words just flow. "At that time? You mean, like, when the Nazis were oppressing the shit out of everybody, right?"

Clyde beams. "I do! Top marks. Oh wait, that's horribly condescending. Scratch that from the record. But totally what I mean. Because that's really the whole problem here. You see, while fundamental to the discovery of The Book, and the founding of MI37, Joseph Lang was also a hideous, hideous, bigoted arsehole of a Nazi. Terrible human being in almost every conceivable way actually. Brilliant thaumatophysicist, but that's about all the positive things that can be said about him. He was kicked out of the organization in 1938 due to the whole brewing war thing. Plus the arsehole thing, I hope."

"So MI37 was founded by a Nazi?" Hannah looks decidedly unimpressed. I would like to be able to take umbrage at this, but unfortunately I'm unimpressed with MI37 right now too.

"Well," Clyde shrugs a few times for good measure. "One of the founders was a Nazi. One out of fifteen I think. Or maybe fourteen. I think it's safe to say that less than ten percent of the people who founded the original MI37 followed the tenets of National Socialism. Not sure how that compares to national averages at the time, don't have the data to hand, but I could look into it, if you wanted me—"

"No." It's my turn to cut Clyde off. "Let's get back to the part where we had to fight a giant clockwork robot that was designed by a Nazi."

"Oh." Clyde stops for a moment, looks around himself, shrugs twice, then comes back to me. "Well, we did that. That was sort of the end point."

I mull this over.

"So," Hannah looks at me, "yesterday you guys fought a giant Nazi clockwork robot?"

Which, in the end, I suppose we did.

"Feckin' sweet, right?" says Kayla.

"Maybe," Felicity says, "we could be a little less self-congratulatory, and a little more outcomes-focused." She points to the schematic. "This is for a prototype. What we fought yesterday was not a prototype. It was real. It was created by a man who for all we know was committed to serving one of the vilest evils to face mankind in the twentieth century. I doubt he stopped at just one."

"But it's 2015," Hannah objects. "Why the piss are they coming out the woodwork now?"

"That," says Felicity, laying both her hands on the table, "is exactly what you lot are going to find out."

8

Work out if the Nazis hid a clockwork robot army somewhere in England. Just another everyday assignment at MI37. I wish I'd made a bigger coffee. In its absence I go with massaging my skull and trying to crack my neck. When that doesn't work, I just study my hands.

"OK," I say, working my way through it. "So two leads. Joseph Lang, and a Scottish pub. Front end and back end of the problem. Front end is located 1935—Lang conceives of this thing and draws up some plans. Back end is yesterday one of the bastards emerging from the ground up in Scotland. So trace the dots forward and back until they join up in the middle. That means two teams—"

I hear muttering and look up. Kayla has leaned across the table and is showing her phone to Tabitha.

She notices the silence and looks up. "What?"

"Yeah," says Tabitha, still staring at the phone and ignoring both of us. "He looks OK."

My eyes narrow. But given the conceivable array of scenarios that could have led to that statement, I decide that I really don't want to know.

"Who looks OK?"

Damn you, Clyde. Damn you.

Tabitha grabs Kayla's wrist and angles the phone toward Clyde. "Potential genetic material," she says.

Clyde's eyes narrow too. I think he's just realized the course he's steered us onto.

"Don't ask," I say. "Please for the love of all that is good and kind in this world, do not ask."

Hannah looks around the room. "This still isn't a hazing ritual, right?"

Felicity seems to be resisting the urge to facepalm.

Watching her struggle through her disappointment in us, her desire for us to, just once, behave like professionals, allows me to slough off one more layer of my hangover.

"This is the kid's thing, isn't it?" I say to Kayla. "If I were to look at that phone, I would see a man you are thinking of trying to coerce into sleeping with you."

Tabitha's hand twitches.

"Do NOT show me," I say. "I just want to say two things, and then move rapidly on. One, I still think it is a staggeringly bad idea for you to retread the path of parenthood. Two, assuming this isn't really relevant to the whole tracking down hidden clockwork robots thing, and that the young man on your phone is not the great grandson of a prominent Nazi thaumatophysicist, then can it please wait until later?"

Kayla grinds her teeth. Close enough to a yes.

"So," I say, trying to smudge out the last of my headache with a palm to my temple. "Two teams. One heads up to Scotland, digs beneath the pub and sees what they can find. The other digs into Joseph Lang, see what we can learn about him."

"Done." Tabitha releases Kayla's phone and grabs a manilla folder off the table. She slides it toward me. "All here."

All right then, so we have a few more breadcrumbs than I'd assumed. I slip a smile over at Felicity. That seems a lot like professionalism.

"So," I say, "do we have any idea where his belongings ended up? Anything not go with him back to Germany?"

Hannah stirs again beside me. "Well, if they kicked the bugger out," she says, "they're bound to have confiscated his research. Least, as much of it as they could lay their grubby fingers on, right?"

Tabitha's expression lies somewhere between grin and grimace.

"His whole apartment," she says. "Confiscated his home. How we have the schematics. But most stuff is still on site."

"On site?" I lean forward. "But he was kicked out in 1938. His apartment can't still be—"

Tabitha stabs a finger at the folder. "Can be. Is. Bloody read that."

"You literally just gave it to me." The words escape my lips before I remember we're trying to be professionals. "I mean, I will as soon as this briefing is over." From Felicity's expression that was too little, a little too late.

"It's actually a rather interesting legal loophole," Clyde starts before anyone can stop him. "You see early thoughts on magic resembled a lot of current popular fears about radiation. There were all these worries about extra-reality contamination around sites of magic. Sullivan's Polluted Ether Theorem of '36 to give it a name, though by any other name it would still be as awfully wrong as it is under that one. There's not even such a thing as ether. The man barely deserves the name thaumaturgist, to be honest, and his Latin was laughable. Not that I want to brag about my own handling of a dead language, but if one commits to the path of tearing reality open, one might as well have the decency to learn one's tools, I always say. Well not always. Just in this one case really. But if I were to talk about it more often, I would say it more often. Because it really is true. Just common decency really.

"Anyway," Clyde continues, somehow failing to pause for breath, "because of that, there were a lot of concerns that the apartments of early government-sponsored thaumaturgists were horribly contaminated and would basically cause anyone who entered them to turn into mutated gloop. So they waited for the contamination to become more diffuse. Except no one knew when that was going to be. Well, not until Barkman got around to refuting Sullivan's theory in '76, though at that point it was basically common knowledge and Barkman was just a glory hound who managed to swing writing the actual paper. But at that point, no one really gave a damn about these old apartments. They were far more interested in creating something that would actually cause inter-reality contamination and turn people into mutant gloop. Really, the cold war was a very odd time for thaumaturgy.

"So the apartments basically stayed protected by these outdated laws that no one's got around to repealing. There's about eighty of them scattered around the country. Mostly in London really. Though there's a concentration up in York too. Big hotbed of thaumaturgy in the late forties up in York, as it happens."

And finally the breath happens.

"So," I jump in as fast as I can, "basically you're agreeing with Tabitha's initial statement of, 'yes.'"

Clyde thinks about that for a moment, opens his mouth, closes it again, then says, "Yes."

"OK," I nod, "so basically we can go there and clean out the rest of his stuff, right?"

Another pause. "Yes," Clyde says. He opens his mouth again, checks my expression, closes it.

"All right then," I say, "let's head over there."

We all stand. All except Hannah. "Wait," she says. "Us?"

I nod. I think I was pretty clear about the whole thing. Hannah turns to Felicity. "You don't have civil servants to…" She hesitates. "Wait. Is *this* the hazing thing?"

Felicity smiles a little sadly. "This, I am afraid," she says, "is it. The entire staff of MI37. We are not quite as grand as you may be used to. Everyone chips in here."

Hannah shakes her head. "Fucking hell."

I look at her again. And there is nothing in particular about her to dislike. But she feels like a stumble in our gearwork. I just hope this case is small enough to allow us to work around it. So she can do her rotation, or penance here, or whatever reason she's turned up, and move on, and we can get back to normal, to stability.

We stand. Kayla flips her phone at Tabitha again. "What about this one?"

"You'd break him like a twig."

A sound makes me glance at Felicity. And she actually did facepalm on that one.

9

All of us except Felicity wedge into the small elevator that leads up from the subterranean confines of MI37 to Oxford's street level.

"What about that pub?" Kayla asks. "Just going to let that go feckin' cold are we?"

This demonstrates considerably more interest in our operational procedures than Kayla usually shows. "You're just trying to get out of carrying all Lang's crap back to the office, aren't you?" I say.

"Fecker," Kayla says as sweetly as she is able, "I could carry that whole building back here without breaking a sweat."

I have never tested the exact limits of Kayla's strength. There is a chance this could be true. That said…

"You are still trying to get out of it, though," I say.

"Feck, yes."

Clyde giggles. Tabitha scowls, though she's been doing that pretty much since birth. Hannah is still trying to look at everyone at once and not appear like she's doing it. She is actually very good at that.

"Look," I say, "Lang's apartment is right here. We'll just pick up the stuff. Then you and I can head to Scotland while Clyde and Tabitha dig through it."

The elevator doors ping and slide open to reveal MI37's front door.

"And me," says Hannah.

I look at her blank faced.

"And me," she repeats. "You forgot me. I'll go up to Scotland too."

"Oh yes," I say, mentally cursing myself. I have to at least fake politeness. I reach out to open the front door. "Of cour—" I start.

And get no further.

Two enormous figures hulk on our doorstep. One has a fist upraised, as if about to knock.

In keeping with the government's desire to keep the whole magic/aliens/oh-shit-what-is-it stuff under wraps, MI37 is a very secret organization. So its headquarters are very secret. So our front door looks a lot like the service entrance to the dubious travel agency next door. It was probably originally painted black, but is buried under such an accumulation of graffiti, fliers, and stickers advertising phone calls with women of ill repute, that it's hard to tell. It would be the sort of doorway someone might hang around in if they wanted to smoke something illicit, except it's right on one of the main streets leading to the train station.

It is, very much by design, an unwelcoming doorway. It is not the sort of doorway one lurks before. It is certainly not the sort of doorway one stands before with one's fist raised.

And if the alarm bells didn't already have me reaching for my pistol and Kayla extracting her sword from its sheath, there is always the fact that the figure's fist appears to be made of solid bronze.

10

"*Nein*! No! Stop! *Achtung*! Please!"

The bronze fist is now an open bronze palm. It hovers inches before the barrel of my extended gun, glaringly on display on the busy Oxford street.

I hesitate. While it's an assumption that probably has its roots in the grossest Hollywood assumptions, I still don't associate asking politely with people who want to kill me.

The second's pause gives me more time to absorb the scene. Two figures. Both of them at least eight feet tall, hunched, wreathed in heavy canvas that falls to the floor... I suppose the word is cloaks, as anachronistic as it seems. It hides their exact forms in shapeless brown folds. Heavy hoods leave their heads in shadow.

But there is still the exposed fist there, making it abundantly clear that these are the kin of the robot we fought yesterday.

"This was mistake," says the robotic shape with its hands where I can't see them. "I told you. We go now." It has a thick German accent, every w replaced with a v. *Vee go now*.

"Uhrwerkmänner," Clyde breathes behind me.

"*Gesundheit*," says Hannah. Her pistol is also drawn, pointing over my shoulder and tickling my ear. Still, that's some surprisingly cool nerves. At this point during my orientation I think I was curling up and crying uncle.

"No," Clyde starts, "I mean that these are them. These are Lang's Uhrwerk—"

"I know what you meant," Hannah says.

"Oh."

"We mean no harm," says the one with its palm extended. "We come because we want to talk. To discuss with you, yes? You understand?"

I am very aware of the amount of weaponry we are showing right on our own doorstep. The bulk of the Uhrwerkmänner hides a lot of what's going on from the cars driving by, but that bulk in and of itself is going to attract some unwanted attention. This is not the place to do this.

"Put the weapons away," I say.

"Seriously?" Kayla and Hannah ask at the exact same moment. Synchronicity between the pair is not necessarily a reassuring development.

"Very much so." I slide my pistol back into its holster.

I hear the sword slide home. A moment later, Hannah's gun stops tickling my ear.

"What do you want to talk about?" I ask the robot. "Yesterday one of you tried to kill us."

A *club descending*. I blink the after-image away and rub my palms dry on my trouser legs.

"Yes," says the one with hidden hands, "yesterday you killed my friend Nils, let us talk about that."

"No, Hermann," says the first, turning away from me, shapes moving beneath the surface of his cloak like tectonic plates. "We are here because we need their help." He turns back to me. "We need you to save our lives."

EN ROUTE TO THE MI37 SERVICE ENTRANCE

I honestly had no idea we had a service entrance. Tabitha apparently did. While the Uhrwerkmänner take the street route, we navigate the bowels of MI37 and pick up Felicity along the way.

"Seriously?" she asks me. "On our doorstep?"

"They say they need our help."

Apparently there is a facial expression for times like these that perfectly mixes skepticism and concern. Felicity provides me with a good opportunity to study it.

"This sort of shit happen to you often?" Hannah asks, hustling along behind us.

"No," says Tabitha at the same time that Clyde says, "Probably more than it does to other professions."

Felicity nods. "Both of those answers."

"Right then."

Another elevator ride takes us to the service entrance and a narrow alleyway. Tabitha studies her laptop along the way. "Nothing on security cameras or satellites. They're alone."

Kayla pulls back an old-fashioned steel grill as the elevator's broad doors sweep open. The two Uhrwerkmänner stand in the alleyway, hunched and cloaked. I can smell something like engine oil and even standing still they emit a faint whirring sound.

Felicity steps forward. She extends a hand. "I'm Felicity Shaw, director of Military Intelligence Section Thirty-seven. I understand you are seeking aid from the British government."

The one on the right shifts awkwardly, looks back at the alleyway's entrance, but the other steps forward slightly. "I told your friend. We are in need of your help. Our lives, they are in danger."

"From whom?" Felicity is brusquely efficient.

The robot hesitates. Then, "From time," he says.

Felicity flicks a look in my direction. I try to micro-shrug, but that's more Clyde's game. She turns back to the robots.

"If I'm going to offer you any form of asylum," Felicity says, "I'm going to need something decidedly less cryptic."

The one nearer the alley exit shifts again. "They can offer us nothing," he says. "This was mistake. I should not have listened to you."

The friendlier of the two turns to him. Clacking German vowels and consonants are muttered in a rush back and forth, one placating, the other grumbling. The friendly Uhrwerkmänn turns back to us. "I am sorry," he says. "This is difficult for us to discuss. We are so used to isolation. Of taking care of our own. This is difficult for Hermann. He feels Nils' loss sharply."

Another explosive burst of German from Mr Tall Bronze and Miserable. I see Kayla's hand twitch toward her sword handle.

"Nils?" Felicity asks when the outburst is over.

The Uhrwerkmänner bobs his massive head, cloak quaking about him. "He attacked you yesterday. He caused much damage. He will not be the only one."

Kayla's hand twitches again. Felicity subtly shifts her stance, squares her weight between her feet.

"Is that a threat?"

The Uhrwerkmänn jerks his hands up, and Kayla's sword is out of its sheath in the blink of an eye. My pistol and Hannah's are hardly a second behind it. But the robot's palms are again up, defensive. He takes a stumbling step back.

"No. No. Nothing like that. No. It is a tragedy. It is why we are here. We are breaking down. We need to be fixed."

Felicity gives me another look. My gun is still out, but no longer trained on the big machine. The one called Hermann seems torn between fleeing for the street and charging us down. But the other one... He sounds genuine. There is an edge of bitterness and sorrow in his voice that I think it would be hard to fake. And honestly, if they wanted to attack us, that moment surely would have come by now.

I nod back to Felicity. For what my opinion is worth. She hesitates another second then nods in turn, this time to the Uhrwerkmänner. "You'd better come in."

11

Prior to becoming a makeshift meeting room, the warehouse-sized storage room at the base of the service elevator shaft appears to have primarily provided a place for old tarpaulins to come and enjoy their twilight years in peace. Steel rafters criss-cross the ceiling, casting odd shadows against the thin fluorescent light.

Slowly the first Uhrwerkmänn removes his cloak, exposing himself foot by glistening foot. As the whole shape is revealed, I feel my heart stutter in my chest. This is yesterday repeating. Its form is too close, too similar. Adrenaline twitches at the corners of my senses. As large as it is, the warehouse suddenly feels too small, too confined. I want a blue sky above my head.

"Hello," says the machine, "my name is Volk."

I am still in possession of enough of my faculties to notice that there are differences between this Uhrwerkmänn and the one that almost ended me yesterday. The eyes are not insectile, but instead each one is described by a round panel of thick glass, like the bottom of a milk bottle. A panel of bronze approximates a nose. Instead of the constantly chattering teeth, its mouth is a thin horizontal speaker bar. There is less exposed gearwork, more panels. In general he seems to be in better physical shape, the metal polished, well-oiled. The clack and whir of his movements sounds smooth, not the awkward guttering clack of the other.

I try to focus on those differences, try to slow my breathing.

The other one, unfriendly Hermann, keeps his cloak on. He hangs back, deeper in the shadows, seemingly trying to gather an extra layer of obfuscation.

Volk looks to Clyde. "You named us, knew us. We are the Uhrwerkmänner."

Clyde claps excitedly, unable to restrain himself. "You were right, Tabby," he says, voice hitting a squeaky register. He fixes his full attention back on Volk. "Are you first generation? Were you really made by Joseph Lang?"

"He was the creator," Volk says.

Clyde claps again. "Oh my God," he says. "This is so exciting. We never get to work with actual functioning samples. It's always descriptions in poorly constructed Greek. Abysmal Greek actually, for the most part. I mean, seriously, I know thaumaturgical research is time-consuming, but would it kill these people to take a month sabbatical and learn how to conjugate a dead language properly?" He shrugs violently. "Sorry, off topic. You need us to save all your lives. Probably more pressing." He shrugs again. "How many of you are there?"

"Once we numbered twelve hundred," Volk replies, his mechanical voice still steady, still sad.

Holy crap. Twelve hundred? Yesterday just one of them was hard enough to take down. My breathing starts to ratchet up again against my will.

An army of them marching. An army of arms raised. Descending.

I shake my head free of the image. Felicity shoots me a quizzical look, but I pretend I didn't see it. I just let Clyde roll.

"Lang was a busy fellow, wasn't he?" he says.

"He needed many of us," Volk says by way of explanation.

Hermann leans forward, lays a massive bronze fist on Volk's shoulder. "They need to know none of this. It does not help us."

"Well," Clyde leans forward, a slightly embarrassed look on his face, "we may need to actually. I mean, I don't mean to be all contradictory—that statement may seem a little disingenuous after I just contradicted you, actually, but I hope you get the spirit of it at least. No need for this to be confrontational, is what I'm trying to say. Probably failing now. But I was aiming somewhere in the general direction of trying to suggest that the more information we have, generally the better it is for us, especially when we're in the life-saving business. I mean there might be a considerable signal to noise ratio, but even the smallest detail might be important."

Hermann grinds his gears at Clyde. There doesn't seem to be another way to describe the noise he makes. He falls back into the shadows of his shapeless cloak once more.

"Look," Hannah suddenly cuts into the awkward silence. "I mean, I'm new at this shit and all, but why are we interested in saving their lives here? I mean this is a giant Nazi robot who attacked you yesterday, right?"

Felicity and I go to speak at the same time, her probably more tactfully than me, but it's Hermann who cuts us off.

"Do not mistake our creator's broken philosophy for our own." If he was disgruntled before, Hannah just managed to push him into full-on pissed off. Not a great start for her, which is pretty much exactly what I feared.

I flap a hand at her to shush. She keeps a pretty tight rein on her expression, but I'm not sure if she's more unimpressed by Hermann's reaction or my own.

"See, Hermann," says Volk, turning to his fellow Uhrwerkmänn, "this is why I need to explain."

Hermann makes no more noise. Volk turns back.

"Lang—he needed many of us to invade Russia. The war there had not gone well for the Germans. The winter had killed so many of their men. Lang believed that we, the Uhrwerkmänner, were the solution. We would not feel the cold. We would not need food. We could march on where men fell.

"He had originally planned to build ten thousand of us. The rebellion came before that. I do not know if he miscalculated our intelligence, if perhaps it was the simple arrogance of a creator, the assumption that we were lesser because we were made, or if he just was blind to the flaws in his ethos. But even though he made us, he did not make us hate. We saw what he wanted us to do, and we rejected him. We would not be tools for Lang and his Nazis.

"They kept us in a warehouse, packed together, one pressed up against the next. It was a night in December when we broke out. They did not seem to have thought of the possibility. We tore down the walls like they were paper. We tore out of their factories. Only a few of us fell. They were too slow to respond, too caught off guard. And we are hard to kill.

"But not impossible. Lang's fury knew no limits. We had defied him. Our maker. He pursued us endlessly. Tank shells rained down upon us. We were twelve hundred. Then eleven. Then just a thousand.

"Most of Europe had fallen by then. Russia believed us invaders. We could find nowhere on the continent to hide. Only England was free. So we fled here, across France, traveling only at night, Lang still behind us. By the time we reached the coast, Lang had cut down a full third of us. Only eight hundred still lived.

"He caught us there, as we fled into the water. We fought, finally face-to-face. Another hundred of us fell.

"So did Lang."

Volk cannot wrangle much expressiveness out of his metal face, but it's impossible not to hear the grim satisfaction in his voice.

"I took him apart with my bare hands." To my surprise it's Hermann who picks up the tale. "He broke so easily in them."

Volk nods to Hermann, a sign of deference perhaps. That seems to fit with the tone so far. I am hearing the legends of a people only seventy years old.

"When we came to England," Volk picks up after Hermann's brief, somewhat graphic interjection, "we did not dare reveal ourselves. Only a little over half our original number remained. We simply wanted to hide and not be hunted. We slipped underground. We hid away. We have remained there ever since."

He rumbles to a stop, the sound of his voice echoed by the churning gears of his chest. And it's a good story. A persecuted people. A boo-hiss villain. The rejection of their maker's philosophy. They come out of it well. But something definitely seems to be missing.

"So," I say slowly, "how exactly does this lead to your friend,

Nils," I look over to Hermann, attempt to judge his reaction, "trying to kill us all yesterday?"

Volk hesitates. I can feel the weight of my pistol hanging just below my armpit. I glance over at Kayla, but there's no need. I sometimes think it's more of a struggle for Kayla to sheathe her sword than it is for her to pull it out. A moment later I realize I should have checked Hannah but I forgot.

"When we came to England," he says, his accent momentarily thicker, sounding more like Hermann, "our total number was six hundred and seventy-eight. Today we number one hundred and forty-two."

He lets the numbers hang there. That sounds a lot like calamity.

"The hell happened?" Tabitha is the first of us to find words.

"We are breaking down," says Volk. "Our gearwork misses its steps. And as it does our sanity slips. We lose our reason and our path. Nils was not the first to be consumed by madness. We have managed to keep so many quiet. Some, it is not as bad as Nils. They turn within themselves. Their madness eats down into their core rather than bursting out. Some we have killed ourselves out of mercy. Others have raged in places devoid of people, their fury gone unnoticed. Some we have managed to restrain and confine where they could do no harm in their final thrashings. And some..." He hesitates, glances at Hermann who shakes his head. But Volk turns back to us and finds words. "Some have left no survivors and we have cleared away the evidence."

OK. An army of Nazi clockwork robots, and now they're all getting an extra-violent version of Alzheimer's. Fantastic. Just...

"What exactly do you expect of us?" Felicity makes the collective question audible. Or maybe she's just trying to cut Tabitha off before she asks how this is her problem.

"Nothing," snaps Hermann. "People have never helped us. Never will. You are useless and we are wasting time here, while our people die. This is a mistake. I have always said so." He puts a hand on Volk's shoulder. "Let us go now before you tell too many other secrets and doom us all. Already they want to kill us so we are no longer problem for them. It is the way of their species."

Volk hesitates. I want to speak into the silence, refute Hermann's claims. Except the thought really had crossed my mind. Old age is taking them in an ugly way. Why not just ease the passing?

"Wait." Every eye turns to Hannah as she speaks up. I try to suppress my wince. "I mean, two things. First off that's a touch judgmental coming from a robot created to shit all over Russian soil, so, you know, whatever. But, like, what about repair... I don't know, repair protocols or something. Like, you must have some idea of how you all work. I mean, just take one of you apart, figure it out, put them back together so they're all tick-tock and not cuckoo-clock again, or whatever."

My wince is no longer suppressed.

Hermann stalks a step forward. "Do you think we are children? Do you think you can lecture us? Do you think you are so much smarter and so much more invested in our fate that you can snap out ideas and we will be so grateful for your great human thoughts? You are children to us. You have no conception of what we have been through, of our pain, our fate. You have not watched hundreds of your siblings, your loved ones, just die. No. So you be quiet, and you leave us alone."

And there's something in the way he says it. Something that suggests that there is something they don't want to say. Some hole in the conversation.

"You fucking came here!" Hannah looks outraged. "You asked for help."

"Maybe we should all calm down," I suggest.

Hermann ignores me. "He came." He stabs a finger at Volk. "I came to stop him from making situation worse. I am doing so now. Volk, come." He turns his back on Hannah, and slams his hand down on Volk's shoulder.

"No," says Volk, even as Hermann spins him toward the elevator, "they have a right to know."

And there it is again—that hole, that avoided topic. And now it has a little more shape and purpose. And I like it even less.

"You, shut up," Hermann says to Volk, marching on.

"Know what?" I ask.

"Nothing," Hermann snaps, still dragging Volk.

"If you think I am just going to let you walk away—" Felicity's voice is flat and hard in the room, cutting through the metallic crunching of the Uhrwerkmänners' movements, "you have sorely underestimated MI37."

"You think you can stop us?" Hermann's voice is as coldly mechanical as his innards.

Felicity smiles. "Actually yes. I do think we have a chance."

Hermann stops. Kayla's sword slides from its sheath as if she has a soft-eject button programmed into it. And then I find my pistol is in my own hand. That's a worrying reflex to have automated.

Volk pulls himself away from Hermann. "This is madness. We need their help. On our own we stagnate and die. You know this." He turns to us. "We need your help, yes, but you too need to help us. There is another of us. He thinks he has found another way to save our race. But he is wrong. I think perhaps the madness has him already, is misguiding his thoughts."

Hermann shakes his head. "Do not tell them. You will only bring our deaths quicker, and now at their hands."

The jury may still be out on Hannah, but she was right, Hermann is a terribly judgmental old bastard.

"What other way?" Felicity is leaning forward. "What is this… other Uhrwerkmänn doing? It's a threat to us, that's what you're saying, isn't it?"

Volk hangs his head. "It is Friedrich. He has taken on the sins of our maker."

"Lang?" Clyde checks.

Oh crap. One of them really *is* a Nazi. This is going to suck.

Volk hesitates again, but refuses to look at Hermann, who fumes silently at his back. Then Volk takes a step forward, crouches down toward our height. "The Uhrwerkmänner are not Lang's only creation. Not the only aspect of his plan. There is also the Uhrwerkgerät. We do not know it. We never saw it. But we heard of it. It was the fail-safe to Lang's plans. If our invasion of Russia failed. Victory at any cost. Even the cost of the earth itself maybe. We do not know for sure. We never have. But it is dangerous. Terribly, horrifyingly dangerous. A bomb out of all proportion with anything created before or since. A tool to make the Americans' atom bomb look like a child's toy."

"Where is it?" Felicity knows how to cut to the chase.

"We do not know. No one does. Not Friedrich either. But he searches. And there is a chance he will find it."

I'm about to pick up the line of questioning, when Hannah cuts in. "And what will the bastard do when he finds the bloody thing?"

Subtlety was apparently not part of Hannah's job at MI6. Which aligns with my experience. And I'd always assumed spies would be sneakier bastards.

Volk glances back at Hermann. The grumpy Uhrwerkmänn looks defeated, his cloak hanging about his frame limply. "You have told them now."

"Friedrich believes the Uhrwerkgerät can save us. He believes it will reset our souls. Many believe him. Many side with him. Because they are desperate, because they will look anywhere for salvation."

Hermann grunts. "We are no bigger fools than they."

"You don't believe what Friedric does, though," I say before Hannah can cut me off. "What do you think will happen?"

"If he finds the Uhrwerkgerät? If he sets it off?" Volk shakes his head. "In that case, I believe he will kill us all, robot and human alike."

12

Help save a species from going violently insane. Or one of them will activate an ancient Nazi doomsday device. Carrot, meet stick. And once more, the role of the mule in the middle will be played by MI37. But now the scenario is laid out before us, I don't see a way to side-step this disaster.

"So," I say, "what stops Friedrich?"

"A cure," Volk says without hesitation. "If you can stop our decline, then Friedrich has no reason to look for the Uhrwerkgerät. No one has a reason to side with him. All the madness stops. All are cured."

And again, despite his inexpressive features, emotion shines out of Volk's face. Hope, faith. He has seen the light. All he needs now is for us to deliver it to him.

Hermann, however, is the piss in Volk's holy water. "You will not find a cure," he says. "We have looked and we have failed. You will not succeed."

I wonder if a cure would remove the stick from Hermann's arse or if Lang just built him that way.

I look around the collected members of MI37. Felicity looks pensive, playing with the arm of her glasses. Kayla's jaw is set. Clyde actually looks excited, bless his poor deludedly optimistic heart. Tabitha looks pissed off, but that's to be expected. And Hannah...

Her expression lies somewhere between Felicity's and Kayla's. Worried but ready. I have an unsettling feeling it might mirror my own face slightly too closely. She should look far more scared.

I'm going to have to look out for her during this. I'm going to have to be looking over my shoulder to make sure she's keeping up with the slurry of insanity this job pours on us. And that means taking my eyes off what's right in front of me. And far too frequently these days, the thing in front of me is looking to turn my spleen into a piñata.

"You will help us, won't you?" says Volk. "Please?"

Hermann's gearwork manages to make a dismissive noise.

Felicity looks at me. I shrug. What else can we do?

"Of course," she says. "You are safe with us."

Hermann starts to laugh. "With you? We will not stay here. I have my people to worry about. I have the disappointment of the false hope you offer to prepare them for. I will waste my time here no more."

Volk shrugs, almost as apologetically as Clyde can manage. "His words, his sentiment, it differs from mine, but the truth is the same. We cannot stay here. We must help guide our people in this time. But we will be in contact. We will help you as much as you help us. I promise."

"How?" Felicity asks. I suspect her job breeds suspicion of empty promises.

"We have a functional radio transmitter," Volk says. "We broadcast on 157.836 MHz and receive on 289.650. We use the Enigma code. We know it is broken, but not many listen."

Radio transmissions. Some black and white scene of a man wearing a flight suit hunched over a vast box of dials as it emits a series of pops and cracks plays out in my head. Something snagged from one of the World War II movies my dad used to watch on Sunday afternoons.

"Excellent," Hermann says, "one more secret given up."

"Fucking radio transmissions?" Tabitha spits, her bile rivaling Hermann's. "We even have a set?"

"Oh yes!" Clyde cuts into my reveries. "There's a set in the third archive room. The one with the taxidermied kraken spawn from that

1963 Pacific mission. The Galapagos Island one. You remember?"

Tabitha arches an eyebrow at him. "I mean, yes," Clyde says.

Volk nods, as if this is the sort of help he's used to receiving, and if it is I really do feel bad for his plight.

"Thank you," he says. "I thank you. Every one of my people thanks you."

Hermann grunts. "Not everyone."

Volk turns to him, a quick twist of the waist, accompanied by a slick whir of gears and a pneumatic hiss. "They do us a great service. Your actions are beneath you."

Hermann shakes his head. "They have done nothing except listen and make a promise they cannot keep. I see nothing to thank here."

I make a mental note that when we find a cure, to think twice before providing it to Hermann. Inorganic and devoid of a functional digestive system or no, the guy is still an arsehole.

Volk and Hermann step onto the elevator's platform. Its steel floor creaks ominously under their combined weight.

And then the elevator starts to rise. The two Uhrwerkmänner being borne away. And it's just us all standing around in a cold storage room, with their mess in our laps, and wondering how the hell to fix it.

13

"OK," I say, even though it's not. It's a way to buy time, to focus attention. All I need to do now is be able to follow it up with something actionable.

Eyes turn toward me.

My brain scrambles to hit top speed. And getting there I realize that not so much has changed yet. We know more, but we still have to fill in the full picture about what's going on.

"Breadcrumbs," I say. "Leading forward and back."

"What?" Tabitha looks like she thinks I'm finally having the stroke she's been hoping I'll have for so long, except the whole thing is now taking too long and is generally inconvenient. "This morning," I say, "hell, less than an hour ago, we were trying to find out about these robots. These Uhrwerkmänner. We had two leads, one in the present, in Scotland, one in the past—Lang's apartment. We needed to follow the breadcrumbs forward and back to see where they joined up.

"But now these guys have shown up on our doorstep so we know where the breadcrumbs from Scotland lead. We know they go back to World War II. We know all that they have to tell us."

"About German clockwork doomsday devices and mad robots trying to activate them?" Hannah asks.

"Exactly," I nod as if she hadn't sounded incredibly skeptical.

"Lang is still in play, though. This is *his* doomsday device. So we still need to check out his apartment. Find out what there is to—"

"Wait," Hannah cuts in. "Really? Like actually, genuinely take their word for this shit and run off to have giant mechanical people beat us up while they hunker down and do whatever it is they're actually doing?"

Oh good. We're less than thirty seconds into the assignment and already Hannah's challenging my authority. That's just marvelous.

"Is there a problem?" I ask her, as patiently as I'm able.

"If I'm the one being beaten up by giant robots then, hell yes there is."

"Girl's got a feckin' point," Kayla adds.

"You," I point to Kayla, "lost all credibility when you started showing people pictures of men you want to impregnate you." I switch the finger to Hannah. "You—"

"Are showing a healthy amount of skepticism." Felicity cuts me off. She smiles at us both. It is not one of those nice, warm, reassuring smiles I've heard so much about. It's the other kind.

I really do have to try harder to be nice to Hannah. She's the new girl. She will say the wrong things. Felicity has asked me to be nice. And just because I keep on having flashbacks to almost dying yesterday, that is not an excuse to be mean.

"Look," Felicity steps toward Hannah, "while this is still military intelligence, what we do here is significantly different to what you're used to. There are far fewer angles, and the threats can be much, much bigger. We don't just protect this nation, we protect the planet it exists on. And there is often not much time to operate in. Follow Agent Wallace's lead," she smiles at me. "He usually knows what he's talking about, even if he avoids the best way to say it. For now, the best approach is to treat what we've heard as true, but it's also best to be looking for angles that are being used against us. We won't see those unless we get out in the field and start searching for them. Does that make sense?"

Hannah looks as if she's chewing through a lemon, but she smooths out her features and nods. "All right then."

Felicity steps back and the floor is mine again. "OK," I say. "Now that's out of the way, let's go toss this guy's apartment."

ON THE ROAD

Clyde and I take his Mini to the apartment. Kayla and Hannah share Hannah's Renault Turbo, because fitting four people who aren't clowns into Clyde's Mini breaks some fairly fundamental laws about physical space and the volume of my stomach.

Music plays for the first quarter mile or so, but then, as we're navigating our way around the fifteenth roundabout, he says, "So Hannah seems nice, I think."

It's not bait, so I try not to rise to it. Clyde is a decent human being and I should follow his lead. So, I say, "Yes," and try to leave it at that.

Except then I say, "Well…"

I immediately regret it. And for a moment I think Clyde is going to ignore it, but then he flicks his eyes off the road and to me.

"Well, what?" he asks.

Damnit. Don't encourage me, Clyde.

"I don't know," I lie. "She feels… off." I have no better words for it. "I mean, I don't think it's her. I think it's the whole dynamic. We have a groove now, MI37. We know what we're doing. This seems like a bad time to throw someone new into the mix."

Clyde nods as Clyde is wont to do. "Have you talked to Shaw about it?"

I shake my head. "I don't think Felicity's going to be amenable to that line of reasoning. I think she's quite positive about Hannah being part of the mix."

"Well, Shaw does know what's best much of the time. Not that I have to tell you that. I'm not the one moving in with her." Clyde smiles happily at that thought.

My palms are sweaty again. I close my eyes. All we have to do is go and get some notebooks and whatever else the insane German thaumatophysicist left lying around. Holiday snaps or whatever. This is simple. It doesn't matter how much experience Hannah does or doesn't have. We are essentially moving men. No one tries to kill moving men.

* * *

OUTSIDE JOSEPH LANG'S APARTMENT

Oxford doesn't really do run-down. Or at least, when it does, it's a very genteel version. The architecture is less crumbling, more just eccentric. Buildings gently sag against each other like friends worse for wear after an evening out. Windows are cracked but never truly broken. Drainpipes look like hazards on a snakes and ladders board. There are modern urban vices of course. But even the graffiti is grammatically correct.

Lang's apartment has all these problems and more, but it is still standing at least—a dilapidated house at the end of a narrow, dead-end street.

Clyde pulls up halfway down the street, behind Hannah's Renault. No reason to get too close, give away to any casual observers what house we're interested in.

Hannah leans on her car door, wearing a lopsided grin. "What took you so long?" she asks, as I unfold from the car.

I try to imagine Felicity's reprimanding face and ignore the jibe. "OK," I say instead, "let's go in, get this stuff."

I head toward the front door, which was once painted red, but is now mostly exposed wood and pale pink flakes. A dented letterbox is positioned at its center like a mouth in need of dentures.

"Wait," says Hannah. "What about, you know, standard sweep and clear? We're doing that, right?"

I clench my teeth. The constant nagging is not really appreciated.

"Kayla," I say vaguely. I always assumed she did that sort of thing.

"Figured you'd finally feckin' notice I did that," is the response. *Felicity's reprimanding face.*

I approach the door, test the latch. The door swings slowly open revealing a dark corridor of the variety usually located in fairground haunted houses.

Someone seems to have installed a hair trigger on the sweat glands in my palms. Even this has them going. This is getting ridiculous.

Kayla takes off. Thirty seconds later she's back at my side. "Clean," she says.

I am—probably rather pettily—quite pleased to see Hannah's

mask slip for a moment. Hardened MI6 field agent or not, it is quite the thing to see Kayla hit something like Mach one coming down a set of stairs. I half expect to see the cloud of her sonic boom still dissipating in the hallway.

"All right," I say, "let's give the place a proper once-over." I lead the way in, flicking the hallway light to no effect. I reach into my pocket and fish out a flashlight—indispensable government agent tool no. 1—and an ear mic that will connect me back to Tabitha in the office—possibly dispensable government agent tool no. 2. I push the ear mic home. The others do the same, Clyde handing a spare to Hannah.

"OK," I say, "we're in. Any suggestions on the sort of thing we should be looking for?"

"Clyde's there, right?" Tabitha's antipathy is tinny in my ear.

"Yes."

"Ask bloody him." Apparently Tabitha has left Felicity's earshot.

As I look to Clyde I can't help but notice that Hannah's brow has furrowed.

"Excellent point," says Clyde, even though it isn't. "Basically on the lookout for anything with writing on it. Paper pads. Spare sheafs of paper. Notes in the margins of books. Even toilet roll. I mean, I realize it's not exactly hygienic, but it's not as if one has used the paper already, it's clean paper, and sometimes a thought does come out of nowhere at an inopportune moment and it's just too good to let it go, and that's just what you have to hand. It's simply practical, I say."

There is a little bit of a silence after that.

"Clyde," Tabitha says into our ears, "share less."

"What?" Clyde looks around, slightly panicked. "I was just… hypothesizing."

"Mmm." Hannah looks dubious enough to demonstrate that she does at least have rudimentary detective skills.

"Kayla," I say, "you see anything resembling an office on your sweep?" That seems like a good place to start.

"Up the stairs, on the left."

I nod. "All right, let's go grab everything that's not nailed down."

We ascend. The stairs creak. The runner is more holes than whole, its original pattern is lost to time. Spider webs tangle with our hair. Our footfalls raise clouds of dust that billow in the beams of our flashlights. Ratty paintings hang at obtuse angles, the occasional glimpse of oil paint catching the light from beneath the layers of filth.

As we hit the landing, I lean on the banister. The wood crunches, rotten, and a chunk breaks away spilling down into the hallways below. Staring down, getting my balance back, I wonder if there really might be something to the contaminated ether theory Clyde dismissed earlier. This place is genuinely creepy.

"Over there." Kayla points to an open doorway.

The room beyond is surprisingly spacious, a couch against the near wall, the others lined with bookcases. Near the room's far end is an imposing desk that seems to have spent the past seven decades resisting the rot that has reduced the area rug that once lay before it into a few moldering strands of cotton.

"All right," I say. "Clyde, you do the desk. The rest of us, start hitting the bookshelves for margin notes."

"Read me the titles," Tabitha cuts in. "I can cross-reference. Look for patterns. Research indicators."

I smile. Sometimes we really can look professional.

I pick a spot, and grab my first book. "*The Origin of Species*," I intone. "Darwin." Tabitha grunts. I flick open the cover, and go to thumb through the pages. They start to dissolve as soon as my fingers hit them, crumbling to dust that spills through the room. I back up, coughing, dropping the book, which lets fly more flakes of brown paper. By the time the whole thing is over, more than half the book is lying in pieces on the floor.

"Erm," I say. "No notes in that one."

From Kayla's disgusted choking, I think she's having a similar experience.

"What's this?" Hannah is standing by Lang's desk holding something vaguely oblong and odd-looking. She is noticeably not checking the books on the shelves like I asked her to.

And this is the moment. Do I lay down the hammer, and try to force her into line, or do I just let it go and hope it doesn't add up, doesn't reach the point where I say go left in a fire fight and she goes right and one of us ends up with an extra hole in our cranium?

It would be better if I'd come from a military background. This is *military* intelligence. Then I'd have a better background in shouting and being obeyed. But usually when I shout I'm just self-conscious, and people look at me as if this is the first time anyone has ever shouted in their presence and they're not sure what to make of the whole deal.

So, in the search for a middle ground, I go with, "No clue. Sort of why I let Clyde handle those things." It sounds more pointed than I'd hoped it would. Sometimes I worry that I'm becoming better at the shooting-things part of my job than I am at the herding-cats part. That is not the career progression I was hoping for.

That said, there is still the throb of a hangover at the back of my head and the vague fear of PTSD.

Behind Hannah, Kayla disappears in another cloud of fragmenting book particulate.

"This is feckin' useless." Whether Kayla's frustration is based on the problem itself or the fact that the problem can't be solved through the application of a sword blade, I'm not totally sure.

"Come on," I say, "this is hardly kicking a clockwork robot's arse. We can do this."

Clyde at least has the decency to chuckle.

And for a moment we really do work together. Like a team. "*Inquiries into Human Faculty and its Development* by Francis Galton," I read off a spine to Tabitha.

"Well, I've got *Mein* feckin' *Kampf* over here," says Kayla before there is the sound of a book detonating. "Oops." She doesn't sound sorry.

"You know," Clyde says from the desk, "this thing actually is very weird." I glance over and he's holding the oblong Hannah was wielding a moment ago. "There are seams and I think…" he tugs on it. "I can't get it apart."

This is usually Kayla's cue to break something, but instead she's standing very still, her head cocked to one side. "Why," she starts, "would three feckin' trucks pull up outside?"

Everything in the room stops. And I suddenly become aware

that there very definitely is something large rumbling outside the front door.

"Three?" Clyde says. "I have to say your sense of hearing really is quite remarkable. One day we really should sit down and test the limits—"

"Shut the feck up."

It's not quite how I would have worded it, but I agree with the sentiment.

Hannah is shaking her head. "I bloody told you lot." I can hear her, not speaking quite loud enough for it to be intended for everyone, but not quite quiet enough to be intended just for her either. "Just bloody trusting bloody Nazi robots." Her gun is out, knuckles white on the grip, finger poised on the safety.

"Hold up," I say. "We don't know anything for sure yet." My message may be undercut by the fact that I'm pulling my pistol while I'm talking.

"Look," Hannah points her free hand at me. "I know you think this is my first day, but it's not. I am *good* at this. This is supposed to be a position I have earned. So if you could stop treating me like some beat copper pulled off the streets and start treating me like a trained government bloody agent, that would be appreciated. Those robots were suspect as fuck, and I told you, and now there is going to be violence."

Violence. I can feel the familiar hum of adrenaline in my veins, and yet something is off. Instead of the urge to smash heads I am looking to the door and trying to calculate how fast I can reach it. I am more flight than fight.

I take deep breaths, too conscious of Hannah's eyes on me, of the good impression I am failing to make. The hand holding my pistol is shaking. I press it to my thigh.

"Violence." I force my voice to be calm. "Yeah, probably. But we cannot jump to conclusions."

"We can make some pretty bloody educated guesses." She is pressed up against the edge of the door, peering into the landing, trying to get an angle down the stairs and to the front door.

OK, I need to stop this catfight and concentrate. Head of field operations. Hannah is in good position. "Kayla," I say. "Any other rooms up here give you eyes on the street?"

Like that, she's gone, a swirling cloud of paper fragments left in her wake.

"Clyde, help me move this desk. I want you to have cover but line of sight on the landing. And Tabitha," I put my finger to my earpiece.

"Can't leave you alone for a minute," she monotones.

"Find something that's going to seriously dent metal."

Then Kayla's voice comes through the earpiece. In a hushed, decidedly un-Kayla-like whisper. Almost tremulous, she hisses, "Oh, holy feck."

14

"There's feckin' tons of them."

Hannah is shaking her head more. And is she right? Is this just a set-up? But Volk and Hermann knew where MI37 was. They could have gone there en masse and taken us out. Why bother to lure us here to do it? There's fewer of us here, I suppose. But it doesn't really make sense.

How Hermann and Volk even knew the location of a ridiculously secure British government agency headquarters is a problem I'm going to leave until I have less pressing concerns.

"It's Uhrwerkmänner?" I ask, taking hold of one side of Lang's desk and starting to heave. I wince at the scraping it raises as we drag the thing's bulk across the floor.

"Either that or there's another group of giant clockwork feckin' robots running around Oxford today." Then, with an intake of breath, "Jay-sus feck. One of them is feckin' huge."

So it is Uhrwerkmänner. Not a wonderful moment for the Trust-Hermann-and-Volk team, but on the other hand they did mention another faction working against them.

"The big one doesn't happen to have a name tag labeled Friedrich, does he?" I ask.

Kayla doesn't bother replying.

Still, this could just be a case of MI37 being in the wrong place at the wrong time. It wouldn't be the first time that's happened to us. But it's an ugly coincidence.

With a grunt, Clyde and I get the desk in place. He hunkers down beneath it, then pops back up, and snags the oblong oddity that Hannah was fiddling with off its surface. He shoves the thing deep into a pocket. "There's something up with it," he mutters by way of explanation. "I mean, I couldn't tell you exactly what. But if I was a wagering man I would lay money that it's no *objet d'art*. Not that I am a wagering man. Bad experience with racehorses at the age of sixteen, not an age when I was flush with cash either. Requires a lot more investment of time than people give it credit, if one's to do it right anyway. Not that any of that is relevant, but there's this whole imminent death thing going on and that tends to make me ramble. Probably noticed that."

I don't comment. I'm having trouble keeping my attention focused. My heart is racing again, and my control slipping away like sand between my fingers.

There is a crash from the downstairs hallway.

"First one's in," comes Kayla's voice. "Bit bigger than the frame."

More architecture crunches. The floor shakes. A smell like gasoline seems to be mixing with the room's funeral-parlor scent.

"So," Clyde says, still hunkered below the desk, "sort of wondering what the plan is here?"

A plan. God, I need to come up with… I put my thoughts under hard rein, force myself to run through my mental inventory of options. We don't know about back doors or windows. That leaves the front door and a handful of windows. Our parked cars represent the fastest way for us to get away, but they were probably a decent clue to the Uhrwerkmänner that they are not alone here. Assuming that they didn't already know that from the mouths of Volk and Hermann.

So, limited ways out, and the Uhrwerkmänner know we're here to take them. Which means there is no element of surprise. In fact even if there is a back door hidden somewhere here, there'll probably be someone there to cover it.

There is a resounding crunch from the back of the house.

"Going to guess that's the back feckin' door," comes Kayla's voice.

Goddamn it. OK, think.

I look to Clyde. "We have about thirty seconds. Grab everything from this desk that you can."

Clyde starts rattling drawers.

OK, that's the primary objective. Now for secondary concerns. God, I hate that our exit strategy is a secondary concern.

"Kayla," I say, touching the earpiece once more. "I need you to draw them away from the front of the house, toward the back."

"All of them?" Normally Kayla is up for any fight. Her hesitation is not helping with the panic at the back of my brain, barking to be let in.

"As many as you can. You're superwoman, remember?"

"Go feck yourself."

OK, that's the distraction taken care of.

"Hannah," I say, "you and I are going to try to defend Clyde as long as Kayla needs to rustle up a decent distraction. Then you, Clyde, are going to blow apart as many walls as it takes to make us a new exit hole. Then we head for the cars and we run like fuck. You too, Kayla. Sound good?"

"Sounds feckin' insane."

Hannah nods. "Affirmative."

So there is something to be said for MI6 professionalism.

"OK," I breathe. "Kayla, wait until—"

There is a crashing sound, and then the scream, "Come get some, you motherfeckin' trash cans!"

Or we could do that.

Chaos erupts beneath us. The room starts to vibrate. Walls crunch, metal screams. There is a grinding like an entire industrial complex coming online. The sound of wood splintering. Harsh German consonants barked out with military precision.

The panic is no longer a dog barking in my head, but one clawing down the walls. It's breaking in to my calm. Sweat soaks my forehead. I palm it away from my eyes. I still don't dare pull the gun up from where I'm holding it firm next to my hip, because the shaking will not exactly inspire confidence.

Clyde is still rattling drawers. He looks up at me, eyes stretched wide. "They're all locked!"

I try to keep a grip on myself but lose it somewhere along the way as the words head from my brain to my mouth. I seize a fistful of his shirt. "You're a fucking wizard!" I yell.

A crunch, louder and closer than the rest.

"They're on the stairs!" Hannah yells and then she opens fire. The whine of ricocheting bullets joins the cacophony coming to meet us.

I move, snap my gun up, taking a shooter's stance, aiming through the doorway. Suddenly my hands are still. This is it, the moment of truth. And for a moment conscious thought flees the building, leaving me blissfully calm and cold, in the grip of muscle memory and routine. Hannah is to the doorframe's left, the muzzle flashes of her pistol lighting the landing in strobe flares.

I catch a glimpse of bronze. I squeeze the trigger.

And then Hannah is in my line of fire, whipping across the doorway, gun clasped to her chest.

I pull my shot at the last moment, desperately aiming upwards. The bullet slams into the doorframe above her head. Pressed to the doorframe's far side, Hannah stares at me wide eyed.

My breath catches. The hollow emptiness of routine falters.

"The fuck?" she breathes. "You weren't counting my shots?" She fumbles the pistol magazine to the floor, pulls out a fresh one.

"How many do you have?" My mouth is on autopilot, filling in requisite bits of conversation. I almost just shot her. Holy hell.

Hannah's professional exterior finally crumbles. She looks like I just broke part of her.

And then the Uhrwerkmänn comes through the door.

Plaster fragments. The wooden latticework of the wall's underpinnings snaps and breaks. Twigs and splinters fly through the air. A beam gives way with a crunch. Cracks tear through the ceiling. The shelving detonates, the crumbling books becoming powder in the air.

It gleams, a bronze and steel monstrosity in our midst. The head is lower than the others I have seen. Its jaw is large and heavy, jutting forward from a pinched face, small dark lenses for eyes. The shoulders are massive, forming almost a complete hemisphere over its shrunken metal skull. The arms are short, but its fists massive. The legs are similarly stunted, a thick mass of pistons and levers.

It plunges one massive fist toward Hannah. She leaps back, slamming her new magazine home as she does so. She brings her gun to bear.

I am one step ahead of her. My pistol booms, loud, despite the concert of chaos expanding beneath me. Shots ping off its massive shoulders, dent the casing about its small eyes.

"Clyde!" I shout. "Time to leave!"

Then I'm leaping out the way, as the Uhrwerkmänn pivots at the waist, feet still planted solidly, and the fist that was aimed at Hannah swings through the air at me. I fall back, slam into the desk, and sprawl back as the fist whips above my head. I go with momentum, roll back over the desk, land beside Clyde in something that is almost a crouch, but slightly more of a pratfall. He fumbles through his pockets, spilling batteries.

"They are surprisingly large up close, aren't they?" he says. "I mean, this Lang chap wasn't one for subtlety. Not that subtlety is probably a huge thing people are looking for in their army of robots. History isn't full of subtle armies. Though I've got to imagine there was one at some point. Stands to reason. Rules of probability and all that. You probably just don't hear about them because of, you know, the subtlety. Maybe ninjas—"

The rest is lost to mumbling as he works a couple of AAs into each cheek.

I leave him to his ramblings and decide to see if Hannah's still alive. I pop my head up above the desk. Then I dive backwards. An Uhrwerkmänn's fist comes down and the desk becomes matchsticks.

"Shit!" I hit the threadbare rug hard. Clyde sprawls. The Uhrwerkmänn's fist continues its downwards trajectory, through the desk, down into the floor, tears through it, opens a great gash in the room.

Hannah is behind the robot, still taking potshots. Then a second Uhrwerkmänn decides that doors are unnecessary, simply plows ahead through the plasterwork. The wall behind Hannah detonates. She joins us on the floor.

Compared to its companion, this new Uhrwerkmänn's head

is massive—a giant wrecking ball of a thing, dripping plaster and wood, eyes placed wide. Aside from that the framework of bronze, the gears, and the sheer abominable size are becoming worryingly familiar.

Hannah manages to turn her tumble into a roll, comes up close to the first Uhrwerkmänn's foot. From where I'm lying on the floor, I take aim at the robot's eyes, try to distract it. One eye shatters as it raises a foot to ponderously kick at Hannah. She rolls back, but only gets herself in the path of the oncoming second robot.

Damnit. If I survive this and Hannah doesn't, Felicity will make sure that I don't live to have my life threatened again. Anyway, it's not like I'm in cover anymore.

"Clyde! The hole! In it!" I bark, and then take off for Hannah.

And somehow as I'm fighting for my life, I find myself hearing Kayla saying, "That's what she said."

A fist comes for me. I dance sideways. Hannah is on her back, crab-crawling away from the second Uhrwerkmänn. It raises a foot, stamps down at her. She pistons her legs, manages to leap back in what resembles a remarkably complicated gymnastics maneuver, landing on her feet. The machine's leg plunges through the floor up to the knee. For a moment it is pinned there by its own misplaced weight. I yank my pistol up, take aim—

And then Hannah is moving, spinning around, up, aiming her pistol and I am in her direct line of sight, and she in mine.

For a moment we are frozen, like two old-school gunfighters in the most messed up standoff of all time. Holy crap, I almost just killed her again. She almost just killed me. I see my own panic reflected in her eyes.

Then she swallows it, goes to her right. I go to mine, and even with my mind battering at the walls of adrenaline and training, screaming on and on about how messed up this, and how it's going to end in my imminent death, I open fire and pour hot lead into the Uhrwerkmänn's gut. My clip goes dry. I slam in another, keep firing.

The Uhrwerkmänn fights gravity and its own leg as my bullets smash concavities and tears into the metal. Its attempts start to grow jerky and uncoordinated.

I turn. The other Uhrwerkmänn is more recalcitrant about being disabled. It's turned a massive shoulder guard to Hannah and her shots around the edges hit thick armor plating or whine off at awkward angles.

Clyde has disappeared, which means he listened to me, which means right now he's downstairs with the majority of the machines, and without any help. Major artillery with two legs though he may be, I'm not sure Clyde should be left to his own devices in a fire fight. Or crowds. Or anywhere sharp objects aren't carefully tended.

"Forget it. Get through the hole!"

Hannah moves slowly. Too damn slowly. She has her gun still trained on the Uhrwerkmänn that isn't spasming and steaming in the corner. Keeps taking shots to keep it at bay as I cover the distance.

"Come on!" I yell, two paces away.

"After you." She looks calm now, or at least as calm as her gritted teeth will allow.

And now perhaps is the time for militaristic yelling and the obeying of my field directives, regardless of whether they're crap or not. "Get through the goddamn hole!"

She blinks once. "Ladies first?" She snaps off another shot.

"Just—" I start and then she casually steps back and plummets down a story. I have time to shake my head before I follow her into the madness below.

15

My first thought is that I should have stayed upstairs. Clyde is hunkered down on the floor, one hand outstretched, head ducked, not looking, eyes pressed tight. An Uhrwerkmänn lies splayed out on the floor, legs wide, its chest crushed. But there are five more in the room, crowding it, encircling him. Hannah is beside him, standing over him, gun held in two hands, arms outstretched. I hear the pistol's report as I land next to her, have a moment to wonder if I'm going to fall into the line of her bullets. That seems to be the order of the day.

Then I'm firing too.

"Come on Clyde! Come on!"

I let go of my gun with one hand, sacrificing some accuracy to make sure I don't sacrifice him. The Uhrwerkmänner are too big to miss anyway.

"I've got satellite." Tabitha's voice is barely discernible over the gunfire, over the grinding of advancing gears. "Uhrwerkmänner in the street too."

"You know what," I say, trying to get Clyde to his feet, "wait until you have good news."

My earpiece crackles again. "Cowa-motherfeckin'-bunga!"

That wasn't Tabitha.

One of the Uhrwerkmänner is standing before a wide archway

that opens onto the hallway, just before the stairs. It tips back its head, lets out a grinding roar. Then a sword juts from its mouth, a blade where its mechanical tongue should be. It spits sparks and metal shards, the roar becoming a clacking stumble of sound. The sword rips sideways. The thing's jaw sways loose.

Kayla straightens, standing on its shoulders.

"That's you in your—" she starts.

Then the Uhrwerkmänn backhands her, sends her flying. Advances with its fellows, its ruined head leaking oil that dribbles down its face.

Oh shit. Their anatomy is not ours. They are inhuman. I glance over at Kayla. She has bounced off one robot's leg, is lying dazed on the floor. But the Uhrwerkmänner are ignoring her, are focused on the rest of us.

The howling Uhrwerkmänn lets out another roar, harsher, half broken, sprays more oil.

Oil.

"Tabitha!" I snap. "Get Clyde a spell that'll set fire to things."

I have Clyde on his feet now. I shove him toward the Uhrwerkmänn he felled before we arrived on the scene. I shake him. "Focus!"

"What? Where?" His voice is slurred.

I point with my pistol at the leaking Uhrwerkmänn. "There."

Tabitha starts rattling off syllables that make no sense. Clyde blinks several times.

Hannah ducks a blow, rolls back, and I have to jump to avoid her tangling with my feet. She comes up. "Can you get Kayla?" I ask.

Our swordswoman is on her feet but still looking dazed. She stands between two of the menacing Uhrwerkmänner.

Hannah stares at me. "Are you bloody insane?"

I shove Clyde at her. "Then make him work."

And then I'm launching myself toward the Uhrwerkmänner.

They move faster than they should. Faster than I can react to. I try to throw myself sideways mid-stride, but then I need to be ducking too, and I can't because my feet are off the floor, and unlike Clyde I am physics's bitch.

A fist catches my shoulder, a glancing blow that makes me think of irreparable joint damage as I spin through the air like a top. I land, still spinning, grind my tailbone into the ground. I howl, smash into something towering and bronze. It comes up, looking remarkably like a foot.

It comes down, still looking like one.

I roll, desperate. And the rabid dog of panic is loose now. He runs, ripping and howling and biting through my mind. I try to get to my feet, but the foot comes down again.

—coming down—

I leap forward, roll, awkward, land flat on my back. Bullets raise sparks above my head. And that's just perfect, even Hannah is trying to kill me now.

I am too deep in my own head to recognize the paranoia even as it taunts me. I want to curl up in a ball. But I can't. I have to keep moving. That's why I'm alive so far. Continual movement.

I'm on my feet, running, not sure if I'm screaming or not. And then there's Kayla, standing right in front of me, her sword swaying in front of her. I swing around her, bounce between a bronze leg and her trim frame.

She rubs her forehead, blinking. "Feck me."

An Uhrwerkmänn stomps toward us. A full-blooded charge. It raises its arms about to bring them down, double-fisted.

—coming down—

Now and then collide. Memories of a ruined Scottish bar overlaying the scene before me. I am frozen. I can't move. I can't do anything.

No. That was then. Not now. *Then.*

I smash Kayla sideways, send her flying. In the corner of my eye I see the fall become an acrobatic tumble, almost a cartwheel, her systems coming online. But I have already disarmed her, have already snatched her sword from her grasp as I sent her sailing. And now I grasp her katana as the fists swing down. I try to use the momentum of our collision to send me back toward the bronze leg.

And I don't have Kayla's strength, or her speed, but I do have a little of her skill. Clyde, when he was an artificial intelligence, downloaded an encyclopedia of sword moves into my brain, and

Kayla has drilled me until that knowledge is not just in my head, but in my muscles. I keep the blade tucked into me, let one fist slam down, missing me, then I lunge. I thrust the point of the blade deep into the joint, twisting, ripping up as hard as I can.

Without Kayla's strength I cannot tear metal sheets, cannot split armor, but even in the thin wiggle room I can lever the blade through, I can feel gears crunching, wires snapping. I wrench the blade free and oils spurts wildly about. The Uhrwerkmänn bellows, and as it raises its arms back up, both fists hang loose. I allow myself a brief moment to cheer.

The Uhrwerkmänn kicks me.

It does not kick me in my ribs, or my legs, or even my groin. It kicks me in *all* of me. My entire body is mashed by the pistoning limb that lifts me across the full length of the floor.

Kayla's sword spins out of my hands. Spittle and most of my sense flies out of my mouth. I almost fly out of my shoes. And then I come down. A crunch and a bang, my mouth snapping open and shut, mashing on my tongue, blood filling my mouth as colored lights fill my vision.

I feel as if I've come apart. I am still legs and arms, hands and feet, head and torso, but the order of things no longer makes sense. I am a jigsaw puzzle scattered across the floor, and my head is spinning far too hard for me to have a chance to solve this problem.

If I work out how my stomach and mouth connect, I think I'm going to vomit again.

My vision is the first thing to come back. I kind of wish it hadn't. An Uhrwerkmänn standing over me. Foot raised.

At least it's not a fist this time. No flashbacks.

Fuck.

The foot comes down.

And then the foot comes loose.

A line of white fire slices through the limb, smashing through armor sheets, metal buckling under the fury of the impact. It drops to the ground less than a yard short of me, the impact jostling my assorted limbs. The Uhrwerkmänn staggers, stumbles, sits down next to me. Kayla stands where it did, oil-soaked blade in one hand.

She holds the other one out to me. "There," she says, "that's how you take off a feckin' limb."

I fight for control of my body, find it enough to reach out my hand to her. She grabs it, hauls me to my feet.

"Spending too much of this job knocked on your feckin' arse," she says. "Going to end up dead that way."

I can't even laugh. I just can't.

16

Kayla drags me to the Uhrwerkmänn that Clyde felled before we entered the room. Hannah stands there, shooting with one hand, shaking Clyde with the other. "I can't focus," I hear him saying. "Say it one more time."

"Concentrate, damnit." Tabitha eschews encouragement in favor of castigation.

"Oh for fuck's sake." My voice is thick thanks to my bitten tongue. But I'm done trying to communicate. The room stinks of gasoline. My pistol is still clenched in a death grip in my hand. I point it at an advancing Uhrwerkmänn, dripping black oil from numerous gashes. I aim at its bleeding head. The first three shots go wide, the next two hit armor, raising sparks. The third shot raises enough to do what I'm looking for.

Flame encases the Uhrwerkmänn's head. It bellows, flailing. Its hemorrhaging arm catches fire, slams into one of its cohorts, forced next to it in the tight confines of the room. Fire rips from one Uhrwerkmänn to the next.

With Kayla still propping me up, I turn to Clyde. "Can you at least blow a hole in that wall?"

He seems to understand me, despite my mangled tongue. At least, he turns, stretches out an arm, and mutters. His arm jolts and bricks spray out into the Oxford street.

"That bloody way!" I am done with this mission. Bloody done.

At least Hannah doesn't question the order. Or try to shoot me in the legs or something.

We careen over the fallen Uhrwerkmänn. Kayla still half carries me. I have a feeling I'm not going to like it when the adrenaline wears off and I can feel all of this. But for now I let the madness of it all carry me along. If I can just keep moving, find my way back to the status quo.

Brick dust clogs the world, and then a cool breeze is sweeping it away. The world is clear and we are free. We skid to a halt, out in the open Oxford street.

Except, no, not quite open.

"Told you," comes Tabitha's voice in my ear. "Street is not a good idea."

And no. No it was not.

17

The Uhrwerkmänn is monumental. A literal monument to Joseph Lang's genius and madness. He stands at least twice as tall as the largest Uhrwerkmänn I have seen before. His head is only a foot or two shy of the windows on the second story of Lang's house.

While the other Uhrwerkmänner gleam bronze, this mechanical man has been painted a flat black. They reflect the light; he absorbs it. Interlocking plates of armor coat his gargantuan form. Not a single gear is exposed. No weak point. No chink to exploit. His head is low-slung, angular, shaped like a knight's helmet of old, a dark narrow slit for his eyes. The armor on his shoulders and chest is worked in fancifully decorative scenes depicting armies marching, tanks rolling, and enemies being crushed to a thick meaty paste. In the center of his chest, a large circular disk bears the likeness of an eagle, its mouth open in a scream. In its claws it grasps a swastika.

This is it. Lang's *Meisterwerk*.

"He's Friedrich, isn't he?" I say.

"I'd guess so," Clyde says. He seems to be recovering himself.

"Fuck me," I hear Hannah whisper. "This job is bloody mental."

That realization, I feel, marks the end of Hannah's orientation period. She gets what the job's about now.

"Oh buggeration," says Clyde. Which is when I notice that one of Friedrich's feet is planted on top of Clyde's Mini. It no longer resembles a car so much as it resembles the sort of mechanical pancake Joseph Lang might have made if he'd been of a more culinary bent.

"All right," I say. "We need to get to Hannah's Renault, and then we need to drive away very fast."

As plans go, I am pleased with the fact that it gets everything into one sentence. The only potential flaw is that it ignores the issue that Friedrich is between us and the car.

Behind us, I hear bricks collapse, heavy mechanical footsteps. The other Uhrwerkmänner have not stopped their pursuit just because we have left the building. We are caught between the metaphorical rock and death-dealing automaton.

"Any suggestions on how the feck we're going to do that?" asks Kayla.

I put my finger to my ear. "Tabitha, find Clyde the biggest spell we have in the database and make it goddamn rain."

There is a pause, and then a malevolent cackle.

Behind us the footsteps grow louder. Before us, Friedrich spreads his arms. "Welcome, little ones," he booms, accent so thick that I can barely make out the words.

"Two car batteries," Tabitha's voice cuts in. "Got access to them?"

I scan the street fast. Clyde's car is totaled, and if we take the one out of Hannah's then our escape plan is buggered. But the Uhrwerkmänner did come here in three large trucks, also parked down the street.

"Maybe," I venture.

"Wait," says Clyde, "you're not thinking about the Viennese Pike are you?"

Again the malevolent chuckle.

Hannah has her gun out again, is pointing it behind us at the encroaching machines. Before us, Friedrich's bulk blocks the street.

"Would you deny us life, little ones?" asks Friedrich. I think he's trying to croon, but the syllables are too harsh, tearing through any pretense of softness.

"Remember how I said I never wanted to try that due to the

high likelihood that I would fry my liver inside my body? Which, while it sounds academically interesting, and as if it would make for a fascinating autopsy, is less the sort of thing I'd like to do to myself on a Wednesday morning," Clyde continues.

"Well," Friedrich continues, unaware of the team's internal debate. "If you would try to deny me, then I can but only try to deny you."

He's a bit long-winded when it comes to his threats, is old Friedrich.

"Is the chance of your liver getting toasty higher or lower than the chance of that Uhrwerkmänn doing to us what he did to your car?" asks Hannah.

Clyde pauses, swallows. "Fair point," he says. "Any chance anyone could help me get a hold of two car batteries?"

"Bloody mental," Hannah mutters again.

I point to the nearest truck. "Hannah and I are on that one. Kayla," I point to the next nearest, "that's yours." I look to Clyde. "Just try to buy us time."

"Can do." And Clyde starts to mutter as the rest of us start to run. He flings out an arm toward Friedrich. I recognize the cadence of the nonsense. The spell Clyde calls Elkman's Push. The one he used to damage the Uhrwerkmänner inside and knock down the walls so we could make our escape.

Friedrich doesn't even flinch. Clyde skids backwards, sneakers squeaking over the surface of the road, arms pinwheeling, trying to keep his balance. Friedrich's laugh is deep and hollow, booming out of his chest.

Shit and balls.

Hannah and I reach the first truck. She tries to get purchase on the lid, but it won't even raise an inch or two.

"Get in the cab," she yells, "unlock this!"

She's got the who's-in-command order mixed up again, but it's probably not time to push the issue.

Kayla's over at the other truck, slicing through steel with her sword, flinging the hood away. The whole supernatural strength thing does seem like it would be terribly helpful.

Clyde is still recovering. The recoil of his failed spell has shoved him close to the three Uhrwerkmänner pushing their way out of the building. All of them are still on fire. One whips a blazing arm in his direction. Clyde dodges forward but oil jets out of the Uhrwerkmänn's injured limb in a flaming stream, spattering his tweed jacket. He howls, drops, and rolls. He comes back up smoking but no longer aflame.

Friedrich continues his advance.

The massive Uhrwerkmänn is in line with Kayla and her truck. She has her fists deep in the engine block, fishing with wires.

Friedrich brings his fist down, a blur of motion, and a crack of displaced air. Kayla glances up, flings herself backwards.

Friedrich's fist buries itself in the engine block. There is a short sharp electrical crack and a momentary spurt of fire. Then his fist comes up. The engine is flatter than Clyde's car. Kayla stands a foot away from the crater he's made, empty-handed. And that's one battery we're not getting.

I'm up at the driver's door, flinging it open, diving into the footwell, grabbing desperately for any handle that seems like it will pop open the hood. It's only going to take Friedrich two more footsteps before he's in line with our truck.

I grab something, yank, hear Hannah shout. She sounds at least vaguely positive. I beat my retreat.

Clyde is still caught between the flaming Uhrwerkmänn and Friedrich. He looks as if he's going to make a dash between Friedrich's legs, then thinks better of it. He glances back at the robots behind him. Thinks better of that. Instead he goes sideways, but that only takes him to the façade of the facing house. For a moment I fear he's going to head into it. This is not a problem we want to bring to someone else's doorstep. It's bad enough we've destroyed Lang's house without us causing the destruction of one whose owners are still actually alive. That is not at all our mandate.

Fortunately Clyde seems to remember that. Unfortunately that doesn't give him many places to go.

"Got it!" Hannah yells, hauling the car battery aloft.

Friedrich advances on Clyde, ignoring us. We actually have a straight shot to Hannah's Renault now. The three of us. Only Clyde is trapped.

I glance back at Kayla. She has recovered quickly, is at the third truck, eviscerating its internal mechanics.

Clyde is trapped. So we all are. I wrench the car battery out of Hannah's hands. She yells but I ignore her. I pitch the car battery up through the air, wrenching my already screaming shoulder. It lands with a heavy thud at Clyde's feet, barely bounces.

"Kayla!" I yell.

And then a second car battery whistles up through the air like a mortar. It comes down hard, slamming into Friedrich's shoulder and ricocheting off without him even adjusting his stride. It lands on its end, next to the battery I threw.

"He has the batteries!" I yell to Tabitha.

Friedrich stands before Clyde. The three other Uhrwerkmänner complete a flaming crescent around him.

Tabitha starts intoning random syllables for Clyde to repeat.

Clyde kneels, seizes hold of both batteries. His arms shake violently, his head bucks back and forth, but I can see his lips move. "*Meshtar mal folthar cal ulthar met yunedar—*"

Friedrich raises a fist.

Clyde's legs start to spasm.

Friedrich's fist comes down.

18

Clyde's lips are still moving.

And then they're not.

Friedrich's fists are a blur. There is the meaty crunch of impact. I close my eyes.

"Holy crap." Hannah's voice, her cockney accent very pronounced for a moment.

I open my eyes.

Clyde is still sitting on the street, still spasming and twitching. Smoke is wafting up from his palms.

Friedrich's fists are a foot above his head. They are still balled. The Uhrwerkmänn is leaning forward, putting all his weight into them. I can hear the metal groaning. But they stay a foot above Clyde's head, not moving, frozen in midair.

And then Clyde's lips start to move again. Metal creaks. Friedrich's titanic shoulders start to shake, picking up the spastic shivering of Clyde's body. And then slowly, inevitably, his hands are pushed back.

Gears start to grind. With a bellow Friedrich eases up on the pressure of his blow. His arms fly back. Beneath Clyde, the ground is starting to deform. Weeds pushing up through the asphalt are pressed flat, leaves are crushed, oozing fluid. Cracks start to run through the pavement. The wall of the house behind him creaks. A windowsill cracks, is crushed down to splinters. An invisible ball of force expands around Clyde.

Friedrich is forced back a step, slams into a flaming Uhrwerkmänn, stumbles, steps on another, crushing it.

"Back up!" I yell, though I'm yelling at myself as much as Hannah and Kayla. There is something transfixing about watching the cracks in the pavement racing toward me.

I back-pedal, my eyes still on Clyde. The truck we just looted groans as the ball of force hits it, starts shoving it down the road after us. I start back-pedalling faster.

Friedrich is pressed up against Joseph Lang's house. The Uhrwerkmänn he trampled is now half flattened beneath the weight of Clyde's spell. I watch as its legs are crushed, then its torso. Friedrich is pushed back another step. Lang's house crumbles around him. Bricks tumble about his legs, beams raining down over his massive shoulders. The start of a landslide.

Clyde's feet are kicking so hard they're starting to blur. His torso thrashes back and forth between the batteries. Somehow he's still holding on to the contacts, but I don't know how.

"Oh crap." The expletive slips from between my lips. Clyde *has* to hang on. Inter-reality friction. If his spell is no longer powered by electricity then—and I don't pretend to understand exactly how—the two realities, ours and the one he's reaching into to craft this spell, will rub together, and the end result will be Clyde going boom in a fairly substantial way.

I slam my finger against my earpiece. "He has to end it," I tell Tabitha. "Tell him to end it, before he shakes himself loose of the batteries."

She understands immediately. "Shut it down! Shut it down, now!" There is uncharacteristic concern in her voice.

Next to me, the front of the truck gives way. I feel something invisible slam into me, send me reeling back. Hannah has turned and is just straight up, running away.

"End it!" I yell at Clyde, though I can't imagine a way he can hear me. "End the spell now!"

The ball of force buffets me again, harder, bowls me over. Friedrich is buried deep in the façade of Lang's house, now concave. Clyde's spell is the only thing still holding it up. And the spell keeps on, continues to expand. I feel a crushing pressure start to roll over my toes, my feet. Bone grinds against bone. I moan.

"Shut it down, you plonker!" Tabitha snaps.

And then it's gone. Everything gone. There is a second of perfect stillness. And then the air rushes back, a thunderclap of sound, dragging down the front of Lang's house, flipping over the truck beside me in a great angry scream of flying metal. Hurling me onto my feet, sending me several running steps back toward Clyde. Friedrich slumps, staggers. Dust is a whirlwind before me.

The truck slams, upside down, onto the street. The quake of the impact tears through my gut. Hannah slams into a tree by the side of the road, peels herself off it, staggers on toward her car. Kayla is already there.

I try to pick myself up, get my bearings. I glance back at Hannah. And has she kept her cool? If she panics and takes the car, we're all doomed. Still, Kayla's with her. Kayla will help keep her sane.

And Clyde. Where the hell is Clyde? He was in the middle of that thing. And from the looks of the swirling maelstrom of dust and destruction filling the street, a lightly flambéd liver may be the least of his worries.

Plus, he has the only object we managed to recover from the house, even if it was just a desk ornament. This fight will not have been worth surviving if we arrive back at MI37 empty-handed.

I need to go back in to the chaos. I need to get him out.

And I can't.

I stand there, and my legs just won't move. I try to get them to go but they simply refuse. Sweat coats my face. I'm breathing hard. And I need to go in there. I need to get Clyde. I focus on that, but other images keep flickering through my head. Bronze fists descending, buildings collapsing, Felicity standing before a house alone, her telling me she wants me to move in with her. All of my pains seem suddenly so much worse, seem to weigh so much heavier. I cannot move for the weight of them. They hold me to the spot. I gasp for air.

I have to go—

I have to—

Behind me, Kayla is slamming her hand down on the horn of the car. "We have to feckin' go!"

I try to answer. I can't get the air.

He's in there. He's fucking dead. If I go in, I'll be… I'll… I'll…

Then, from the swirling cloud that fills the street, an eddy becomes a shadow, becomes a hunched over figure, becomes Clyde, hacking and coughing, stumbling forward.

His hands are red, blistered, every hair on his head is on end, and his eyebrows are smoking slightly, but he is alive. He is Clyde, and he is still standing.

He paws dirt from his eyes, stares around wildly, sees me.

"We can go now, right?" There's a slightly hysterical edge to his voice.

Something crashes behind him, invisible in the swirling chaos. Clyde jerks, flinging his head around to look over his shoulder. He starts to run.

My limbs come loose. I run too. Pell-mell, like the proverbial bat straight out from Satan's dusty arsehole. I fight to keep in control, to not just run over Clyde. Instead I grab his shoulder, pull him with me.

Hannah's car starts moving. And we are not there. She is leaving without us. She is abandoning us to our deaths. She is—

She is turning the car around. A swift three-point turn, and Kayla flings doors open. I throw Clyde across the seats, dive on top of him. Hannah applies her foot to the accelerator, and we take off, leaving only dust and disaster in our wake.

19

BACK AT MI37

One of the advantages of dating Felicity is that she allows me to apply the ice packs before we do the debrief. Also, Clyde needs to be taken for an MRI scan to make sure he's not char-broiled his intestines. Meanwhile, Tabitha is sent on a begrudging sandwich run, and I take painkillers, and walk myself through a self-assessment for concussion. Basically, if you can read it, you don't have one.

Kayla spends most of the time telling me not to be "such a big feckin' nancy". I prefer that to the time she spends staring at her phone saying terrifying things like, "No, he's too pretty," and "Aye, that's a bum, that is."

Clyde returns around the same time Tabitha brings the sandwiches back, with a foul-smelling cream all over his hands and a surprisingly chipper attitude.

Hannah sits quietly, applying ice and bandages in equal measure. Having consumed her sandwich, she pulls herself out of her chair and stumbles stiffly off in the direction of the office kitchen. She comes back with a cup of something brown. She takes a sip then spits out a long stream of fluid into one of the trashcans. "Jesus," she says, disgust painted clear upon her face, "what the bloody hell is that?"

Clyde and I exchange a glance.

"Coffee," I venture.

She shakes her head. "That is not pissing coffee. That's pissing piss that is."

I'm not sure why—maybe it's just the residual adrenaline in my system, or perhaps my desperate desire to forget my moment of total paralysis—but I take mild offense to this. The MI37 coffee is indeed shitty. It does indeed taste a little like cat urine. But it is our coffee. It is the coffee of brotherhood. Clyde and I have saved the world drinking that coffee.

"I think Tabitha tested it once," Clyde says, "and actually compared to most coffees you'll find that the urine content is actually quite low."

Hannah looks at him like he just dealt her sanity a blow it didn't need to take. "Most coffees?" she says.

"Look," I say, "I'll admit it's not the finest brew, but…"

"It is awful," Clyde agrees. "Which is what makes the urine thing so surprising I think."

That is not the point I am trying to make.

"Is this how you fight off the monsters then?" Hannah asks. "Just throw a mug of this stuff at them and see them bugger off to the mothership."

I think there might be a veiled criticism in there… Either that or a desperate attempt to put this morning's events into some sort of context. But I'm not sure if I'm up to feeling charitable.

"Ooh!" Clyde claps. "We should totally try that. And, as an interesting adjunct, it does seem that there are a number of realities containing entities that are theoretically soluble in caffeine. Unfortunately the nitrogen in our atmosphere causes them to detonate, so no one's been able to test—"

"Look," I say, wanting to get back to the suddenly important cause of defending MI37's shitty coffee, "it's a perfectly acceptable beverage. It's there for keeping us awake, and for improving reaction times in the field. We need…" I reach for something else caffeine could theoretically help with.

"Course," says Hannah, "if you don't drink the piss, you could just sleep through the invasion and avoid danger that way." She throws a wink at Clyde.

He grins. "Another excellent point, actually."

He is not helping.

"Look—" I say for the third time.

Which is when Tabitha passes the kitchen. She is holding a glass jar in which something unspeakable floats in formaldehyde. She looks at us.

"The hell you drinking the coffee for?" she asks. "Tastes like piss."

All in all, I am rather glad when Felicity pops her head in and tells us it's time for the debrief, even if moving my legs does feel like trying to coordinate two planks of wood.

Back in the conference room, I run through events while clutching a fresh ice pack to the back of my head. I outline our arrival, the poor state of the books, the arrival of Friedrich and his robotic cronies—

"Because Volk and Hermann sold us up shit creek and nicked our paddle too," Hannah cuts in. "Like I said they would."

Her ice pack is on her shoulder.

"That doesn't make sense," I say. "Why come here, ask for us to go there, and then attack? Why not just come here in force?"

"They couldn't come here in force. They had to make nice and lure us into the open."

"It still doesn't make sense. They have no argument with us." I feel like Hannah is reaching here. MI6 has honed her professional paranoia to too sharp an edge. It would have been better, I think, to bring in someone fresh, with fewer preconceived notions. This job demands flexibility of thinking.

"You know what really doesn't make sense? You almost shooting me twice. I noticed you hadn't mentioned that yet."

Oh, so that's what this is about. "You stepped into my line of fire twice."

"You don't know basic pissing fieldwork! You didn't count my shots. And you're the bloody field lead!" She's still sitting down, has her arms folded, and she's trying hard to keep the professional mask in place, but it's fraying at the edges. She's letting a little too much passion into her voice.

I open my mouth to defend myself, when Felicity says, "Look," her voice like a cleaver severing the strands of our argument. "Let's focus on what actually happened. We do not yet have proof that Volk and Hermann betrayed us. There are multiple explanations. Coincidence is one of them, but I'm not a huge fan of that theory. Hermann and Volk knew where we were, maybe this Friedrich character does as well. He could have surveillance on us. Or he could have it on them. They told us their broadcast frequencies, maybe Friedrich knows them. He was one of them once. And while they told us they were using encryption, the Enigma code was broken in the forties. We can't discount betrayal, but we can't say it's a certainty at this point, and Arthur's arguments make me question whether it truly is likely."

Hannah does not look happy about this. I try to not look too happy.

"As for fieldwork," and here Felicity's gaze shifts to me and I start feeling decidedly less smug, "that's not been an area of concentration for us. Until recently everyone has had," she pauses, searching for the right word, "a rather unique skill set, and coordination hasn't been an issue. It's also not Arthur's background. Any pointers and tips you have on how we can increase our efficiency in that aspect of our work would be very helpful, I'm sure."

She's still looking at me when she finishes talking. I decide to nod rather than point out that another solution is for us to get rid of Hannah because we were getting along just fine without her. Because it's not as if she didn't help at all. She did. She held more than one Uhrwerkmänn off my back. It's just I don't know that we couldn't have handled it without her, and I would have come far less close to almost shooting a co-worker in the head if we hadn't had her along.

Hannah nods as well. It is not a full declaration of peace but at least it's a momentary truce.

Finally, Felicity turns to Clyde. "And what exactly did we manage to retrieve after all this destruction of government property?"

Clyde either doesn't catch her tone, or doesn't recognize it, because he gives an excited smile and starts fishing around in his jacket pockets. He tugs a few times and then yanks out the desk ornament Hannah found.

"This!" he says with an absurd kind of glee. He sets it down on the table. It is about a foot tall, and an inch wide and deep, with narrow channels running down its sides. A series of nearly invisible diagonal lines slice through those channels, and at each slice, the channel is offset slightly, so the flow of it is broken into a series of steps weaving back and forth, the pattern of steps different on each side.

Felicity stares at it. "That?"

"Yes," nods Clyde, "that."

Kayla squints at him, then at Tabitha. "You sure that feckin' MRI said he was fine?"

"Is there," Felicity ventures, working her fingers back and forth across the table, possibly in search of a neck to throttle, "something about that particular…" She stumbles over what to call it.

"Desk ornament," I supply.

Felicity closes her eyes, seems to need a moment to absorb this additional detail. "That desk ornament," she manages, "that makes it worth all the attendant fuss that was involved in getting it?"

Clyde hesitates, cocks his head to one side, staring at the object. After a few seconds' contemplation he straightens. "I'm not sure," he says blithely.

Felicity's jaw works.

"Said he's not sure," Tabitha cuts in rather abruptly. She's staring at Felicity, as if daring her to vent her frustration. "Might be. Might not. Give him time to analyze."

Clyde beams. "Thank you, Tabby. Very kind of you to say. And very nice to get a vote of confidence. Can make all the difference that can. Really. I read about it somewhere. The impact of collective belief on outcomes. Of course, I do think there was a chance the author had been committed to a mental health institution at the time of publication, but that's more often the case than not with this sort of material. It was well-referenced as I recall. Though a lot of it was to CIA documents that, when I had a chance to check them out, were largely redacted. Bit of a shame. I had this terrific idea surrounding government propaganda and the flavoring of pancakes, but—"

He looks up and sees us staring at him.

"Maybe another time," he finishes.

For a moment Felicity pushes her hands to her temples. I want to reach out to her, stroke her arm, do something to help her ground herself, find her feet in all of this. But she is more than strong enough to do it herself. When she pulls her hands away her jaw is set, her eyes clear.

"You." She points to Clyde. "Find out everything you can about that… desk ornament. I want to know anything it has to tell us. Use techniques the Americans wouldn't dare to use on terrorists if you have to. Make today worthwhile.

"You." She points at Tabitha. "Get on satellite footage, CCTV footage, on damn YouTube, and find out if we can see where the hell those Uhrwerkmänner either came from or went to. I want to know where they live and then I want to drop a bomb on it."

There is a fire in her eyes now, steel in her voice.

"You." She turns her finger on Hannah. Hannah seems to fight the urge to look startled, and doesn't quite land on interested. "I want to do a team-building exercise tonight, and I need you to pick a place for us to do drinks. ASAP."

The order is given with such military force that it takes me a moment to sort out what it actually is. A team-building exercise? But tonight is for lying horizontal on the couch, complaining bitterly about aches and pains, and listening to Miles Davis at excessive volume. I am very sure it is specifically for that. I need that. I need my head straight. I froze up today. That can't happen again. And where alcohol has failed me in the past, Miles has always had a good chance of success.

"Team-building?" I think the constant shifting terrain at MI37 is finally beginning to fatigue Hannah. "Like, bevvies and shit?"

Probably not exactly how Felicity would have phrased it.

"Along those lines," she concedes.

"Banging." Hannah grins.

"Tonight?" I ask, trying to sound like I'm being reasonable, and not contrary. Unfortunately, there is a small chance I may have already been undermined by my earlier behavior. "Are you sure?"

My head throbs. I think I preferred it when the pain was just due to alcohol.

"Yes, Arthur," Felicity says. "The cohesion of the team is important. I think that became clear today." If her tone grew any more pointed it would prick me.

Kayla leans forward in her chair for the first time since the debrief began. She stabs a finger at Hannah. "Pick somewhere with some decently feck-able men, all right?"

Oh, well, that's just perfect.

SHORTLY

Felicity snags me in the corridor as we traipse out. Hannah has told us she will email out a meeting spot later, once she's had time to think about it some more.

"Hey," Felicity says, "do you want to go home and grab some supper first? I think we have some left over tortellini in the freezer."

I look down at her. The woman I love. *Home.* She said home. She means her place. No, *our* place. She is asking, in her own way, to look after me.

And I can't say yes.

If we go back, I will have to fill out the holes in my report. All the things I didn't want to say to my boss, but have to confide in my girlfriend. That I froze up today and risked my friend's life. That there is something outside of me, but somehow part of me, some fear that grips me so hard I can hardly breathe. That every time I look at her, think of *her* place becoming *our* place, I feel its fingers about me.

I don't have time for those feelings. I don't know what is going on in my head, but it has to stop. I need to kick myself back into alignment quickly. And I need peace for that.

"I was thinking…" I start. Which is all I have. I try to force my brain to engage. "I was thinking… maybe I could get a head start on packing up some of my stuff to bring over to your place. Sorting piles. What to put into storage. What to chuck. That sort of thing."

"Oh." Felicity's face falls for a moment, then brightens. "That's a great idea. Thank you, Arthur." She leans up and pecks me on the cheek.

If any of what I'd told her was true, I suspect I wouldn't feel like an arsehole right now.

"It's mostly going to be me making a mess and finishing up crappy microwave pizza," I say, elaborating on the lie. "Why don't you go home, have some of that tortellini and I'll catch up with you at drinks?"

Something flickers across Felicity's face. Indecision, perhaps, though that's not normally her style. Then she smiles again. "OK, yes. Maybe that's for the best."

An odd way to phrase it. The guilt battles with my relief. Guilt loses. I lean down, kiss her forehead, and walk away.

AN UNGODLY HOUR, OUTSIDE AN UNGODLY-LOOKING PLACE

The Park End night club in Oxford appears to have very little to do with the up-scale residencies in London, and a lot more to do with girls who don't look old enough to drink wearing clothes that don't look suitable for public display.

Hannah stands in line with them, clapping her gloved hands, and rubbing them together for warmth. She's wrapped in a long thick woolen coat, but where her legs emerge they are bare, and she's wearing heels that look like they might double as stiletto daggers.

Actually given her training they might do that…

Clyde and Tabitha stand next to her, both looking like they came from the office, which I suspect they did. Clyde waves me over.

"Hey," I say, trying not to say anything that sounds as old as I feel right now, "how did it go looking at that desk ornament?"

"Oh!" Clyde beams. "Quite well, I think. Tabby was the one who really cracked it open. Not literally. Well, I mean, there was a very funny incident with a hammer, but that worked out pretty well all told. And I promised to not make any more references to The Cure that could be misconstrued in a negative light. So, you know, problem solved."

"None of that," Hannah cuts in. "No bloody work chat. I've had more than enough of that today. This is after-hours bollocks this is. I want you all to get shit-faced and tell me who's porked who."

"Oh," says Clyde. "That's easy. Tabitha and I dated before I died and went insane. And Arthur is dating Felicity. Not sure on the porking status there, but it doesn't really seem an area I want to intrude upon. That said, I mean, it's been a year and she wants him to move in, so if one were to make an assumption—"

"Shut up," I say. It is a little abrupt, but I have exhausted my mental list of polite ways to get Clyde to stop talking.

Hannah seems unsure if she should appear amused or slightly disturbed. "Bloody incestuous lot, you are, aren't you?"

"They're feckin' disgusting."

I look over my shoulder to discover that Kayla has arrived. Then I keep on looking because apparently not much of Kayla's wardrobe decided to arrive with her.

Ever since I have known Kayla she has been encased in flannel and denim. I have a suspicion that grunge was kind of a big thing for Kayla. I think I can count on my fingers the number of times I've been able to see both of her eyes looking out from under her bangs. As a side note, they both looked equally murderous on all occasions, ending a bet Tabitha and I had going.

But not tonight. Tonight she is wearing something narrow and dark, that hangs off one shoulder and clings desperately to her on the way down. And then it stops halfway down her thighs, and there is pretty much just leg for quite a long way until some rather elegant wedges adorn her feet. And her hair... something has happened to her hair. It is shiny, and pulled back loosely, with a subtle fifties vibe worked into it. There is a lot of skin, and, well, I have always known that Kayla is terrifyingly athletic, but she avoids the mildly freakish look of a body-builder. She is muscled, but leanly. She has more... shape than I would have imagined. If I'd ever imagined. I hadn't. And yet now, despite my best efforts, it is very hard to deny that, in fact, the whole effect... it is... attractive.

"Damn, girl," Hannah's abrasive tones cut through my surprise, "you are going to fucking kill on that floor tonight."

"The whole feckin' point," Kayla says. She reaches into a tiny bag she is clutching in one fist. She jams out her phone at Hannah. "These three," she says. "Meeting them here."

All of which leads me to believe that Kayla approaches dating in much the same way she approaches a swordfight. It's a slightly daunting idea.

"Let's see them." Tabitha elbows toward Hannah and the phone screen.

Thankfully that is the moment I feel Felicity slide her hand up my spine. I turn, kiss her. A moment of respite from the world. Then, all too quickly, it's over and Felicity is looking past me, taking in the rest of the group. "Oh, Kayla," she says, "you do look lovely."

Kayla shrugs. "I feckin' know that."

I lean down, kiss Felicity's head, and take the opportunity to say, "How long before we can leave?"

She leans back, looks at me ruefully. "Come on," she says, "you faced down a horde of Nazi robots today. You can take on a dance floor."

STANDING NEXT TO A DANCE FLOOR

"On second thoughts," says Felicity, "that was a terrible idea. Let's find a seat."

In front of us, a thick mass of Oxonian youth bounces about like dice in a cup to the rhythm of a bass line that is more felt than heard. To be honest, it all looks rather violent. And not my sort of thing at all.

Yet, for some reason, my foot is tapping.

I should hate this. I came here ready to hate this. I was mentally prepared for that. But, watching the teenagers dance, I see a sort of abandon in them that resonates with memories of my own youth. I never went to a club like this exactly, but I definitely remember back when I was a student—beers and music, and... other things that a former policeman will not talk about. A time when I used to let music move rather than cocoon me.

It has been a long time since I danced with anyone, but I would rather like to coax Felicity Shaw into that twisting mass of humanity.

She, however, is heading toward some stairs and hauling me after her. The others follow us.

"Drinks," I manage to make out Hannah saying. "Nice one."

The upstairs of Park End features several bars, a second dance floor, and a circular balcony that looks down on the floor below. Kayla and Hannah position themselves on the edge of the balcony and peer down. Felicity races toward a table and the two chairs next to them, then stares down a gaggle of teenage girls who get there at the same time.

"I'll grab some drinks," I say, nodding toward the mobbed bar as she slumps down.

Tabitha and Clyde stand next to each other, looking awkward. A lull in the throb of the music lets Clyde hear me, he looks up gratefully. "I'll come too."

There is an art to getting to the crowded bar. It involves a lot of shoulder and elbow work, and has to be subtly done if one is to avoid injury. It's a knack, and again something I used to have a modest amount of skill at. It takes me a while to get through the first two rows, but then all of a sudden I'm at the bar, and I can only vaguely hear Clyde—lost behind me—asking people if they would mind getting out of his way, perhaps, maybe, please. I smile slightly. Despite all my expectations, I think I may be enjoying myself.

Two minutes later, I am clutching three pints, a glass of wine, and two bottled drinks with the names of fruit on them. I grab Clyde from the back of the bar crowd where he's still being thwarted by his own politeness and drag him back to Felicity and the others.

"Thanks, love," says Felicity. She takes a fairly substantial sip of the wine.

Hannah and Kayla are looking over the edge of the balcony, down at the dance floor. "What about him?" Kayla points.

"Not exactly my type." Hannah shrugs.

"Well what's your feckin' type then?"

It strikes me that it took saving the world twice before Kayla treated me in a way that even approached mild disdain. Hannah has managed to get right in there.

Which is a good thing of course, and would be a silly thing to be jealous about if I were actually jealous. But it's not helpful that Hannah is encouraging this procreation plan. It's not healthy behavior on Kayla's part.

"My type?" Hannah squints at Kayla. "Well, it's erm…" It is one of the rare occurrences when she looks less than sure of herself. I try to pretend I'm not eavesdropping. "Slightly less male," she finishes.

My attempt to look as if I'm not paying any attention is betrayed by my eyebrows shooting up.

Kayla stares at Hannah hard. "You like the ladies, then?" she says finally.

Hannah nods.

Kayla eyes momentarily tighten. Hannah has that professional shield up, a carefully manicured neutrality. Then Kayla breaks into a broad grin.

"This is feckin' perfect. You are going to be the feckin' greatest wingwoman I've ever known." She grabs Hannah by the wrist. "Come with me now." She drags her toward the stairs leading back down to the main dance floor.

I look over at Felicity. "Did you…?"

She shrugs. Which I suppose is all that little revelation really deserves.

Clyde and Tabitha keep intermittently looking back down the stairs and then taking large sips of their drinks. They seem to be avoiding each other's eyes.

"Very interesting music from a structural point of view," Clyde says at last, shouting to make himself heard. "I mean, on one level it's very formal, but there's so much room for looseness within those strictures. Not my normal fare, but really rich in influences. Almost a bricolage-like approach, if one will allow a comparison to the visual arts."

He stops as abruptly as he started. Stares into space. I nod, mostly to be polite. Everyone else seems to be doing pretty much the same. Personally, I just think it's a terrible song that just happens to be ridiculously catchy, and to possess a curious power over my hips. They sway from side to side without my approval. On an additional note, I think this might be the best I've felt in days.

"Bit light for me," Tabitha says, still not looking at Clyde. She takes another sip of her beer. She's almost finished it.

"Well," Clyde smiles, "it's not Dvorak, is it?"

Tabitha still doesn't meet his eye. "Probably not."

Both of them take large sips. They stare into their empty pint glasses. Clyde puts his down on the table, seems not to know what to do with his hands, and picks it up again.

Tabitha turns to him, hesitates. He turns to her. The moment hangs. Felicity and I try to freeze, be nothing more than human furniture. Tabitha glances away then back.

"Wanna dance?" she says finally.

"Well," Clyde says, shoulders already pistoning, "erm, I mean, what I was going to say was—"

Tabitha grabs his arm.

"Yes," he finishes.

They descend, leaving Felicity and me behind. I stare after them. And even with the music bludgeoning some of the rough edges out of my mood, I still feel doubt gnaw at me over that one. They have walked that path before and it didn't lead anywhere that tourists would like to send postcards home from.

"You think they'll…" I start.

Felicity doesn't move, just watches the stairs. "I don't think we have any right to comment," she says after a while.

"I don't think they should," I say.

She nods. "They have history." Finally she looks at me. "Keep that to yourself, though."

I smile. Always sensible. My Felicity. I sit in the empty chair next to her. It stops my hips from further misbehavior at least, though my toe refuses to stop tapping. I take her hand in mine.

"So, everyone is dancing…" I tilt my head in the direction of the dance floor.

Felicity grimaces. "I realize this whole thing was my idea, but I just… I can't. It's, God, they're just… Everything is sticky. And loud. And very, very young."

She's right. I'm all of thirty-five, and in this crowd I look almost geriatric. Except part of me feels like the youth is rubbing off on me.

"You're the most beautiful woman here," I tell her, wrapping her fingers in mine.

She smiles, indicates her face with her free hand. "But this," she waves a hand at her face, "takes me much longer to achieve than it would take them."

I smile. "Don't spoil the illusion for me."

The free hand slaps me gently.

"Come on," I say, "let's dance a little. It'll be terrible, but we'll be team building." I grin at her.

Felicity straightens her back. "I am the head of a major division of the Ministry of Defense. I cannot be seen dancing in night clubs."

"Yeah," I say, "but if anyone recognized you as the head of a major division of the Ministry of Defense then you'd be no good at your job." I lean forward. "And I happen to know you're very good."

That earns me an eye roll. "Come on, let's get this over with."

We descend to the dance floor. I have no skill in this arena. Fortunately, I have found that the key to socially acceptable dancing is not skill. Instead it's something closer to what gets me, barely trained as I am, through encounters with terrifying monstrosities beyond the ken of my fellow man.

As Felicity starts to sway to the beat, I ask myself:

What would Kurt Russell do?

He'd pop it and lock it like a champ, and then he'd drop it like it's goddamned hot.

So I dance exactly like that. Not with style, not with class, and certainly not with grace, but with a sort of abandonment that ignores the fact that I am surrounded by other people. It's freeing, letting go of the social niceties, just letting the music bring something buried out of me. Moving how I want to move. Unfettered by fear.

I whirl around Felicity in a flurry of poorly coordinated limbs. I grab her hand and fling her back and forth. She looks as if she's caught between terror and hilarity. It's not a terrible place to be. I pull her close, kiss her, and then fly away. And nobody spares us a glance. We're just two more idiots in the night.

For one beautiful moment there is only this. Only now. Without worries about what's been and what's to come.

Then laughter interrupts me.

Hannah is standing on the edge of the dance floor, almost doubled over. I grind to a halt.

When she manages to straighten, she is breathing hard. She points at me, dissolves into giggles, then finally recovers long enough to say, "Oh, oh my... Oh, you dance like the oldest man on earth. It's fucking brilliant." And then she's stumbling toward the bar, bouncing off girls and boys with laughter and smiles.

I stand watching her.

Felicity comes and takes my hand. "We can go now, right," she says. She sounds tired.

"Yes," I say. "Yes we can."

20

THE NEXT MORNING, BACK AT MI37

I stare at nothing across the conference table, eyes half-lidded. Kayla reflects my look back at me. She's back in plaid, hair sagging in front of her eyes. Her hands play with her phone, turning it round and around, but she doesn't seem to be up for looking at it. She stifles a yawn. Hannah sits next to her. She looks exhausted too, but somehow smug about the whole thing.

Only Felicity, for all her complaints last night, looks alert and chipper. Well, alert and mildly annoyed. She checks her watch for the tenth time in as many minutes.

"We agreed nine a.m., didn't we?" she says for the fifth time. She knows we did. I nod slowly anyway.

Hannah rolls her head to look over at Kayla. "So," she says, "how'd it go with that third guy last night?"

Kayla looks down at her phone and grimaces. "Same as the other feckers. He was a looker, so that was nice. Not stupid either, though to be honest, in retrospect the night club seems a bit of a feckin' stupid place to go if you want to make sure someone's not a dumb feckin' arsehole."

Hannah nods sagely. "For most blokes, talking to a girl at a club and not exposing yourself as a dumb arsehole is a pretty high commendation, I think."

Felicity surprises me by uttering a brief, "Amen to that."

I check my watch. Where is Clyde?

"It's the feckin' arm wrestle that makes them puss out," Kayla decides to say at that moment.

I exchange a glance with Felicity. She looks less surprised than I think most people who have been in any sort of successful social interaction should look.

"Have you considered," I start, "that trashing a prospective boyfriend in a public arm wrestle—"

"I'm not looking for a feckin' boyfriend." Kayla looks at me as if I just asked if she'd like to take a dump on the conference room table. "I'm looking for a good genetic sample. This is simple feckin' Darwinism, and you better feckin' remember that."

We stare at each other for a moment. I'm not entirely sure what one says in this sort of situation. Nothing in life has prepared me for how to deal with a eugenics approach to one-night stands.

Felicity is checking her watch again, and I smell freedom. I turn to her. "Why don't I go down and check the lab, make sure they didn't get held up." Possibly with more enthusiasm than decorum would suggest.

Felicity nods. "Yes," she says. "This is getting ridiculous."

That is definitely one word for it.

MERCIFULLY FAR FROM CONFERENCE ROOM B

I always find the MI37 lab to be depressingly mundane. Long benches and stacks of scientific equipment; a Bunsen burner mostly strangled in its own rubber piping; a chemistry set that sits in a sink glistening wetly rather than bubbling and steaming; over-sized microscopes; laptops open to nonsensical databases. It is depressingly short on obscure tomes and fantastical creatures preserved in formaldehyde.

Lang's desk ornament sits on one bench, surrounded by a pair of calipers, a bundle of pipettes, and a hammer. Modern thaumaturgical science at its finest.

Of Tabitha and Clyde there is no sign.

I'm about to turn around and head back upstairs when I hear a noise from the supply closet. I pause, strain my hearing. The noise comes again, a sort of muffled thump, followed by some almost inaudible… word? Is that someone talking?

I take a step toward the closet door. There's a label on it saying in bold black letters, CAUTION, CONTAINS CAUSTIC MATERIALS. Then underneath someone has scribbled in red Sharpie, *That means you, Clyde.*

The noise comes again. A sort of rattling thump, then something else I can't quite make out. The sound of movement. And then, a muffled… what? I can't even tell if it was a human sound.

I pause, my hand inches from the closet door's handle. This is not just any laboratory. It is MI37's laboratory. Literally anything could be in there. And experience has led me to believe that if something could be anything then it is almost always something unspeakably awful.

Just in case, I draw my gun.

Another thump. The loudest so far. Something heavy colliding with… a shelf perhaps? Is someone tied up in there? Actually, that wouldn't be that bad given all the other things that could be behind the door.

Slowly, as quietly as I can, I twist the handle down, and ease the door open an inch.

And then I see. And I… I… I…

Oh God.

There is a lot of pale white skin.

And black.

And thrusting.

And Clyde's arse crack.

I let out something like a strangled cry of horror. Of all the things I could… no… no… oh dear God, no…

At my utterance, Tabitha shrieks. A high-pitched banshee howl. Oh God, I wish it was a banshee.

I stumble away, but in my haste I've forgotten to shut the door and it starts to swing open wider. I slam my hands over my eyes, momentarily debating the wisdom of clawing them out of my head altogether. My retinas are forever unclean.

"Oh good golly God," which is apparently what you say at exceptionally traumatic junctures if you're Clyde.

"Get out!" Tabitha screams. "Get out!"

"Did you need anything, old chap?" In his panic Clyde appears to have reverted to a 1940s stereotype.

I can't think. Behind my eyelids I keep seeing that narrow line of horror again. Tabitha's hands clawing at Clyde's back. His head thrown back—

Oh God. Oh God. I think I'm hyperventilating.

"Felicity was wondering if you were going to attend this morning's briefing session about—"

I realize that I'm talking, that my mouth is moving even as I back-pedal blindly across the room. I smack into a bench, half fall onto it, lie there like a turtle. I need to take my hands away from my eyes to get up properly, but I can't quite bring myself to. But if I don't then I'm trapped here longer.

"Oh yes!" says Clyde, sounding like he's on the edge of hysteria. "The desk ornament. Of course. Be up in, well, erm… I don't know… Shall we say twenty minutes?" His laugh scales up through octaves.

"Get out!" Tabitha screams again.

I manage to flip back over the table, land on the floor, and start in a belly crawl across the floor toward the door, steadfastly refusing to look behind me.

Tabitha's screams follow me out the door.

TWENTY DEEPLY TRAUMATIC MINUTES LATER

When she finally enters the conference room, Tabitha looks remarkably together. Her hair is even gelled into its two devil horns. The eyeliner is applied as thickly and neatly as ever. Every earring is in place. Even her scowl seems no different from the one she wears to the meeting room every day.

Clyde rather ruins the impression.

While not exactly neat at the best of times—Clyde has

somehow managed to make it to thirty without learning how to use an iron—today's look is a study in post-coital dishevelment. His shirt is buttoned wrong, pale white skin showing through the gaps. His tie hangs loose, on top of one half of his collar. One sleeve of his tweed jacket is rolled up to his elbow, though I have no idea how that could have happened. And somehow his trousers are on backwards.

Felicity stares at them. "What the hell kept you?" she asks.

I decided to not go into the details. I just told her Clyde had said they'd be twenty minutes, and then tried desperately to not think about why. I wish I knew which bit of my frontal cortex to jab the screwdriver into.

I wait for Tabitha and Clyde's answer with a sick sort of anticipation. It is like the train wreck you cannot help but stare at.

"Accidental spill in the lab," Tabitha says, channeling the rage of coitus interruptus into the words. "Took forever to clean it up."

"Caustic fluids lab, again," Clyde says with an apologetic shrug. "Lost quite a bit of clothing to the accident. Which is why I had to get dressed again."

That last bit seems like a rather unnecessary detail, but the story is well rehearsed at least. I can almost convince myself that Tabitha was just helping him clean up… caustic fluid.

I flashback again. No, I cannot quite believe that story. No matter how hard I try. I just cannot.

Felicity shakes her head. "Seriously, Clyde? Again? I think I'm just not going to let you go in that closet ever again."

"Good idea," I say before I can stop myself. Felicity stares at me, confused. "I totally agree," I trail off.

"Well, erm…" Felicity is still staring at me. "Thank you for the support on that one." Her eyes flick to Hannah, who seems to have a far better idea of what I walked in on, and who is smirking deeply.

"Maybe we can finally get down to it?" Felicity says.

"The presentation," I snap out. Oh God, I need to get more control over my tongue.

Felicity is staring at me again. "Maybe a little less caffeine tomorrow morning," she suggests.

"Yes," I say. "Of course. Just thought we should be specific about what it was. When you said…" I stop talking again. That would probably be best.

Hannah's smirk deepens.

"The presentation, totally, of course." Clyde seems to realize halfway to the front of the table that his trousers are on backwards. "Oh bugger," I hear him whisper.

He navigates his pocket awkwardly, reaching back around his thigh. "Is that a desk ornament in your pocket or are you just pleased to see me?" He titters, high-pitched, looking wildly around the room, before retrieving the item and tugging it out.

I reconsider whether the decision to not claw out my eyes was really such a good one.

From the way Felicity is looking at me, I think she's started to realize that something is a little off here.

"OK." Clyde sets the ornament down on the table, smooths his hair down three times in a row. It springs back up, ignoring him. "So the desk ornament. Did a little digging, dated the thing to the 1930s, so contemporaneous with Lang. In fact we have reason to think he might have been the designer. Mostly, I do have to admit, because he initialed it at the bottom. Not exactly Sherlock Holmes levels of detective work. Though to be honest, I think expecting that of anyone is a little absurd. I mean that's only really workable in fiction where someone knows the results and is backward engineering everything. It assumes omniscience really. Which, actually, makes me think of a number of experiments I'd love to run. I need to remember to write a proposal up for them, because I really do think even limited omniscience could have some very interesting combat implications. Not just violent and strategic, but also empathic. Maybe get us to some more peaceful solutions. Not that any of that is relevant of course, but if I tell you, then perhaps one of you will remind me." He looks around hopefully.

"The ornament," Felicity prompts.

"Oh yes. Well, ran some initial tests on it. Metal. Quite interesting alloy actually. Poor conductivity, which generally suggests it's not a magical object."

"Wait," Hannah holds up a hand, "is this all a long build-up to this being a desk ornament, or is there a good bit?"

Tabitha's eyes lock onto Hannah and look ready to deploy surface-to-air missiles.

"He's fucking explaining."

Ah, young love.

"Well, to be fair," Clyde says, "and I do think fairness is an important place for us to start from. Not that that's really a revolutionary idea. Fundamental starting point of at least a few major world religions that I can think of, anyway. But, to Hannah's point, I could probably cut..." He pulls a notebook out of his pocket, flicks it open, and scans a page. "Well, about the first twenty minutes of this if you just want to cut to what it does?"

"God, yes." Felicity echoes the sentiment of the room. Well, the sentiment of everyone except possibly Tabitha.

"Well, it's interesting actually. Totally Tabby's idea. Moment of utter brilliance on her part. You see it's all to do with the asymmetrical grooves on the sides." He indicates the lines that stutter back and forth down the long sides of the ornament. "You have to line them up, you see. But there's no way to actually do that. The way the thing pivots you can't do it."

He starts to wrench at it. With a series of grinding clicks, he transforms the ornament into a twisted polyhedron that vaguely resembles a drunk tower of Pisa. He waves it at us. "Useless, see?"

Hannah's eyes narrow. "This is the bit where it does something, right?"

"Trust me," I say, "this is the short version."

"Giving context," Tabitha snaps. "Important to *understanding*." She makes it sound like the last term is going to be a bit of a reach for Hannah and myself. I'm not entirely sure I deserve to be painted with the same brush here.

"Oh, yes," Clyde says, "got a little sidetracked, but I really do want you to understand how brilliant Tabby was here. Would never have got here in a hundred years. Well..." He considers, "Actually a hundred years is probably a viable time frame. Terribly long time, actually, a hundred years. I mean if you consider the twentieth century as a whole for example. We hadn't even hit the World Wars going into it, and we were in the digital age at the end. Plenty of unthinkable things had been thought. Mind-boggling actually. So, yes, probably would have thought of it in a hundred years. Just trial-and-error by that point. Fifty years... Erm, ten, well, erm, maybe... probably would have taken me a week or so. That's probably accurate. But, well, world on the line and all that, speed being of the essence probably. At least, I assume it is. It does tend to be in these situations. World-ending threats do always seem to be on a tight timeline. Maybe that's why they fail so often. If they just gave themselves more time to plan it all out. I don't know... Anyway, Tabby really cut the time down, that's what I'm trying to communicate."

"How?" Felicity's one word is a gong ringing out loud against the background babble.

"Oh, hadn't I got there yet?" Clyde looks genuinely surprised. "Sorry. Gives you a sense of how overwhelming Tabby's brilliance was, really. Totally leading me—"

"How?" Felicity's voice rings out again.

"Oh yes," Clyde says. "There I go again."

"HOW?"

Clyde blanches. "You have to twist it through realities," he says in a rush. "The physics of it don't work out in our reality, but with a little..." He pops a silver-cadmium battery into his mouth in a surprisingly smooth motion, and then twists at the ornament again.

There is no grinding this time. Instead there is a crackle and the sound of things sliding smoothly. In Clyde's hands the ornament seems to... fold, somehow. It is shorter, longer, sections glide through each other as if suddenly insubstantial. It spits blue sparks.

And then Clyde spits the battery out, and is holding a simple rectangle again. In fact it looks exactly like it did before. Except now the grooves along the long sides are perfectly aligned.

"Sooo..." Hannah drags the word out. "Basically it's a magical Rubik's Cube?" As much as I think Hannah could be giving out a slightly more positive vibe this morning, I am also wallowing in a similar amount of underwhelm-ment.

Tabitha grins. "Not exactly."

Clyde sets the ornament gingerly down on the table. Suddenly the base of it is suffused with blue light. It spreads up the grooves, growing brighter as it goes, almost white at the tip. Slowly the four corner sections seem to almost ripple. And then it blooms, a flower opening steel petals, spreading back with a series of mechanical clicks to reveal a column of blue light within, that shines brighter, brighter, a tiny newborn sun in the heart of the room, flooding it with cold light.

My vision burns, whites out, something deep in the base of my skull seems to click, and I wince, bracing for pain that doesn't come—

And then it's over. Then we're standing in conference room B, staring at Clyde who's standing in front of a rectangular desk ornament with a series of stagger-stepped grooves running up its four long sides.

"Neat, right?" says Clyde.

There is a long pause. Hannah breaks the silence. "Is this one of those things that's much cooler when you're high?"

"It's a key!" Clyde stares at us as if he can't believe we didn't get it.

"Maybe," I venture, "this is where that context might have been useful."

"Told you." Tabitha shakes her head.

"Huzzah!" says Clyde, pulling his notebook back out of his pocket. "I mean, yes, of course. You see a lot of this stuff is years ahead of its time. The whole folding the column through space to align the grooves. There wasn't a working theory on that until the late sixties. *Theory.* I think the first documented case of someone successfully doing it isn't until the late seventies. And Lang was doing this back in the thirties. It's incredible!"

"The light," Tabitha cuts in. "Not actually the important bit. Side effect of putting out strong thaumatic frequency."

"Thaumatic what?" Hannah is fighting the cross-eyed look.

"Just go with it," I say. "Even after they explain it, it won't make any sense."

"Well," says Clyde, utterly oblivious to my snark, "each reality has its own thaumatic frequency. I mean, that's the theory, about how we're reaching through realities. It's all to do with aligning the frequencies of the thaumatospheres, creating a junction. That's how the composite reality works, pretty much. It's this massive symphony of thaumatic resonance. All the frequencies meshing together to make one whole."

Hannah is definitely looking a little askance at the world right now.

"Told you," I say.

"And Lang, well he must have been a master at manipulating those frequencies. I mean this thing is quite ingenious."

"Tabitha," Felicity cuts in, "maybe we can cut to layman's terms."

Tabby tears her eyes away from Clyde, glowering. "Fine," she says. "Luddites. To do with pocket realities. Lang made one. Little section of some other-where, tucked off from the mainstream composite reality. This is the key. Unlocks it. Lets you in."

Pocket reality. My job is full of things that sound awesome right up until you have to actually deal with them.

"So," I say, "that thing opens a door into another reality?"

Clyde nods enthusiastically. "I know! It's brilliant." Then his brow creases. "Again with all the caveats about Lang being an absolute arsehole of the highest magnitude. It really is a shame."

"And what's in this reality?"

Tabitha looks at me like I'm an idiot. "Don't know. Haven't been there. But what would you put in a secret reality only you can access?"

Hannah leans forward, both elbows on the table. "Secrets," she says, her grin broad.

And yes, that does make sense. A hidden key for a hidden pocket of reality. It's not exactly going to be something he created to deal with his lack of closet space.

Which leads to the next question.

"OK," I say, "so now we have a door to kick down, how exactly do we find it?"

21

Tabitha looks from me to Clyde. "Fucked system," she says very deliberately.

I realize that it would be very hard to tell if Tabitha ever spontaneously developed Tourette's.

Still, Clyde reaching across the table and high-fiving her is probably a fair sign that didn't just happen.

"The what?" I manage.

Tabitha rolls her eyes at my ineptitude. "Functional Userface for Counter-Thaumaturgy. F.U.C.T. FUCT system."

I glance at Felicity. She shrugs apologetically. "Unfortunate acronym."

Hannah is laughing silently to herself, shoulders shaking. "God," she manages, "I can't bloody tell if this is the worst military intelligence division or the best. I really can't."

Felicity's face hardens. Tension knots around the corners of her eyes. And something is going on. Something more than just her desire to make Hannah feel at home. I should have asked her about it on the way home from the club last night, but it's hard to launch into what you know will be an exhausting conversation when you're already exhausted.

"Best." Tabitha stabs the word across the table. "Fucking obviously."

Kayla shrugs. "Meh."

I resist the urge to bounce my forehead off the table's surface. Instead I say, "I realize that getting us back on track is a perilous and likely fruitless thing for me to try, but what exactly is the F.U.C.T. System—" I am careful to simply spell out the acronym, "—and how do we use it?"

"Database," Tabitha says, flipping her laptop open. "Created in the early eighties, during magical arms race. Government got paranoid. Worried about thaumaturgical bombs. Dirty magic. Wanted an early-warning system. Created the FUCT system." She doesn't spell it out.

"In case we were ever fecked," Kayla contributes. Hannah snorts. Tabitha rolls her eyes.

"It was a huge undertaking, actually," Clyde cuts in. "Really quite impressive. I mean, assuming you're the sort of person who is impressed by the scale of government-sponsored undertakings. You might not be of course. In fact, it might be fair to assume that you're not. Can't really see it being everyone's cup of tea. Might have been poor word choice on my part. Maybe I should have gone with 'noteworthy,' or possibly even 'surprising,' though that also makes some assumptions about your expectations from the government. Very tricky thing this whole language nonsense."

"Focus," I suggest.

"Oh yes," Clyde says. "Well, essentially they mapped the thaumaturgical frequencies of the United Kingdom. Went around, took a lot of measurements. Not an easy thing to do by any means, because, well, what they discovered was that it fluctuates. The thaumaturgic resonance of any one place has a certain amount of wobble. And thaumaturgic activity in an area can throw the wobble even further out of whack. I mean, our own activities… we're changing that map ourselves. That's why I try to log all magical activity at the end of every month. The system has an algorithm built in to try to grow over time, but it's very tricky. Still, at a large scale it's still pretty accurate. Best thing we have. London, for example, has a pretty constant background resonance of forty-seven to fifty-two Woltz."

"Waltz?" asks Hannah. "You have to dance to measure magic?"

"Oh no," Clyde says with a guileless shake of his head. "Spelled with an 'O' instead of an 'A.' Named after Eugene Woltz. Estonian chap who developed the whole system. Defector from the USSR. Probably explains why the FUCT acronym is what it is. English as a second language and all that. Probably someone should have mentioned it to him. But, ah well. Anyway, a nice chap, though unfortunately rather violently dead. Tends to be a habit with pioneering thaumaturgists. That's why I stick to the tried and true. Too much respect for keeping my spine within my body to be a real pioneer, unfortunately."

I'm not sure that last sentence really deserves an "unfortunately."

"But," I say, "if the system is so inaccurate, can it really help us?"

"Yes," Tabitha cuts in. "Obviously. Why I mentioned it." She shakes her head, momentarily overcome by the sadness caused by my mental inadequacies. "Pocket reality. Stable anomaly. Shows up."

Hannah and I both say, "Erm," at the same time.

"Oh," Clyde cuts in. "So yes, the wobble. It makes picking up fine fluctuations difficult. Actually buggered the whole system from being able to do what it was meant to be able to do. The system has a very bad name because of it."

"Worse than FUCT?" I ask, slightly dubious.

"Well, that is the bad name," Clyde says.

That makes about as much sense as anything.

"But, what it is good for is spotting large scale patterns and anything stable. London is a large scale pattern. We get the consistent Woltz reading for it. Anything big like that isn't going to change much. Except Sheffield. Sheffield's just weird. But, also anything that's going to be stable for a very long time is going to be easy to detect. Like a pocket reality that's going to exist indefinitely. Going to be, by definition, incredibly stable. Needs to be so the key can get into it."

"And we know the... frequency... of this reality."

Clyde reaches awkwardly into another rear-facing pocket and pulls out something that looks like a microphone that the Jetsons would own. He hands it to Tabitha who plugs it into the USB slot of her laptop. "Do it," she says.

Clyde slips another battery under his tongue, mutters, and

twists. The key gyrates through realities, aligns, unfolds, emits its light. Tabitha holds the scifi microphone up to it.

"Got a reading," she says as the light blinks out. "Three hundred and eighty-four point oh six nine seven Woltz."

Her fingers fly over her keyboard. She grins. "And a match. Three hundred and eighty-four point oh six nine seven Woltz."

She spins the laptop around so we can see. In the center of an incredibly convoluted interface is a window where a series of interconnected blue lines intersect and diverge in a pattern that in no way resembles anything recognizable.

"Erm." Hannah and I harmonize again. I flick a glance in her direction but she isn't looking at me. I'm not sure what I'd do if she was looking at me. I can hardly accuse her of stealing all my best lines.

Tabitha zooms in heavily. Starts to zoom out. Slowly I start to see a vaguely familiar pattern.

"Wait, isn't that the Underground?"

"That's near Hammersmith, ain't it?" Hannah is leaning forward again, a look of tight concentration nearby.

Tabitha examines her screen. "Yeah," she says, something that almost sounds grudgingly impressed. "Service tunnel. Got the GPS."

"All right then." Felicity claps her hands. "Field team, you have your target. Tabitha, you stay here and run the forensics suite on that ornament, see if we can learn anything else about it."

We all stand, start milling toward the door. My heartbeat has picked up. Is this how I always feel before a mission? I've lost confidence in my body's reactions.

As we reach the door, Felicity taps Clyde's arm. "Fix your trousers before you go," she says. "You look a bit of a fool."

THREE HOURS LATER AND TWENTY METERS DOWN

I always assumed that walking onto the London Underground tracks would be accompanied by crowds of aghast men and women, shrieking sirens, and officials in neon yellow safety vests bellowing that you were too young to die. Apparently, though, if you just stroll along with enough confidence no one gives a damn.

The space feels narrow and cold. The smells of wet wood, gravel, and concrete are tight around us, along with a foul undercurrent that lies somewhere between stale urine and the cabbage that used to get served at school lunch. Graffiti is thick on the walls—taggers' names in bold ballooning fonts, professions of love and hatred, an image of Hitler and Nelson Mandela making out.

Metallic clanging echoes down the tunnel, impossible to locate.

"Was that close?" Clyde asks. His voice jumps through several different registers. Considering how his morning went, I'd expect him to be a little calmer.

Still, the tracks do seem to be emitting a faint hum.

"We're close, right?" I ask, trying to keep my voice flat.

"Here it is." Hannah has been leading the way, seemingly at ease with our trespass. She swings her flashlight to the right, illuminates a paint-crusted door. She fishes out a ring of keys, selects one. "It's great the stuff MI6 gives you," she says. She slips it into the lock.

It doesn't turn. "Oh bloody hell," she says. "I hate it when they get like this."

The tracks are definitely humming now. Squeaks and clanks bounce down the tunnel walls toward us.

"Kayla," I say, "maybe this is one for you."

"I've got this," Hannah says, still jiggling the key. "Give me a moment."

A loud screech—wheels changing tracks—that does not come from far away.

I think about Hannah's request. Not for very long. "Kayla," I say. "Now, please."

Hannah is still bent over the lock when Kayla's foot hits the door. Metal screams. It flies open, ripping the keys out of her hands.

Hannah stands indignantly. "Was that entirely necessary?"

Behind her the yellow glow of headlights starts to illuminate the tunnel.

"Yeah," I say. "I kind of think so." And then Clyde and I are bundling after Kayla into the service tunnel as fast as our feet will carry us. I look back. Hannah stands there, shaking her head, and then finally, finally steps into the tunnel. Two seconds later, an underground train fills the tunnel behind her in a scream of sound and rushing air.

Over-confident or just stupid—I try to work out what impression Hannah is trying to make on me. Or maybe it's not for me, because Kayla fist bumps her for some reason.

The door opens onto narrow stairs that take us another thirty feet down, before opening up into a much larger space. This tunnel—the one that supposedly houses Lang's pocket reality—is three tracks wide, and lit by intermittent service lights, strung together by thick orange cable. The space feels almost luxurious after the confines of the tunnel above. It even smells better. Lang sure knew how to pick his subterranean lairs.

"Should be about a hundred yards this way." Clyde points, glancing down at a rather sophisticated GPS device Tabitha outfitted him with. "Then we'll try activating the key."

We make our way forward, the silence slightly awkward. Kayla whistles. A noise devoid of tune. It doesn't help.

I'm trying to work out a way to talk to Hannah when she hesitates. I almost walk into her back.

"What's that?" She flicks her flashlight over to one side of the tunnel. I peer. Something glints. Something metal. Something big.

Behind me I hear Kayla's sword leaving its scabbard.

And it takes me a moment, but... It's a leg. A vast robotic leg.

An Uhrwerkmänn's leg.

"Oh, I was really hoping this would be a quiet little jaunt into another reality." Clyde sounds profoundly disappointed. "The furthering of human knowledge and understanding. Why does everything have to be about violence?"

"OK," I whisper. "Hannah, you—"

She's already rolling her eyes when a vast grating voice booms down the tunnel toward us.

"Is it coming?" the Uhrwerkmänn calls. A Germanic gravity to its vowels.

I'm not a hundred percent certain, but I'm pretty sure that means it knows we're here.

"I wait f-or it but it never c-omes." The Uhrwerkmänn hitches oddly in the middle of words, sputtering through speech.

Then it stands. As massive as all its kin. I hear the battery bouncing off the back of Clyde's teeth. I draw my pistol. And oh shit, here we go.

"I wait and I wait, but it never comes."

The Uhrwerkmänn steps into the light. Narrow frame, long limbs. Damaged too. One shoulder is exposed, gearwork clacking, pneumatic tubes wilting around the joint. Large convex dents mar its domed skull.

But it stands tall. There is a sense of... nobility in its slow forward pacing. Something in the angle of the skull, in the bearing of its mangled shoulders. And though most of it is caked in grime, in places the metal still gleams brightly.

Volk's story flashes through my mind. The Uhrwerkmänner refusing to be seduced by the Nazi philosophy. Sacrificing themselves rather than oppress others.

"I've got a clean shot," Hannah whispers.

"They twist, you know?" says the Uhrwerkmänn, shifting conversational gears without warning. "They twist and they twist, and they twist."

Clyde glances at me. I've lost track of Kayla.

The Uhrwerkmänner's hand hangs unmoving in the air between us.

Curiosity overcomes me. "What does?" I say, loud enough for it to hear. It's not like I'm giving our position away.

"Oh, you had to bloody ask." Hannah shakes her head slightly. Her gun never wavers.

In answer the Uhrwerkmänn bends its arm, grasps one finger of the hand, and twists. There is an audible snap of shearing metal.

It's not flesh. It's not blood. But still, I wince.

It stares at the finger, torn loose from its hand, its immobile features expressing as much melancholy as they can. Then it lets the digit fall, tumbling onto the track. It looks up at me again.

"Maybe that will bring it sooner. Maybe it likes to eat them."

There's almost a question in that last statement. An edge like pleading.

"I've still got the shot," Hannah says.

It stands there, perfectly still, staring at the fallen finger. A shudder runs through it.

Hannah glances at me. "That thing is one slipped gear from losing it."

And no. No it's not. Jesus. Irritation is a rough spike tearing through my mood. "Oh just stand down already," I snap at her. "It's fine."

She hesitates.

I sigh. In front of Clyde and a deranged robot was not at all where I wanted to have this conversation. "Look," I say. "I appreciate that you have more field experience than me. I really do. But if anything is likely to antagonize this bastard it's the fact that you're pointing a gun at it. Now, I realize that you don't agree with that assessment, but honestly the way this whole thing is set up, I'm your boss. I may make a mistake from time to time, but I'm better prepared to fix it if I know where the hell everyone is, and what the hell they're doing. I can't make contingency plans if I can't count on you."

Hannah looks at me. Her gun is still up. "You're asking me to endanger myself," she says. "And you. And him." She nods at Clyde. "And Kay—well, OK, probably not Kayla, I get that. But you're asking me to knowingly put myself at risk on the say-so of some bloke who just admitted he doesn't know what he's doing half as well as me. You get that, right?"

The Uhrwerkmänn spasms to life once more, takes a twitching, jerking step toward us.

I am trying to be reasonable. I run that mantra through my head. What would Felicity say?

"I'm asking for a little trust," I say. It sounds Felicity-like.

"You almost shot me yesterday," Hannah points out. "Twice."

Another faltering step from the Uhrwerkmänn.

"Erm… don't mean to interrupt here—" Clyde starts up.

"I know." I manage to override Clyde, and talk to Hannah without gritting my teeth once. "And that's exactly what I'm looking to avoid. That's why I'm asking for you to trust me. So we don't repeat yesterday."

"I trusted you more yesterday." Hannah appears to be pretty far from the soft, warm trusting place. "Your case files seem to have left out a lot of the specifics of your successes."

"But they were successes. They may have been unorthodox—"

"Unorthodox!" Hannah bites back bitter laughter. Another step from the Uhrwerkmänn.

"Look," says Clyde, "maybe this isn't the time for politeness after all, because I really think—"

"If you weren't there," I say, my calm slipping away, "you don't get to judge. I have lost a lot of friends over the past year getting my job done, and—"

"Yeah, and I don't want to be one of them," Hannah barks back.

"Trust me," I snap, "you are not my friend."

Another step from the Uhrwerkmänn, it is only six yards away now. Close enough to smell the oil leaking out of it.

Hannah stares angrily at me.

"You," I say to her, "are my subordinate. Now I gave you an order. Put the bloody gun down."

Her hand wavers.

The Uhrwerkmänn looms.

And then the Uhrwerkmänn collapses.

It lets out a slight gasp, almost a sigh, and then just slumps to the ground. Metal limbs clang against metal railtrack, a discordant xylophone. A deep ticking sound in its chest grows in magnitude then grinds, squeals, stutters, and finally stops.

After a moment everything is still.

We stare down at the Uhrwerkmänn's massive corpse.

"What just—" Clyde starts.

Then Kayla steps out of the shadows. She's wiping oil off her sword blade, leaving long black streaks on the legs of her jeans.

"Unorthodox distraction, aye," she says. "But I appreciate it." She sheathes her sword, grins. "Stealthy like a feckin' ninja," she says. She points at Clyde. "You had bollocks all idea I was there, right?"

Clyde is still blinking.

I'm still staring at the corpse. Even now, even disheveled by madness and death, there is still a nobility to the body. It wasn't going to attack us. I'm still sure of that. I think it just wanted us to understand. Because it couldn't. It wanted us to understand so we could explain everything back to it. And instead we killed it.

There's a bunch of reasons why we do what we do at MI37. Right now we're trying to stop a mad robot from setting off a Nazi doomsday device. But I think what we're losing along the way is that we're trying to save someone too. The Uhrwerkmänner need us to succeed to survive. To not lose their way, like this one did.

We suddenly seem very far from our goal.

22

"Here," Clyde says.

This stretch of tunnel looks no different from any other. Still, it's where the GPS says we should be. We dutifully obey our electronic master. Clyde pulls out the reality key, sucks on a battery, twists. Blue light floods the space around us.

Again I feel the slight thump at the base of my skull, some bass beat in the rhythm of the universe. But this time it reverberates. Deep and sonorous. Painful. A headache ripples out to encase my skull. My vision seems to shimmer. For a moment there isn't one tunnel in front of me, but a myriad of tunnels. Myriad realities. Nausea twists through me, sharp and sudden. Blue light floods everything.

Then it's gone. Everything. The pain. The nausea. The blurring of my vision. I am just standing, bewildered in the absence of my own suffering, trying to figure out what just happened.

Apparently nothing.

I stare about looking for evidence of a shift in... anything. But it's the same dull tunnel. The same drab walls. It might have been a spectacular light show, but it didn't seem to do much.

Everyone else seems as confused as I do. Flashlights play on our surroundings looking for something different.

"The Uhrwerkmänn's gone," Hannah says. Her flashlight's circle of illumination flickers over an empty section of track. She looks at the key in Clyde's hands. "Useful for tidying stuff up, I suppose. The psychotic murderer's handy-helper?"

For a moment I imagine a pocket reality full of dead bodies. I blanch.

Then I see it. My flashlight comes to rest pointing at a wall. "That wasn't there," I say. "Not before."

A door. An unimpressive one. Small, shabby, and made of gnarled wood. However, right now I wouldn't mind if it was small, shabby, and smeared in Lang's fecal matter. It's new. It's a chance this trip isn't just about Kayla euthanizing a robotic race.

"Kayla," I say. She crosses the tunnel, grabs the handle. While having her open the door means she is more likely to get hit by whatever abomination is behind it than anyone else on the team, she's also more likely than anyone else to survive.

Hannah looks at me. "Shouldn't we…?" She taps her hand on her holster, nods at the door.

"You are very keen to draw that thing," I say. I get the impression the indulgent tone isn't appreciated.

Kayla kills any nascent bickering by applying her shoulder to the door. It flies open, swinging easily on well-oiled hinges. Kayla takes the three short sharp steps into the room. Somehow, in the intervening nanoseconds, she has her sword out of its scabbard. Hannah fills the doorway behind her, pokes her gun over Kayla's right shoulder.

The door opens onto a short corridor—maybe a yard long—before the space opens out. Blue light floods everything. Slowly we advance.

The room is circular and achingly tall. The ceiling is distant, five or six stories up at least, the walls coming together to form a high peaked dome, like a vast, elongated egg. Every inch of the walls, from floor to that far-removed ceiling, is lined with books. The short corridor at the doorway was actually just a narrow channel cut through the shelves.

Books are jammed into the space. Spines upside down, back to front. Titles in English, German, French, Italian, Russian, Japanese, Korean, Latin. Titles in alphabets I don't recognize. Books jammed in backwards so only the pages peer out at us, all browning with age and neglect. Some curled and tattered. And not just books. Curled scrolls, sheaves of loose writing, newspapers, notepads, maps. I see a stack of what appear to be movie posters. There's even one shelf that appears to be dedicated to rolled-up tapestries.

The floor is similarly cluttered. Yet more books in tattered piles. Empty picture frames. A few old hurricane lamps. A gas mask. It feels as if I have somehow stumbled into an overly complex I-spy photograph. I can't tell where the blue light is coming from. It seems simply to suffuse the place.

Kayla and Hannah stand in the center of the room, weapons still drawn.

"You two done threatening the books yet?" I ask.

Hannah slowly puts the gun away, not bothering to look sheepish. "Yeah," she says, "because a rather-sorry-than-safe policy is totally the one we should be following."

Clyde isn't paying any attention. He stares around the room. I think this is what he imagines heaven looks like. I am close enough to hear him whisper to himself, "Oh good lord. I have to show this place to Tabby."

I put a hand on his shoulder. "This is good work," I tell him. "This has to put us ahead of that Friedrich arsehole."

He nods, but then a frown clouds his face.

"What is it?" I ask.

"I was just wondering…" He rubs the back of his head, ruffling his hair. "How the hell are we going to get all this back to the office?

BECAUSE THE MOUNTAIN WON'T COME TO MUHAMMAD

"Could call someone about this," Tabitha says. "Oppressive work conditions, this is. Unsanitary. Plus the wireless signal down here is about as existent as the square root of minus one." When no one responds she shakes her head. "Fucking philistines."

She ducks back down below her makeshift desk, set up in the middle of Lang's underground tunnel. I happen to know for a fact that Felicity has organized for her to have a wired connection so fast it makes photons worry that something might be catching up to them.

Clyde sits cross-legged at the desk's base making his way through one of the stacks of books Hannah, Kayla, and I have retrieved from Lang's study. He has informed me that he'll be sticking to the Latin texts as Tabitha's ancient Greek is better than his.

Felicity stands next to me, surveying the mobile field office we've set up. "This is good," she nods. "This gives us an edge."

"I hope so." This job has taught me that unbridled optimism is usually an invitation for the universe to deliver a swift and savage blow to the balls.

"You should set up some perimeter security," Felicity says. "In case Friedrich uncovers details about this place, or about the key."

I gaze into the blank darkness of the tunnels. I picture the unsettling image of them gazing back.

"Do you think he'll stop?" I say. "Friedrich. If we find this cure the Uhrwerkmänner are looking for?"

Felicity is quiet for a moment. "I don't know," she says after a while. "I mean, that's what he says he's doing. Looking for a cure. So if we do it... he should. But... He's on the sort of journey people have trouble stopping."

I glance over at the Uhrwerkmänn Kayla killed. "God, I hope he does stop," I say, with more feeling than I intended.

"Looking for a bit of peace and quiet?" Felicity's smile is further from sympathetic and closer to mocking than I'd like.

I wrestle with that. Try to find the right words. "Looking for... a stop to pointless struggle," I say. "And being pulled into other people's pointless struggles. Why can't people just be satisfied with what they have?" I reconsider that last bit. "At least, why can't giant Nazi robots be satisfied?"

Felicity shrugs. "It's like a fire fight," she says. "Stasis is death. Nothing ever stays the way it is." She pats me on the back. "We don't fight for stasis, Arthur. We fight for the best change possible. And sometimes that's still a shitty change. Sometimes we just fight for the least bad outcome." She wraps an arm around me, squeezes.

I squeeze her back. It's a little half-hearted. "Not exactly a motivational speaker, are you?"

Another shrug. "Fine then," she says. "Just think about how your paycheck is dependent on you fighting the good fight instead then."

THAT EVENING

Back in the upper underground tunnel, I hold the door open, so Felicity can slip past me onto the stairs leading back down below. Bags of Chinese food weigh my arms down. Felicity holds several steaming cups of coffee.

"We should tell Volk and Hermann about this place," I say as we descend.

"I don't know." Felicity's ahead of me and I can't see her face, but she sounds dubious. "I think you're right that they're on our side, but I also think their network is leaky as hell. Anything we tell them will get to Friedrich sooner or later."

Kayla waits at the bottom of the stairs tapping her phone. "I'm wasting feckin' time here." She doesn't bother looking up. "Never be able to fix up a date for tonight at this point."

"Aren't you meant to be on perimeter guard duty?" I ask.

"Feckin' doorway," Kayla says. "Feckin' perimeter. Feckin' guarding it."

Felicity nods. "I've got sweet and sour chicken for you when you're ready."

Kayla grimaces. Hopefully her chicken is heavy on the sweet side.

We put the bags down on Tabitha's makeshift desk, which has been drowned in Lang's papers. Clyde sits in the middle of what might well be a book fort. Even Hannah is reading. I peer over her shoulder. It looks like gibberish.

"*Beowulf*," she says without looking up. "The Old English original version. Had to translate it my first year of uni. Only book in Lang's stash that I recognized. Learning bollocks all from it. Just like back when I was at uni, actually."

Felicity holds out a box toward her. "Chow mein."

"You two learned anything?" I look to Clyde and Tabitha. Tabitha is sitting at her desk, Doc Martens propped up on its formica surface. She peers over the edge of the journal she's reading.

"Himalayas," she says.

My eyes have a momentary meeting with Felicity's. They confer.

We come up lacking. "Maybe a little more information?" I ask.

"Well," Clyde cuts in, "these are all Lang's personal papers. We thought we'd start with them. Educated guess. Well, not formal education. No Joseph Lang Studies offered at Cambridge unfortunately. Not that I'd likely have studied that. Wouldn't have had the foresight to see their application, like as not. Not many people would, I suspect. Which probably explains their absence from the curriculum come to think of it. Tough to organize an entire undergraduate course when you don't think anyone's going to take it. Beating one's head against the administrative red tape, I'm sure. Not that there's ever been much literal red tape involved in the bureaucracy I've encountered. Maybe it's something to do with communists. The Reds. They seem keen on bureaucracy. Though the tape... well that could be metaphorical, I suppose..." He stares off into space.

I give him a moment, check on Tabitha. She's gone back to reading.

"The Himalayas?" I prompt him.

"Oh yes, sorry." Clyde shrugs twice. "Well, we thought we'd start with Lang's papers on the grounds that those might contain the most personal information. The Uhrwerkmänner being an idea original to him and all that. And, well—" His hand indicates the walls of paper around him, "—turns out he was quite a loquacious fellow. Which isn't said to cast aspersions, just an observation. Though some of the things he got loquacious on..." He makes a face. "That lot," he says indicating the paper wall behind him, "is basically filth."

"Racist fuck," Tabitha comments without looking up.

"Amen," Hannah mumbles, her mouth full of noodles.

"Maybe," Felicity says, taking advantage of the momentary lull, "we could get back to the word, 'Himalayas.'"

"Oh yes," Clyde nods. "Well the stuff that isn't filth, a lot of it is journals. There's really very little technical stuff in them. I mean there's some fascinating meanderings on the nature of reality, and some very odd math around it. A rather unwieldy combination of philosophy and poetry mixed around it all, but nothing which is really solid practical information."

Tabitha jams a thumb at the door to the pocket reality. "Personal, not professional."

"Professional?" I still need more.

"This seems to be where he kept things that were of personal value. A library of the non-functional. This wasn't a workspace," Clyde elaborates.

"And the workspace?" Felicity asks.

But I have it now. "Is in the Himalayas."

"Bingo." Tabitha turns a page, keeps reading.

"A valley in the Himalayan foothills in Nepal. We mapped it on Google. Looks like there might be some sort of temple or ruins in the region. It's a little vague."

Now the information is out on the table, it looks a little wonky. "He just jaunted off to the Himalayas to do work?" I ask. "In the thirties?"

"Well," Clyde says, "it is where they found the book. So it was likely funded research. First by MI37, and then by the Germans after that. They sent a few expeditions there. Mad for all this occult stuff, they were. I think I heard there was an expedition looking for Atlantis there. Which doesn't make much sense from what I know of the legend. Seems like you're traveling in the opposite direction from Atlantis as soon as you start heading up, but I guess it's not really my area of expertise. Someone must have thought it was a good idea at the time."

"You mean," Hannah sounds a little surprised, "you're not going to tell me that the existence of Atlantis was confirmed during the sixties by a cabal of LSD-toting college professors from Denmark?"

"Oh no, not at all. Atlantis is still a big mystery. Though you're pretty close to the way the existence of Jotunheim was confirmed, except that those professors were all Swedish."

"Shut up." Hannah flicks a noodle at him.

Somehow I feel like I should have been part of that conversation, as if my role was somehow usurped.

"So," I say, trying to reassert myself in the conversation, "we need to go to the Himalayas. A valley in the Nepalese foothills."

"Yes," Felicity says.

"What? No!" The objection approaches us at speed from the stairs back up to the London Underground. Kayla arrives, phone pointed accusingly at me. "Are you trying to feck me?" she asks. "Because I am trying to get fecked, and it is a scheduling feckin' nightmare, and I cannot have you fecks dragging me off to feckin' Nepal. I've got too much shit coming up. No." The last word is said with the sort of emphasis normally reserved for the cocking of pump-action shotguns.

"Have you considered," I attempt, "that getting impregnated isn't the best way to repair your relationship with Ephie?"

"Have you considered shutting up before I give you a sword enema?"

Well… now I have.

"Have you considered a sperm bank?"

All eyes fall upon Clyde. He immediately begins shrugging. "Oh gosh. Speaking out of turn. Which assumes turns in conversation. Which would actually make the whole social interaction thing a lot easier to navigate if you ask me. Not that you were. Hence this whole mess and—"

"Shut up," Kayla tells him. "Then start up again. Just about the sperm bank thing."

"Oh," Clyde studies his hands. "Just considering, you know, that the whole dating thing is fraught with all sorts of problems of the sort that can't easily be solved with pointy bits of metal. Also wondering if, perhaps, maybe, well… possibly, I suppose, if maybe the dates were actually a distraction from the business of, well, getting down to business. Just, you know, considering that your goal isn't actually a loving companion to spend your tender years with, but rather a simple repository of genetic material. Might be a quicker way to get to the aforementioned genetic material, I thought. Cut out the whole middle man, so to speak. Or any sort of man, really. Replace him with more of a turkey baster sort of apparatus."

There is more silence. I cannot quite bring myself to look at Kayla. For fear of turning to stone.

"Felicity always said you were a feckin' clever bonce," Kayla says finally. "Guess you do have your moments."

In all honesty, I suppose he does too. It's just this is one of the moments when I wish I could slap him.

"Aaaaanyway," Felicity says, revealing that this is also one of the moments when I wish she hadn't mastered the whole "unreadable expression" thing. Still, not knowing what she's thinking does leave the door open for us to launch an informal intervention into Kayla's family planning.

Instead, though, Felicity goes with, "Tabitha, Clyde, I'm going to need you to assess and pack up any essential texts for our trip to Nepal. The earliest flight won't be until sometime tomorrow. We'll all be accompanying you two as a protect—"

"Not going to fucking Nepal." Tabitha has her hands on her hips, indignant. "Researcher. You have a new field agent. I stay fucking home. My fucking job description."

Felicity wheels on her, with a suddenness that catches me off guard. "Yes, Tabitha," she says, and there is a whip crack to her words. "You do. You go. This is not a bloody discussion, it is marching orders. There is a very dangerous, very desperate machine out there looking to unleash God-knows-what on the world. And you and Clyde are what stands between him and success. Lang was a scientist, a thaumaturge. Understanding his work is what is going to save us here. All of us." She sweeps an arm savagely at the ceiling, at London and England above. "So you will understand it. You will do everything within your power to fix it. Because that is what we do. We fix problems other people can't. We do the things only we can do. *You* will do the things only you can do. And if you can't do it with a smile on your face, maybe you can do it with my boot up your arse."

There is a very long pause. Tabitha shuffles her feet and glances at Clyde, who shrugs in a way that resembles a tortoise ducking its head. I stare at Felicity, trying to work out where that came from. Felicity's tolerance for our bullshit is normally far greater than that.

And then I notice that Felicity isn't looking at Tabitha. She's looking at Hannah. Hannah who has her face buried in her box of noodles, and who seems blissfully unaware.

"Bloody hell." Tabitha breaks the silence. "Fine then."

"Good." Felicity's expression is tight. She seems a little embarrassed by her outburst. She takes half a step toward me then stops. She pushes strands of hair back behind her ears. "Let's get going then."

23

ON THE M25, HEADING TOWARD OXFORD

"So," I say, "what was all that about then?"

Felicity has been fairly quiet since we left the others packing crates of manuscripts down in the underground tunnels. To be fair, she's been tapping away on her phone trying to guarantee military transport as early as tomorrow. She looks up, her mouth a tight line.

"What was what?" she asks.

"I think that's the closest Tabitha's come to having her head bitten off since that incident at Didcot power station."

For a moment the line of Felicity's mouth softens. Then it tightens again. "We need to do good on this one, Arthur," she says. "Better than we have been. We need to do this and look good."

Look good. I weigh that. I add it to the look I saw her giving Hannah. The scale tips.

"OK," I say. "What's all this got to do with Hannah?"

Felicity looks away, stares out at the string of rear car lights strung out before us, glowing red breadcrumbs leading us in circles.

"You two need to find a way to work together. I need peace between you two."

I don't have to be a former detective to notice that that isn't an explanation.

"Why?" I push. "Why can't we just throw up our hands and say it was a nice idea, but Hannah's a bad fit and we'll keep our eye out for someone else?"

"Because they'll shut us bloody down if we do."

Felicity's words ricochet off my ears, bounce off the windscreen, and tear great bloody holes in my calm. I feel my foot slip down on the accelerator. The engine revs with my shock.

"They'll fucking what?"

My emotions are slipping gears again. I try to rein them in. The cat's eyes at the center of the road slip by faster and faster.

"Shit." Felicity puts her head in her hands.

"They'll shut us down? If she's a bad fit?"

Felicity doesn't look up. "If she gives us a bad assessment," she says to her lap.

"She has the power to shut us down?" I'm still trying to grasp it all. It doesn't make sense. We've been doing so well. We've saved lives. We've made a difference. Why jam a stick in our spokes now and blame us for tripping?

"She doesn't know." The bitterness is rank on Felicity's tongue. "No one's meant to bloody know. You're not meant to know. In the words of the Prime Minister, 'don't even tell that one you're keen on.'" Her laugh is bitter. "And I thought, well screw him. I'll tell Arthur. But then you've been so… preoccupied or… God, I don't know. But I'm trying to be the good girlfriend and give you space, and let you figure it out. And I thought maybe the added pressure wouldn't be the best thing. I trust you. But it's like you're trying to screw this up, Arthur. Like you're actively working against me."

"The Prime Minister." I'm still reeling here. Hannah has the power to shut us down. The car ahead of us is coming up fast. I shift lanes. The blundering thrum of the tires over the cat's eyes. I wipe one palm on my trousers, try to get a better grip on the wheel.

"When he wanted to see me. He told me. He said he was impressed. Said he wanted to give us an opportunity. One of MI6's best and brightest. She was to come over for a few months, see how it all went. Assuming the experience was a good one we'll get more like her. We'll get a bigger budget. We'll finally be everything I dreamed this department could be."

That all sounds like good things. Then the other shoe drops.

"And if it doesn't work out?"

"Then maybe it would be for the best," she says adopting the haughty received pronunciation tones of our country's political leader, "if MI37 was rolled into MI6 for more centralized oversight. Avoid some of these close calls." I think she is close to spitting into the footwell.

MI37 rolled into MI6. Into Hannah's mothership. And of course, I'm sure she'd like nothing better. Except MI37 would be as bad a fit with MI6 as Hannah is with us. We'd be the grit in their shoe, and it would only be a matter of time until we were discarded by the wayside.

"What would happen to you?" I ask. "If…" I can't quite bring myself to utter the scenario.

"Oh, I'd be officially in charge for a while at least. But there would be 'oversight.' And eventually they would find a reason to shunt me out of the way. And then I would find myself wandering through a maze of side-jobs and increasingly obscure positions until I wind up behind a desk reviewing reports about how many paper clips they're importing to Iran this month and trying not to kill myself for want of something to do."

It's a good thing we're having this conversation away from her orchids. I think this would wilt them.

"Shit." I don't have another word for it. "Shit. Shit. Shit."

Felicity finally looks up, looks at me. "You're not over-confident either." It's a statement, not a question.

"She's a bad fit." Red lights start to blur together in the lane next to us. "We're being set up to fail."

"Bad fit?" Felicity sounds like she doesn't understand. "Arthur, she's exactly like you. That's why I thought this might work."

"Like me?" I take my eyes off the road. I can't believe Felicity would say that. My foot slips down a little harder on the accelerator. The vibration of the car helps to ground me. "What are you talking about? She couldn't be less of a team player if she tried."

"You mean she follows her instincts? She challenges the accepted rules?"

I risk a glance away from the road. Felicity's eyes are an open challenge. "I mean she's going to get me or her or someone else killed."

"She's the most trained field agent out there."

"She's trained for the wrong thing."

Felicity grabs her head. "Arthur, fucking listen to me. You *have* to get on with her. You *have* to try harder. If we get absorbed by MI6 then, as things stand, it will be your fault. You are the point of friction. I've never seen Kayla take a shine to someone more quickly. I think Clyde may be incapable of disliking people at a fundamental biological level. Tabitha… is Tabitha. But whatever this problem is that you have with her, you need to get over it. I honestly don't care if it's justified or not. You have to get on with her or everything we have here is at risk."

"Everything?" The monumentality of the word lands in my lap like a rock. *Everything.* Jesus, when did this ground shift on me?

But Felicity is already shaking her head. "Not…" Her hand flaps back and forth in the gulf between us. "You and me. Jesus, I just asked you to move in with me."

God, that does not help. It should. Of course it bloody should. I know it should. And I know she's right and I'm in the wrong, and that doesn't help either. I feel like Lang's reality key. Nothing on me lines up. And there is no magician willing to twist me through reality and into a shape that aligns.

We fly through darkness. Rear lights are a red river beside us. The car rocks as we pass others on the road.

Felicity puts a hand on my shoulder. "Slow down, Arthur." And then, as I start to finally ease off the accelerator, "This isn't an attack. It's a request. It's me asking for help. OK? Help me save MI37. If Hannah really is that bad then once it's safe we'll get rid of her. OK? We save the world. We save MI37. Everything's good. Everything goes back to normal after that. OK?"

"OK," I say, though not loudly, and not necessarily with the conviction I should muster. Because I feel brittle right now. Ever since that incident in the Highlands something in my head has been wrong. And the way I am now I don't know how far I can bend to accommodate Hannah without snapping.

But I slow down, and I join the other cars, and slowly we find our way back to Oxford.

OUTSIDE FELICITY'S APARTMENT

"Aren't you coming in?"

Felicity stands on the curb, framed by the car door, her hair lit by the street light, brown strands painted yellow. She looks puzzled.

"I just—" I start. I have rehearsed this in my head as we piloted our way through the quiet twisting streets, but now the moment has come I hesitate. I am running out of excuses to not stay over. And part of me does want to stay over. But I also need some calm right now, some stability. If I'm to do what she asks of me, if I'm to finally extract my head from my arse, then I need to do it in my own space. I need to do it on home ground, somewhere I'm not worrying about making a commitment that will leave Felicity a bloody widow.

God, I'm doing it again.

"If this is about what I said in the car..." Felicity starts.

I force a grin on my face. "Only in a way," I say. "I just... if we're going to the Himalayas tomorrow, I want to be prepared. I want to go back to the office and look at all the stuff we have on Lang there. Make sure there's something the others aren't missing while they're down in London."

Hell, that may even be a good idea. The thought buoys me a little. "I'll just be an hour or so. I'll be next to you when you wake up."

A little distance. A little alone time. And it will be good to wake up beside Felicity. That may be exactly what I need to calm down and be reasonable about Hannah.

"OK," Felicity says and she smiles. "That's good, Arthur. We're going to be good, right?"

"Hannah will be amazed by our poise and professionalism."

Felicity looks dubious. "If we could just aim for borderline competent that would probably be enough. No need to get ambitious."

I smile. Genuinely this time. "OK, love."

The smile she returns is broad. "I like it when you call me that."

A QUIET WHILE LATER

Down in conference room B, I stare at the Google Maps image on my laptop. A lone valley in the Himalayas. Utterly isolated.

Like me here, in MI37 at midnight.

The offices are quiet at the best of times—a space built for a hundred people housing only five. With just me here, there's a sort of comforting desolation to the space. And I'm not learning anything here that I couldn't have learned back at the apartment, but it's nice all the same.

I get up, stretch my legs. I think I saw some folders about Lang down in the laboratory. If I bundle those up then this won't look so much like what it is—me wasting time. But I'm glad I came here.

I whistle as I walk down the empty corridors, try to imagine the sounds transmuted into a trumpet's solo wail. My fingers tap the ghost of a drum beat on the wall as I walk.

It's coming back to me. My center. My balance. Felicity was right, in the car. I need to get over myself. There *is* a way to get along with Hannah, as obnoxious as she is. Everyone else is managing it.

That stupid bloody robot up in the Highlands throwing me off my game.

I picture it again, here in the reassuring hallows of MI37. The event seems distant when framed by concrete walls and lit by fluorescent strips. Manageable. It was just another close call in a long series of close calls. I have lived through those events.

Felicity was right. She's always right.

My feet carry me to the lab and I suffer a momentary flashback to the ungodly sight of Clyde's naked white arse bobbing up and down. Jesus, that was this morning. I saw that *this morning*.

And I thought almost having my brains clubbed from my skull was traumatizing.

Abruptly I'm laughing. Not a small chuckle, but something

deep and hard. As if some primal clasp has slipped on a chest deep in my gut. I have to hold onto the side of a table to steady myself. My eyes are leaking.

Tabitha and Clyde. In the bloody closet. Oh Jesus. Oh God.

I'm on my knees before I recover. And my sides hurt, and my knees are weak, but I really do feel better. Catharsis via hysterics. Hell, if it works, I'll take it.

I scan the room, still chuckling. And there are the folders. I pick one up, start leafing through. It better look at least vaguely relevant. And, yes, there is the word Uhrwerkgerät. I leaf through other pages, but it's all in German and I don't know the German word for Himalayas.

"Shit." I curse as a piece of paper nicks the pad of my thumb. A thin paper cut. I stick the digit in my mouth and taste blood.

A thump from behind distracts me from the cut's sting. I spin around, already reaching for my gun.

There's no one there. I am alone.

I hesitate. Did I really hear something? I strain my ears. You have to break through five or six ridiculously complicated security locks to get down here. I must have—

Another thump. Distinct this time. Undeniable. Something heavy... two heavy things colliding.

Then silence. I am overly aware of my heartbeat. My breath.

"Hello?" I call. "Is anyone there?"

No answer.

Nice one, Arthur. If anyone thought they were alone down here, there goes the element of surprise.

I'm glad Hannah isn't here to point that out to me.

Another thump, and I get a bead on it this time. I spin, face the closet door, with the, CAUTION, CONTAINS CAUSTIC MATERIALS, sign tacked on it.

"No way." The thought emerges audibly. But it can't be. Not twice in one day. I cannot be trapped listening to Clyde and Tabitha go at it twice in one day. The world is not that cruel.

But then it strikes me that Clyde and Tabitha are still back in London packing up Lang's paperwork. Even if they had a very weird and very specific fetish involving that exact closet then they couldn't have beaten Felicity and me back to Oxford. There's no way. Which means it can't be them in the closet.

Another thump.

I level my gun. I wish I had a sword. I'm better with that, but there's a certain impracticality to walking around Oxford with one strapped to my back. Not that I'd ever dream of telling Kayla that.

I approach the door slowly. And for the first time in a while, I am holding my gun with a steady hand. I am ready for this, whatever it is.

Well, I'm ready for it to be whatever, I suppose.

I pause two paces away, steel myself to grab the door handle and fling it open.

Whatever is on the other side beats me to the punch. The door swings open while I'm still a yard shy of my goal. I leap back even as I jab my pistol forward.

But there is nothing there. Just shelves and shadow. My gun threatens an empty room.

I stare deep in, searching. Step forward.

Nothing.

And then something detaches itself from the darkness. A chunk of reality flaking away, walking forward. Shelving, plaster, crates. It's as if someone was sitting there wearing an outfit painted to blend in precisely with the view of someone standing exactly where I am now. Like some extended art joke. An example of near perfect camouflage suddenly revealed. Even as it moves, it's still difficult to determine exactly what's going on. I think I make out... an arm? A leg?

And then—because, of course, they always do—things get weirder. The costume starts to lose its color, starts to fall away. Not clothing falling away item by item, but a slow unraveling, like string pooling on the floor, revealing beneath...

It is a figure. I got that much right. But it is not anyone or anything I would go so far as to call human.

It is a human-shaped hole in reality. It is a man-sized piece of... space? The figure is flat and featureless, its skin night-sky black, spattered with stars.

Is this more camouflage? But I can think of nothing like this.

No practically manufactured item. No, this is something Other. Proper, upper-case, mess-with-your-head, MI37 WEIRD.

Of course, this is the point where any rational person would take off after their sanity, running and screaming up through the corridors and passageways.

I go with saying, "Hello?"

The figure raises a hand. Points at me.

"Arthur," I say. "Agent Arthur Wallace." I clarify. I think about it, and then throw in, "Of MI37. We save the world. Mostly from things that look like you."

It pauses. We stand there, two sides of a deeply fucked up mirror. Its jaw works. An echo of my own speech?

And then its voice comes.

"Beyond the collapse—" it says.

Oh God. Oh no. Jesus, its voice is doing something to my head. It's opening holes in my brain. Opening up space.

The syllables send me to my knees. I try to bring my hands up to cover my ears, but my muscles are spasming wildly. My eyes start to twitch and roll. I lose sight of it, but the words don't stop. Won't stop.

"—I am you."

I can feel blood coursing from my nose, down my chin. The taste of copper fills my mouth again. The figure's words fall through space into my mind.

And then everything goes dark.

24

"Arthur? Arthur? Arthur!"

Hands. Hands shaking me. What the—

And then it comes back to me. The crushing grating agony in my mind. The unspooling of my sanity. The creature. The figure.

"No!" I yell, and kick my legs backwards. I grab at whoever is talking to me, try to drag them back, drag them clear.

"Hey! Calm down! Get him! Grab him!" A confusion of words around me. A smothering blanket of shouted concern and snatching hands. Someone pins my arms, holds them in an iron grip. I buck and yell. They have to get out of here. This is not safe.

"Hey, hey, hey, hey." A low rush of words, a flutter of syllables against my ear. Felicity's voice. "It's OK, Arthur. It's OK. You're OK."

And that grounds me. That brings me back. It's over. Whatever the hell it was, it's over.

They help me to my feet. Felicity, Kayla, and Clyde. Clyde rubs at his hip where I caught him with a flailing arm or leg.

"Sorry," I say.

He shrugs. "Oh no, quite all right. Could have happened to anybody. Probably happening to hundreds of people right now. I mean probabilistically speaking. Seven billion people on the planet. At least a hundred being kicked by flailing friends. Stands to reason. It's going to happen to you at some point or other.

Why complain about it? That's what I always say. Well not always. Doesn't happen often enough for me to say, 'always,' but you get the gist of—"

"I do," I cut him off.

Felicity is peering at my face, horror-struck. "What the hell happened?"

And my face does feel odd. I reach up, touch my chin, my upper lip. They are coated with something crusty and dry. I rub at it. Rusty-looking flakes come away on my fingers.

And then I remember the blood. Pouring out of my nose. I look down and see my shirt is soaked.

"We have to get you to a doctor," Felicity says. "This could have been some sort of seizure, or—"

"No." I cut her off sharply. Too sharply. My own worry reacting to hers. "I mean… no," I say more softly. "It's not that."

And I explain. When I finish Clyde is rubbing his beard, tracing the line of his chin. "God, that sounds so familiar. I'm sure I've read something like that before." He moves to one of the lab computers, starts clicking. "I wish Tabby was here."

"Keep it in your pants," Kayla mutters, but Clyde doesn't appear to hear her.

"Oh damn, that reminds me," Felicity says. "I should tell Tabitha and Hannah to stop checking the pubs for you."

"You had them checking pubs?" That's not a great default location for people to check for you.

Felicity shrugs. "You seemed out of sorts last night, and we didn't need everyone searching here. Plus I'd called the hospital and you weren't there."

Pubs. Third on the list. OK, that actually sounds reasonable.

"I'm so sorry you were worried." I take her hand.

"I'm so sorry you almost had your brains bleed out your nose."

In the background, Kayla makes gagging sounds. I wonder if it's possible for someone to be allergic to human affection.

"Yes! There it is!" Clyde says from his computer. He turns to us, beaming. "Tabby would be very proud of me. Normally I'm horrible with her databases. Though they were much easier when I was an AI. But anyway," he shakes his head, "future echoes."

A quick glance around the room assures me that I'm not the only one who has no clue what Clyde's talking about.

Clyde seems to reach that conclusion around the same time as me. "Oh," he says, "right. Well, they've only been theoretical up to this point." He rubs the side of his head, mussing the hair.

"Wait," he looks at me, "Arthur, did you hurt yourself in any way just before the thing appeared?"

I think about it. "Erm, well," it feels silly, but usually withholding information leads to supernatural horrors trying to eat my spleen, so I say, "I did get a papercut." I show him my thumb. Kayla makes gentle scoffing noises.

"On what?" Clyde is intent. "This is very important."

I shrug. "I was just checking some of the stuff we had on Lang. And I found some stuff about the Uhrwerkgerät, and, well… then, I suppose."

"Oh." Clyde doesn't look very happy. "Oh poop sticks."

I want to question the curse, but his expression keeps me focused.

"Why?"

"Well," he says, "like I say, future echoes have been theoretical up until now, though there's been some pretty solid math to describe them. They're this rather odd feature of composite realities. Like ours, for example. Pretty obvious example to go with, I admit. But they only happen when there's a fairly massive disruption to multiple realities within the composite. An event so large that it distorts other realities in the composite. An act of violence that extends beyond the realities initially caught up in the mess. In other words echoes, or ripples spreading out from the disruption, moving forward and backward through time and space."

"That doesn't sound feckin' fabulous," Kayla puts in.

Clyde shakes his head. "Not at all. Sort of frog in a microwave sort of bad. If you assume the frog is a large portion of reality that you're generally quite keen on continuing to exist. But it does make sense given that Lang was an expert at manipulating realities."

"What's Lang got to do with it?" I wish Felicity's face would go back to neutral. Her absence of calm is beginning to leak into me.

"Well, a future echo is usually triggered by something related to the main event. In this case it was Arthur hurting himself while doing something related to the Uhrwerkgerät."

I almost don't want to ask. But I have to. For my job. For my sanity. "Which means?"

"Well…" Clyde shrugs, a violent spasm. "This is all theory, you realize. Best guesses and all that." His face twists. "But the most obvious inference is that the Uhrwerkgerät is going to go off, and when it does it's going to kill you."

25

Oh.

Oh shit and balls.

The silence that greets Clyde's utterance grows. And grows. A crushing eclipsing vacuum of sound. And I need someone to fill it. To stop it. Because I...

I...

I...

"We find it and we stop it." Felicity rescues me. Pushes against the crushing gravity of it all. "That's our plan. That's what we're going to do."

"Erm..." Clyde clears his throat. "God, this is the bit where I hate having read about this stuff, but it was a Friday night and it was late and there was nothing good on TV, and I was sort of a bit down about the recently-having-been-a-supervillain thing at the time, and there was a sort of grim fascination thing going on. And please understand, I really don't want this to be the truth, it just happens to be the theory supported by pretty much all the evidence.

"You see, if the echo has arrived then that means that the Uhrwerkgerät *has* to go off." He stares about, looking for someone to nod and say it's OK. No one does. He plows on anyway. "It's like a ripple in a pond. If you see the ripple then you know someone threw a stone. Here we saw there was a future echo, so we know there was a detonation. We can't have had one without the other. So basically the manifestation of the echo means the detonation is sort of, well, one doesn't really want to use the word 'unavoidable' but pretty much it's unavoidable."

I sit down. My legs just go out from under me. The floor comes up and smacks me in the arse. My death. Predestined. Signed, stamped, post-marked, and delivered love and kisses from the universe. Reality is conspiring against me.

There is chaos around me again. Felicity is shouting something again. Clyde is backing up, hunching his shoulders defensively. Kayla has her sword drawn for some reason and is eyeing the closet door.

I can't hold onto their words. I can't hold onto anything. Not even my own fucking life.

Jesus.

I am going to die. I mean, I was always going to die. Death and taxes and all that crap. But… I mean, soon, right? Before my time, I suppose. I am going to die young and I don't even have a good-looking corpse to leave behind. Felicity might disagree, but…

God, Felicity. She's…

Actually she's going to die too. This bomb is going to go off. Clyde just said it. It's predetermined. It's already happened. We just have to catch up to it. A detonation powerful enough to distort reality. Felicity's not going to survive that. No one in MI37 is. England isn't. Hell, Earth might not.

What do we do? What the hell do we do, when there's nothing we can do?

"Ephie." The name cuts through my fug. Felicity has rounded on Kayla. She grabs her by the lapels of her flannel overshirt. "This is reality magic. Get Ephie. She's a Dreamer. She determines what's reality. She is reality magic. Get her here. Make her fix it."

"That wee bitch?" Kayla's expression is incredulous. "She can't do shite for this."

"Get her!" Felicity's voice breaks slightly.

"It's not like that. I can't just go to her. I just call her and if she's not being an uppity wee shite she feckin' comes."

"So fucking call her." Felicity still hasn't let go of Kayla's shirt.

"She won't come."

"Call her!"

Kayla hesitates, then sighs. "Ephie," she says loudly. "Ephie!"

Nothing. I sit in the lab soaked in my own blood and misery and Kayla's call goes unheeded.

"Again," Felicity demands.

"Ephie!"

Nothing.

"Again."

Kayla looks miserable. It's so unexpected and unguarded a look, I almost turn away. This is Kayla's pain. Pain she can't stab or hack away. Pain she's so defenseless against she's trying to bury it under another pregnancy.

"Ephie!" Her shout is hollow in the room.

Nothing.

"Again." Felicity is merciless.

Kayla's expression twists. She finds her anger. "The wee bitch isn't listening to me!" She's almost shouting. "She's got her head shoved up her reality-bending arse so feckin' far she can see out of her own eyeballs. She can't do shite for us. Forget her."

Then Kayla seems to notice that she's breathing hard, takes a moment to steady herself, rests a hand on Felicity's arm. "We'll go to the Himalayas. Clyde and Tabitha will find something feckin' there." She nods at me. "We'll fix him. It'll be all right. You ken?"

Felicity holds her for a moment, not relaxing a muscle. Then she sags. Kayla catches her with her other hand, props her against a lab table.

"It's all theory and shite," she says. "Thaumaturgical bollocks. We'll kick them there, make 'em squeal, and all this shit will be sorted." She looks to Clyde. "Right?"

"Well," Clyde retreats to the far side of the computer. "I mean, I suppose if we're going to learn any more about the Uhrwerkgerät anywhere it's going to be there. And Lang seems to be the expert on this stuff. Maybe if he made theory into practice then... well, I don't know... I think the fact that I don't know is sort of the point. So I need to find out. Could totally be a way to save Arthur. And the world. And everything." For a moment he looks like he actually means it. Then he glances down at the papers he pulled up on the computer. The sight of him blanching gives me less confidence.

"It's what we do," I hear Felicity mutter. There are a few lines of hope drafted around her eyes. She looks down at me, takes a breath. "It's going to be alright," she says.

I start laughing. I don't know what else to do. I see it again. The figure of night and stars standing before me, destroying my mind.

"Of course it is," I say. "Yeah. Totally."

"You'll be OK," Felicity says. "I promise you."

They're words divorced from their meaning by the absurdity and cruelty of the world.

But what is the other option? Curl up here? Maybe I can use those words. At least for a little bit. And then denial will kick in and I can coast on that.

Coast on it up until the moment when I am violently blown up. Oh Jesus.

I take Felicity's hand, hold on tight.

"It's going to be all right," she says.

"It's going to be all right." I repeat the words back to her. I even try out a smile. It's not so hard to fake. I feel I've been practicing it the past few days.

"Yes. It will be." I think Felicity's smile might even be genuine. She may really believe me. "Now," she says, "let's go to Nepal and sort this shit out."

26

BRIZE NORTON AIR BASE

Clouds roll in as we make our way south to the RAF base just outside Brize Norton. Rain spatters the car windows. Felicity drives. Tabitha and Clyde sit in the back of Felicity's minivan trying to hide the fact that they're holding hands.

Someone on the radio jokes at the Prime Minister's expense. Felicity laughs. She is sunshine despite the rain. It's as if everything is already fixed for her. She was quiet earlier. But then after a few miles she coughed and made some quip about Kayla and pregnancy. Something about needing a man with balls of steel, and how composite metals typically had a low sperm count. It's been smiles since then.

Maybe it's genuine. Maybe it's denial. I'm just glad she seems better than she did back at the lab.

We approach the air base. It is large and fenced off. We start to trace its circumference, finding our way to the gate.

"What the hell?"

Felicity's tone makes me look up from contemplating my own navel. Two massive figures stand by the road, their shapes barely discernible beneath heavy brown cloaks.

Volk and Hermann. How the hell did they get here?

"Careful," Tabitha says from the back seat. "Could be anyone."

And actually she's right. Those cloaks conceal the figures' true identities. They're too small to be Friedrich, but that's about the only robot we can rule out.

"Should we keep driving?" Clyde asks. "It seems a little impolite and all, but, well, we can't be completely sure that they're here for us. Well, that said, I suppose if one starts down that road, well it's very difficult to be completely sure about anything, isn't it? I mean one is constantly reliant on one's own senses, and there's just so much evidence demonstrating how they really aren't as reliable as we'd like to think. What if one has gone mad in the night and doesn't realize it? I might not even be in a car on my way to the Himalayas right now. I might be in my kitchen talking to two watermelons and a spatula and hallucinating wildly. I mean when that's a possibility, what is certainty?"

I'm not sure if that's rhetorical or not, but it's definitely a pause. "I'll see what they want," I say to Felicity. "You keep the engine running."

"I'll come too," she says. "Tabitha—"

"No." I put my hand on her arm, practice my smile. "The one good thing about knowing a bomb is going to kill me is that I can be certain that these guys won't."

"That's not going to happen," Felicity says. It sounds like a reflex.

"Actually—" Clyde starts from the back seat, but the car is already slowing. I open the door as we roll to a halt, hop out into the rain.

The two hulking Uhrwerkmänner turn to face me. The gravity of their movements makes me feel small and fragile and full of extremely squishable organs. My pistol feels unhelpfully small. I need to find some sort of missile launcher I can carry around without raising eyebrows.

"You are leaving without us." There's no mistaking that grating resentment. These are my guys.

"Hello, Hermann," I say. "Lovely to see you too."

I can't tell if he grunts or slips a gear. "You abandon your task," he says.

He is buried deep in his cloak again. The thick cloth is sodden, clinging to his angular frame, yet it still obfuscates more than it reveals. Volk, on the other hand, pokes his head forward, round glass eyes protruding, rain dripping down their surface.

"You have found something?" He sounds hopeful, eager even. The *yin* to Hermann's despondent *yang*.

"Maybe," I say. "We're not sure. We want to check it out."

"See, Hermann!" Volk slaps his companion on the back. "I told you it was so. They are coming closer to the solution we all search for."

Another grinding grunt from Hermann.

"How did you know we were going to be here?" I ask them. If I can find that out, I might be closer to working out how Friedrich and his mechanical posse intercepted us at Lang's apartment.

"You mean so you can keep us out of the loop next time?" Hermann spits. "So you can keep whatever secrets you find close to yourself and share them with no one else? We shall tell you nothing."

Seriously—does he act like a jackass on purpose?

"I ask," I say, starting to wish I'd brought an umbrella, "because last time we told you where we were going, your friend Friedrich turned up and tried to endurance test our spines, and I want to know if the leak is on our end or yours."

"You accuse us?" Hermann's voice is a knife blade being sharpened. "You dare? With no understanding? With no concept of our sacrifice, our battle? You say we are betrayers?" He straightens, limbs unfolding beneath his cloak. He looms over me, ten feet tall or more.

The bomb will kill me. Not him.

"I'm saying it's a possibility," I say, looking up into the overhanging darkness of his cloak. I put no malice into the words, just let them hang.

Hermann's weight shifts suddenly. A foot coming forward, an elbow swinging back.

"No, Hermann!" Volk shoves his bulk between the two of us.

For my part, I stand my ground. *He can't kill me. It's predetermined.*

"How did you know we'd be here?" I ask again. "Because the leak could also be on our end—"

"So he admits it!" Hermann froths behind Volk's outstretched arms.

"It's another possibility," I say, still keeping my voice flat. For once I feel in control of something. Hermann's hysterics are terribly predictable. "It would be unintentional," I hesitate, "obviously. But you being here suggests our communications aren't as secure as we thought they were."

"See," says Volk, turning his back on me, voice placating, "this is concern. The same as ours. We work together."

A wodge of oil arcs over Volk's shoulder, lands in a thick puddle beside me. Which means Lang even designed a way for them to spit. That seems a little unnecessary.

"Calm yourself." There's finally an edge to Volk's voice. And then a string of German words that I don't understand. "*Du machst dich lächerlich.*" Then he turns to me.

"We have hidden for many years. Underground. Where you do not look. You have tunnels everywhere. You abandon them over and over. These hidden, forgotten spaces are ours now. They go many places and allow us to hear many things."

I hesitate, working out the implications.

"There are tunnels below MI37?" I ask. "You just stuck a glass up against the wall and listened to us talking?"

Volk nods. The speaker-bar that is his mouth twists slightly— the suggestion of a smile. "Not just below MI37."

Well, that's not creepy at all.

"You are a fool." Hermann spits again. Not at me this time. It spatters over Volk's cloak, leaving an ugly stain on the side of his hood.

"But you haven't seen Friedrich or any of his cronies down in the tunnels with you?" I say, ignoring Hermann.

Volk shrugs. "There are many tunnels. We cannot be in them all at once."

Not quite the "no" I was hoping for. There are still no definitive answers.

"OK," I say, "that's your show and tell over with. My turn." And so I lay it out for them. What we found beneath London, our plan to go to the Himalayas and do more research. I leave out the bit about the future echo. That feels personal. And likely to cause Hermann to have another hissy fit.

"So you have nothing," Hermann says when I'm done.

"Well," I snap back, "I do think I have a bit of a cold now that I've been standing in the rain for ten minutes telling you about all the shit we've been through on your behalf." This, I remember, is why we normally let Felicity do the talking. She keeps her temper on a tighter rein.

"Forgive my friend," Volk says. "It is hard to watch our people die. We are anxious for news."

My anger ebbs. I think I have a little insight on that sort of stress now. "I understand," I say.

There is a moment while everyone pulls themselves together a little bit.

"So," Hermann breaks the silence. "Where is this plane? When do we take off?"

"We?" I say. "This—"

"Of course we," Hermann snaps. "You do not think we will let you simply run off and abscond with what we need. You will show us the way and we will retrieve it. I will not have you fail again as you did at Lang's house."

"Hey," I say, whatever momentary calm I enjoyed evaporating, "we've been on this less than a week and gotten further than you. So a little fucking gratitude might not go amiss."

"Is everything all right?"

A voice from the car draws all our attention. Felicity is standing by the driver's door, shielding her eyes from the rain.

"Fine," I call back. "Just discussing Hermann's desire to come with us to the Himalayas."

Felicity's mouth makes an "o."

"When do you take off?" Hermann calls. "Your friend," he spits the word, "is reluctant to tell us."

"Well," Felicity hesitates. "It might be hard to disguise your presence in Nepal, and—"

"We are coming," Hermann insists.

I look to Volk. "Come on," I say, "help me out here."

"We are most anxious to retrieve the papers," Volk calls to Felicity, "and eager to be of assistance in any way we can be."

It doesn't sound like any more of a request than Hermann's statement. The tone is friendlier, but that's about it. I sigh.

Felicity sees me do it. "Runway Bravo," she calls. "Half an hour."

RUNWAY BRAVO. HALF AN HOUR

The RAF seems a touch surprised to find two mechanical giants in the middle of one of their hangars. To be honest, I am too. They declined a ride from us and we left them by the side of the road. The idea that the pair of them can bypass military defenses so easily as to have beaten us here is a little worrying.

Still after a brief standoff where the pair of them are threatened by fifty or so soldiers with rifles, and alarm klaxons sound from every corner of the base, Felicity manages to smooth things over.

Eventually the base chief disperses his men with mutterings about "irregular bollocks." A vast Hercules carrier plane waits for us, which at least solves the problem of where to store Volk and Hermann. Despite his immobile features, Hermann still manages to give me a dirty look as he gets on board.

"Friendly bugger, ain't he?" says Hannah.

She and Kayla drove up together in Kayla's car. They arrived only in time to catch the tail-end of the excitement.

I remember my conversation with Felicity the night before. About how Hannah unknowingly holds MI37's future in her hands. About how important it is to be nice to her.

Then I remember how I'm going to get blown to bits in a few days, and how that is probably the only thing Hannah will ever remember about me.

So I don't bother replying. I just get onto the plane, sit down, and wait for the future to get a little closer.

* * *

THREE HOURS LATER

As far as in-flight entertainment goes, military aircraft are shit. Instead of a movie, I get to listen to Kayla discuss the desired genetic traits of a sperm donor with Hannah. Apparently she is looking for someone "intelligent and shite", "not a fatty," "with none of that genetic disease bollocks," and with "a tiny wee bum."

"Are tiny wee bums genetic?" Hannah asks her as I attempt to have the seat swallow me.

"Better feckin' be."

"I've always liked a good curve myself."

"Yeah, but you're looking for an entirely feckin' different gender."

"True."

This is apparently enough to pique Hermann's interest. "It is inefficient, your way. An inelegant means to procreate."

"The feck?" Kayla looks at him with something close to open disdain. Felicity's up in the cockpit chatting with the pilot so nobody checks Kayla's attitude. I probably should, but honestly Hermann has it coming.

"You strive for something greater than yourself, for something worthy of preservation. But it is all random. It is all chance. You have no control over your variables. You have no idea if you will produce perfection or a mewling useless grub."

"Oh," Hannah brightens. "I thought you'd rejected your creator's philosophy? Eugenics still OK with you is it?"

Hermann grunts from the depths of his hood. "Eugenics is just a variation on a theme. Biology is inefficient to the point of being useless. I am talking about design, mechanics. Our creator's purpose was warped, but his tools for advancing himself, his race, they were correct."

Volk shakes his head. "Why do you seek to antagonize always, Hermann? They are our friends."

"They are convenient allies for as long as it suits them." Hermann sneers. "Betrayal is the natural state of the biologic. History has taught us that."

"Build a baby?" ask Kayla. "Hell, you find me the doctor and you sign me up."

Hannah shakes her head. "Nah. That'd take all the fun out of it." She smiles.

"Aye to that."

It would probably be smarter to hold my tongue, but I do at least have the certainty of death by bomb, not by Kayla-wielded pointy thing, so I wade in. "Don't you think," I say, "that you should, maybe, try to patch things up with Ephie before you just have another child? I mean, all other healthy-relationship concerns aside, she's a reality-bending demigod who is likely to take badly to you trying to quite literally replace her."

"She can shove it up her arse."

I look around for allies. Which is when I realize I am short on them.

"Where did Clyde and Tabitha go?" It seems like a good enough way to change the course of the conversation.

Hannah's grin broadens. "They headed off to find the 'bathrooms at the back of the plane' about half an hour ago. Imagine they're quite enjoying the inefficiency of biology at this point in time."

I blanch. Betrayed on all sides, I head to the cockpit to find Felicity.

AND ANOTHER TWO HOURS

When Clyde does have the audacity to show his face up at the cockpit, he is thankfully alone. I don't think I could meet his eye if Tabitha was right there as well.

"Arthur," he says, "if you don't mind, I would love a brief word. Well, in all honesty, knowing myself, as I think some king once advised someone... Or maybe it was just a line in that *Matrix* movie. The one with all the leather and slow-motion. Oh God, now it sounds like high-end pornography. But it was a big Hollywood blockbuster, I swear. But anyway, well, demonstrating in fact that, this being me, it may not be a brief word. But not a completely protracted word. Perhaps a word as brief as I'm likely to make it. Or a medium word. Not a word like 'antidisestablishmentarianism,' but also not a word like 'and' or 'to'. A sort of middle ground."

Felicity turns her head to hide the fact that she's smiling.

"Go ahead," I tell him.

"So, the whole earlier incident with you sort of insulting Hermann and him losing his temper, and you saying that you knew you weren't going to be killed by anything except the bomb."

"Yes," I say. It seems like the one silver lining to all of this. There's nothing to worry about right up until the end.

"Not actually true."

Clyde tears away the silver lining, bunches it up in a ball, and proves it to be kitchen foil.

"You see, it's not as deterministic as that. You're *supposed* to be killed by the bomb as far as reality is concerned. However, you could still be killed by something else. Totally a possibility."

Oh crap. I start to sag again.

Felicity shakes her head. "We're sorting out the bomb thing."

"Erm…" Clyde looks dubious, then shrugs. "Yes. Of course. But the thing is, if you do die, Arthur, it'll actually be worse than, you know, regular usual death. Well, caveat that. I mean, firstly, unlikely to be a regular usual death given our line of work. Probably an abominable snowman crushing your head into your chest cavity or something awful like that. And secondly, I mean, for you there's a probably a pretty definable upper limit for how awful dying can get. At a certain point it's just dying. Not that… I mean, I don't want to undersell how awful you dying would be. It's very awful. It's just, well… the experience for the dying person pretty much standard, I imagine. A singular experience. At least looking at it from a biological point of view. But I'm not talking about you. Actually trying to talk about everyone else in the world. Which may or may not bother you, but I'm hoping that, given your choice of profession, you are the sort of fellow who cares about his fellow man even in the act of death. Because, well you see, as mentioned, you're supposed to die by the bomb." His eyes flick to Felicity. "At least at this moment in time. So, if, say, *before* we sorted that out, the whole abominable snowman, head-chest cavity scenario were to play out, or some variation upon that theme, well that would violate reality and the future echo. And that in turn would lead to a paradox. I mean, why would that future echo have occurred if that wasn't what killed you?"

I am suddenly very aware that I'm thousands of feet up in the air in what amounts to a tin can manufactured in the fifties, and that no one has given me a parachute. "Paradoxes not a good thing then?" I check.

"Depends on the scale. I mean at best you're looking at minor amounts of reality changing. Not many accounts of when that happened as it's hard to detect, writes itself back into history, but you know, sort of loss of a nation and its population. Elimination of a genetic line. Shifts in the turning points of history. Standard time-travel disaster sequence."

"That's the *best* case?" I check.

Felicity tries to jump in. "Isn't this all a moot point?" she asks. "We're going to sort this all out." She makes it sound like the threat of me dying, tearing reality apart, and scattering the pieces about like confetti is on a par with keeping a library book out too long.

"Well the worst-case scenario," Clyde barrels on ignoring Felicity, "is a self-perpetuating paradox. One that's so problematic that resolving it leads to more paradoxes which then need to be resolved. But then the resolution of those leads to further paradoxes, et cetera, et cetera, so on and so forth, down the dominos all fall, everyone watches it on YouTube and is very impressed, and then reality collapses in upon itself, is no more, and not only is everyone dead, but they never existed in the first place, and neither did anything else."

I chew on that for a bit. "That is a pretty bad worst-case scenario."

Clyde nods. "Sort of why no one really messes around with reality magic. Leave it to the Dreamers and other professionals like that."

Felicity shakes her head. "This is a totally moot point."

But it strikes me that Clyde is worried enough about the event that he just had sex with Tabitha in the back of a crowded plane just so he could get it in one more time.

And yet, what else is there to do? What does this change? My death is imminent one way or another. Just keep on fighting the good fight, until it's not good anymore.

"You're right," I say squeezing Felicity's hand. "Moot point. Doesn't matter at all."

27

TRIBHUVAN INTERNATIONAL AIRPORT

The plane brings us down in a broad flat bowl of land. The city of Kathmandu spreads around us. For a moment, standing in the plane's doorway, the peaks surrounding it don't look that large. Then my sense of scale adjusts. I gawp.

Hannah pushes past me and I remember I am a hardened government agent. I shut my mouth.

"OK," I say as my feet meet solid ground once more. "Due to the whole lying in a bloody heap thing the other night, I am a little behind on our next steps."

Tabitha grunts as if the typical-ness of this has just aged her an extra five years. "Car rental. Drive two days. Catch a bus. Drive a day. Get off the bus. Hike two days. Arrive. Get papers. Do it all backwards."

"Five days?" I ask. "We can't get a helicopter or something just to whisk us up and dump us there?"

Hannah reaches over and pats my stomach in a way that might possibly be OK if we were in any way friends. "Too much time behind a desk?" she asks.

"Too much time elapsing while Friedrich and his bunch of screw-loose nut-jobs work on creating the bomb that is going to kill me," I snap at her. Again, diplomacy seems like a waste of time given my agenda. Hell, if everything goes as the future has apparently dictated, there won't be an MI37 for Hannah to end. I can say to her exactly what comes into my mind.

Hermann and Volk are clanking down the Hercules' back ramp. "For once he speaks something resembling the truth," Hermann barks.

Felicity, standing behind me, puts a hand on my arm. "It takes the time it takes. We can't commandeer the military here. It's Nepal. But it's OK. We'll sort everything out." There's a sort of Zen calm to her as she says it. As if this place is already rubbing off on her. Or as if she's in some sort of mental shock and not dealing with reality at all. I might be more worried about resolving these sort of long-term issues if I had any faith in there being any sort of long term to worry about.

As it is, I suppose I get to spend five days with my girlfriend traveling through beautiful countryside in a foreign land, to a place in the Himalayas seen by only a handful of other people. There are worse ways to spend your final days, I suppose.

FIVE DAYS LATER

We round a bend in the trail and suddenly a valley is exposed to us—lush untouched vegetation filling it, a warm green blanket dotted through with spikes of vibrant color. Epic mountains rise, thrusting majestically up into the sky. The serrated teeth of the world. Clouds skid and collide with sheer rock, roiling up in thick rolling banks of white. It is an epic view.

It can also kiss my arse.

"We have to be nearly there," Felicity pants, leaning heavily on a makeshift walking stick which has already given her three splinters and me five.

"There is no end," I tell her, desperately trying to stop the backpack from digging any deeper into my flesh. "This is karma. We must have done something awful. Some decision we made in the past is responsible for the drowning of a million kittens."

"Green fucking hell," Tabitha mutters.

"Well, it is quite a beautiful view," Clyde hazards.

"I will slap you," Hannah says. It is one of our rare moments of agreement, but considering our decreasing ability to talk to each other without using curse words, I don't tell her so.

Volk offers no comment. Hermann manages a sneering chuckle. I would offer to slap him as well, but ever since I discovered that my early demise could cause the destruction of all reality, I've found myself becoming less antagonistic with people who could potentially backhand me into oblivion.

The first day in the car was mostly OK. Even if the air conditioning was broken. And the radio. And the suspension. Looking back on it, even that was OK. There was a sort of camaraderie in hating that car. And Volk and Hermann were towed in a trailer behind us so I didn't have to put up with the latter's snark.

The second day was not so good. If we had been able to sleep better perhaps. In a hotel that had mattresses for example. And fewer lice. But the camaraderie became rather bitter that day. Clyde kept saying nice things to Tabitha of course, but considering their mutual grunting had been audible through our hotel's paper-thin walls, it didn't hold much charm.

The bus was a definite step down. The suspension may have actually worked until Volk and Hermann clambered on board. But it was the chickens, I think, that were my breaking point. Not only was the noise deafening, but Hannah was allergic to them. She spent the entire fifteen hour ride either telling us about the fact or producing a volume of snot which seemed untenable given her size.

And now the hiking. We started almost with a sense of excitement. We were finally leaving mechanized hell behind us. Apart from it turned out that slowly broiling to death in our own sweat in a chicken-filled, allergen-contaminated hell-bus was infinitely preferable to slowly broiling to death in our own sweat in a forest filled with insects the size of our thumbs. All of us bleed openly from the bites. And on top of that, someone appears to have jammed a small semi-detached bungalow into my backpack.

How Clyde and Tabitha were up to having noisy sex in their tent last night, I have no idea. If I didn't have to listen to it, I would almost admire their stamina. As it is, I would gladly spay them both.

And to top it all off, Volk and Hermann are immune to both the insects and the exhaustion. They just keep grinding on.

Volk at least offered to help carry some of our equipment, but Hermann just watches and sneers. I keep expecting him to call us "weak fleshy things" or something like that.

As we contemplate the view and the shittiness of the hiking, Kayla comes jogging back. Her unique physiology puts her in a class closer to the Uhrwerkmänner when it comes to weathering the journey, but she is somehow less smug about it. Possibly because Hannah seems to be suffering as much as any of us.

"About another hour, then you'll be right on top of the feckin' thing." She's been scouting ahead. On her own she probably could have been at the lab in two days or less. Why Lang chose to put himself through this every time he wanted to get some research done, I have no idea.

"Oh thank God." Hannah collapses onto her knees. "Tea break. I demand a tea break."

"Come on," Kayla chides. "Another hour and you can rest all you feckin' want."

Hannah clutches her hands together. "Mercy," she mock begs.

I look at Felicity. She shrugs. "Just another hour," she says.

I groan but she's right. Resting will just make starting up harder. I want this done with. "Come on," I say. "Just a little bit more."

This is not a popular suggestion, but we push on.

Kayla falls into step with us. "Bit of a militaristic-looking sort of place for a feckin' research lab," she says casually. It doesn't sound like casual fact.

"What do you mean?" I ask.

"You know," she says, "sort of imagined something quite feckin' dull. Square and shite. Maybe a little sort of European mountain home or some Heidi bollocks. But it's like a fort carved out of the stone. Very feckin' impressive."

"He was a Nazi," Hannah points out.

"Yeah, but his feckin' mountain castle wasn't," Kayla objects.

"Tainted," Hannah says with a shake of her head.

"Can we go back to the part where his lab is actually a fortress," I say. "Does that not strike anyone else as odd?"

Felicity looks over to Clyde and Tabitha. "Did the notes say anything about the lab itself?"

"No." Tabitha doesn't even look up from her plodding feet.

"Just mentioned the place by name. The *Ort wo gute Dinge sterben*," Clyde elaborates. "Bit of a mouthful. Though I do have to say that his prose style really does obfuscate a lot of his meaning. Not one to use three words if fifteen and a complex metaphor involving pineapples will do the job."

"He likes to rhyme," Tabitha comments, as if this is possibly his greatest crime against humanity.

"Could be a reclaimed space," Hannah suggests, moving back to the more relevant matter of the fort itself. "Old space, moves in, takes it for himself."

Kayla nods, but I'm less sure.

"That seems remarkably free of paranoia for you," I comment. Felicity flashes me a look, but I am tired, aching, and need to let off steam. Sniping at Hannah seems like a viable option.

"Oh," Hannah says blithely, "I'm all for nerve gassing the place before we step inside."

"Oh good." I nod. "Because two crimes against humanity make a right."

"Anyway," Felicity cuts in, attempting to stamp out the argument before it can really catch fire. "Let's just all be on the lookout for trouble, shall we?"

FIFTY MINUTES AFTER THE UTTERANCE OF FAMOUS LAST WORDS

We spot the trouble less than two hundred yards from our goal. This particular iteration is female, about five foot two tall, stands in the middle of the trail, and wears nothing more than a small skirt.

"Tour guide?" I hazard.

Felicity grunts, staggers to a stop, and drops her backpack on the ground. "I am too tired for this shit," she says.

The woman before us is wiry, and muscled in the same way as Kayla. Her nut-brown skin has a healthy, ruddy glow to it. Dense black tattoos twist over her arms, across the top of her chest, down between her breasts, and then spread over her stomach. Something between script and tentacles.

Her face has been painted, a stylized pattern. Black is smeared around her mouth and nose. As if she has been feasting on coal dust. The rest is white except for black dots that make exaggerated eyebrows. White dots drip down from her chin. Her eyes float, cataract-white in the white make-up.

"OK," I say. "Not to go all judgmental about a book based on its cover, but she doesn't look totally friendly."

"Couple of beers in you, you'd feckin' love her," Kayla suggests.

Despite her exhaustion Tabitha still has her laptop out and open in under three seconds. Her fingers fly across the keyboard. "Shitty face painting database," she mutters. "Take much longer?"

The woman reaches behind her back and from somewhere or other produces a singularly prodigious sword. It makes Kayla's look substantially more toothpick-like than usual.

"Stupid weapon," Kayla comments. "Too feckin' slow."

"Not to be contrary," Clyde says, "but doesn't that rather depend on the wielder?"

Kayla shrugs. "I'll feckin' gut her, no worries."

"Couldn't I just shoot her instead?" asks Hannah, which is hardly the attitude I'm trying to foster.

"Sure," Kayla says, stepping aside.

"No!" I say as Hannah pulls her gun. "Nobody is shooting anybody until—"

"Wait," Tabitha says. "Hit. Seventy-four percent likelihood. Ashmortok sisterhood. Limited to the Himalayan region. Associated with the Book discovered here in the thirties. One that led to the founding of MI37 and all that. Seemed to be dying out in the forties. Reinvigorated in the early fifties. Primarily European immigrants. Co-opted a lot of the National Socialism precepts from the disbanded German party. Sort of fit with their whole death cult thing."

The woman licks the blade of her sword. Black blood wells

from her tongue. She spits it at us. It starts to boil on the ground.

"You know what?" I say to Hannah. "Just go right ahead and shoot her."

28

At almost exactly that moment, a lot of bad things all happen at once.

Four figures leap from the trees that tower over either side of our trail. Men and women alike, wearing facepaint and little else. They are silent, the only sound the rustle of foliage behind them.

The blood the woman spat on the ground before us boils up, a great black cloud steaming off it. Thin gelatinous tentacles rise up from its surface. Eight-foot-long strands whip back and forth, block the path ahead.

The spitter herself charges toward us, through the cloud of thrashing blood.

Hannah shoots her.

The shot snaps through the whipping blood severing strands, and slams into the woman's neck. Flesh rips and blood explodes out of the wound. She drops, gurgling and thrashing. That's actually rather reassuring.

Then the four jumpers land, and are upon us.

Felicity leaps back. A blade falls close enough to slice a button from her shirt. She tries to get her pistol up but her assailant—a wiry little man with curiously long nipples that are possibly the most horrifying thing I've seen since I joined MI37—slams an elbow into her wrist and the weapon goes flying.

I get my own gun up and blow a fist-size portion of his brain into the forest beyond the path. That's quite enough of him, his violence, and his creepy nipples.

Of course, defending Felicity has left me open to death by hideous gutting. I drop and roll as a blade slices the air above me.

Despite the size of their blades, which are broad enough to resemble absurd anime props, our attackers move with terrifying swiftness. I on the other hand move with agonized lethargy.

I had intended to come out of my roll in a cat-like crouch. Instead, I come out flat on my back, panting.

The blade reappears in my field of vision, starts to fill it.

I roll sideways. The blade hammers into the ground next to my head, slices down into it several inches.

That buys me time. My attacker heaves on her blade trying to free it. I heave to try and get my body into a kneeling position. We both get there at about the same time. She raises her blade. I raise my pistol. My bullet beats her downward strike. She topples over backwards, carried by the weight of her weapon.

I struggle to my feet, survey the scene. There are more of the bastards now. Hermann and Volk are almost covered in them. Three are clambering up Hermann's back. He throws himself backwards, lands on his spine. Blood and bone go crunch.

Volk for all his humble nodding and placating smiles seems to have no problem burying his fist six inches deep in a man's chest cavity.

But swords bite at them. Volk's chest plate is notched and pitted. He leaks oil from a gash in his thigh. Sparks are spitting from Hermann's shoulder.

The rest of MI37 are doing even worse. Tabitha is just sitting on the ground with her laptop clutched over her head. Clyde slumps over her, pawing clumsily at batteries lying spilled on the ground. He gets one in, mutters, and a looming cultist spirals through the air, limbs finding new angles to exist in.

Felicity and Hannah are back to back, firing. Felicity's magazine runs dry. She fumbles for another. The cultists close.

I fire with the wild abandon of a man too tired to give much of a shit. There are probably moral implications to my actions, and ramifications that I will have to live with for at least a little while.

There are perhaps faces that will haunt my remaining dreams. But, goddamn it, I bloody hate death cults.

I shoot, shoot, shoot again. The attackers are whirling dervishes. Mostly I miss but one bullet snaps a knee in two, sends one crashing and screaming to the ground. I catch another in the chest and he collapses.

One of the attackers, broad-chested, abdomen streaked with lines of black and white, stands over his fallen comrades chanting. He holds out his prodigious sword one-handed and I swear I see electricity crackle down the blade. Where our attacker's blood has spilled, black mist begins to boil.

A black whip slashes at me. I duck back, but I'm too slow. A line of pain opens up along my cheek as the skin splits open. Blood pours down my cheek.

Shit. Shit. I can't die here. I don't want to be remembered as the jerk who accidentally ended the whole of reality.

Well, I suppose if that happens there won't be anybody to remember me, but still, goddamn it, I don't want to die.

More blood whips at me. I stagger back, trip over my own exhausted limbs. A whip smashes the ground before me. I leap sideways, collide with something, someone, bounce back, trip, bite dirt.

"The hell?" I manage, trying to twist and see what I hit.

I should have bloody known.

Hannah stands there, panic edging in at the corner of her professionally calm eyes. She holds out her gun to me. "I'm out." The panic is seeping into her voice.

"Goddamn it," I say struggling to my feet. I reach for a spare clip but I don't have one.

Shrieking, a largely naked man descends upon us. His speed causes his loincloth to flap in a manner that leaves far too little to the imagination. He brings his sword down.

Hannah ducks under the blow, comes up close to his sweating barreling body, and drives her fist up into his throat.

"You," she says, following up with a cross to the man's temple. "Are." Her elbow follows her fist, crashing into his skull. "Not." Her knee buries itself in his crotch. "My." She cocks a fist. "Type."

With a slurred roar, the little man slams a fist into Hannah's throat. She staggers back. He follows up with a flurry of kicks. She blocks, but weakly. The little man whips up his sword.

Hannah lashes out with a leg, steps on the inside of his ankle. He squawks, goes down, and lands back-first on his sword.

He dies noisily.

Hannah stares at me, eyes not quite focusing. "Erm." She blinks. "I think I really need your gun." Her voice sounds hoarse after the blow to her throat.

The thing is, though, I need my gun. There's no way I can practically use one of the death cult's swords. They must weigh in excess of fifty pounds. I have no idea how these people are managing to wave them about with such deftness. It's absurd.

I look up. Clyde is still crouched over Tabitha. He looks exhausted. The pair are encircled by steaming, whipping blood. He sends kinetic blasts at it, sending it spattering, but it just rises up from where it falls, diffused but far from destroyed.

Herman and Volk resemble disturbed ant hills, churning with seething masses of cultists. Volk's hand emerges, the arm behind it dangling assailants, plucks a cultist off Hermann and flings her bodily across the trail. She collides with a tree, her back cracking audibly.

Felicity is crouched at the edge of the path, lining up shots. She shoots slowly but steadily, efficiently. But it's not enough. She's being shut down.

Kayla. Where's Kayla?

And then she arrives in my view, skidding to a halt, feet kicking up clouds of dust. Her whole body is smeared with streaks of gore. She spits a wad of blood at my feet.

"What are you feckin' waiting for? Give her the feckin' gun."

As if she'd been standing over my shoulder the whole time. I look down at the weapon. "But," I say. "I sort of need to be able to defend myself." It doesn't seem that unreasonable.

Kayla rolls her eyes. "Feckin' fine then."

She whirls to the side of the road, slashes at a tree. A branch falls. Her blade flies. Five, six, seven cuts maybe.

She tosses the hacked-off branch to me. I'm so startled I barely have time to react. It is four feet long, wickedly sharp, and aimed directly at my liver. Still the lizard brain overcomes my shock, jabs out a hand in time to catch it.

"Wait," I say, "seriously?" It is in the end, a stick.

"You doubting my feckin' work?" Kayla's sword is leveled at me. And I am very much aware that the fighting is moving back toward us fast.

"Erm…" is the best I can manage.

"What the feck are you waiting for? You can feckin' defend yourself now. Give her the feckin' gun."

Dumbly I throw Hannah the gun.

"See," Kayla says, "that wasn't that feckin' hard, was it?"

"Thanks," Hannah says to Kayla, proving that she does actually know the word.

A cultist launches himself at us. Hannah ducks, he sails past her. I yell, jab my stick in his general direction.

There is a meaty thwack. When I open my eyes, I have speared the man directly through the throat. He dangles there gurgling his last.

I rip the stick free. The flesh of his neck parts with shocking ease.

Kayla nods. "Good, now go feckin' kill things with it."

I don't need to be told twice.

29

Felicity is hemmed in. She snaps off shots with increasing speed. Where one cultist falls, another steps in. They are mindless in their relentless assault. She runs out of bullets, scrambles for a fresh magazine.

The cultists charge.

I slam into them like a wrecking ball. Kayla's wooden sword whips through flesh, tearing muscle, ripping at bone. I catch the first one low in his back, wrench sideways and send him tumbling and tripping through his own spilling guts. The blow carries on, smashes into another thigh, bites deep. The woman yells, spins, whips her massive blade at me as she falls. I leap sideways, my stick gouging a great funnel of flesh from her as I do. Her screams spill with her blood.

The cultists' charge falters. Felicity drops her gun. I see it clatter on the gravel of the trail. She closes distance, ducks under a blade, gets inside their reach. She punches the same way she shoots. Short sharp jabs, aiming for nerve cluster, for weak points. A knife strike to a man's wrist. His sword drops. The other hand buries a stiff finger into his Adam's apple. He follows his sword to the ground, gagging. She whirls, ducks another blow. Her cupped hands clap down hard either side of a woman's head. The woman howls, reels away, blood streaming from her ears.

Three more. A sword whips up in front of my face. The tip of my nose screams pain. Blood is running down from a cut across my forehead. I try to blink it away.

It is the big man with the electrified sword. The one who set the blood to steaming. I thrust at him. Maybe if I can end him, I can end his spell.

He bats my blow away, the momentum of his massive sword sending me reeling sideways. There is a massive spark as my stick meets his sword. Wood blackens. His blade is still electrified.

My mind scrambles as fast as my feet. The current is still active. He's sustaining whatever spell is animating the blood. If I can get him to drop the blade... Even better, if I can do it before he drops the spell...

Electricity, as explained to me, is the lubricant needed to reach between realities. Without it there is what Clyde and Tabitha refer to as "inter-reality friction." In my experience that largely resembles the spell-caster blowing up.

I redouble my attack, feint left, feint right, then go in hard left again. I want to get in close, inside the reach of the cultist's blades. These bastards are useless at close quarters. But my opponent knows that too. He pushes me back. I feint again. I step forward and in.

The flat of the cultist's blade smashes against my shoulder, sends me flying. I jam out a hand, skid over earth, skinning my palm. My mouth feels full of blood.

By the time I get my bearings he's coming at me. The sword is held high over his head. His mouth is wide open, an utterly silent howl of victory. His blade descends.

I jump forward, toward him, desperate. Close the distance. But I don't close it enough. Oh shit. Oh nuts. I whip my stick upwards in a flat arc.

Wood bites flesh. I feel the tug of resistance, then free air.

His wrists. I just chopped through both his arms at the wrists. Holy shit. Kayla really knows how to carve a stick.

His sword flies away over my head, flipping end over end, arcing down, bisecting a cultist perfectly, balls to brow. Blood is a monochromatic rainbow launching from my attacker's truncated arms.

The spell. He didn't drop the spell. And the electricity is gone. And I got in close.

Realization strikes me just before the detonation does. It catches me full in the face. I am bowled over massively. I eat dirt, gasp at sky, eat dirt. I am a ball of flying pain. I can feel chunks of the detonated cultist digging into my skin.

I land on my back. The sky spins.

Around me—more explosions. The steaming pockets of blood all detonating, like small land mines. The valley rings with the cacophony of violence.

I don't know how long it is until I can pick myself up. The world seems curiously silent now. Everyone is standing dazed. Somehow I am still alive. Given the pain I'm in, I'm not sure I'm glad. Still, at least I haven't rewritten reality just yet.

I see Felicity stand, her features obscured by dirt and blood. And that galvanizes me somehow. While she's still here, I do have something to fight for.

A cultist struggles to his feet before Felicity. He bares his teeth. They have been sharpened to fine points.

She shoots him in the head.

God, my job is weird.

"To me!" I yell. "MI37, to me! Make for the fort. We can defend the fort! We can do this! MI37 to me!"

I start to jog forward. It's as much as I can manage. Running is beyond me, as much as I need to do it. Felicity falls into line beside me as I pass her. Then Clyde and Tabitha are up and with us. Tabitha still clutches her laptop to her chest. A chunk of plastic has been gouged from its case, obscuring the manufacturer's logo. Clyde's face looks scorched, blast marks giving him panda eyes. Kayla and Hannah fall in with us too. Kayla has Hannah by the wrist, helping pull her along. Behind us I hear the pounding footfalls of Volk and Hermann. I glance back. They are stumbling too now, wires and pipes hanging ragged from them. Hermann has a cultist's dead body caught in a jagged knee joint. The body flops obscenely.

Around us, cultists stagger back to their feet, into a run. They flock after us, a great ugly wedding train of murderous fuckers.

We are haggard and bewildered. Only the fact that we're more used to being blown up than they are seems to have given us an edge. My limbs scream at me that death would be better than this. But whatever inner core of sheer obstinate stubbornness has kept me alive so far makes me stay on my feet.

We stagger round a curve in the trail and Lang's lab is before us. A yellow stone fortress hacked into the mountainside. Our goal. Our safety. Our savior. Little more than a hundred yards away.

Except it is not safety. It is not our savior. It's where the bastard cultists are coming from.

30

At this point I think it's probably not unreasonable to just curl up and accept the beating the universe clearly wants to give me. Rock, hard place. Frying pan, fire. Pick whatever damn metaphor you want. I am the whipping boy and reality is the dude with the whip. Except… if it whips me then reality stops existing… so the reality is… wait… Maybe I'm beyond metaphors.

"Oh fuck." Tabitha sums it up far more succinctly than I ever could.

We have a moment, maybe two. The forces before us are surprised to see us. The cultists behind us are just as stunned that we're somehow still alive.

"OK," Hannah says. "How much ammo do we have left? We have to conserve—"

"Shut up," I snap.

"Arthur!" Felicity sounds shocked.

"The hell?" Hannah doesn't really sound less shocked.

"Just shut up and let me think." I'm spinning, scanning for options. I can count my life expectancy in seconds. Reality's isn't much longer.

"Off the path," I yell.

"I don't think—" Hannah starts.

"I'm the goddamn field lead!" I yell, grab her by the collar and heave.

Then I'm in among the trees. The foliage is thick, heavy. Branches and leaves slap at me. I slap ineffectually back. I've seen Kayla use her sword like a machete but I can't get the trick of it with mine.

Volk and Hermann overtake me. Their bodies punch holes into the foliage. Saplings are crushed beneath their feet. MI37 stumbles in their wake.

Adrenaline does funny things to time, to perspective. The world narrows down to a timeless tube. There is only the space directly ahead of me. And I plunge into it for an indeterminate, aching time.

"This way. This way, you fools!"

Hermann's harsh consonants clatter into my consciousness. I turn my head to see him. The world feels like one of those awful dreams where you need to do something quickly but everything moves like treacle. An infinite sluggishness.

We must be running parallel to the slope of the mountain. Foliage is still to our left, but on the right it's given way to an increasingly sheer wall of stone. Hermann stands at the entrance to a narrow fissure. A natural cave.

"Wait," I pant. I'm terrified of stopping, unsure if I'll be able to get going again if I really do grind to a halt, but my body's needs are starting to scream. I stumble toward him, trying to remain in motion. "It's a dead end," I say, "we'll be trapped."

"No." Volk's head emerges from the cave's darkness, shocking in its abruptness. "It is a tunnel. It goes deep."

"It's our best bet," Hannah says. "Come on."

I hesitate. Not because she's wrong, but because… for bloody stupid reasons, I realize. I hustle into the tunnel.

The darkness is sudden and absolute. I stagger, crash against stone. "Slowly, you imbecile," Hermann snaps. "We must be quiet now."

I try to regain some semblance of control over my limbs. Describing my success as partial is generous. Each step feels like falling. My chest heaves.

I glance over my shoulder. The cave entrance is a sharp wedge of whiteness. The world beyond is bleached by the sun. What happens out there is invisible to me.

"Come on." Hannah's hiss is harsh, bouncing off the cold rock walls.

I reach out, feel along the wall. I drag my toes over the ground with each step, waiting for something to bark my shin, for my head to strike a ledge. But the floor is surprisingly smooth.

I have questions—Who built this? What the hell is our plan? Does anyone have a glass of water handy?—but no energy to ask them. I just stumble along, using the ponderous thump of Volk and Hermann's footfalls to chart a path into increasing darkness. Twists and turns take us away from the light of the cave entrance. My eyes probably should have adapted by now, but there's nothing for them to adapt to.

Exhaustion comes in increasing waves. Some deep tidal move gaining power. My hands shake, my legs.

"Have to…" I manage to get out, but a third word is just too much.

"Not yet." Hermann's voice is harsh and surprisingly close. "I will not have them taking you so you can spill our secrets to them."

Fortunately, "Bugger off," fits into my exhaustion's two-word limit.

"Here," Volk calls from up ahead. "We can stop here."

Hermann mutters to himself. Perhaps my hearing is heightened by my enforced blindness, perhaps Hermann is just pissed off, but I definitely catch, "…always contradicting me…" before he stomps off.

I stagger toward Volk. Blind as I am, I can sense the space around us changing, some difference in the air temperature, in the timbre of my footsteps.

I bump into something large and metallic. It takes me a moment to realize it's Volk's hand. "Sit here," he says. His palm is surprisingly gentle against my chest—and a significant portion of my abdomen—as it guides me. "Rest."

I don't need telling twice. A moment later someone sags beside me.

"Felicity?" I say, reaching out.

"Oh, Jesus, get off me."

Hannah then.

"Maybe we can risk a little light here," says Volk.

There is a grumbling sound from Hermann, then a hawking noise. A moment later a ball of flaming oil arcs through the air and lands with a heavy splatter. Globules of light flicker, revealing a large, rough cavern.

Behind us a neatly round hole marks the tunnel we entered through. I lie on the ground between Hannah and Tabitha. Clyde is sprawled opposite, next to Felicity. Kayla squats on her haunches looking mildly disapproving. Hermann and Volk hulk over us.

Clyde looks up at Hermann. "Oh," he says, "it's a *flamethrower*. You know, I was thinking, I knew Lang was into making you guys all anthropomorphic and everything, but building a mechanism that allowed you to spit oil seemed a touch above and beyond what was really necessary for verisimilitude. I mean, not that I'm one to guess about the inner workings of a man's mind. My degree is in chemistry. Not a psychologist by training or inclination. Maybe spitting was part of some important childhood trauma that was mixed up in the whole id, ego, super-ego complex that was Joseph Lang. I have no idea. But a flamethrower. That makes a lot more sense."

Hannah shakes her head tiredly. "Of course it was a bloody flamethrower. What the hell else would it be?"

I decide not to mention that I had shared Clyde's curiosity.

Hermann launches a few more gobs of flaming spittle into the cavern. The light is yellow, guttering. Under better circumstances it might give the whole event a campfire-like feel. But right now, though, the ambience has more of an I'm-exhausted-and-surrounded-by-puddles-of-flaming-spit vibe.

"All right," I say, when I have the breath to speak at any sort of volume. "Let's take stock. Where are we? What have we got?"

"Where are we?" Hannah laughs. "We're in the middle of a bloody cave in the middle of bloody nowhere surrounded by murderous magical assholes. And what have we got? No bloody extraction plan. No goddamn plan at all. Just like all your goddamn pissing missions." She shakes her head. "Jesus, this was meant to be a promotion, not a death sentence."

It's that last part that needles me. Because of all of us, who's had their death preordained?

"Fine then." I throw up my hands. "What would you do? What would the great and wonderful Hannah Bearings do to get us out of this pickle? I fucking abdicate."

Felicity starts to work the heel of her palm against her forehead. Kayla looks like she wishes she'd brought popcorn.

Hannah stares at me. A desolate look. And there's a part of me that feels sorry for her then. She shakes her head.

"I don't know. I don't know any more. This is too late. I would have done it all differently up front. But now… here… I mean they spit fucking magical blood. What the hell do you do?" She looks away from me. "I don't have any fucking answers for you. Aren't you always harping on about how you're the field lead? About how you've got the bloody experience?"

It feels like a very hollow victory.

"Let's just go through the backpacks," I say into the silence. "Figure out what we've got left."

We pool our belongings. For shit that weighs so much, it seems very paltry all of a sudden.

"Maybe at night," I say, looking at the pile. "Maybe we can slip out and away."

"Away?" Volk sounds puzzled.

Hermann snorts, sends another flaming spitball into the cave. It lands a little closer than I feel is necessary. "They are talking about running away," he says. "They are talking about abandoning us."

Volk twists his head to one side, looks down at us. "Is this true?"

I shrug, feeling awkward under the massive weight of his stare. This feels like kicking a massive mechanical puppy. "I don't see another way. We are absurdly outgunned here."

"No." I expect it to be Hermann, but it's Felicity. I look up at her, and there is a glaze of determination on her face that almost borders on madness. "We came here to learn to fix things." Her voice is tight. "We *have* to fix things." She stares directly at me. "The Uhrwerkgerät will not go off. Ever. *Ever*. Do you understand me?"

The future echo. Denial. This is a conversation that's knocking at the door of Felicity's mental defenses, asking politely if it's OK to move the wrecking balls into place.

And what do I do in the face of love like that? "OK," I say. "We'll stay. That's OK. We'll do that."

The fierceness does not leave Felicity's face. Her nod is tight and sharp.

Volk leans back, nods. "See," he says to Hermann, "I keep telling you. There is nothing to worry about."

Hermann says something that sounds both very German and very offensive.

Hannah shakes her head. "You lot are bloody crazy."

My eyes narrow, and I turn to look at Hannah. Words boil in the back of my mouth. Felicity grips my arm, shakes her head.

"You lot see if you can rustle up a meal," she says in a voice that fakes calm about as well as Dick Van Dyke fakes a cockney accent. "I want to talk strategy with Arthur."

She pulls me deeper into the cave, still with that tight fierceness in her eyes. The one that insists reality conform to her will if it doesn't want a sound kick in the crotch.

"So," I start, as friendly as possible, trying to set a cheery tone despite the circumstances.

"What part of 'the future of MI37 rides on a good report from Hannah Bearings' was confusing to you?" Felicity hisses.

I wince. This is likely to proceed poorly. Felicity is still planning for a future I can't imagine.

I fumble for words. "I'm sorry," I say, always a good place to begin.

She glares at me. "You're going to say 'but,' and I have no room in my life for 'but' right now."

I decide to not say "but" after all. Instead I hold my tongue.

"Listen to me, Arthur," she says. "The safe path forward is very narrow and fraught with many dangers. I do not need you shoving us bodily toward one of them. We get out of this intact. Alive. MI37 unharmed. That is what we do. That is what defines MI37. That is why we must survive. Because the world needs people like us. Tight, close, and efficient. Hannah has to be part of that. You have to let go of whatever it is you have against her and let her in.

That has to happen for MI37 to survive. And the world needs that if it's going to survive."

Her words are all waves battering against the rock. Eroding away at my nihilism, but too slowly. I can't find a way to let her break all the way through.

"I'm sorry," I say to her. And that's honest, because I am sorry that my behavior hurts her. I am sorry that I cannot find a way to bend on this. I am sorry that I cannot see the way forward that she can. But all those other truths will just get me in trouble. So I keep it short and simple.

Felicity narrows her eyes. I don't think she trusts me. "I don't want you to be sorry. I want you to change your attitude."

I nod. "I understand." I hedge my answers.

Her eyes don't soften.

"I understand," I repeat. I lie. To the woman I love, I lie. Because why spoil what future she has left with the truth?

She holds the stare longer. "Good," she says finally.

I reach out, pat her arm. "I wonder if Hermann will let us roast marshmallows in his mouth?" I ask.

She rolls her eyes. But the groan becomes a grin. Disaster averted.

Just in time for another one.

"I mean late! Fucking late! Why I used the word. Late. I am late."

All heads snap to stare at Tabitha. She is standing staring at Clyde. The top of her head barely comes up to his chin. She is leaning forward, buoyed up by her anger. You can almost feel the heat coming off her.

Clyde is sputtering, shoulders pistoning, strangely out of sync, too thrown off course to even shrug properly. I think we all are. This domestic crisis has no place in our current predicament.

"But…" he splutters. "We… Just last night… I mean… How… When…?"

Felicity claws at her face. "Are you kidding me?"

Clyde is still processing. "You mean… when we… we…" He stares at his hands, vaguely thrusts one hand at another.

"Stop talking." Tabitha is shaking her head. "Mistake. Made a mistake. Shouldn't have told you."

I think she's told more than Clyde now. Everyone is staring. Kayla is grinning. Hannah looks almost as bewildered and aghast as Clyde. That's probably the more appropriate response. This couldn't be more mistimed.

"Fucking thought you should know. Fucking wrong." Tabitha grimaces.

"What?" Clyde is horrified. "No! Of course you should have told me, Tabby. This is huge. This is amazing. This is us. This is life. We made life. You and me. We... We..." He steps toward her, hands out ready to embrace her.

Apparently this was not the reaction Tabitha wanted.

"Get off me." She slaps at his hands, back-pedalling fast. "Get the fuck off me."

Clyde comes up hard, as if slamming into a brick wall. "What?" He is back to confusion.

I turn to Felicity. "You have to stop this. This is awful."

"Me?" It's Felicity's turn to look horrified.

I sweep a hand around the room. "Who else?"

"I don't want you to touch me," Tabitha is snapping at Clyde. "You can't touch me. You can't..." She sweeps her hands down the length of her body, hesitating over her midriff. "You've already..." But she can't get the words out.

Felicity grunts. "At some point I'm going to have to hire somebody for their tact." She takes a deep breath, then louder, calls, "Tabitha, shut up."

To be fair, I think that was a level of tact that lay within my grasp.

Clyde blathers on, seeming not to notice. "You don't mean that," he says. "I mean. I don't mean... What I meant was, was I don't want to put words in your mouth. Understand the whole putting things into you is a bit of a sore point right now, in fact. Probably shouldn't be drawing attention to it, actually. But I guess what I mean is that I'd really ask you, well beg you actually, to just reconsider the whole thing here. I mean, we could—"

"Clyde, you shut up too," Felicity snaps, advancing on the pair. Kayla, Hannah, Hermann, and Volk have formed a semi-circle around them—an audience looking at the show. Hermann is quietly shaking his head.

Felicity levels a finger like a pistol. "Time." She points at Tabitha. "Place." She points at Clyde. Then the finger circles above her head, pointing at the ceiling. "Not here. Not in this postal code. Not in this fucking country. Not until this crisis is averted. Not if either one of you wants to avoid being spayed."

"Like to see you fu—" Tabitha starts, stepping merrily into the face of Felicity's anger.

The sound of Felicity's hand slamming into Tabitha's cheek echoes around the room. Tabitha takes a step back, eyes wide.

"Hey!" Clyde takes a step forward. He stops, brought up short by the barrel of her forefinger.

"You put it back in your pants," Felicity snaps. "We could all take a break from your grunting."

Confusion crosses Clyde's face, terror fast on its heels. His eyes go wide. "You could hear..." he manages.

"I'm half convinced that's how the death cult knew we were coming." There is no humor in Felicity's voice.

Clyde crumples into himself. All the fight gone from him.

Felicity turns to Tabitha. "I shall be expecting your HR violation form indicting my actions here on my desk upon resolution of this Uhrwerkgerät fiasco. I shall be formally reprimanded, my salary docked, and yours will have an end-of-month bonus. That will be the end of the matter. You will not expect regret on my part, and I shall not experience it." She turns to face the larger group. "If any of you think we are here for anything other than the retrieval of Lang's papers, if any of you think anything other than a successful outcome is acceptable—" She turns and looks at me for that one, "—then you better think again. There is one ending to this I will accept, and I will bitch-slap the shit out of anyone who gets in its way." She looks up at Hermann. "And that includes you, you tin-can asshole."

Silence reigns. And God, I love her so much in this moment.

Felicity stares at everyone in turn. "Now someone fix a damn meal," she snaps. "We'll need our strength for what's to come."

31

SEVERAL AWKWARD HOURS LATER

My makeshift torch gutters in a sudden gust of air. Shadows leap on rock walls.

It could be quite dramatic. Unfortunately, however, I made my torch by soaking one of my sweat-drenched shirts in Hermann's oil-phlegm and the stench bellowing off it rather undercuts the moment.

"You should change your feckin' diet," Kayla says. "There's something feckin' wrong with you if your shirts smell like that."

It was my suggestion to explore the cave system while waiting for night to fall. Three tunnels lead out the back of the cavern we'd found. Felicity took the first one with Hannah, looking for an opportunity to smooth things over. Hermann and Volk took the second. So I, in my infinite wisdom, picked Kayla to help me explore the third. That left Clyde and Tabitha with a little time to talk things over while they guard the camp. Or Tabitha with ample time to murder Clyde. One of the two…

God, I don't even know what to think there. I mean… Clyde… Didn't they just start…? I guess it's been almost two weeks. But… Clyde a father? Tabitha a mother? I mean… I've seen Tabitha dote on her laptop. But another living thing?

Jesus.

"Which one you want?" Kayla brings me back to the present. We've come to another fork in the tunnel. This place seems riddled with them.

"Right," I say. I always say right. It's a system. Plus the tunnels twist enough that we have yet to circle back on ourselves.

Kayla uses her sword to score an arrow into the wall, pointing the way back to camp. She examines the sword's edge before slipping it back into its scabbard.

"Feckin' labyrinth, this place," she comments as we start off again.

"No Minotaur, though."

Kayla turns to me, cocks an eyebrow.

A second later a roar echoes down the tunnel toward us.

"I feckin' knew it." She shakes her head, resigned. "You had to feckin' say it."

I shake my head. "No. No way."

We both strain, listening for something else, any other clue. "It was something else," I say. "Organic. Water or, I don't know, rock heating, cooling, something like that."

"This isn't a feckin' house built in the seventies." Kayla's expression indicates her opinion of me, never very high, just dropped a couple more notches.

"It was not a Minotaur."

Kayla winces. "There you go a-feckin'-gain."

But there is no roar this time. I shake my head, more confident now. "Sound probably bounces oddly down here. All this rock."

Kayla snorts. "You have no feckin' idea what you're talking about, do you?"

I shrug. "Not that much different from usual."

Another snort. "Feckin' hark at you. Weren't you all piss and vinegar earlier putting wee Hannah in her place?"

It's my turn to be incredulous. "Wee Hannah?" I echo.

Kayla flicks her hair slightly. "She's a good inch shorter than me. She's wee."

I'm honestly not sure that's true. Still I get a sense I know where this conversation is going to go, so I decide to just cut it short. Kayla probably won't have to insult me so much that way.

"This is where you tell me I'm being too harsh on Hannah and need to chill out, or some Scottish variant, right?"

Kayla doesn't even bother looking at me. "I don't give a flying feck at a rolling feckin' donut what you think of Hannah. Don't give much of a shite about what you think about most things, you uppity little feck. And Hannah's a big girl, she can take care of herself."

"You just said she was wee," I counter.

"And you're a pedantic feckin' arsehole, but I wasn't going to harp on it," Kayla says without any apparent rancor. Or at least with no more than her usual amount.

This sort of flat acceptance of my belligerence brings me up a little short. I have no place to put my indignation. We trudge on a few more paces in the torches' flickering light.

"Why do you like her?" I ask eventually. Kayla has only ever tolerated me. But she likes Hannah, and I can't bring myself to. But I'm not above considering that issue might be on my end. At least not entirely.

Kayla shrugs. "I don't know. She makes me laugh. She knows the right moment for a wee bit of the old ultraviolence. She's another girl on the team who isn't Tabitha. That lass can be a bit feckin' abrasive on a Monday, if you catch my drift."

I do. But, "There's Felicity," I say, feeling somewhat honor-bound to defend her in her absence.

"She's the boss of the team. She's not on the team."

"Who's the pedant now?" I ask.

I earn a genuine grin for that one. As we approach another fork in the path.

"Right," I say, pointing.

Kayla scores the rock and we move on.

"Look," she says. "The universe has preordained you for death. Pointed its big old feckin' finger at you and said, time's up. That's some heavy shite. You need to be an arsehole from time to time, be a feckin' arsehole. Just stop trying to find a way to feckin' apologize for it all the time."

As she says it we round a corner and step into an abrupt shaft of light. I blink, the sudden illumination bleaching everything out.

As my vision returns, I see the ceiling of the tunnel splits here, a deep fissure in the rock, as if the finger of God slammed into the clay of the world and retreated, leaving this pit of light. The sun must be almost directly overhead. The walls are rough and ragged, yellow stone stained with seams of brown.

Behind us, the tunnel twists back into darkness. Before us—

"What's behind that, do you think?" I ask, pointing at a large boulder that blocks off the far end of the fissure.

Kayla looks at it, weighing it up. "You asking me to show off, is that it?"

"You mean, demonstrate your inhuman weirdness?"

"I have an alternate feckin' physiology because I was head-fecked by aliens, you feck. Be a little feckin' sensitive."

"You just belittled my imminent death."

Kayla shrugs. "Past. Future. Totally different. Yours might never happen. Mine definitely did."

I roll my eyes. "Just move the boulder already."

And then there's another roar.

We both pause. It's louder here. Something unnatural to the timbre.

"It's coming from above," I say, not at all sure it is. "It's a mountain lion or something." Kayla just stares at me. "Weird echoes," I finish up. It's less convincing than it was the first time.

Kayla looks back to the boulder. "I shift that thing and a Minotaur feckin' guts you, I get to say I told you so."

I sigh. Knowing my luck it's half likely to happen. Still, at least the subsequent paradox-ridden death of reality will wipe the smug grin off Kayla's face. "Deal," I say.

Kayla puts her shoulder to the massive boulder, heaves. It grinds, moves. Kayla dusts off her hands.

I wave my torch into the revealed depths and fail to illuminate anything much. I stand there, hesitating. On the plus side, I am not gored by a Minotaur.

"Get in there, you big jess," Kayla says.

Fine then. The cavern is cold after the warmth of the fissure's sunlight. It smells of wet stone.

"You hear that?" Kayla asks.

I freeze, listen intently. And then, yes, I do. A faint whispering sound. A barely audible rustling.

Just in case, I pull my pistol.

"Jumpy feck."

"You know what," I say, "of the two of us, I still don't have superpowers."

"Whatever."

I sweep my torch around trying to probe deeper into the darkness. Two tentative steps in and the beam of light catches the edge of a wall. It glitters oddly, almost glistens.

And then it moves.

I jump about six feet back, but it's already too late. Whatever the hell it is, it's awake.

There is an explosion of movement, a flurry of shadows. The rustling surrounds us, consumes everything. I try to point my pistol everywhere, fail to do so.

It's not just one thing. It's many. They're everywhere.

"Fuck!" I shout.

And then I realize. They're butterflies.

"Oh, Jesus."

My professional pride flutters past, flies out the cavern entrance. I holster my pistol. Kayla smirks.

"Imminent death," is my excuse.

The butterflies are a cloud around us, filling the space. They land on me, wings whispering against my skin.

The rays from the cavern's entrance catch their patterns. And there is something entrancing about them after all the darkness and rock. I stare. Then something about the wings catches my attention… Where are the whorls of color? The bright eyes and warning lines? Instead of the expected patterns there is something more intricate, more delicate.

I reach out my hand. A butterfly alights. I pull it close to get a better look.

A forest. No, a jungle. Its wings show a jungle. A tangle of trees and vines. I can see birds flitting between trees, sunlight dappling their bodies.

"The hell?" I pull the butterfly closer. At first I think it must be a painting, but… no. It's actually the pattern on the butterfly's wings.

Another one lands. It shows a building. The fort. The one that housed the death cult. The one we were trying to get into. The butterfly takes off. Another lands. This one shows a dark tunnel of rock.

"Are you seeing this?" I ask Kayla.

"Feckin' weird-arse butterflies."

I take that as a yes.

I stare at them as they settle on me, take off again. I see rivers and lakes, distant cityscapes. Then, as we stand there, the butterflies begin to get used to us and our light. They settle back on the wall of the cavern.

I approach slowly, peer at them. They have grouped themselves. All the jungle butterflies together. Butterflies with dirty paths painted across their wings strung out in a long winding line. And here, I see a cave entrance. Butterflies with black rock, and narrow twisting passageways, clustered here. I pick out the butterfly showing the fort with a cluster of similarly patterned creatures over to my right.

A thought lands in my mind, spreads its wings. I take a step back, let my light play over the scene.

"Holy shit," I say.

"What?" Kayla is checking the grip of her sword, oblivious to the wonder before us.

I point at the butterflies. "They're a map."

32

HAVING RETRIEVED THE OTHERS

"No bloody way."

Hannah stares at the rock face as billowing butterflies settle back to rest. "That's bloody mental."

"*Papilionis mappa*," Clyde breathes. "I mean I'd read about them, but this technique's been lost since the early twelfth century. I think it was Aramadeus the third…"

"Shut up." Apparently Tabitha and Clyde did not exactly bury the hatchet during the time I gave them. Unless it was in Clyde's crotch.

"Of course, love," Clyde says immediately.

"Don't fucking call me that."

"Of course, l—" Clyde catches himself. "Tabby," he finishes.

Tabitha, apparently unwilling to look at Clyde even to scorch him with her ire, instead glares malevolently at the butterflies.

Felicity approaches the wall. The butterflies' wings flutter at her approach, the map rippling. When they subside she peers closer.

"So where are we?"

I point to a yellow triangle in amongst the dark rock-patterned butterflies. "I'm pretty sure that's the fissure we just came through to get in here. So we follow this path—" My finger starts to trace a line of paler rock along the backs of the butterflies, "—and we come out here." Two side-steps and my finger lands on the cluster depicting the fort.

"Just right turns?" Hannah sounds incredulous. "You just took right turns and you happened upon this?"

"Is there a problem?" Felicity speaks before I do. I have yet to find out how her chat with Hannah went.

Hannah stares a minute longer. "No." She shakes her head slowly. "I just. I mean... I don't know."

"Good." Felicity's smile is tight. "OK, so it looks like—"

She is cut off by another one of the roars Kayla and I heard earlier. It is louder now. Closer perhaps. Booming and rolling around the room, sending the butterflies into a flurrying cloud of motion. They whip and whirl around us.

"What the hell *is* that?" Felicity looks around.

"Mountain lion," I say, but with less conviction than before. It didn't sound like a mountain lion. It didn't sound organic at all. "Or maybe the rock shifting. Or water." I shrug. "I think all the rock is distorting the sound."

"Minotaur," Kayla says with a simple nod.

Felicity narrows her eyes. I shake my head in warning and she leaves wisely alone.

I turn to scan the cave for the tunnel the butterfly map says leaves this cave. As I do so, something in the way Volk and Hermann are standing catches my eye. Some discrepancy in their mechanical body language.

I try to figure out what it is. "Do you recognize it?" I ask, pointing to the map.

Volk glances at Hermann, then bends his head toward me.

"No," Hermann says loudly, and Volk comes up short. "It is meaningless to us." Hermann looks hard at Volk.

I look to Volk. "No secrets," I say. "Right?"

Volk doesn't say anything for a moment then straightens. "That is what I was going to say," he says. "Nothing else. We do not recognize it."

I stare at them for a moment, but I trust Volk. And maybe I was just misreading the body language thing. They aren't human after all.

"Always wanted to get in a scrap with a Minotaur," Kayla tells no one in particular.

"Yes," Felicity greets the utterance. "Well, if everyone's had their say then I think we have a path forward. So let's get ready, march on this fort, and kick the living shit out of everyone inside it."

33

ONCE OUR ARSE-KICKING BOOTS ARE ON

"Two more lefts and we should be there," I say, glancing at the directions I've scribbled down. I try to inject my voice with confidence. It turns out maps made out of magically evolved butterflies are a bit inconsistent when it comes to scale. Well, either that, or I'm crap at writing down directions. I'm really banking on it being the first of those options.

Another roar echoes around us. They've been coming more and more frequently, slowly growing more distinct but still defying identification. It is something like a ripping noise. An almost mechanical tearing. A sound out of place in this world of rock and moss.

"You know," Hannah says, "at some point that's going to get pretty bloody disturbing."

We keep on walking. We make the first left, then the other. A tunnel leads ahead, revealing nothing but shadow and darkness.

Hannah pipes up again. "You sure this is the way?"

"Just following the directions," I say, and for Felicity's sake leave my comments at that.

"You fuck up the instructions?" Tabitha asks, taking a slightly more direct route to this conversation's end point.

"Feel free to go back and double check," I snap.

"You know, I don't really think that's totally appropriate, Arthur," Clyde says, slightly apologetic. "I mean, considering Tabby's condition."

The sound of Tabitha grinding her teeth almost drowns out the next roar.

"Is it me or does it seem like we're walking toward that noise?" Felicity asks. Potentially attempting to change the subject.

But then abruptly the tunnel widens. The pool of our torches' light is no longer abutted by walls, but fades off into darkness.

"Maybe," I say, turning to Hermann, "a little more light."

He hawks massively, and with a degree of ostentation that probably isn't necessary. And a thick wad of flaming oil sails across the room to splatter against a far wall.

It is indeed another cavern, smaller than the one where we made camp, but distinctly more endowed in the large bronze door department.

The door is a large oval set into one wall, broader on the horizontal than the vertical. Swirling lines cover it, twisting and tangling, as if the metalworker who wrought this great thing had a pretty substantial hard-on for paisley. The world takes all sorts, I suppose.

"Seems a little lacking in handles," Hannah comments, bringing her usual level of optimism to proceedings.

"Seems like this place is a little feckin' lacking in Minotaurs to battle," Kayla comments, bring her usual level of unnecessary violence to proceedings.

As if in response to her call, another roar booms into the cavern. The loudest yet. I swear I feel the air pulse with the noise. Kayla's head snaps to a shadowed corner of the cavern. She stalks toward it.

At the same time Clyde and Tabitha are moving toward the door. I can't argue with Kayla's instincts, but we definitely need someone covering that pair as well. That's the direction the magic-imbued death cult is in.

"Another tunnel over here," Kayla calls. She cocks her head. "Think I can hear something."

"Getting closer or further away?" I ask.

"Which do you feckin' think?"

Shit and balls. I turn back to Clyde and Tabitha. "What sort of time frame are we looking at with that door?"

"More you talk, slower we go," Tabitha barks back. Clyde gives me a slightly reproving look. I assume for having bothered Tabby. I need to tell him not to do that. If I'm getting tired of Clyde's mother-hen act, then Tabby is almost certainly going to throttle him with his own urethra within a week.

On the plus side, there's a decent chance of the universe ending before then, but still…

"Can you help?" I ask Volk. Just rip the door open or something.

"The cultists would hear," Volk points out, a degree of apology to his voice. And he's right: they would, and we are seriously outgunned.

"Just so you know," Hannah says picking up on the theme, "I have, like, three-quarters of a clip and then I'm bollocksed."

"Just so you know," I say, "you have my gun." I wanted to bring my wooden sword but apparently wood doesn't hold an edge the same way as steel. And when Kayla tried to trim all the bone bits and hair off the edges a few fairly fundamental cracks reduced the thing to three short sticks of no conceivable use in a fight.

Hannah looks down at the gun, with at least a sliver of panic on her face. I should probably take less satisfaction in it. "But—" she starts.

"Don't worry," Felicity cuts in. "You keep the gun." She tosses hers my way. "I have some hand-to-hand combat training that should help. And Arthur will have six shots at his disposal with which he can secure a new weapon."

It's my turn to look slightly panicked. I don't want to give Hannah a chance to see it, so I try to mask it with officiousness. "Any sense for what's coming?" I say, approaching Kayla.

"Yeah, a feckin' carnival with fourteen clowns and a troupe of pygmy jugglers. Who do I look like, feckin' Tonto?"

I look at the still-closed door and decide it's probably not worth asking how that's going.

Felicity sidles up to me, slips an arm around my waist. "Stop worrying," she whispers, "I once saw you kill a giant mutant dog with a pointy stick."

It's true enough. Except, "I don't have a stick," I say.

The moment stretches out. Nervous shuffling feet. A growing rumble from the corridor Kayla is watching, one that even I can hear now. Another roar tears through the space. And Hermann and Volk definitely share a look on that.

Just like they did the last time the sound came. Back in the cave with the butterflies. It wasn't the map that they recognized. It was that noise.

"What?" I ask them. "What is it?"

And then at the same time, Clyde says, quite loudly, "Oh, I see," and Kayla says, "Incoming!"

Behind me, the door starts to rumble open.

From the shadowy corridor before me, I hear the distinct sound of metal striking rock.

"Oh crap sticks." Clyde's voice is leaden behind me.

"Oh feck in a handcart." Before me, Kayla blurs into motion.

The moment is frozen. A tableau in cold, unmoving marble to illustrate to wayward children the exact meaning of the phrase "between a rock and a hard place."

Behind me: the door is half open, rolling back into rock, blue light shining out of the swirling lines that decorated the bronze surface. Beyond it, a group of thirty or so death cultists look up in our direction.

Before me—Friedrich emerges, hulking, filling the tunnel mouth, for a moment resembling some monstrous child being birthed into the cave. His head scrapes the tunnel ceiling. Sparks scrape, rock complains, metal screams. An ugly booming, roaring sound. A terribly familiar one.

My eyes fly to Volk and Hermann. And they knew. They knew. I knew that they knew something. That moment, that look. It was a decision to not tell us. To not bring us to this moment in full awareness.

But why? Are they the traitors Hannah suspects, or just the desperate people I want to believe they are?

But then there is no time for why. Because far too many people are trying to kill us at once.

34

WITH SIX SHOTS TO SECURE A WEAPON

Well, I'm certainly not going to pick a fight with Friedrich when I only have six pistol rounds to my name. And short of shooting Hannah in the back, that leaves me with the cultists.

They are jerking to their feet, scrabbling up from the moments of repose they apparently enjoy while in the company of their ridiculous, prodigious swords. I sprint toward them. Within seconds they are sprinting toward me.

In the breach, Tabitha stands behind Clyde, not cowering exactly, but hardly offering resistance. Clyde's arm is outstretched, his mouth moving. His arm bucks, as if absorbing recoil. A cultist's forward charge is abruptly reversed. He flies backwards, body snapping against architecture. Clyde lets the spell fly again, again.

He can't get them all, they swarm past him. One closes on Felicity, swinging his sword in a flat horizontal arc aimed directly at her midriff. She ducks, rolls beneath the blade, closes the distance. And, again, up close the cultist's absurd swords are more a hindrance than a help.

Felicity rises out of the roll. The heel of her palm strikes the cultist's Adam's apple. He drops the sword, staggers back. She catches him a quick blow to the side of the temple with her left hand, and as he staggers right, she pivots on one heel, spins, and slams a foot into the opposite side of the man's head.

She's had some hand-to-hand combat training. I shake my head. Felicity makes Chuck Norris look like an amateur. And she does it in hiking boots.

I charge into the fight, pistol up. As soon as a target looks big enough, I fire. I need to clear a space, a moment's breathing room.

One cultist drops, a ragged wound where his jaw was. I catch another in the shoulder. He drops his sword but keeps running at me. Right up until Clyde's spell catches him in his midriff and sends him jagging sideways across the floor, head and heels clattering over the rock. We come together, forming a tight knot.

A cultist lunges and I fire yet again, the bullet smashing into his chest, sending him reeling back.

Another comes, I aim, fire.

Nothing.

Six bullets. No weapon secured. And to make matters worse, I've just proven that Hannah was right when she said I should count my shots.

The cultist's sword lances toward me, a searing blow aimed low, aimed to gut me, to be hard to avoid. My weight is off from the firing stance. All I can do is go with momentum, falling toward the blade, desperately trying to twist as I do.

I smack against the flat of the blade as it passes me, feel the upper edge, slice into the underside of my flailing arm. The wound is hot and bright and threatens to eclipse everything. I hit the floor. More pain. I grit my teeth. Close the distance. That's what Felicity did. That's how to survive without a weapon. And I have to survive.

But I'm too slow, too dazed from my impact with the cave's stone floor. The distance is not small enough, and my attacker too quick. I'm on my hands and knees when the next sweep comes. He pivots like Felicity, letting the weight of the sword carry him around. I drop to the ground again, smack my chin, blink lights from my eyes. The cultist has his back to me, still spinning, is bringing the sword up to bring it down in a heavy two-handed arc.

I don't bother getting up, I roll, twisting my body. *Close the distance.*

The sword is above the cultist's head when I hit his ankles. It's not a hard blow, but his balance is precarious, and he doesn't need much of a push.

With a yell he trips over me, carried by the weight of his sword, feet actually leaving the ground as he's whipped up by the momentum. The tip of the sword smashes into the ground six inches from me. Desperately hanging onto the handle, the cultist is cartwheeled around, a blur of flailing legs and naked flesh.

And then he completes his three hundred and sixty degree circuit, smashes back-first into the vertical edge of his own blade.

The two halves of the cultist go sailing over my head, land in separate bloody heaps.

Gingerly I pick myself up. The sword is leaning at a slight angle after the impact of its former owner. The handle points toward me.

I reach out and grab the hilt. Weapon secured.

35

The back of the cave is filling with Uhrwerkmänner in a way that I tend to associate with imminent death. Hermann and Volk fall back.

Friedrich dwarfs them. Before him, they are a child's action figures. He smashes a fist at Volk. The Uhrwerkmänner dances back, surprisingly light on his feet, but comes up against the edge of the cave. He barely ducks Friedrich's follow-up blow. The monstrous Uhrwerkmänn's fist plows into the rock, sending shrapnel shards flying. They dent and pit Volk's armor plating.

In the moment while Friedrich recovers his balance, Volk is on him. He delivers a flurry of blows to Friedrich's midriff. Gears whistle, his fists blur, metal screams.

Friedrich backhands Volk halfway across the room.

The noise is deafening. Like a car crash. Volk rolls, comes up on his feet. Like a badass. Apparently he went to the same hand-to-hand combat training course as Felicity. Still, one of his shoulder guards is mostly scrap, hanging uselessly off his shoulder.

The spot on Friedrich that Volk was whaling on looks like it's been lightly buffed. This fight just doesn't seem fair.

Friedrich starts advancing on Volk.

A gunshot joins the cacophony of battle. A ricochet sparks off Friedrich's sleek head. Another shot, just as ineffective.

Friedrich turns and looks at Hannah, standing puny before him, pistol gripped uselessly in her hands.

She fires again. The bullet pings off Friedrich's skull. He keeps staring at her. The sort of stare that precedes very bad things.

I stumble toward her, dragging the massive sword after me. It clatters and jumps over the rocks, like an anchor weighing me back. But it's the only weapon I've got.

Hannah gets off three more shots before I get to her. Friedrich is on the move. She's lining up the fourth. I slap her hands away.

"What the hell do you think you're doing?" I yell above the sound of the battle. "You said you have three-quarters of a clip. You might as well be spitting paper wads at him!"

She turns to me, eyes blazing. "I am buying bloody time for Hermann."

My brows crease. I glance back at Friedrich. He is ten yards away, closing fast.

And then I see Hermann, in the air, leaping, up above Friedrich, then coming down toward him. Like a basketball player going for the slam dunk.

As he comes down Hermann delivers a hammer blow to Friedrich's chin. I almost expect to see Friedrich's head spin and his eyes roll back to reveal dollar signs.

As it is, Friedrich is mostly stoic about the experience.

One of his hands fires out too fast for me to track, smashes into Hermann's gut. Metal screams. Hermann's body jack-knifes around Friedrich's fist. Then, with a flex of pistons, he flings Hermann away.

"You buy Hermann any more time and he's going to get killed," I snap. "We need to get the fuck out of here."

The skin around Hannah's eyes tightens as she stares at Hermann dragging himself to his feet. One of his legs trails badly as he limps a retreat.

Volk has another Uhrwerkmänn caught by the throat and is ripping streams of cogs and rubber piping from a gash in its midriff, but two other robots are circling to his left and right.

Kayla seems to be having fun at least. She is astride a fallen Uhrwerkmänn repeatedly stabbing it in the back of the head.

I look back to the other fight. It is blurring into this one. Several cultists are hacking down an Uhrwerkmänn, its limbs lying around it in spreading pools of oil. Another Uhrwerkmänn is wearing most of the upper torso of a cultist on its fist like a glove.

Felicity, Clyde, and Hannah are at the edge of the cavern, pushed up against the wall. Felicity ducks one sword blow. Tabitha screams, holds up her laptop.

A sword blow bisects the machine. Sparks explode everywhere. Tabitha screams again, louder this time.

Clyde spins, sees the cultist preparing a backhand sweep of the swords, and steps toward him. His hand is held out, is inches from the cultist's face.

Electricity crackles over Clyde's teeth as his speaks his spell. The convexity of the cultist's face inverts, becomes concave. As he drops to the floor his skull becomes a bowl full of blood.

But Clyde's rage has cost him his situational awareness. Even as I start toward him, the pommel of a cultist's sword smashes into the back of his head. He sprawls. The cultist flips her blade up.

My scavenged sword still feels like an anchor. I try to get it up in front of me, but I don't have the time to take the weight, to work it all out.

Instead I keep running, put my feet down and push. The cultist's muscles bunch as she prepares the killing blow. My feet pound on unforgiving rock.

The sword starts to descend.

I barrel straight past the cultist.

My sword, pivoted out at an angle, clattering over the rock, slices into her ankle. She screams. Staggers. Her blow goes wide.

I stagger to a stop, manage to turn despite the momentum of my sword. The cultist is on the floor, screaming, gripping the jagged stump of her leg.

Damn, these swords are sharp.

Felicity is caught between two cultists, unable to close on one without exposing herself to the other. Clyde is still on his hands and knees shaking his head.

Tabitha is staring at the separate halves of her laptop and weeping. Openly weeping.

We have to get out of here.

"Hermann!" I bellow, but the battle is too loud for him to hear me. He and Friedrich are on opposite sides of the cave, tearing cultists from their bodies. Friedrich hurls one at Hermann, and the body leaves an obscene red stain down the Uhrwerkmänn's body as it slumps to the floor.

I run toward him, as fast as my sword will let me.

"Hermann!" I scream again.

This time he hears me, flicks his head in my direction, some approximation of annoyance on his approximate features.

"The oil!" I jab my finger at the fallen Uhrwerkmänn. "Set fire to the oil!"

It's all I can think of. A desperate stab at buying us time so we can beat our retreat.

Then he spits. A stream of liquid fire leaping out from between his teeth.

It is like someone turned the lights on in hell. Maddened cultists coated in ink and blood scrambling on the walls, dancing between fallen bodies, the air full of their sharpened blades. And among them—maddened Uhrwerkmänner, vast hulking ruins of machinery, coated in rust and blood, bits of bodies smeared across their limbs.

The flame from Hermann's spit reaches the fallen Uhrwerkmänn. There is a soft whoomph. And then the louder, angry clap of detonation.

The shockwave cracks me across the face, sends me spinning. I eat floor, taste stone and sweat, oil and blood.

When I come up, Kayla is wiping her mouth, spitting. Beside her a cultist half picks himself up. Without even looking, Kayla spears him through his skull.

Jesus, we have to get out of here.

"Move!" I scream, lungs burning. The room is filling with smoke from the Uhrwerkmänn's splayed flaming corpse. "MI37 to me! We have to move!"

Felicity is picking herself up beside me. Blood runs from gashes in her forehead and cheek. Tabitha is lying on her back, still clutching the separate halves of her laptop, still staring at them. Clyde grabs her underneath one shoulder, hauls. Blood runs down his arm, leaves a stain on her dark skin.

Kayla is moving, has Hannah in a vice grip. Hermann and Volk follow. Friedrich's bellow chases them.

We push past stumbling cultists, through the bronze portal, into the belly of their fortress. The room is all yellow rock and hard edges. My over-sized sword skitters over the floor, tugging at my shoulder. Two corridors lead away, one left, one right.

"Left," I yell. Experience has taught me that when you have absolutely no information to go on, decisiveness trumps wasting time trying to apply logic. Especially when you've only got a two-second lead on the bastards trying to kill you. We jag left—

—straight into a group of cultists charging toward the sound of fighting. Seeing us, they hesitate.

Kayla doesn't.

She barrels into them like a sword-wielding bowling pin and limbs fly like struck nine-pins. I bellow with exertion hefting the leviathan sword above my head. The laceration in the bottom of my right arm screams pain. I scream too.

A cultist has turned her back, has turned to face Kayla. I bring my sword down. I bisect her to her sternum. Her feet splay. Her own sword drops lifeless to the ground.

One down.

I go to tug my sword free. It doesn't move.

To my left and right cultists close.

Oh shit and balls. I heave on the sword once, twice more. But it is too heavy, too firmly embedded in the bone. Shit, shit, shit.

One cultist swings laterally, the other straight down. Because they're assholes, I imagine.

I drop the sword, leap backwards as fast and as hard as I can.

I have to live. If I die then reality dies. I have to live.

Right up until reality dies.

God, this is messed up.

A sword skims over my face, a sting of pain from the tip of my already injured nose as it bounces off the flat of the blade. The descending sword catches on my shoe leather, sends me tumbling.

I lie on the floor. Blood is flowing from my nose again. I'd probably be more concerned about that if wasn't lying prone on the ground with two cultists poised above me.

I glance around. Help? Anyone? Ferris Bueller?

And there's Hannah. With a pistol. She points it first at one cultist and then another.

And she doesn't pull the trigger. She switches her aim, back and forth, back and forth. There's a helpless expression on her face.

She sees me staring.

The cultists' swords go up.

She shrugs, infinitesimally, her lips move. I can't hear her but her words are plain enough to read. "Only one shot."

So fucking take it. But I'm through giving advice for her to ignore.

The swords are above the cultists' heads. The moment their balance is weakest.

I push hard with my hands, lift my head, my legs, spin on my arse. My feet connect with one cultist's ankles, a moment later my head with the other's. The world spins a moment. I lose track of the falling swords.

I don't knock the cultists over, but I do knock their swords wide. One blade lands an inch to my right, the other closer to my left.

Finally the shot rings out. A cultist falls to the floor.

One down. Thank God for small mercies.

Even as the second cultist tugs to free his sword from the trench it's gouged in the floor, I am rolling forward and up, pushing myself to crash into his legs. He goes down, tumbling over me.

I hear the meaty smack of him landing face first on his own blade. Two down.

I stand up. Everything is shaking. Around us the cultists have fallen. The smell of gunpowder is heavy in the air. I raise a shaking hand to my nose. The pain is excruciating. But the shape of my schnozz is still the same. Only skinned.

All in all, the fight probably took about ten seconds. Unfortunately, our lead was only about two.

That booming screaming roar comes again, almost so loud it sends me reeling. An Uhrwerkmänn fills the corridor around us. A cultist clings to its back, howling and smashing. He sees us, lets out a shriller scream.

"Run!" I bellow again. "Run!"

36

A MINUTE LATER

I collapse panting. This is better than fighting with my backpack on, but not by much. We are horrendously outnumbered. I had rather conceived of this as a stealth operation. I honestly believed that a secret underground passage would lead to a secret doorway. This is to stealth what McDonald's is to dieting.

We're in a small square chamber. It is surprisingly decorative given the spartan aesthetic that seems to dominate here. There is a geometric tapestry in reds and maroons hanging from one wall and red flowers in an earthenware vase sitting on a blocky table cut from the same rough yellow stone as the fort itself.

Kayla is pressed against one wall. She peers around one corner. "I think we're finally free of the feckin' bastards."

Volk and Hermann hulk in the middle of the room. They have made the sneaking thing significantly harder. It's been like trying to sneak down corridors while accompanied by two pieces of farming machinery. One of whom complains loudly much of the time.

"I do not know why we ever asked for your help," Hermann grunts. "This is pitiful."

I ignore him. Pointing out that he's only managed to get this close to Lang's papers because of MI37's efforts is only likely to set him off further.

Rather to my surprise, the one who seems to take his criticisms most to heart is Hannah. She flinches away from the Uhrwerkmänn, shaking her head. Kayla takes two steps toward her friend, reaching out a hand, but Hannah flinches away again. She seems to fold in on herself.

"Hey." Kayla's severe allergy to sounding in any degree soft or sympathetic makes the comfort sound harsh.

"No." Hannah shakes her head. "Just… no." She looks around the room, a pained expression. "I mean… just, what the bloody fuck is this? I mean… There's no intel. There's no plan. This is shit creek and it's like we all just sat around and made time for burning paddles before we even got here. And it's always fucking like this. Always. And… and…" She wrestles to find an expression to express herself. Nose wrinkled, lips curled. Some awkward place between disgust and sadness. "And you all seem so fucking comfortable here." She's aghast. "Like this is how it's meant to be." She points at me. "Even bloody him. He bloody took on two sword-wielding lunatics and won. And I couldn't even pick one to bloody shoot in the face. I mean what the hell is that? That bloody… *clown* outclassed me. Hugely. I mean hugely. It was like I was a bloody rookie. And… Jesus." She sweeps a hand around the room. "This is wrong. Everything you do is wrong. But I've read your file. And you do good shit. And I can't do it. I bloody can't. I'm bloody good at my job. I was promoted into this. This was a big bloody deal. And it's going to fucking kill me. Because I can't fucking hack it. And that…" She points at me again. Struggles to put her disdain into words, "…that fucking muppet is good at it." She shakes her head. "I don't understand. I just don't. And it's doing my head in something bloody awful."

I would comfort her except for, well, the constant barrage of insubordination and know-it-all comments.

"You're not feckin' useless." Kayla takes another step, rests the outstretched hand on Hannah's shoulder. "Period of feckin' adjustment and all that shite. Takes a while to get used to the weird shite. You should have seen him when he first got here." She nods at me, because apparently I'm just exhibit A for the prosecution today. "Abso-feckin'-lutely useless he was. Couldn't even get the safety off his gun. Now he's all right. Took him a bit, but baptism by fire and shite. If he can pick it up, you sure can."

Hannah looks unconvinced.

Felicity, on the other hand, just looks a little bit pissed off.

"Maybe," she hisses, "we could all work on the interpersonal dynamics when we're not trying to hide from not one but two packs of homicidal nutjobs. Better yet, you could have done it when I bloody suggested it." Her gaze sweeps the room, and again I fail to avoid the ire.

Personally, if the timing were better, I might take this as a positive sign. Hannah is acknowledging that she's no good at this and, begrudgingly, that we are. If she just threw up her hands and said, "Well that lot can take care of that shit, I want no part of it," then MI37 would be back in the right hands.

"OK," Felicity says when no one feels the need to snark back at her, "we've got some breathing room."

"Time to find the papers," I say. "Anybody got a good sense for how deep we are into this place?"

Tabitha, who has been trying to find the spot in the room farthest away from Clyde, snaps, "Probabilistic mapping algorithms. Would be using them if some magical asshole hadn't totally failed to protect the things most important to the woman whose life he seems determined to ruin." She wields the two halves of her laptop at Clyde. It is his turn to flinch away.

"I think the humans must be rusting," Hermann comments to Volk. "We will need papers on how to fix *them*." It's the first time I've heard him sound amused.

"Hush," Volk chastises.

Hermann just snickers.

"Well," Clyde says into the ensuing silence, "most forts are built on an asymmetrical pattern to prevent attackers who breach the main gate from making a straight run to the good stuff. Create more of a killing field. Which is not the sort of encouraging term I suspect anyone wants to hear. Maybe be better if there was some nice euphemism for it. Poppy field perhaps. Though maybe that word's a bit tainted. Actually, tainted is a bit of a tainted word, if you ask me. All sorts of nasty connotations to that one these days. Yick. But I, much like a fortress attacker actually—funny coincidence—am a little off course. Was going to say, at least, I am saying it now, I suppose. Got there in the end. Avoided the killing… erm, poppy field of my own distractions. Anyway, where was I? Oh yes. The main gate of the castle was central. So I would anticipate an inner wall with a gate to the left or right, and then any sort of keep to be on the opposite side of the gate. Probably toward the back of the whole complex. Then the chamber would be hard to access inside that keep. Given that we're subterranean probably down rather than up. I mean, just playing the odds here. And the way the tunnel took us came in near the back left of the fort. At least if my sense of direction still stands. And we've been meandering around here and found nada, so if we headed that way, and went down a few floors, that might be a best bet. If one trusts me. Which, totally understand if you don't. Whole laptop disaster. So sorry about that. Not the sort of thing I would allow to happen to any live cargo Tabby had. Should she be carrying some sort of basket of kittens, or crate of chicks, or… well, erm…" He shrugs violently. "Say, a child."

There is a slow exchanging of looks.

"Probabilistic mapping algorithms," Tabitha says eventually. "Same results. Less mouthy."

Felicity and I exchange a glance. "Well then," I say, pointing in the same direction as Clyde. "That way then."

37

TWO FIGHTS, EIGHT SERIOUS LACERATIONS, AND FIVE DEAD BODIES LATER

Gasping for air, dripping blood and sweat, and thoroughly bloody sick of this ridiculously sized penis-extension of a sword, I crash to the bottom of a flight of spiral stairs. I bounce off one wall, spin into a broad room. Kayla is already there. The rest of MI37 follows swift on my heels. Hermann and Volk come last, taking a lot of the important-looking structural components of the stairs with them. Ominous cracks spread through the rock walls. Hopefully there's an alternative exit.

"Did we lose them?" I call back to Felicity.

"Like fuck." The constant threat of death seems to be damaging the part of her that normally controls her language. That said, I can see at least three gashes on her that look like they need stitches. If she wants to curse, I think she has an excuse.

I wish I had time to comfort her. Personally, I'm finding the imminent death thing is actually distracting me a little from, well… the other imminent death thing, I suppose. But I've had less time to be morose about the new threats.

"Is this it?" Hermann asks. "Or another of your dead ends."

And well… I take the time to take stock. We're in a broad room.

It's not deep though. And… well, there is a massive oval door to help give the place an ante-chamber sort of feel. The door itself resembles the one that got us into this whole mess. Lying on its side covered in swirling paisley patterns.

"Oh crap," I say. I seem to have developed bad associations with doors that look like that.

Behind us, the sound of fighting encroaches. Another deafening roar widens the cracks in the walls.

"The door," I say, pointing. "How long?"

"Oh," Clyde looks about, shrugs, "erm, well the last one took us a couple of minutes and we, sort of, in a manner of speaking, by which I mean, very directly and in all the obvious ways, we were assisted by Tabby's, erm…"

"Computer," she finishes for him, acidly. She holds the two halves aloft once more. I have no idea why she's still holding them.

Another boom of ugly steel-based death resonates above us.

"What about this feck?" Kayla asks.

I spin around to see who on earth she could be talking about. I only catch a blur as she whips into motion. Then she's across the room, reaching around a corner. There's a shrill scream and suddenly she's dragging a small spindly man back across the floor toward us.

The man is stark naked, and unfortunately one of the first things I get to learn about him is that he has been completely shaved. Not a speck of hair on him. Anywhere. Bright blue tattoos swirl over his body, matching the patterns on the door. I also quickly learn that they cover him completely. Some tattooist needs to learn when to stop.

"Yes!" Tabitha cries as Kayla drags the man kicking and screaming across the floor. "All makes sense now." She turns to Clyde, a victorious expression on her face, but it sours as soon as she lays eyes on him. She turns back to Kayla, grimacing. "Key. He is. For that door."

The man wrestles and twitches in Kayla's grasp but can't get free. She shoves him toward the door.

"How the hell is he a key?" I say to Tabitha. This seems like a fundamental idea I'm missing.

"No clue," says Tabitha. "But read in my database before…" another acid glance at Clyde, "cryptic then. Makes sense now. A man is the key."

Oh hell, that's about as good an explanation as I usually get.

Kayla shoves the man closer to the door, pulls her sword. "There you go," she says. "Feckin' open it."

The man stares at her, shaking. A string of syllables that make about as much sense to me as my DVR instructions spill out of him.

"I don't think he speaks English," I say.

"Bet he speaks feckin' this." She brandishes the sword.

"Clyde," I say, "you don't happen to know any nifty translation spells do you?"

Clyde shuffles his feet, looks anywhere but at Tabby.

"Database," she mutters in a voice that could grind granite.

"Sword it is then," Kayla says, sounding a little too cheerful for my tastes. She takes a step toward the tattooed youth.

He takes an instinctive step backwards.

Another vast tremor shakes the building. I stagger a step. Suddenly Kayla's sword isn't the only weapon pointed at the youth.

He puts a hand on the door. It glows. Yellow light cracks through the deep bronze carvings. It seems to linger at certain points. Geometric patterns illuminated. Networks of hexagons and swirling lines.

And it seems to collect too, pooling on the youth's body, swirling around his tattoos. The light glows, grows, is nearly blinding. I take one hand off my sword handle to shield my eyes. The youth is glowing like a lightbulb, his head thrown back. The door itself looks almost on fire.

Then the light flares, too bright. The world a shade of yellow that is almost white. Someone lets out a cry caught between pain and bliss.

When my eyes recover the light is gone, the youth is nowhere to be seen, and the door is grinding open.

"There," says Kayla, "told you he'd understand the sword. Universal feckin' language."

38

"Inside. Fast," Felicity snaps. But we don't really need to be told. I can hear feet on the staircase behind us. The metallic sort that shake loose stones free.

Hermann and Volk lead the charge this time. Uncharacteristic eagerness possesses them. They duck through the low entrance, momentarily blocking the view of the room, then I'm pushing in behind them.

It's another study, but neater than Lang's last one. It possesses a sense of order and tranquility I normally associate with tombs and cathedral chapels. None of Lang's personal brand of organizational chaos. This is a curated, cared for selection of texts.

The room is large, as wide as the foyer but deeper. A path is worn smooth in the rough rock floor. Low tables delineate its edges. They are made of wood in opposition to the stone furniture that dominates the rest of the fort. On each table are textbooks, spread open, much annotated, diagrams scribbled in the margins.

At the end of the path, raised slightly on a central stone dais is a table. More books are stacked upon it. A series of large, thick journals bound in browning leather.

Beyond that a subterranean river scours its way through the back of the room. Dark passageways lined with white froth punctuate the walls to either side of the room. The rest of the room is as typically barren as the rest of the place.

"Not going to gain much renown as interior decorators, are they?" Clyde says at my elbow. "Though I suppose, being a secretive death cult, renown isn't exactly what they're looking for—"

"Shut up," Tabitha snaps. "Time. Essence."

To emphasize her point, several Uhrwerkmänner land at the base of the stairs behind us.

"Shit!" I say, ever eloquent in the face of danger. Still my curse gets folk moving, no longer taking in the room, just running pell-mell toward that desk and its contents. They have to be the papers. They have to be what we came for.

Hermann gets to them first, sweeps the table with one massive hand, scoops them all up in one go. He reaches down to a panel on his thigh. Something extrudes from a fingertip, is inserted into some socket. A moment later the panel pops open. The journals disappear into a hidden cavity.

"Hey!" Hannah snaps.

"You cannot carry them all, and I have no trust in you," Hermann says without hesitation, popping the panel closed.

At least he's not a bullshitter.

A sound like the world collapsing behind us. I spin around. Two Uhrwerkmänner are in the doorway. Behind them... It resembles a landslide. The rock of the stairs collapsing. A sound like a train trying to dry hump a mountain.

Even before I see his massive shadow emerging from the cloud of dust, I've worked out that Friedrich is here.

Kayla pushes to the front of the group, faces him. "Any of you fecks bother to work out an exit strategy?"

Hannah is shaking her head. "Bloody, bloody, bloody—" She doesn't seem like she's going to get any further than that though.

I scan the room. And there really is only one choice.

Shit and balls.

"The river," I say.

It's a frothing black nightmare. A gushing stream spat out of one cavernous hole and swallowed into the darkness of the other.

Before us, the two Uhrwerkmänner spread left and right,

making way for their boss so he can come and personally mash us into oblivion.

"Just wanted to remind you," Clyde says, looking at the river, "not to add undue pressure, but your death at this juncture might bring about the end of reality as we know it."

"Fully aware," I tell him. "Why I'm going to do my best to avoid it."

"Bloody, bloody, bloody—" Hannah is still working her way toward the next half of that sentence as she pegs it past us and leaps into the frothing waters. When she comes up she's already fifteen yards downriver, almost out of the room.

"Tabby, I'll—" Clyde starts. I think she jumps just to cut him off. He plunges in after her.

Behind us, Friedrich bellows in frustration. His footfalls accelerate.

"Idiot fleshy things." Hermann is in the water before me, then Volk. Titanic explosions rock the surface of the river as they enter the waters, but its force is enough to barrel even them along. And that passageway better not narrow up ahead.

Then it's just Felicity, Kayla, and me. Friedrich is charging. The floor shakes with the force of him. With the bass of his rage. And somehow I am still waiting for Felicity to go first, to make sure she is all right.

Then Kayla is pushing us both in, carrying us with her. And all I hear before the water closes over my head are three bitter words. "Stupid, silly fecks."

39

A moment of near crippling pain. Cold that the Arctic must surely be jealous about. It crushes me, obliterates me.

Then my head breaks the water. I glimpse rock flying past me. A massive howling Uhrwerkmänn full of rage. Then walls close about me. A fist clenching. Darkness enveloping.

The terror is almost as absolute as the blackness. There is no sense of space, of how close I am to dashing my head against the wall. There is only the implacable force of the river. It pounds at me. The water closes over my head, opens, closes, opens, like the mouth of some great fish gasping its last on some frozen shore. I wait to break a limb. There again, I'm so damn numb, I'm not sure I'd notice.

Ahead I hear the clang and crash of Hermann and Volk as they smash against the walls. I want to call to the others, but there is no chance to get a breath. No chance to call Felicity's name.

And then light. Stabbing. Fierce. Rushing toward me too fast. And no, I cannot be going that fast. I cannot. That's not—

And then out. Out into light and air. Spat out by the river like some vast gastric rebellion. The light is too much. I have no sense for time, space. Just the water is gone. I am flying through the air now. Only my speed remains constant.

And then water once more. Swallowing me again. It closes

over my head. But it no longer pounds at me. My speed has been robbed from me by the impact. Now I simply sink down. Into bottomless space.

My lungs burn. A pain that forces focus.

A lake. A river. Something. The subterranean river burst from the rock into a waterfall, spat me out into the sun, and now I am wasting all this successful fleeing business by subsequently drowning.

Swimming is difficult when you can't feel your legs. But there must be something in muscle memory. Or in the remaining air in my lungs. Because my head breaks the surface and I gasp air.

Eventually I make it to the shore. We all do. Even Hermann and Volk, wading up out of the lake, wreathed in weeds and with several small fish snagged and flopping on their recently tattered metal edges.

I lie on my back in the dying heat of the day, Felicity beside me, my friends scattered around me. And Hannah.

"All right then," I say to the exhausted crowd. "We got what we came for. Let's call this a success."

Laughter isn't really the response I was looking for, and Hannah's seems unnecessarily bitter to me.

I do my best to ignore her. "Tonight we make camp," I say. "Tomorrow we hike back to civilization."

"Our packs?" Tabitha doesn't even bother to pick up her head. "Our supplies? In a cavern." She flops a hand over her head to point to the mountain and the waterfall behind us. "Up there."

And, I have to admit, that could be a problem.

"Feckin' jessies," Kayla says, reaching out and plucking a limp fish from the end of a spindle of metal that juts from Volk's thigh. "Live off the land. Make a raft. Do it like we should have the first time around."

And I'm tired, and beaten, and badly cut in a number of places, and half-drowned still, and hell, that's a good enough plan for me.

40

FIVE DAYS LATER

As beautiful as Nepal is, I cannot say that I am sad to see it drop away beneath me. The Hercules air transporter takes to the air like some magical metal whale, and we begin the final leg of the journey home.

Not that the journey back to Kathmandu was *that* bad. It was significantly better than the journey away from the capital. It was downhill for one thing. And we did it almost entirely by raft. Kayla made it the morning after our escape from the fort—a surprisingly large and sturdy thing, capable of toting even Herman and Volk, who made for powerful polemen pushing us along with the current. Well, Volk did most of that admittedly. But it left Kayla and Hannah free to spear fish, and Clyde and Tabitha free to study the journals we retrieved from the fort.

I'm not sure I'd call it totally functional research. Tabitha refused to put away the two halves of her laptop. Clyde sat further and further away from them each day, until his feet were trailing in the water. And then Kayla speared something almost as long as the raft with teeth to match, and Clyde decided to find another spot to mope in. Fortunately, Tabitha doesn't seem to have lost any data. At least that's how I interpreted, "In the cloud, moron."

As for me, there honestly wasn't much to do. Sit back and wait for my new stitches to heal. Felicity was in a surprisingly good mood. She seems to have taken our successful retrieval of the journals as proof positive that news of my oncoming death has been greatly exaggerated. And, lying on my back, slipping down some nameless river in some nameless valley in the back of beyond it was occasionally easy to let fear sublimate into hope.

Hannah can scoff, but we have what we came for. We're that much closer to success. And with the roar of the Hercules' four prop engines propelling us toward the clouds it's time to come up with a game plan.

I lean forward from the bench where I'm perched in the plane's cavernous fuselage and look at Clyde and Tabitha. They sit opposite each other, the full width of the plane between them. Clyde studies one journal intently, three more stacked at his feet. Tabitha has three open on the plane floor.

"So," I say, "how's it going?"

"Ah, well, I mean," Clyde looks up from a legal pad full of notes, warming up his word factory, "as I believe previously described, Lang not the easiest experimental thaumatophysicist to understand. And that's not exactly a crowd much lauded for their crystalline prose. Not to disparage their many accomplishments. Very important subset of folk are experimental thaumatophysicists, and interesting and remarkable in a great many different ways. As are all people really, I think. Don't mean to imply there are any dull people in the world. The miracles of one's inner life and all that. And really what we find interesting is a very subjective measure, and not one that I think would stand up to any sort of rigorous quantification. Though I have read a couple of interesting papers on quantifying subjectivity. All a bit flawed in my opinion, but noble efforts. Much like the efforts of experimental thaumatophysicists to parse their theories into prose. But all that said, and with a number of warnings about presumptive thinking on my part, one can't help but feel that Lang rather delighted in obfuscation."

"Total jackass," Tabitha adds. "Lang was."

Clyde nods several times. "Yes, yes. Very valid conclusion based on the available evidence."

"Don't fucking patronize me." I think it's the first time Tabitha has made eye contact with Clyde in almost a week.

Clyde looks horrified. "Oh no, of course not. Wouldn't dream of it. Though, I suppose could be an unconscious thing. But God that would be horrible. Totally going to make it a conscious thing." His look of horror intensifies. "Not that I'm going to consciously patronize you. The opposite of that. At least, well, the opposite that is being consciously unpatronizing. Not the opposite that is being unconsciously patronizing. Doing that already. Or might be. Don't know. Going to fix it. I'm all over it, Tabby. Very responsive to advice. I mean, I am." He flashes teeth at her in what is likely meant to be a smile.

She has returned to her journals and doesn't look up.

"So," I say, attempting to rescue the conversation, "it's not going well?"

From the back of the plane Hermann lets out what I interpret as a mechanical sound of disdain. I don't think he has the requisite anatomy to fart.

"Oh, wouldn't necessarily put it that way," Clyde says. "Definitely making progress. Just sorting the signal out from the interjected attempts to mathematically prove the superiority of German gerunds to other languages is a touch tricky, especially when he's attempting the whole thing in rhyming couplets."

So Tabitha is right. Lang was a jackass. The Nazi thing probably should have clued me in.

"Rather a lot of unnecessary metaphor use, as well. Especially in his engineering notes."

Tabitha grunts. "Pretty sure no part of Hermann should be referred to as a *Liebes-pumpe*."

"A what?"

"My love pump," Hermann says, without any apparent emotion.

Part of me wants to ask, but not enough to outweigh the part of me that is blanching.

"Ooh!" Against all that is good and holy in the world, Clyde sounds genuinely excited. "I haven't read that bit. Don't suppose you could share your notes when you're done with it, could you?"

Tabitha grunts.

An ugly thought strikes me. "Wait," I say, "you two have been sharing notes, right?"

Another grunt from Tabitha.

"Well…" Clyde drags the word out. "I wouldn't exactly say it's a typical one-on-one direct comparison of research findings. Rather a sort of unstructured, erm, kind of, well…"

"No," Tabitha summarizes for him.

I think I know why Felicity rubs her temples so much. "Jesus," I say. "I realize that you two are going through a rough time right now, but seriously, please, demonstrate the smallest modicum of professionalism. Talk to each other. Instant message. Something."

"Can't instant message," Tabitha says pointedly. "Laptop chopped in two."

"Then *something*." My teeth are grit. Maybe some sort of anxiety medicine would be helpful. If I can get the prescription filled before bloody Ragnarok, or whatever.

"Come on," I point at Clyde. "Go and sit next to her. Talk to her." Of the two of them, I'm more likely to have success getting him to move. And that'll be a start.

Without ever actually meeting Tabitha's eye, Clyde shuffles across the fuselage. I slump back beside Felicity.

She pats my leg. "Good work, love."

"We'll see."

She rolls her head until it rests on my shoulder. "It'll be fine," she says. "Probably have it figured out by the time we get back to England. Save the Uhrwerkmänner. Put this whole end of the world nonsense behind us. And then you can move your boxes over to my place."

Oh Jesus. My boxes. My completely nonexistent boxes. Maybe it would be better if I did protract this crisis a bit. Just so I have time to pack.

"I'm just going to shut my eyes," Felicity tells me. "Try to catch some sleep before we land." She nestles her head closer against my shoulder, sighs slightly. Relaxes.

Relaxes.

And long after Felicity has slipped into sleep, I am staring at Clyde and Tabitha reading, never exchanging a glance, and feeling my stomach roil into knots.

BRIZE NORTON AIR BASE

England is damp and gray and reassuringly mundane. It feels comfortable, like one of my dad's cardigans. It even manages it with two hulking World War II-era robots standing on an RAF base runway. I stretch, feeling joints pop, trying to realign after almost ten hours on the plane. It's mid-afternoon, time for a good jetlagged kip, and then some vigorous world saving bright and early tomorrow.

"OK," says Hermann, advancing on Clyde and Tabitha, "you will give me the journals now."

"Wait," I step forward. "The journals they're in the middle of going through to fix *your* problem? The ones we need so we can keep on doing the job you asked us to do? The ones we just almost died about eight times each in order to retrieve? Those journals?"

Hermann shakes his massive head. "You use too many words. You waste my time." He holds out a large bronze palm. "The journals. Now."

"No," I say flatly. Hermann's snark and attitude I'm willing to put up with. Directly interfering in my ability to take a nap in the next hour or so is something else entirely. "We need those if you want us to provide any sort of effective help and you know it. Because it's bloody obvious."

Hermann snorts laughter. "Effective help? That is what you call this parade of disasters you have led us through? You have had your fun. Now we will take the journals and do this properly."

Volk lays a hand on Hermann's shoulder. "Let me handle this."

"Handle this?" Hermann snorts. "You are almost as laughable as the these fools."

Volk shakes his head. "Why do you always have to make everything more difficult? If you had not always been this steel-headed I would think your gears falter."

Apparently that's what passes for a smackdown in Uhrwerkmänner society.

"Do you want the journals or not?" Hermann asks him. His accent makes it "vant," like some 1980s movie villain.

Volk sighs, turns to us.

"Actually—" Clyde steps forward before Volk can speak. "This whole need for journals, and possessiveness, I mean, not trying to belittle anyone's motives or anything at all like that. Don't want to get us all off on the wrong foot. I mean, this whole interjection is sort of an attempt to course correct. That is to say, I don't wish to imply anyone has knocked us off course. Not at all." He shrugs twice at Hermann, who looks at him, bewildered. Clyde bumbles obliviously on. "It's more that I can see us coming to a fork in the road ahead and I wish to ensure we remember to turn the steering wheel. Probably comes across like the worst sort of backseat driving now that I've made that comparison. Metaphors really aren't my strong point. Not like checkers. Very good at checkers. Well, that is to say, not to brag, but objectively speaking my win-loss ratio is far more than two standard deviations above the norm. But metaphors, completely rotten."

"Clyde..." I manage to slide a warning note into the conversation.

"Oh yes, my point," Clyde says. "Good point. Yours. Not mine. Well, hopefully mine is, but I probably shouldn't be the one to judge. I was just going to say that based on our whole back-and-forth, putting-minds-together thing, that Tabby and I may have this all figured out and the whole journal-possession thing may be a moot point."

Standing nearby, Kayla shakes her head. But I hear her say under her breath, "He feckin' gets there in the end."

Volk is more exuberant. He claps Hermann on the shoulder hard enough to make him take a step forward. "This is wonderful news. Do you not say, Hermann? This is all we could have hoped for. Everything comes to fruition. Just as we knew it would." He seems utterly guileless in his enthusiasm.

Hermann harrumphs.

"Excellent," Felicity claps her hands. "Well then. Change of plans. Let's jump on this now, and we can solve everyone's problems." She beams from Clyde to Volk and back.

I feel myself pursing my lips. And God help me, but I think I might be closer to Hermann's response on this one.

"Wait," I say, "really?"

Clyde nods. "Oh yes, you know, me and Tabby, once we get together. Greater than the sum of the parts. Well my part anyway. Tabby's part is of the highest order. Really lifts my part up. Wait... that sounds... didn't mean it that way. Of course."

And there it is, the grit in my sandwich. How desperate is Clyde in his desire to make Tabitha think of their union positively? How much will he over-emphasize, and exaggerate?

"The guy who wrote mathematical prose poems and took tangents without warning? You just double checked each other's notes and it was all fine?" Admittedly, it was a ten hour flight, but Tabitha and Clyde were pretty far from their end goal when we took off, and I can't imagine their collaboration was that efficient. "Tabitha?" I look to her, silent so far.

She looks like she's been sucking on a lemon, but that's not exactly different from normal. "Maybe," she says eventually. "Could work."

"Then what are we waiting for?" Volk asks, moving away from the group, toward the air base's gates. "We must go now."

But I'm still not sold. "'Could work' is not quite the same as 'will work.' And it's not like we don't all have pretty intimate history with magical shit going wildly and spectacularly awry. Shouldn't we double check this one a couple of times?"

"And wait for Friedrich to find us again?" Volk asks. "He has been on our heels the whole time. We cannot wait. Your little man and lady," he points to Clyde and Tabitha, "they can save my people."

We're rushing, I know we're rushing. Too many people just want this to be over. Hell, I want this to be over. But I want it to be really over. Not just another screw-up that gets us in deeper.

I look to Felicity. Felicity is strong, and smart, and sensible. Always has been, always will be. "This doesn't strike you as hasty?"

Felicity smiles. "Listen to Clyde," she says. "When was the last time you heard him be that definitive? We're going to fix this. Everything's going to be taken care of. Just like we knew it would be."

Strong, and smart, and sensible. Except when it comes to me and the universe foretelling my death.

Or am I worrying too much? Everyone seems to think I am.

And maybe there's a point when professional paranoia, just becomes paranoia... Didn't I accuse Hannah of having exactly that problem?

I cast around, looking for any ally left. For a moment my eyes meet Hannah's. She stands there, pensive, hands clutched behind her back. And she agrees with me. I can see it there. But she won't say anything to help me. It's gone too far for that. And it's gone too far for me to ask her for help.

"There," Felicity says. "It's settled. Come on, let's get this sorted out."

41

THREE HOURS LATER, SHEFFIELD

Felicity's hand shakes me awake. "We're here."

Here, it turns out, is a rather shitty-looking abandoned factory, in a rather shitty-looking industrial wasteland on the edge of Sheffield.

For a moment we sit there. It's started drizzling again. The sort of rain that doesn't fall but simply hangs in the air waiting for you to walk into it. The factory windows have all been knocked out. Only half are boarded up, the remainder gaping witlessly at the world. Graffiti has been scrawled over almost every square inch of exposed brick, but nothing more erudite than a pop lyric, and nothing more artistic than a rather carefully rendered picture of a turd.

There is a crunch of tires on gravel as Kayla pulls up beside her. Hannah sits next to her in the passenger seat. Tabitha is barely visible behind fogged windows, curled up on herself sitting in the back seat. Behind me, I hear Clyde move as he shifts to stare out the window at her.

I direct my attention back to the derelict factory. "Doesn't look like much," I say.

Felicity shrugs. "It's the address Volk and Hermann gave me. And we still have half the journals." Four leather-bound journals sit on the back seat next to Clyde, the partial number a testament to the continuing distrust between MI37 and the Uhrwerkmänner.

"Speak of the devils," I say. Two shapes emerge from the factory's shadowy interior. "Well," I correct, "the devil and Volk."

And we really do need to learn more about this tunnel system of theirs. We left Brize Norton at the same time, the pair of them heading off over fields, and yet here they are ahead of us.

Their whole movement around the country confuses me, in fact. How the hell did Friedrich find us? Did he just overhear that we were going to the Himalayas? Or did he find his own path there? Is someone in the Uhrwerkmänner camp betraying us? If so, wandering into their parlor may not be the best idea.

But on the other hand, doesn't Friedrich want the same thing as Volk and Hermann in the end? Doesn't he want his people saved? The difference in opinion is on how best to achieve that. If we can show him that there's another way to stop the madness taking the Uhrwerkmänner, won't he stop?

There are too many other unanswered questions for me to know. Again, I doubt the wisdom of rushing in here. Except Felicity is already getting out of the car.

"So," I hear her say, "this is where you've been hiding all these years."

I turn back to Clyde. "You're sure about this?" I say. One last attempt to apply the brakes.

"Totally," he says. He's still staring out the window at Tabitha as she uncurls from the back of Kayla's car, brown tattooed legs poking from baggy multi-pocketed shorts, unseasonable in the autumn chill.

"You're talking about saving the Uhrwerkmänner, right?" I say.

"Right," he says, still sounding distracted, still not taking his eyes from Tabitha.

He gets out of the car. After a moment, I follow.

"Let's get this over with then."

OUT OF THE RAIN BUT IN THE DARK

The factory's interior is no prettier than its exterior. Broken tiles, moldering boxes, and mouse shit coat the floor. Old ceiling tiles hang like wilting foliage. Shoulders hunched, Volk and Hermann lead the way through the mess.

"Love what you've done with the place," Hannah says to no one in particular.

The Uhrwerkmänner lead us from one cavernous space to another. They don't call a halt until we are deep into the building. The room we stand in is much like the others—large, decaying, and distinctly malodorous. The only difference is a piece of machinery, roughly the size of a three car pile-up, that long ago became an unidentifiable amalgam of rust.

Hermann sets his shoulder against it, heaves. "This way," he grunts.

With a grinding shriek, the metal hulk scrapes across the floor. It is not, I realize, organic to the room. It was placed here. It is, in fact, a colossal trapdoor. One that would require inhuman strength to move. The sort of strength a massive robot might possess for example.

The machinery shifts to reveal a ragged hole in the factory's floor.

"Well, that doesn't look feckin' ominous at all," Kayla says.

"Come on." Felicity is brusque. "We want to get this done."

Most of us anyway. Some of us still have doubts.

Still, I do my job and am the first one to the edge of the hole. Its edges are serrated—a mess of tattered tile and crumbling cement. I look down into darkness.

"It is not far," Volk says. "I will lower you."

Gently he reaches out a hand, grasps me about the waist. His fingers encompass me from thigh to midriff.

It feels remarkably like putting my head in the jaws of a lion. The sense that if he wanted to, Volk could end me right now. But he doesn't. His grip, instead, is gentle, lifting me slightly, then lowering me down until I am just a few feet from the floor. I drop the last bit, stare into the blackness.

My eyes have started to adjust by the time the rest of MI37 are standing beside me. Hermann jumps down followed by Volk. Their metal feet boom against the concrete floor. Volk reaches up, heaves the rusting machinery back into place. The darkness is complete.

Light gutters above us. A bright yellow flame. The pilot light of Hermann's flame-spit-thrower thing.

The space is narrower than the room above, shallower. The ceiling curves slightly, a broad, shallow arch. Below my feet, two sets of tracks are set into the flat concrete floor.

"Was this a subway?" I ask. At one point I would have assumed that couldn't be, that everyone would know about a subway system built in Sheffield. At this point, I'd be surprised if Sheffield doesn't have a fairly substantial secret history.

"We laid the tracks," Volk says. "It speeds us."

Eyebrows arch throughout our group.

Hermann steps forward, forcing Clyde and Hannah to dance out of his way. He puts one foot on each rail of the track.

"It is easiest if we carry you from here," Volk says. Hermann grunts, but then points to Kayla, Hannah, and Tabitha. "I will take you."

"Like hell," Tabitha spits.

"Get on!" Felicity snaps. We all turn to look. She looks a little surprised by her own outburst. Still she does her best to mask it. "There is no time to waste. The lives of the Uhrwerkmänner, and our own teammates are in the balance. We can remove that threat. Move." And she does it all without even glancing at me. Though I don't know if that's enough to fool anyone about her priorities.

Still scowling, Tabitha allows Hermann to pick her up and set her standing on his foot, hands gripped tightly to a plate of metal on his leg.

Volk sets me up on his back, beside Felicity. Clyde he sets standing on his foot, before holding him in place with a large hand.

"This," he says, "may seem a little disconcerting at first."

Something grinds in his feet. He shifts his weight. He... grows. Not much. Maybe an extra six inches. But mounted on his back, I am very aware of the change. In the pale light, I peer at Hermann's feet, try to work out what's going on.

"Wait..." I say, "do you have built-in roller skates?"

"Oh of course," I hear Hannah say from in front of me, the sound of resignation in her voice. "Why wouldn't the Nazi magician build his robot army with roller skates? Stands to bloody reason."

"Well," Volk acknowledges, "it is something like that."

And then we're off.

The closest thing I can think of is the tunnel under the Himalayas. But instead of water whipping us along, it's two tons of German engineering and magic. Wind batters at me, the only sense of movement in the all-encompassing dark. Hermann's pilot light is all but invisible. I think we are going downhill but it's hard to tell.

And then, seemingly almost as soon as it starts, the trip is over. Yellow, electric light blooms around us. The tunnel opens up. A passage leads off to the side, stairs leading down. Hermann and Volk slow. Sparks spit from beneath their feet, and then they are stepping off the tracks, taking a couple of jogging steps. They set us all down.

"This way." Volk points to the stairs.

We hesitate. But Felicity is right. We're committed now. No reason to waste time. Get this over with. Get back to trying to get back to the way things were.

I take the steps two at a time, leaving the light of the tunnel above, heading toward a second source of illumination below.

I can't quite tell what I'm looking at until my foot hits the final step. And then I stop. Then I stare.

A vast cavern. Massive beyond my comprehension. A cavern the size of a small town. A ceiling a hundred yards above my head. And the space between. It is full of Uhrwerkmänner. A hundred of them at least. And buildings. Thrown together structures of steel and wood. A vast encampment of them.

Behind me the others reach the bottom of the stairs, join me in the gawking session. Volk and Hermann follow swift on their heels.

"Ah," Volk almost sighs. "Home."

42

"Hot bloody damn," Hannah breathes. "It's bloody massive."

She's not wrong. But it's not just the space. It's everything. It's the scale of the buildings, the streets. It's like a shanty town for homeless giants. Uhrwerkmänner stamp between massive amalgamations of rusting iron and tarnished bronze.

As I look at them longer, the more I understand Volk and Hermann's desperation. As beaten up and battered as the two Uhrwerkmänner who accompanied us to Nepal now appear, they are shining paragons of health in comparison to the rest of the crowd. These Uhrwerkmänner walk hunched over. Their limbs shake or simply drag along after them. I see one who stops every three paces and lets out a scraping metallic bark. Another's head jerks violently back from side to side with every step it takes. Hermann's bitter despair suddenly makes a little more sense.

We all stand there for a moment, taking it in. The scale of it. The place. The problem.

"OK," I say. "Let's get this all sorted out. Tabitha, Clyde, what do you need?"

There's a pause. People still absorbing everything. It's an odd sensation to not be the one most disoriented by the shock of the new. "Come on," I say. "These people need our help."

And I'm the one hurrying us along now. Because maybe there

is hope. Or maybe because even if I can't believe in a chance for myself, I believe these... people... robots... whatever the hell they are, they deserve a chance. They were dealt a shitty hand, but they've done their best with it. We should do our best by them. And we're here now. So maybe there is the chance of an end to all of it.

"Erm, well, OK, yes," Clyde says. "Tools. That's sort of the big one. It's actually a lot of mechanical tinkering. Shouldn't need a welder or anything like that. Just pliers, screwdriver, a wrench or two, maybe a cutting tool of some sort."

"And a volunteer," Tabitha throws in.

"Oh yes." Clyde nods. "One of those too."

There is a pause.

"Is one of those a problem?" Clyde asks. "Probably should have mentioned all that before we got here. Rather caught up in the moment, I'm afraid. But the hammer... well, a lot of things can be used as a hammer. And the cutting tool might not be wholly necessary. The screwdriver might be a dealbreaker, though, so—"

"Why a volunteer?" Hermann's voice is pitched low, less friendly than even his usual belligerent tone.

"Oh." Clyde, apparently oblivious to basic social cues, smacks the side of his head. "Probably should have mentioned that too. Would lose my head if it wasn't attached to my neck. Which, actually, is pretty obvious. I mean clearly some sort of violent decapitation would have to be involved for any other arrangement. No other kind of decapitation actually. Well, is that true? Probably not, though I can't off the top of my head think of a non-violent method. Lack of imagination on my part, I'm sure."

Hermann steps toward Clyde. Another step and he'll squash him. "Explain," he growls.

"Wait, wasn't I doing that? Totally meant to. Bit of a preamble, I suppose. Probably not the time or the place. So, yes, this whole volunteer thing. Fairly important. You see the process Lang describes is an internal one. An unlocking of potential he calls it. In a very literal manner apparently. It's a little hard to tell from individual mentions, but once you see the pattern over the course of some texts all these oblique references start to add up. It's to do with realigning certain fundamental pieces of gearwork, and repurposing some other material. It's a little hard to tell to be perfectly honest. But once we get stuck in, I get the impression it'll all be very straightforward. And there's a lot of magic involved, which tends to straighten out most kinks. Well, apart from the times when it veers off at a horrible right angle and obliterates bits of the coastline or something. But like I say, very confident about that. And Lang is very clear about that being 'the solution' to problems."

"Wait," I jump in. "Not the final solution, right?"

"Oh no," Clyde shakes his head. "He capitalizes that. All sorts of ick."

"Be fine," Tabitha says. "Mother bloody hen."

Again, Hannah's laugh doesn't need to be quite that bitter in my opinion.

We've started to attract attention, I notice. Uhrwerkmänner at the edges of the shanty town are grinding to a halt. Or at least as much of a halt as they are able. A couple point. The clack of metal vowels in a language I don't understand.

Volk is staring at them. As sad an expression as he is capable of making etched into his features.

"I'll do it," he says abruptly. "I volunteer for you."

"You trust these, these…" Hermann struggles to find a word. "*Schwachkopf.*"

Well, that doesn't sound complimentary.

"If they say it will work," Felicity's voice is strident, "then—"

Volk holds out a hand, placating, silencing, but he's looking at Hermann. "I believe that our people are desperate. That I am desperate. Hope is here. Within reach. I will grasp it."

Hermann shakes his head. "You are *Schwachkopf.*"

Whatever the hell that word means, Volk seems to take it without rancor.

"You must not despair, my friend," he says. "That is what Friedrich did."

Hermann shakes his head again, but he holds his tongue.

Volk turns to look down at Clyde. "Come, my diminutive friend," he says, "do what you need to do. Save me. Save my people."

AN HOUR LATER

Decrepit as they are, the Uhrwerkmänner are pretty resourceful. They've produced a vast array of tools: hammers, mallets, wrenches of all possible varieties, a rainbow of screwdrivers. They've even jury-rigged some seating, and now crowd the edges of a broad, makeshift amphitheater.

Volk lies on his back in the center of this circle. His chest casing has been peeled back. He did it himself, using his own hands to splay sheets of beaten bronze. Clyde is perched on the Uhrwerkmänn's midriff, spidery legs bunched beneath him, knees jutting. He wrestles in the chest cavity, his actions obscured by Volk's jutting bulk. Occasional bursts of oil spurt up, spattering Clyde's face and hair. He rips out a piece of pneumatic tubing, tosses it to the trash-strewn floor. I can't help but wince. The audience regards it stoically. All except Hermann, who stalks the edges of the circle. I'm not sure if he looks like he's looking for an opportunity to attack or escape. Do machines have a fight or flight system?

A disturbance at the edge of the circle announces Kayla's return. She carries a matte black box. Felicity's car battery. Clyde swore he'd only need about half the juice in it. Felicity said he could have it all if it would help.

I stand next to her, fold my arms, use the gesture as an excuse to squeeze one of hers.

"Still feeling confident?" I ask. If she is, maybe I will too.

"Still feeling like this is a necessary attempt," she says. Which isn't quite the same thing.

"Long shot, or total shot in the dark?" I press.

"Clyde and Tabitha are very good at what they do." Felicity continues with the non-answers.

"Clyde and Tabitha are in the middle of a huge lovers' spat," I point out. "That may not be entirely conducive to their best work."

She turns to me. Her eyes are pained. "What do you want me to say? We're always trying for the long shot. Those are the circumstances under which we operate." Her expression softens a little. "At least we've proven we have a pretty good aim."

It's a good line. And this is the part where I smile and nod and go along. Except I remember again the mad Uhrwerkmänn's fist falling. I remember the man who was a tear in reality. I remember inevitability.

But I look around. I see the jittering, twitching crowd. Don't they deserve a long shot?

So I don't smile. And I don't nod. But I shut up, and let things carry on.

Clyde is staring at an oily fistful of cogs. "Erm…" he says and glances at Tabitha.

"Don't care," she replies without looking up.

Clyde regards the cogs once more, shrugs. "Ah well." He dumps them on the floor.

Volk jerks. "This… it… progresses well?" The words drip out of him like leaking oil.

"Oh, erm, yes, totally. Nothing to worry about in the slightest," Clyde says, lowering almost his entire head into Volk's chest cavity. A large array of important-looking objects are spread on a table to his right. Approximately a crap ton more than you could ever take out of a person and hope to keep them alive. Volk, it appears, was built tough.

"OK," Clyde continues. "I'm going to be rearranging a few things." He glances at a sheaf of notes. "Let me know if anything feels like it's terribly wrong. I mean, it might be meant to feel that way, I don't know. But it'll be good to know if it correlates to something actually going horribly wrong and we have to try this out on someone else." His eyebrows shoot up. "Not that I expect anything to go wildly astray. Or even slightly astray. Well… OK, I should probably concede that slightly astray is statistically fairly likely. But not incorrectably astray. Just thought I should clarify the sort of astray I mean. Don't want to be unclear. Though, thinking about it, most of my attempts at pellucidity are what leads to obfuscation, so maybe I should stop that. But what I'm trying to say is that this might feel weird and that you should give me a shout if it feels too weird. Horrible bedside manner that I have. Apologies about that. Though Bedside Manor would be a great name for a doctor's house. Not that that's relevant, but…"

He comes up out of Volk's chest cavity with a fistful of pneumatic pipes. "OK, just need to put a few things back in new places…"

Silence from Volk.

"I say, Volk, are you quite all right?"

Volk's head lies limply to one side.

"Oh." From Clyde's expression that is not a good "oh."

Hermann stops stalking, advances. "What have you done?" He's not quite shouting, but he's close.

"Minor, erm... sort of mass paralysis. Probably." Clyde peers back into Volk's chest. "Unless, I... No, that's still intact."

"Which you shall cease to be if—"

Kayla, Hannah, Felicity, and me all take a step forward. A group rattling of sabers.

"Calm down," Tabitha says. She has pried open a panel in what passes for Volk's waist. "Motor control loss. Will do it to you. Watch you shit oil over yourself. Unless you want to sit down?" She doesn't bother looking at Hermann either.

Hermann hesitates. Tabitha spins a screwdriver in her palm like a gunslinger at high noon.

Hermann backs away with a grunt, resumes his pacing.

"All right," Clyde says, still looking around Volk's chest. "Just put this back in the new alignment." His arm scrabbles around outside Volk's form, grabs a tumorous mass of cogs and jabs it back into the body. "Then pull on this." He grabs something, yanks, grunts. "I say, Kayla, could you lend a hand."

Kayla rolls her eyes. Then in two leaping strides she has straddled Volk. "Feckin' show me."

"If you could just pull—" Clyde starts.

Kayla reaches in, yanks. For a moment cords knot in her neck. Then with a crunch, Volk's head disappears inside his body.

"Oh," Clyde says. Still not a good "oh." "Erm, didn't expect that, but OK. Now, maybe twist..."

Kayla doesn't let him finish. Again her muscles bunch. A panel creaks open in Volk's side revealing a shallow channel. His arm pivots and aligns, lying flat and sunken along his body.

"OK, this is weird." Clyde consults his notes. "How about..."

He continues giving Kayla directions. She carries on yanking. Slowly Volk's body reorganizes itself. Panels opening and closing. Sheets of metal extruding and enfolding.

"Like a bronze chrysalis," Felicity comments beside me.

That's more poetic than I can manage. To me it looks more like a bronze coffin.

"All right," Clyde says. "Just need to connect this to… Well, that doesn't make sense. Tabby, don't mean to, well, I mean, of course you're totally sure you wrote this all down correct—"

"Yes," she says. Apparently no one is willing to let Clyde finish a thought today.

"Well, OK." Clyde rustles about in the chest cavity. "Just need to wire him up now. Tabby, if you could help me with the battery…"

The large box flies at him with alarming speed. Clyde lets out a shrill whimper, but Kayla snags it out of the air before impact.

I look at Volk again. And this just doesn't seem right. He doesn't look right. He looks like an amputee victim or… I don't know. I mean, this was built into him. Lang designed all this to be possible. But Lang doesn't strike me as the most charitable of people. He designed the Uhrwerkmänner as soldiers. As weapons. Apotheosis-mode doesn't seem like something he would have taken the time to build in.

Though maybe… a repair function? That would make sense, I suppose. They were soldiers.

But something about that doesn't sit right.

But I don't have any other ideas, and it's not like I'm the one who has read Lang's journals.

The solution. That's what Clyde said. A solution to…?

Clyde is still talking to himself. "…and that clips on there. OK." He looks at his notes. "Tabby, terribly sorry to bother you, but this incantation. Is that a *vishnu* or a *veshnu*? Can't quite make it out."

Tabitha grunts and walks away.

"Well," Clyde tells her back. "No worries, I'll figure it out."

Alarm bells are ringing in my head again. I step toward Volk, lying there, suddenly seeming small, feeling more *other* than he ever has before. "You're *sure*, right?" I ask Clyde.

Hermann stops again, lunges toward us. "You said you were sure." He is accusatory, the threat of violence clear in the set of his shoulders.

"He is sure," Tabitha says. "Arthur's not. Ignore Arthur. Not his area."

Hermann hovers, wavering between the desire to pull the plug and the desire to see this over and done. For once, it seems Hermann and I are of the same two minds.

After a moment's awkward silence, Clyde breaks it. "Well," he says, "I'm just going to go ahead and say that spell now." He clips the wires leading from Volk to a battery, then clips on a second pair. Clyde holds the second set gingerly.

"*Mirehel bal mun keltar bar multarek mel pishtar. Bol gollon el nimtess shin.*" Clyde forces his tongue through the gibberish phonemes of magic. "*Col veshnu bal tenkoo. Al balrat mol collat. Tempra cal.*" Without warning he grabs the live contacts. He manages one more word, maybe another, his head thrown back, howling. A jagged white spark spears out of his open mouth, arcs up, down, strikes Volk.

What is left of Volk begins to emit a dull grinding sound. A painful meshing of gears.

Every muscle in me tenses. I want to move, to push into action, but I have no idea which way to jump. I only know that the need to feels imminent.

Clyde makes another cawing sound. Lightning juts from his jaws, slams into Volk. The grind picks up an octave. Volk's frame starts to rattle.

Around us the other Uhrwerkmänner seem caught in the moment. Too much rides on this moment. They are trapped by it. Hanging between fear and hope.

Clyde's scream is awful. He falls to his knees, body convulsing. A thick stream of electricity explodes out of him. He projectile vomits it across the room. It slams into the crowd, blows the seating apart. Robots sprawl, scatter, desperately clambering over each other to escape.

I move half a step toward them, but there's nothing I can do. I can feel the weight of my pistol in its holster beneath my armpit. But can I really shoot Clyde? This may be victory. This may be an end.

Clyde, jaw stretched wide, turns slowly. The lightning doodles destruction across the floor, approaching Volk.

Hermann is open-mouthed. He lunges toward Volk. The spitting stuttering lightning bolt brings him up short.

He turns toward Clyde.

Clyde's spasming body finally makes its circuit. He vomits electricity at Volk, connects.

Hermann closes the distance.

The grinding from Volk becomes screaming. A metallic shriek like nails on a chalkboard. His limbless form bounces and crackles. Sparks spit out of him, hit the ground, hit other Uhrwerkmänner. Hermann is a pace from Clyde when one smashes into the side of his head. He is driven wide of Clyde, goes down on his knees.

The solid beam of white that connects Clyde to Volk stutters, blinks in, out, in, out of existence. Volk is glowing. Blue light shines through cracks in his carapace. Seems to shine even through the metal. And yet even as he starts to glow the air around him darkens. He is a single bright spot in a spreading ink stain in reality.

Felicity's fingers squeeze deep into the flesh of my arm.

This does not feel like victory.

This does not feel like an end.

The lightning blinks out of existence. For a moment it seems like the room has been plunged into pitch darkness. But as I blink away after-images, no… Things are… normal? Not quite. Clyde is on his knees on the ground, still shaking slightly, still twitching. He has dropped the cables connecting him to the car battery. The clamps steam.

The Uhrwerkmänner's jury-rigged seating is in ruins. Great holes are blasted in it. The Uhrwerkmänner themselves lie in gently jerking heaps, slowly, awkwardly picking themselves off each other. I can't tell if their hesitance is the palsy in their movements or fear. Maybe it's both.

Felicity's grip does not lessen on my arm. Kayla has her sword drawn. Tabitha has taken cover behind a collapsed Uhrwerkmänn. Hannah stands staring with a sort of horrified fascination frozen on her features.

Hermann is on his knees, next to Clyde, staring.

And Volk simply lies there. No more darkness around him. No more blue light. No different from before the spell started. Just that odd bronze box, folded in upon himself. Headless.

The Uhrwerkmänner unfold themselves, find their feet. And Volk just lies there.

Was that it? Was that our big moment? Am I off the hook now? Am I going to live? But I can't quite put the words into speech yet.

Hermann is the first to talk. "What have you done?" He stands, towering above Clyde. "What did you do to him?"

"W... w... well, we, erm. I... I... I... I mean p... perhaps," Clyde stammers.

"What it said to do," Tabitha cuts in, standing. "What Lang's notes said. We did that. What you asked us to do." There is not an atom of apology in her.

What Lang's notes said to do. Lang's *solution*. Something is very wrong.

"This?" Hermann is caught between mockery and horror. "I asked you to make my friend *this*? I do not remember that request. He wanted to live. He wanted to save. He wanted to—"

"*BECOME.*"

The word booms around the makeshift amphitheater. It seems to fill the whole hidden cavern. It bounces off the Uhrwerkmänners' shanty-town walls.

Every head turns. Human and machine moving as one. Back toward the cavern's entrance, the stairway. I shift, trying to see what is coming. And part of me already knows. But I keep telling it to shut up and just be wrong.

But it's not. It never bloody is.

And, striding into view, comes Friedrich.

43

Oh shit. Oh balls.

"No," Felicity says next to me. If she grips me much harder she's going to break the skin.

But yes. Here he comes. Vast and towering. Dwarfing the Uhrwerkmänner that dwarf me. And his army comes with him. A sleek shining wake behind their flagship, HMS *Asshat*.

They stand in stark comparison to the jittering mob Hermann and Volk lead. Well... Hermann at this point. I'm not sure what Volk is doing. It looks suspiciously like the mechanical equivalent of a coma. But Friedrich's forces are rigid. Their steel gleams. Their marching is synchronized. Not one of them looks like it's on the verge of asking if I'm its grandson.

"Volk dreamed," Friedrich booms. "He dreamed of a better life. A better future. He dreamed of escaping the limits of frailty. Of becoming better. Of becoming more. Of becoming what our father designed him to be."

"No," Hermann shouts. "No, you leave. You are not welcome." It is a futile wail against Friedrich's massive boom.

"Our father was misguided, twisted," Friedrich carries on regardless. "His tragedy is all the greater for the goodness that lurked within him—the spark of love that he bore us. Love that he tried to betray, but never fully could."

He stares meaningfully around the room. His sloping axe-head of a face taking them all in. "Lang locked within us all the opportunity to ascend ourselves, our degeneration," he bellows. "He built within each of us the chance to be perfect."

He sounds more like a preacher than a warlord. Or a cult leader perhaps. There is a dark charisma lurking in his chest. His voice is expressive in a way that his face can never be.

"Get out!" Hermann rails. Friedrich's forces begin to ring our ruined amphitheater. Some push onto the central stage, surround what's left of Volk.

For some reason they ignore us. Perhaps we are not a threat. I certainly don't feel like one. Kayla may feel differently though.

"You betray all that we strove for!" Hermann is still shouting. "Everything we achieved when we walked away from our father. You are capitulation. You are cowardice."

Hermann, it seems, has big old brass balls.

Actually, I realize, it's possible that he literally does have them.

"I am success." Friedrich enters the ring. His voice crashes against Hermann. "I am victory. I am everlasting. And you are defeat. You kneel at my feet."

"I will nev—" Hermann starts.

Two Uhrwerkmänner kick out his knees. There is a violent crunch of metal, the sound of something thick snapping. Plates in Hermann's legs buckle as he slams down to the ground.

"You kneel." Friedrich's voice is rich with satisfaction. "As Volk told me you would. As Volk promised me."

The operator in my gut hits the down button. It plummets toward my ankles. *Volk?* Oh no. Oh crap.

"You lie," Hermann spits.

"Volk wanted this. This moment. He believed in this. He saw the futility in you. In all of you." He sweeps one colossal arm around the room, at all the Uhrwerkmänner. "He saw your doom. And I welcomed him to my fold. But he said, no, he would not come with me. He told me he would remain here, to guide you toward me, toward this moment. Toward the victory of our race over death. Toward apotheosis. Toward *becoming*."

"No," Hermann is saying over and over again. "No, no, no."

"How was I always able to find you?" Friedrich asks. "How was I always one step ahead of you?"

God. It's far from being the worst part of this, but all I can think is that Hannah was right. I am never going to hear the end of this.

"The tunnels..." Hermann starts, but his defiance is finally waning.

"You believed that?" Friedrich scoffs. "Then madness already eats at your reason. You are already lost."

Goddamn it. I believed that too. There's a chance that having had reality ripped out from under my feet so often, I have become a touch gullible.

But Volk? Of the two Uhrwerkmänner it was *Volk* who betrayed us? Shit and balls. God, if I survive the next few minutes I'm going to be left with some serious trust issues.

I glance over at Hannah.

OK... with worse trust issues.

Hermann himself has lapsed into silence. The rest of the Uhrwerkmänner are silent, horrified spectators.

Friedrich smells victory, switches back to his original topic. "Volk knew in his core that our father would not abandon us. That his love would triumph over his evil in the end. He knew the promise our father had made us."

Friedrich steps forward, standing directly at the base of Volk's body. His legs are set wide, his massive chest pushed out. Every inch the conquering hero. He bends, picks up Volk in both hands. Without any discernible effort he hoists several tons of metal above his head.

"Behold," he booms, "our absolution. Behold the Uhrwerkgerät!"

44

Beside me, Felicity groans. "Oh, you have to be kidding me."

Everything we fought for. Everything we strived to prevent. And we just handed it to Friedrich on a silver platter. We bloody crafted the Uhrwerkgerät for him in front of all the people we were meant to save.

And I let it happen. I knew we were rushing this. I knew Clyde and Tabitha were dysfunctional. And I let events ride over me. I let fear rule me. My goddamn fear of death. And it's that fear that's brought the future echo's promise closer.

I am such a fucking jackass some days.

"This!" Friedrich bellows. "This is the power inside of us. This is the power of *becoming*. Volk has embraced it. One of the best among us. The one you trusted. He saw this truth and ran toward it with open arms. Do not betray him. Do not betray yourselves. We were promised more than decay and dysfunction. And we can embrace that promise. Come with me. Redefine this world. Reclaim yourselves. Your birthright. Be all you can be."

A solution. Lang was writing about a solution. But Lang's concept of a solution is a fucking reality-destroying bomb. And we didn't take the time to get the context, to get the level of understanding we needed. We just plunged in. Because we're desperate.

Hell, there might not even be another solution to the

Uhrwerkmänner's problems. We only have their word that there was one. And if we're desperate, what are they? They stare at Friedrich now. A broken people. This last scrap of hope ripped away from them.

And they'll go to him. Volk's betrayal, real or not, has broken Hermann. There is no voice of resistance. There is no path to take other than the one Friedrich offers. Transform themselves into this bomb, to the vague hope it promises, or just lie down and die. God, in their place that's probably the straw I'd grasp at.

Unfortunately, in the place that I'm actually in, that all leaves me rather fubarred.

Friedrich lays Volk's limbless body down on the operating table, slowly, almost reverentially.

He's going to keep talking. He's going to keep going until he convinces them. And we're just standing here watching him.

Why is the right thing to do also always the really dumb thing to do?

I step forward, out of the huddled ranks, pushing between the legs of Friedrich's loyal Uhrwerkmänner. Felicity tries to pull me back, but I twist away from her.

It takes a moment for Friedrich to register my presence. I am very aware that I am surrounded by twenty or more robots all of whom could kill me with almost no effort whatsoever.

But something has to be said.

I clear my throat. It's hard to read Friedrich's expression, but there's a chance it's more amused than murderous.

"You realize this is all bullshit, right?" I say. My voice sounds pathetically small in the wake of Friedrich's colossal boom. But I keep going. Because I don't know what else to do. Because even in the face of death, we keep on thrashing. Some idiot response built into the lizard brain and reinforced by too much Hollywood bullshit.

"I know you lot have been buried down here for a long time," I say, "but up on the surface we have this thing called an infomercial. It's where a slimy fucker does his best to sell you something you don't want. And he'll go on and on for hours, and he'll say anything he can, tell any lie he thinks is feasible, just to sell it to you." I point straight at Friedrich. At his knee caps, actually. "That's this bastard."

I take a breath, hold it for a moment, expecting some great foot to come down like it's the end of the *Monty Python* credits, to be reduced to the simplest of slapstick humor.

But it doesn't come. I don't know why the hell he's doing it, but Friedrich's giving me the floor.

"This Uhrwerkgerät he's so excited about. It's just a bomb. That's all. A big one, yeah. I'll give it that. But that's all it is. It goes boom. Things die. And you know the thing about bombs? There's not much left of them at the end. They don't ever get a chance for an encore. Friedrich says he's got your best interests at heart but—"

And that's as far as I get.

It's not a violent end, not a savage one. It's laughter. Friedrich's laughter simply drowns me out.

"Look at him!" Friedrich booms. "Look at how small he is. How pathetic. Look at your oppressor. You live down here in squalor. Because of him."

Which seems a little unfair.

"He says he has your best interests at heart. But since they first bombed us, shot us, hounded us, killed us, when has humanity ever had our best interests at heart?"

Ah, now I know why I'm still alive. I'm the straw man. The argument to be torn down.

Friedrich stares at the assembled Uhrwerkmänner. "He is scared now. Because he knows this is his end. The age of man is done. It is our time. Our time to rise. To *become*."

"I'm fucking scared," I shout back, "because I know where this ends. Sure, yes, with my death. But I'm not alone. We all die. You blow up reality itself. You pull the thread on the whole goddamn tapestry, you self-righteous jackass. You end everything. Me. Them." I point at the assembled Uhrwerkmänner. "You." I point at Friedrich. "We all die. Because you know what you're doing about as much as I do."

That was the future echo's promise to me. This ends badly. For everyone. I just got the heads up first. Lucky me. I am the guy with the sign reading "The World's Ending" standing on the street corner preaching to the uncaring crowds.

Except maybe, just maybe, this time they're desperate enough to listen. And sometimes people just need something to cling to as their reality fractures.

Friedrich is laughing again. "He is pathetic," he booms. "He is desperate. His time is over."

And he raises one massive hand.

Oh shit.

Because I am not the straw man. It's simpler than that. I'm the fly, and he's the swatter.

45

Friedrich's hand descends.

For a moment I am back in a bar in Scotland, watching a wooden beam come down. Watching death coming, unavoidable.

A massive crash. Steel on steel.

And I'm alive.

I look up. And there is Hermann. His right arm is a mangled ruin. But it holds Friedrich's fist a yard or more above my head.

"No," Hermann says.

"No?" Friedrich sounds more curious than annoyed.

"No," Hermann grunts, arm creaking down. The gap between my skull and imminent death becomes noticeably narrower. I scramble backwards.

Even as his right arm is crushed, Hermann twists and smashes his left fist into the side of Friedrich's skull. "You are a liar!" He lands a blow. "You are death!" Another. "You are betrayal." Another blow. "And I will fight you until I fall."

"Then you shall fall."

Friedrich lands a massive backhand across Hermann's midriff. The Uhrwerkmänn sails over my head, lands with an epic crash.

And that's it, that's the moment.

It's on.

Friedrich's troops fall upon the cowering Uhrwerkmänner.

Many go down, hunkering. Metal hands clutched over metal skulls. Friedrich's troops grab them. Like so many neanderthals claiming their brides, they drag them across the floor by legs and arms.

Other Uhrwerkmänner turn and simply flee as fast as they can. Not many make it far. Their own limbs betray them. Decaying gearwork makes them slow. They limp, and they hobble, and they are brought down.

And a number simply surrender. Hold up their hands, bow their heads, and start marching to the beat of Friedrich's drum.

And a few, just a few, stand and fight.

It doesn't go well for them.

I see one Uhrwerkmänn, ten feet of bronze and steel, land a titanic blow. A steel chest plate buckles beneath his fist. Gears burst from its edges spilling glittering onto the floor. Friedrich's footsoldier stumbles back, grabbing at his gut. Oil spurts rhythmically from its mouth. The Uhrwerkmänn raises a fist in victory.

Three of Friedrich's men pile on to him. Their fists rise and fall, a steady rhythmic pounding. One of them stands, heaves on something, twists. The Uhrwerkmänn's victorious arm is ripped from its socket. Friedrich's man starts to whale on the Uhrwerkmänn, using the limb like a massive flail.

"To me!" I yell to MI37. "To me!"

The place is chaos, and we are barely even bystanders. The scale of this fight is beyond us.

Someone probably should have mentioned that to Kayla.

She ignores me utterly. Sword out, she flies at one of Friedrich's Uhrwerkmänner. Her sword lands in a hip joint, and she twists like a gymnast, hoisting her whole body six feet up into the air, standing upside down on her hands, clenched on the sword's hilt. Her legs smoothly wrap around the Uhrwerkmänn's neck and she pivots her body up, sword wrenching free through pneumatic tubing that whips and curls in the aftermath. She uses her momentum, spinning around the Uhrwerkmänn's neck, until she sits astride its shoulders. She leans back, hanging upside down for a moment. Her sword lies along the length of her body. Then her stomach muscles flex and she sits bolt upright, the sword blade finding the joint at the base of the Uhrwerkmänn's skull, driving home, until it bursts out from beneath its chin.

The Uhrwerkmänn stumbles forward a step, then crashes to its knees. Kayla rips her sword free and rolls down its back as it falls face first into the dirt.

OK, so maybe we are still in this fight.

Tabitha and Clyde are with me. Felicity and Hannah too.

"Here," says Felicity, "catch." She reaches into a jacket pocket, tosses me a matte black cylinder.

I catch it, stare. "Is that a grenade?"

Felicity nods. Her penchant for carrying grenades with her at all times is beginning to worry me. I mean... does she take them to the supermarket? Is she ready for facing down an enemy emplacement somewhere in the frozen goods aisle?

Hannah looks at Felicity expectantly.

Felicity grimaces. "I'm really sorry. I only have two."

Hannah shakes her head, somewhere between resignation and disbelief. "Fucking typical."

I scan for Friedrich. There's a bastard who could really use a combustible suppository. Something to shift that rod out of his arse.

He's halfway across the room. Volk... the Uhrwerkgerät tucked under his arm. And that's not good. We need that back.

I take off at speed. Around me, massive bodies smash and crash against each other. I dart left, right, trying to keep on as straight a course as possible, trying to gain on the massive Uhrwerkmänn. But with legs three times as long as mine, he doesn't even have to try to outpace me.

Two Uhrwerkmänner stumble into my path. I twist between the legs of one, bouncing off one limb, twisting to avoid being crushed by the other as it scissors back, the body above rocking back under the impact of a hammer-blow punch to its jaw. Then the legs of the second Uhrwerkmänn block my path. I plunge right. The first Uhrwerkmänn sweeps the leg. I hurdle its oncoming limb, land, glance up to see the second Uhrwerkmänn has been less nimble. It totters above me.

I dive to the ground, duck, roll. The Uhrwerkmänn lands two inches behind me. Dust kicked up from its fall covers me. I scramble to my feet hacking and choking.

I see Friedrich. He's at the stairs, ducking into darkness, still far too far ahead of me. I dig deep, try to find another gear.

I hit the stairs, my feet pounding. But by now other Uhrwerkmänner are ahead of me. One of Friedrich's soldiers has an Uhrwerkmänn by the foot and is dragging him up step by step. The body crashes up and down, filling the corridor with sound. I make time, reach the fallen Uhrwerkmänn. I jump, land on its broad chest, keep running. I launch myself at the captor's arm. I land hard, my chin bouncing off steel.

Damnit, Kayla makes this shit look easy.

The Uhrwerkmänn senses my arrival. It's probably the way I slammed into his arm. He looks down at me, grunts. He drops the leg he's dragging, pulls back his arm. I wrap my legs around the limb, trying to hang on. Then I realize that he's about to smash me into the wall of the stairs and see how much of me he can leave there.

I let go. Above my head his arm slams into the wall. I lie on the floor and hurt for a moment. The Uhrwerkmänn looks down at me, roars.

Well, hell, it wasn't like I was going to catch up with Friedrich anyway.

I lob the grenade up, a soft underhand toss from a lying position. It's a good thing I played cricket in school. The grenade hits the back of the thing's metal throat.

A hard flat bang decapitates it.

The shockwave slams me harder into the floor. My spine gets all intimate with a number of my organs. The world goes out of focus for a while.

By the time I make it to my feet, the fight is over. Hermann and the non-psychotic members of the Uhrwerkmänner race have definitely lost.

If they looked halfway to the grave before, now the Uhrwerkmänner look like it's only their necks that are still poking out from the soil. On the other hand, that's considerably better than a large number of their friends.

I pick my way between mechanical body parts. Felicity, Clyde, Tabitha, Kayla, and Hannah stand in a small knot near the ruins of the amphitheater. Kayla is soaked in oil from head to foot. An all-singing, all-dancing, all-murdering silhouette. For a moment I flash back to the future echo and my step falters. But we've misstepped enough in the past few days. Time is increasingly of the essence. And there's no room for me to stumble anymore.

But the promise of that figure. It's more real than ever now.

God... Felicity... She had so much staked on this... this... supposed victory. God, that word almost makes me laugh. This was supposed to be a *victory*. Jesus.

They watch me come, all of them. A silence that grows more oppressive as I approach. Some surreal tableau. Man and machine and the furniture of defeat.

"Why?"

It's Hermann who breaks the silence when I am still twenty yards away. I stop, not understanding the question, quirk my head to one side.

"Why have you come back?" he asks. His voice is flat, uninflected. He sounds more machine now than ever. That spark of animation knocked askew in the fight.

And still I don't understand.

"What further indignity do you have to wreak upon us?"

What? Seriously? I tap my chest, just to be sure. "Me?"

For a moment Hermann is utterly still. Utterly silent. I fear the spark of life may have been snuffed out entirely.

"YES! YOU!" The words explode out of him. He is barely able to contain the rage of them. He hurls his body into them, arms thrashing. "All of this! You bring the Uhrwerkgerät to our door! You hand it to Friedrich. You end us. You end our hope. All of it is you!" He sags, staring at me, the energy trickling out of him. "What do you have left to do? Tell me." He straightens, finds the energy to scream once more. "TELL ME!"

But again... really? I tap my chest for a second time. "Definitely me you're talking about?"

He takes a step toward me. I see Felicity reaching for her shoulder holster. Kayla is pulling out her sword once more. But I've survived worse than Hermann's anger.

"You're sure it's me you're yelling at and not your betraying, backstabbing, shit of a friend who sold you up the fucking river?

You sure you want to accuse the only fucking help you have left?" Hermann isn't the only one who can get in touch with his inner bloody rage. I gave blood for this fucking machine. Repeatedly. I am sick of his shit.

Hermann isn't cowed. "You are the ones who turned him into the bomb. Into the end of hope. It was you who promised a solution." Hermann spits. His pilot light flicks to life. Flaming oil splashes down, no more than a few yards to my left. "Lies! All of it lies!"

"That wasn't even me!" The injustice of it probably shouldn't sting. And I certainly don't want to take his finger of blame and point it squarely at Clyde and Tabitha. But come on. I was the one actually trying to be the voice of reason here.

"Still you lie!" Hermann yells. "You cannot stop. You are full of lies! It spills from you."

The Uhrwerkmänner peanut bloody gallery offer no bloody commentary on this. They seem content with standing around looking shell-shocked. Though, to be fair about three-quarters of their buddies were either just killed, kidnapped, or coerced into defection.

"We covered the bit where we're your only allies, right?" I mention.

Hermann laughs. "Our allies? You think we want your help?"

"I think," Kayla interjects, "that you might want to watch your feckin' tone."

Hermann looks down at her. At every oil-soaked inch of her. Clyde hoists a fistful of batteries out of one pocket. And just for a moment we look like a bunch of people you do not want to fuck with.

"Get out," Hermann spits. "You are not welcome here. We do not wish for allies such as you."

I just stare at him for a moment. Because… just, really? It seems so absurd. And I get that we screwed up here. I get that the Uhrwerkgerät is our fault. But the fact that they even had something to screw up was because of us. And if they want to clear this up, they will need us. When there were four times their number they were already monstrously screwed. The odds did not improve for them today.

"Get out," Hermann repeats. And there's no fight left in him.

But he won't beg either. The pride hasn't been beaten out of him yet. So he just repeats the words, in the same flat tones that we started. "Get out."

I throw my hands up. "I just…" I look at Felicity. I've seen her in better moods.

"Come on," she says. She's holding a tight rein on everything. The tension is clear in her voice.

I shrug, turn on my heel, and walk away.

46

We're almost back at the abandoned factory before I trust myself to speak again. We've trudged along the tunnel in utter silence. Tabitha has stalked well ahead of the main group; Clyde, far behind. Felicity has a thousand yard stare. I fear it's going to leave a crater when she crashes back to earth.

But I can't keep my incredulity bottled up any more. "Me?" I say. "Us? He accused us? Friedrich was right there going through the A to Z how of Volk had screwed us all over, and his takeaway message is that we're to blame?"

Getting it off my chest doesn't even really make me feel better.

"What the *hell* else was he supposed to do?" Felicity's words fly out like a lash. I almost wince at the blow.

"What?" I manage.

"We made the goddamn bomb in front of them. Friedrich has been searching for it, and it didn't exist until *we* made it for him. Us. Of course he goddamn blames us. We're to blame." Red spots mar her cheeks. Her gaze stabs violently around the group. Tabitha. Clyde. And then lingering on Hannah. Hannah whose report will, without a doubt, damn us.

And finally Felicity's gaze comes to rest on me.

"This was meant to sort everything out. This goddamn bomb is meant to kill you."

She says it as if it's somehow my fault.

"I was the one person saying maybe we should hold off and double check," I protest. "That was me."

For not the first time in the world, the technically accurate answer is not the correct one. But what should I do? Tell her it's going to be OK? I haven't had the luxury of that conviction for a long time. Tell her that the universe is probably going to end before Hannah has a chance to sink us? I can't say I'm wholly convinced that would help.

While I try to figure it out, Felicity's rage moves on. "And you damn two," she says, simultaneously trying to cast her ire both to the front and the back of the group. "You bloody attest to me that you have this sorted out. And then this? Because Tabitha's goddamn panty liner is dry a few days too long? That's why the world is ending?"

Jesus. I'm not even convinced Kayla would go that far. Maybe this is what the inevitability of death is. The joy of living without consequences. Short-term solutions are suddenly applicable to every problem.

"I know."

It's not the response I expected. It's not even the person I expected to respond. It's Tabitha, standing at the front of the group. Not bristling with rage. Not ready for the fight. But small, and bitter, and wretched. And I would have thought that if any of us wanted the world to end it would be her.

But her confession, whatever motivates it, seems to take the wind out of Felicity's sails. Her rage sags.

"Let's just get out of here. Work out what the hell we do next."

Kayla uppercuts the substantial amount of machinery that blocks our exit out of the way, and slowly we drag ourselves out of the bowels of our defeat.

TWO HOURS LATER. ON THE ROAD

Felicity was uninterested in giving the other members of MI37 a lift back to Oxford. Instead, they ride with Kayla. Which must be fun. Not that sitting, staring at the rain hitting the windscreen, and listening to some interminable dirge on Radio Three is actually a barrel of giggling schoolchildren.

Finally, thankfully, Felicity punches the stereo off. In fact, she punches it so hard the little LCD display cracks. She doesn't seem to care.

It strikes me that this is the moment when the boyfriend says something comforting.

"It's going to be—" I start.

"If you say 'all right' you're going the same way as the stereo."

I nod. "Fair point."

Tires thrum. Rain drums. I start to miss the radio.

"We need a plan," I say finally. "We just need to work out how to move forward. That'll put things in perspective."

"In perspective?" There's a hollow shock in Felicity's voice. "You're going to die."

Well, that's one way to derail a conversation. Just deliver a punch to my keenest fears as directly and harshly as possible.

"Yeah," I manage eventually. "The whole it-being-prophesied-by-the-universe-in-a-way-that-is-so-profound-it-echoes-forward-in-time thing sort of brought that home to me."

Ahead of us, a stream of braking cars paints the rain running down the windscreen a violent crimson.

"But... But... But..." Felicity is unusually hesitant. I look up from my hands in my lap, realize she's crying. Tears run down her face, pulling her mascara south.

The cracks in me, in my head, my heart, go just a little deeper.

"But we were meant to fix it," she says. "Like we always do. And everything we did... everything we went through... Except it's still going to happen. It's still going to fucking happen."

"Yeah," I nod. And I should have more than that, but I don't. I am hollow. And in the absence of words I should reach out to her, comfort her. But I can't even do that. I am paralyzed by the weight of it.

"There's no way to move forward," she says, utterly desolate, utterly remorseless in her grief. "It's all pointless."

The cars continue to brake. We grind to a slow, slow halt. She sits there, like a paper doll the world has crushed up and thrown away.

I turn my gaze to stare out at the sodden world. "Remember back in September?" I say. "We went to that new Italian place. It was a really sunny day after all that rain so we decided to walk. But it was halfway across Oxford. And then I spilled the meatballs down my shirt. I mean, just completely. I don't think I could have got more on me if I'd tried. And you would not let us call a cab, despite the fact you were laughing so hard you could barely walk."

"Yes," Felicity says, her voice salt-lake-bed flat. "I remember."

"I was so happy then," I say. "I remember thinking, this is perfect. I don't ever want anything to change. I want it to be like this forever."

Felicity nods. Almost imperceptibly.

"It's all fucking changed," I say.

A long silence after that. I don't really have anything to add. Apparently Felicity doesn't either. Maybe there is nothing. It's just a fact. Inevitability.

"You want to know something stupid?" Felicity says as the traffic suddenly lurches back into motion.

I almost manage a smile. "Sure."

"Tomorrow's our one-year anniversary."

Oh Jesus. That is… I don't know. It is galvanizing enough to make me finally reach out and squeeze her leg. She reaches one hand down from the steering wheel to squeeze my hand back, then replaces it.

"At least we made it that far," I say. It sounded cooler in my head.

"I just… I just wanted to share my life with you," Felicity says. She's still not looking at me. Eyes on the road ahead. "That's all."

It is an enormous thing to say. I mean, I knew it, I even reciprocate the feeling. But still. To just state it as if it's nothing. As if it's just simple.

"And now all this shit." She lays on the horn, suddenly and viciously, blaring her way between two cars, forcing her way forward through the traffic.

"I'm just… I'm paralyzed by it," I say. "I haven't…" I shake my head. But somehow I need to reciprocate her honesty. "I haven't even started to pack. I can't. I can't see the future."

Felicity brakes hard. My head snaps forward, body pulling tight against the seat belt.

"You haven't what?"

There is an edge in Felicity's voice that was lacking. A sharp edge tearing through the emotional numbness.

Shit. Wrong confession. Too big. I should have gone with the fact that it was me who left the MI37 fridge door open overnight that one time or something.

"It's just…" I try to explain, but already my ability to hit the right emotional tone has gone. The moment is over. "I mean, the future is fucking terrifying."

"I asked you about moving in well before that future echo showed up. You told me you were packing well before it showed up. You lied to me."

Oh crap. We're establishing a timeline now? This reminds me of the murder investigations I used to run. And I'm not a good enough liar to get away with murder. It's probably easier if I confess now, beg for leniency.

"This whole job is a death sentence," I start. "I mean, do you really imagine that a day comes when we get to quietly retire from this and live in a little thatched cottage somewhere in Devon?" OK, maybe that image was a little too specific… "Or do you imagine a poorly attended funeral, the only mourners people almost at the end of their own short trips to an early grave?"

Felicity nods. It doesn't resemble her agreeing with me so much as it does the clockwork of rage winding up. A pendulum's unforgiving tick.

"And how long have you felt like this exactly?"

Alarm bells are ringing in my head. It's a trap! It's a trap!

Contrary to popular opinion, honesty is not always the best policy. There is definitely a time and a place for a well-placed white lie. Unfortunately in this particular time and place that lie is not as simple as stating that you read online that the door suction on fridges can lessen over time and suggesting a replacement part be ordered. And while the correct piece of conciliatory fiction is probably out there somewhere, I'm buggered if I can find it. Which leaves me with the unpalatable truth.

"Since Scotland," I say. "The first Uhrwerkmänn. Back in the pub." And then, because surely a little pathos cannot hurt, "I almost died."

"That was the day I brought up the whole idea of moving in together!"

I am beginning to think of the timeline as something alive. Some insidious snake conspiring against me.

"I'm so sorry," I say. My last possible tactic. Full-on apology. "I thought I could deal with this all on my own. But things haven't exactly been getting better."

"On your own?" Felicity nods again. She's still not agreeing with me. "After I pour my heart out to you and ask you to move in with me? To twine your bloody stupid life with mine? Your immediate reaction to this appeal to live a shared life is to keep everything to your bloody self?"

I need to start watching movies with fewer explosions and more talk-y bits. Maybe I could find some examples of what I'm meant to do in these situations.

"I think we got away from the bit where I'm destined to die," I say. But if I want to rescue this with humor I'm going to have to be a hell of a lot funnier than that.

"You selfish *arse*."

Felicity punches the stereo again. The LCD cracks further.

"And now a real treat," the DJ tells us. "We've got a full hour of Gregorian chant coming up."

"Felicity, I..." I start.

She cranks the volume and drowns me out.

47

THE DAY OF THE ANNIVERSARY

To say things are uncomfortable at work is a little bit like saying that being suspended over hot coals can make you sweaty.

The best way to make amends for this—for everyone to get back on everyone else's good side—is for us to find Friedrich, formulate a plan, and kick his arse. We are however rather falling at the first hurdle.

I have set Tabitha and Clyde to working on likely locations for Friedrich's hideaway. This, unfortunately, involves discovering every large underground space in Britain. And since digitalization has not been a priority at MI37, that means trying to dig up every map we have. And that everyone else has. And when Tabitha is refusing to acknowledge Clyde's presence on earth, the whole thing becomes a touch time consuming.

Tabitha, however, is not the only one denying the existence of others. After silently dropping me off outside my apartment last night, Felicity went straight to her office this morning, closed the door, and has not opened it since. Earlier, I stood outside it for five minutes but could never picture what would happen after I knocked on the door. The future was utterly blank to me.

After that, I retreated back to the conference room. Kayla and

Hannah sat there. Kayla tapped at her phone. I didn't want to ask. Research isn't her thing. She's a field operative. Unless there's something that needs its insides moved to its outsides she doesn't usually get involved.

Which left Hannah. I stared at her. She is a top-class MI6 agent. She should have good ideas on how to track people down. She has likely had extensive training on the subject. I should ask her how to run this operation. But our relationship seems a bit beyond that point.

"We need to know about the Uhrwerkmänner," I said instead. "Something to help Kayla and Clyde narrow their search down."

"Yes." No inflection. She might have been agreeing with me, or mocking my statement of the obvious. All the liveliness had gone from her.

"Help with that," I said. I opened my mouth to add something else. I don't know what. A word of encouragement, advice. A question perhaps. But I just couldn't. Her appearance on the team heralded this whole operation. And I know that's just coincidence, but part of me can't help but blame her.

I turned my back and walked away.

And now I sit here in a long-abandoned office, and stare at my computer. On the screen I have open a copy of the London *Times* dated to August 1963. Pinned to the wall on my right is a large map of England. A full five feet tall. Beside me is a box of tacks with bright red heads. I have spent the day going through newspapers looking for anything, any evidence of the Uhrwerkmänner's existence. Any story that could possibly be attributed to them. Looking for locations, for any cluster of activity.

There is not a single pin in the map.

Everything is too vague. Any story that could conceivably be them is too full of ambiguities to convince me. I know now that there are simply too many things that go bump in the night for me to definitively say of one incident, "Yes, this is them."

I can't see the future, and now I can't even make out the past.

I should go out. I should buy Felicity something. A new orchid perhaps. Or a seed. Something symbolic. Something that requires time. Even if we don't have it. A peace offering. Something to make it clear that I still love her. No matter how caught up in my own shit I get.

God, I need her help with this.

I consider going back to her office door. Knocking. But I can't go empty-handed.

I go to the conference room, but no one is there. I consider going down to the lab to tell Clyde and Tabitha that I'm stepping out for a moment. But I think their frostiness might bring the paralysis back—too palpable a reminder of our failures.

I'm almost at the elevator that leads up and out of the MI37 offices when my phone buzzes in my pocket. A text message. Felicity. My heart booms, a solitary burst of thunder, my abdomen becoming an aching void. My finger punches the screen.

"Conference room. Now."

As three little words go, they are not over-brimming with romance. I check the top of the screen. Five recipients. This is unlikely to be a romantic rendezvous. My heart sags, crushes the organs that now seem over-stuffed into my gut.

I check my watch. Somehow it has become 6:30 p.m. Maybe I'll have a chance to visit a florist after this latest crisis is over. There must be somewhere in Oxford that sells flowers late at night. Maybe we can do our anniversary tomorrow. Erase today. Pretend it never happened.

Tomorrow. Ha.

Clyde and Tabitha are already in the conference room. They sit across from each other. Clyde stares at Tabitha. Tabitha stares away, at the corner of the room.

And Felicity. She is there too. Standing at the head of the table, tapping her toe against the floor.

I take a seat. Try not to copy Clyde's impression of a teenager mooning over his unrequited love. Then I worry I've gone too far in the Tabitha direction. I glance at Felicity, then away. At her, away. Then I worry that all this is making me look a jittery coke head.

I look at my watch instead.

Hannah arrives, bustling, energetic. She fidgets in her chair. But she doesn't bring any conversation with her.

After another miserable minute, Felicity looks to her. "Where's Kayla?" she asks.

Hannah shrugs. "No bloody clue."

Felicity sighs, pushes hair out of her eyes. "Well this can't wait," she says. "We have an Uhrwerkmänn on Jericho Street. One of the crazy ones. And in about half an hour the students are going to be on that street in force. Go and take care of it."

And that's it. She turns to go.

"Wait," I say. It leaps out of me. Unplanned. Almost, but not quite unwanted.

Felicity waits. She doesn't turn around, but she waits. "Is there a problem?"

God, I wish I'd had time to buy her that orchid.

"No," I say eventually. Lamely. "We're on it."

Hannah grunts, but Felicity doesn't say a word. Just walks away.

48

JERICHO STREET

There is a simplicity to a direct threat. It may be only tangential to the larger problem of the Uhrwerkgerät, but it is something to directly strike out at. There is no tomorrow here. We just hit this mad machine hard and walk away.

I almost enjoy the run to Jericho. Oxford traffic prohibits any sort of rapid progress by car and so we handle domestic emergencies on foot.

We scrabble around a corner onto Jericho. Felicity didn't give us an exact address, but finding the ten foot tall robot wreaking wanton destruction isn't the trickiest bit of detective work I've ever done.

Hannah is the first to skid to a halt. I get the feeling she could have outrun me more completely than she has. I'm not sure why she didn't. Maybe survival instinct. I'm sure she'll be as satisfied as me to shoot something today, but the Uhrwerkmänn could cause serious bodily harm should it choose to get up close and personal.

Clyde and Tabitha arrive shortly after. They may have got here quicker, I suspect, if Clyde had held his tongue.

"—no need to worry, is all I'm saying," he finishes as they slide to a halt beside us.

Tabitha is clutching her new laptop to her chest. It has a matte black case. As she turns it protectively away from Clyde, putting her body between it and him, I see the streetlights catch on a pattern traced in a more reflective shade of midnight. A skull or a snake. I don't quite catch it before the light flees the laptop's surface.

"I'm just saying…" he continues. "Well, knowing me, probably not just saying anything. Wittering on about all sorts of things probably. Like now, actually, come to think of it. This is exactly the sort of thing I'm talking about. But I just mean to say, forgetting all the other blather, and I hope this doesn't come across as combative. Meant as a point of discussion certainly, but one that opens onto vistas of frank and respectful communication. But I just wanted to say, in a manner of speaking, that judging a chap based on one minor lapse of judgment, which I might add—well I *am* going to add—which happened during a fairly intense bout of combat. Fisticuffs and all sorts were involved, I assure you. Well, no need to assure you, you were there. You saw them. The fisticuffs themselves. Themself? No themselves. Both sound odd. But that's not what I'm getting at. An ancillary point at best. But it seems a bit harsh to judge me solely on the fate of one laptop given the depth and breadth of our relationship. And I have apologized. One momentary lapse."

Tabitha narrows her eyes. Like a shark before it tastes your tibia.

"Two lapses," she says and taps her stomach. A hard flat slap. One containing no compassion for any spark of life that nestles inside.

That actually shuts Clyde up. Which is helpful because it gives me a chance to say, "Maybe we should be focusing more on that."

I point. Their eyes follow my finger. They see.

The Uhrwerkmänn is in the middle of the street. Its bulk is picked out by streetlights. It is on all fours. It kicks and smashes at the road. An ugly spastic crawling.

"Gone!" it screams. A sound on the edge of legibility. A sound like a knife being sharpened in the back of its throat. Its colossal fist smashes into the tarmac, leaves a crater.

As satisfying as it will be to slap this thing personally, I do double check, "Any word from Kayla?"

Hannah just shrugs.

Tabitha pulls an earpiece from her pocket, jams it in her ear. "Kayla," she says. "Bothered to show up yet?"

She shakes her head at me.

"All right," I say, "we'll do this the slightly more painful way then." For the first time in a while things feel easy. Thoughts coming easily. "First we set up a containment zone. Enough people have seen this bloody thing already. We stop it from moving any closer to the town center. Tabitha and Clyde, you two get behind that thing. Clyde, you'll—"

"No."

Tabitha's refusal detonates the bridge beneath the train of my thoughts.

"What?" I manage.

"Not going with him." She doesn't even bother looking at Clyde.

I try to find the right expression to put on my face. Angry seems unlikely to work. And sympathetic is never an emotion that seems to survive contact with Tabitha's emotionally caustic hide. I go with some amalgamation of conciliatory and conspiratorial. "Look—" I start.

"Send him on his own. Probably impregnate it. Screw up its life. Patronize it until it self-destructs."

Clyde, who seemed as if he too was on the verge of opening his mouth, instead chooses to remain silent.

"Well," I say, "that doesn't seem to be an entirely likely scenario…"

"I've got this." She taps her earbud. "Don't need to be near him to give him information."

"Tabby." An unfortunate wheedling quality has crept into Clyde's voice. He knows better than me how disastrous that is. He cuts the plea short and settles for looking disconsolate instead.

I'm not the only one who's going to benefit from kicking robot *derrière*, I think.

"OK," I say. "Look, Clyde, you stay with me. Tabby and Hannah can go—"

"No." It's Hannah this time.

"Jesus," I say. "When the hell did this become a democracy?"

The Uhrwerkmänn lets out another cawing screeching, "Gone!" and scrambles a few yards down the street. I can see two kids leaning out of an upstairs window staring down at it. Wonder fills their eyes.

Hannah shakes her head. "Whatever. Just makes no bloody sense for me to be behind it. Because Clyde—he doesn't need back-up. He can shut off the street himself. Use some of his bloody magic to… I don't know, fuck with my head and poke the Uhrwerkmänn in its rusty arse or something. Then you and I are the shooters up front. It's going to take both of us to dissuade it from coming into town. Better yet, Clyde's in front and we're behind. That way he can push it away from the town center instead of toward it. We slow its retreat and do damage. Then you shove Tabitha up on the rooftops in case it tries to go that way. Or just for a good observation spot. Give her good view of the field of engagement so she can prep Clyde with the right spell." Another shake of the head. "Bloody obvious."

You know, it would be nice if someone didn't second guess me all the bloody time, as if I hadn't done this before.

"Look," I say, "how the hell do we just shove Tabitha up on the rooftops? Unless you brought a stepladder with you."

"Actually," Clyde says. "I do know a spell…"

Damn it. I mean, I know he's helping. It's just he isn't.

The Uhrwerkmänn saves me from recriminations. It plunges its fist into a shop front. Glass crashes. A burglar alarm wails. How are we still standing around talking about this?

"Just get behind the damn thing with Tabitha," I say. "It's ten foot bloody tall. I'm sure even Tabitha can shoot something that size."

"Don't have a gun," she says. "Would prefer rooftops."

I claw my fingers down my face.

"Fine," I say finally. "Get up on a roof. But Clyde is not bloody helping you. Clyde, punch that thing in the face. Hannah, get behind it."

There is hesitation. "Now!" I bellow.

Batteries fly into Clyde's hands. He palms them into his mouth.

Hannah and Tabitha are slower. Tabitha stares at the rooftops. "Well, how the hell…?" she says.

"I don't know!" I snap. "Maybe get behind the bloody thing like I bloody suggested."

The Uhrwerkmänn is suddenly backlit. Something coming up the street behind it. A truck perhaps. Red light fills the space, turning the robot into a manic, mashing silhouette.

"Gone!" it screams, dragging the sound out, prolonging the auditory agony. "Gooooooone!"

"Oh this is perfect," I mutter. Witnesses rear-ending an Uhrwerkmänn are exactly what I need. I yank out my pistol and empty a clip at the damned robot. I'm not sure how much damage I do, but it certainly feels good.

Beside me, Clyde does his thing. A spattering of nonsense syllables and something slams into the Uhrwerkmänn's drooling chin. It is rocked back, up onto two feet, and then back, sitting down on its arse, dazed. Clyde skids back along Jericho Street's bumpy tarmac, sneakers squealing in protest.

Behind the Uhrwerkmänn, the truck slams to a halt. I wait for it to flee. But it sits there.

And why the hell would a truck back up the street toward the insane Uhrwerkmänn? That doesn't seem sensible.

Oh no.

I almost expect it, but it doesn't make it any better. The massive shadow shape moving between the Uhrwerkmänn and the truck.

Oh shit.

"Friedrich's here!" I yell. "Engage! Engage!" I jam another magazine into my pistol, start charging, firing. And now would have been a really nice bloody time to have some people positioned behind that Uhrwerkmänn.

The back of the truck opens up. More silhouettes. And not one of them has the decency to be small.

The maddened Uhrwerkmänn manages to get out one more "Gooooone!" before its minimally more rational compatriots are upon it. There are at least four of them. They pin its arms and legs.

Then Friedrich is there as well. He plunges a fist toward his struggling victim's chest, flings a sheet of metal aside. His fist descends once more. Machinery follows, caught in the glare of streetlights. Dripping oil painted red by the brakelights of his truck.

I'm running, moving as fast as I can while still maintaining something that resembles an aim. I empty a second magazine into Friedrich's arse. He ignores me.

Damn it, I know what he's doing. This is the very definition of bad. Friedrich's followers heave on limbs. Metal screams, but the body starts to twist, reconfigure itself.

"Clyde!" I scream. "Something big!"

"*Ushtar mol koltar fal ectum bal melsith—*" Clyde's garbled words ring out in the street.

Friedrich wrenches on one more internal organ. Blue light starts to flood the street.

Shit and balls.

"*—bel telsin!*" Clyde screams.

Suddenly every streetlight goes out. The brakes on the truck die. Only the glowing blue light of the reconfigured Uhrwerkmänn… no, of the Uhrwerkgerät lights the scene.

Except, wait… there's a second blue glow in the street. Coming from the back of the truck. And in that thin light I see that the new Uhrwerkgerät isn't exactly the same as the old one. Volk was a teardrop of metal. This Uhrwerkmänn has become more of an arc. An arm or perhaps a leg is perpendicular to the rest of the body, pointing into the radius of the curve. And this isn't a new Uhrwerkgerät. It's a new component of the same one.

Two glows… Two components of one bomb…

Volk is in the back of that truck.

Further analysis is cut short by Clyde's spell roaring into full effect. Darkness is only the first of the absences to open up in the street before me. A sucking vacuum grabs at me, starts to drag me down the street faster and faster.

Friedrich reels, staggering back from the newly rendered component of the Uhrwerkgerät. I hear something crunch. And goddamn it, Clyde actually hurt him. This could still turn out to be a good goddamn day.

And then it really hits me. Yes, yes, this could be a damn fine day. Because if this Uhrwerkmänn is only a component of the whole then that means Friedrich isn't done. That's why Friedrich was kidnapping other Uhrwerkmänner. He needs them to finish building his bomb. To make it bigger. Friedrich's work still isn't done.

Which means there still might be hope.

"*Schnell!*" Friedrich yells. I'm close now. I can see the crumpled plate of armor on his left flank. The dragging tension of the spell lets up. I skid to a stop, take aim, searching for weak points.

I change where I'm aiming. Friedrich isn't the primary target. Those metal bastards holding the bomb are. I open fire. It's still not enough. They reach the truck, slam the new component of the Uhrwerkgerät into the old.

The blue light intensifies.

Clyde is howling mad nonsense behind me. That same dragging vacuum fills the air. It pulls me toward Friedrich. And I want to shout no, he's not the target. He's not what's important here. But it's already too late.

Because there's another crunch from Friedrich. Because another plate of armor is damaged, the edges are peeled back, more weak points exposed.

Because we have the monumental Uhrwerkmänn's attention now.

Grinding one fist into another, Friedrich turns and advances upon us.

49

In a James Bond movie this is the moment when I would do some truly epic shit. Probably shoot an Uhrwerkmänn in some minuscule weak spot, causing it and all the other robots to detonate in a cascading chain of explosions, while I surf a shining piece of wreckage down the street toward freedom.

Personally, though, I've always subscribed more to the Kurt Russell school of movie hi-jinks. And as absurd as many of his antics are, Kurt Russell is also a man who can recognize a sensible moment to turn and hoof it.

So I do that.

Possibly not a moment too soon. The sound of Friedrich's fist striking the spot where I just stood physically assaults me. Tarmac seems to quake beneath my feet. Gritty shrapnel smashes against my calves and thighs.

I hear the damaged plates of Friedrich's stomach grate as he straightens, prepares to launch another blow. Even if he misses with this one, I suspect I am unlikely to survive a third attempt. I need cover.

I scan the street. Hannah is the first thing I see. "Covering fire!" I yell, dashing left. I need a storefront, a restaurant. A door I can burst through.

"Negative!" I hear her yell as I retreat. "The Uhrwerkgerät!"

What the hell?

The whistle of Friedrich's fist past my ear is almost enough to turn my bowels to water. I see the outstretched fist in my peripheral vision for a moment, then I am running past it.

That was the second time.

Somewhere in the back of my head, I can hear a calm reasonable voice reminding me that if I die from something that isn't the Uhrwerkgerät then I'll cause the end of reality as we know it. That all those lives will be on my recently deceased conscience. I decide that I'll kick that voice's arse later, but right now it needs to take a ticket and wait its turn.

And then a door. A restaurant door. The clientele at the front tables leaving their costly meals and pressing up to the windows, trying to work out what the hell is going on out there.

The slight wrench of metal is all the warning I get.

The people in the restaurant see me coming at the last moment. A dull shape rocketing toward them through the glare of the restaurant's lights.

My leap sends me flying at the large plate glass window, head tucked down, arms above my head. Glass shatters unwillingly. The crack runs up and down the length of my spine, scrambling my head and scorching my tailbone.

I skid through glass. People scream. I feel my clothes and flesh tear. There isn't really time to care. I pick myself up, ignore the swaying in my stride. I raise my arm—

My gun... Where is my gun?

I see it lying in the glass shards, bend down, scoop it up. Restaurant-goers back away from me. People are shrieking. I am beyond being able to make work it all out. The only thing that matters is that Friedrich is out there.

I start shooting through the window I just smashed.

Another scream. This one from outside.

A moment later, Hannah crashes through the restaurant door.

"Jesus fuck!" she yells. "Did you even aim at anything?"

I force my eyes to focus on her.

"You were going after the Uhrwerkgerät," I say. My voice sounds slurred even to me.

"Couldn't get to it. Doubled back to save your stupid arse. And then you shot at me."

"At Friedrich," I correct.

Hannah pulls her suit jacket out to one side. A neat bullet hole punctures the front and back.

"Missed me by a fucking inch. You idiot."

"When I give an order and you don't obey it, I don't know where you are," I yell.

People are all around us, staring. This is not the time for arguments. I step away from Hannah and this madness. Step toward the night and the battle and the Uhrwerkgerät and everything we actually need to get done here.

Next to me a man, more adventurous than his fellow diners, has edged ahead of me, peering out into the street.

"Get back," I yell at him.

Too late.

The restaurant's remaining windows erupt as Friedrich backhands the entire façade.

The adventurous man flies into me. What is left of him at least. His bones have given way under the pressure of Friedrich's blow. The meat of him has pulped. I am smashed backwards by someone who now resembles a very large hamburger patty.

Revulsion rolls over me and I roll over the floor. Together we smash through tables, chairs, legs. My head rings.

I skid to a halt. Above me the world spins. I wait for it to come back into focus. When it does something is wrong.

I must be hallucinating. I am next to a table, looking up and Kayla is there. A spaghetti noodle is halfway into her mouth, dripping tomato sauce. A man is standing nearby, backed up against the wall, a look of pure terror on his face.

Hallucination-Kayla shakes her head.

"I should have feckin' known," she says.

50

I close my eyes. Reopen them. No, Kayla is still there.

"What the—" I manage before my lungs give up and decide to just gasp for a bit. Some distant part of my brain is registering that I am covered in quite a large volume of someone else's blood. The man standing behind Kayla looks like he wants to climb up the wall and hunker up near the ceiling just so he can get further away from me.

From the look on Kayla's face she is not overly pleased to see me.

I realize she is wearing the outfit she wore to the nightclub. The one that is form-fitting and skimpy. I can't quite work out what is happening.

"Do you feckers," Kayla says, biting savagely through her noodle strand, "have any feckin' clue how hard it is to assess someone as a feckin' potential sperm donor?"

This strand of questioning is not helping me get my bearings any faster. Screams are coming from the front of the restaurant; the sound of Friedrich removing important structural parts of the building's façade.

"No," I manage. My body is singing with pain.

"I have to have Tabitha hack the donor clinic's feckin' databases. I have to find someone local who isn't a feckin' genetic cesspool. I have to find him online, solicit a feckin' date out of him. And once

I've done that. Found an actual candidate to be the father to my feckin' child. Then you fecks..." She trails off. Overcome by bile, I think.

Behind her, the man trying to climb the walls has decided to share his horror at me with his horror at Kayla. She follows my gaze, sneers scorn at him. "Don't feckin' worry, pet. No way you were going to get any. Not sure how you made the donation in the first feckin' place. Thought you had to have some balls for that."

Another scream from the front of the building. The pop-pop-pop of Hannah's pistol. Shit. This probably wasn't the time to leave her alone up there.

I look to Kayla. There are many questions. Not the least of which revolves around the fact that she had Tabitha hack a fertility clinic's database. So many levels of wrong. But more important is my need to get in the fight now.

Unfortunately, due to the mild cranial scrambling of my most recent injuries, what actually comes out is, "How the hell do you even hide a sword in that outfit?"

Kayla closes her eyes. She seems to find my idiocy painful. "You don't," she finally spits. She reaches across the table, grabs a steak knife. "You make feckin' do."

51

Kayla launches herself across the room. I manage to get to my feet, scramble in her wake. The center of the room is almost clear of diners now. They press up against the walls, slowly creeping toward the back of the room. Survival instinct versus the paralysis of sheer terror.

The sensible response in other words.

I on the other hand move rapidly and in the wrong direction. I plant one foot on a chair, launch myself, crash down on a table. I leap from one to the next. Tablecloths skid beneath me. Cutlery flies. Crockery smashes.

Hannah is on her back at the front of the room. She's clutching her left shoulder, pistol lying discarded on the ground. Friedrich's arm is still reaching through the devastated front windows, scrabbling after her.

It reaches up above her. Ready to swat her into oblivion.

I aim my pistol.

Kayla beats me to it. She leaps almost a third of the length of the room. Her body arches back, arms raised above her head, steak knife clutched in both fists. I really hope it's one of those Japanese knives. The ones that make soda cans look like they're made of butter. Except this doesn't look like it's that classy a restaurant.

Kayla slams into Friedrich's hand. A red-headed battering ram.

She plunges the knife down, punching toward a seam in the metal, ripping, tearing.

Friedrich's swat is arrested. The bee-sting stab of Kayla's knife holding him still.

Abruptly he whips his hand back and forth, shaking it with improbable violence.

Kayla rides the bucking bronco of his fingers for about two seconds, which is at least one and a half seconds more than seems possible. Then she's flying toward one restaurant wall. She spins in midair, manages to get her feet beneath her. Then she is leaping away, somersaulting backwards, landing on her feet.

Friedrich's hand retreats. She flings the steak knife after it and I see it slam into the joint between two fingers even as she snatches up a second knife.

Then it's not only the hand pulling back. Friedrich steps away.

The bastard can be hurt.

The front of the restaurant is pure devastation, glass, and brick, and splintered tables. I land in the mess of it as Kayla pulls Hannah to her feet. Hannah grimaces, spitting curses. When she's finished she manages, "Bloody clipped my shoulder."

Kayla nods quietly, a look of surprising empathy on her face. Then she violently wrenches Hannah's arm up and back. Hannah screams. There is a pop that makes my stomach shudder.

Kayla nods. "Right as feckin' rain," she says.

Hannah is still gasping. But there's not really time to waste. "After him," I yell, pointing in the general direction of all things clockwork and brutal.

And then, just to make sure nothing can get any worse, Hannah and I manage to collide with each other as we go through the goddamn window.

I land hard, and mostly face down. Still I get the better of it. I collided with Hannah's injured shoulder.

She howls again. She manages to fit a lot of four-letter words into it.

"Oh God, are you all right?" Suddenly Clyde is there, running out of the burgeoning darkness. He comes to a halt beside Hannah. "Well I guess obviously not. The whole screaming thing. Bit of a giveaway, I suppose. Should be asking how I can help." He levers Hannah to her feet. "I mean, well, now I am helping. And you're back on your feet again, so that's good. No worse for wear, I bet. Made of tough stuff."

Why does he sound like some terrible TV dad version of himself?

Hannah steps away from him, starts down the street. I can hear the pounding of giant metallic feet and the revving of a truck engine. "Come on!" She sounds impatient. "They're getting away!"

I start after her. I've lost track of Kayla, but that probably only means she's ahead of us. Probably armed with a can opener this time.

"Oh!" Clyde says from behind us. "I can help!"

Even as I run, I brace myself. Clyde's help has not, historically, been as helpful as promised.

Hannah suddenly yells. She's running hard, despite still needing to hold her shoulder. But now her feet are pedalling wildly through thin air. She lifts up into the sky.

"What the bloody arse hell?" she yells. "Put me down!"

"But I'm lifting you onto the rooftops," Clyde calls from behind us.

I glance over my shoulder. Clyde's eyes are blazing sparks of white light in the night, casting illumination onto his upraised palms as he lifts them up. With each inch they ascend, Hannah gains another foot.

"You'll have tactical oversight," Clyde says. Then, again with that odd paternal smugness in his voice, "Plus you're injured and this will keep you out of harm's way."

"I will bloody shoot you in your bloody face if you don't put me bloody down this bloody minute!"

Hannah is actually aiming at him.

Jesus. This is so not the time…

"Do it." Tabitha's voice is flat as a judge's gavel landing.

"Don't do it!" I snap back. I don't think she will but better safe than sorry.

"But Tabby…"

The steady ascent of Clyde's hands falters. Hannah jerks wildly through the air. At least it's probably throwing her aim off.

In the background the truck's engines rev again. I can't hear Friedrich's footsteps any more.

"...I'm protecting her," Clyde continues. "I'm keeping her safe. Being responsible." He's talking with his hands now. Hannah whips back and forth through the air above my head. "I'm trying to show you..."

He pauses, trying to find the words. His hands pause with him. Hannah hangs into the air, about a foot above my head. The truck's lights blaze. The sound of it rolling into motion.

"Put her down, Clyde," I say, but he's lost in his confusion and misery.

"They're getting away with the pissing Uhrwerkgerät." Hannah's voice is full of frustration.

"Put her down!" I say again, trying to break through.

"You're being a stupid selfish idiot who's messing up the whole goddamn mission," Tabitha tells Clyde. It is less than helpful.

"I've got the shot."

In the chaos I almost miss Hannah's words. But then they catch me. In Clyde's moment of paralysis she's gained her equilibrium. Her pistol is gripped in both hands. One eye closed she sights down the barrel.

She's going to shoot it. Shoot the Uhrwerkgerät.

I'm not a demolitions expert, but I'm pretty sure nothing good happens when you do that. Hannah probably knows that too, but desperation has the better of her.

"No!" I yell. I launch myself into the air, snagging at her trailing foot.

I grab it, just as she fires. The shot explodes out into the night in a cloud of flame and cordite fumes. It lances through the intervening space.

It hits the Uhrwerkgerät.

And bounces away. The sound of the ricochet sings out in the night. A sharp clear sound, strangely sonorous in the space between the old stone houses that line Jericho Street.

I'm sure that will leave a mark, but it hasn't ruptured anything. The bomb isn't going to kill us all tonight.

And then, as the truck accelerates away, the night unspools before my eyes.

Oh God. It's happening again.

A future echo.

It's like the backdrop to a movie. As if the whole scene before us is some scene painted onto cloth. And someone has pulled the thread. And behind the world, behind the thin scrim of reality, is just the emptiness of space. A sucking rushing void. I see stars glinting, impossibly distant.

And this unreality is so much more real than the paper-thin buildings around me, this petty pretense of existence. This is absolute, implacable, unstoppable. It is everything we are not. And it undoes me.

The void in my vision becomes the void in my mind. Gaping lacuna of thoughts and emotions. The echo is eating me up, consuming the flickering flame of light and passion.

My face is bloody. Vessels rupturing around my eyes, my ears and nose. The blood covering my face, soaking my shirt. But it's so distant. Such an unnecessary concern. In the face of this. This absolute. This undeniable. This truth. This implacable, unstoppable future.

And then it is too much. It overwhelms me. I fall to my knees. I see Hannah lying face down in a pool of her own blood. I hear Clyde hitting the floor. Tabitha's voice moaning, "No, no, no, no, no, no," in the earbud in my ear.

And then the darkness consumes everything.

52

GOD KNOWS WHEN

When I come to, the pool of blood I lie in has started to congeal. For a moment I lie there, breathing shallowly, encased in my pain.

Friedrich is getting away. Taking the Uhrwerkgerät with him.

I have to get up.

I heave. The blood resists. Things I'd rather not rip do so anyway. I think I just left half my eyebrows behind on the asphalt. I grab for my gun.

But the truck is gone. Long, long gone. Police sirens are rushing to fill the space it has left.

The future echo was more powerful this time. Why?

Because we're getting closer to the point of origin. The ripples in the fabric of space and time getting larger as we approach the actual disturbance, each one rocking the boat of my existence to a greater and greater extent.

Because we're up shit creek, basically.

I look around. Clyde is lying on his back, still out. The front of his jacket is covered with blood. Tabitha is further away, curled up fetally in the light of a streetlamp. Kayla spread-eagled and shadowed fifty yards ahead of me. The glint of the steak knife still caught in her hand.

And Hannah. She sits a few yards from me, head in her hands and pressed between her knees.

"Are you OK?" I ask. I don't go to her. The gulf between us is too great.

She looks up. Her face is a horror show. Blood has seeped out from around her eyes, the lashes matted together, the whites bloodshot. It has flowed freely from her nose, painting a sad clown's carnival make-up around her lips. It has soaked her shirt, her trousers.

"Do I bloody look OK?"

I shake my head. "Not really, no."

"So why the bloody arse hell are you asking me?"

I actually think about that for a moment. "Because I'm the field lead. Because you're part of my team."

Her sardonic laugh is barely audible this time. A bubble of ironic mirth just managing to surface through the mire of… of whatever the hell it is that Hannah feels. Disappointment? Frustration? That can't be too far from the mark, I think.

"God," she shakes her head. "You are, by far, the worst agent I've ever come across. Ever. I mean, you are truly terrible." The laughter is stronger this time. "But you know what really gets me? Your crapness isn't even really the problem. I might be able to work with it eventually. I think I could get you to pay attention to me in the end. Learn some basic fieldwork. It would suck, but I've been undercover in Kandahar for six months before, I can do suck. What I can't do is bloody hopeless. Because it's not you. It's all of you. It's this whole dysfunctional shit show of an agency."

"The police are coming," I interject. "We should wake the others. Get out of here." I don't need to hear this. This is for Hannah really, not for me.

"Shut the fuck up," Hannah says. The first real hint of emotion beyond dull disappointment creeping into her voice. "I'm talking. And I really, really hope you actually listen, because it's about the last time I talk to you." She pushes her hands deep into her hair. "You're a disaster. I covered that. But what else would anyone expect you to be? You're a police detective who has never received a day of training in his life. Apparently none of you have. There is no attempt to educate, to immerse you. Just the hope that the skills you have are enough." She's becoming animated now, voice gaining decibels. "And if they aren't, well, shit, sorry, I guess we gambled the fate of the world on the wrong bloody group of idiots. Our bad. But at least there's no culpability because no one can complain about your total and utter failure when they're all fucking dead!"

Her cheeks are flushed now. "You want to know what the real problem is?" She finally releases her head long enough to shake it. "You don't, because you're banging her. I mean, Jesus." Now the head shaking has begun it seems it's here to stay. Behind us Clyde starts to stir. "I mean," Hannah continues, "don't even get me started on that. Actually, no. Let me get started. I mean first off it means she should be discharged immediately. You are bloody military intelligence. That sort of thing is *not* OK. And if you want an example of why it's not you've got Clyde and Tabitha right there in front of you as a walking, talking, bloody real life instructional bloody video. Jesus. You let them screw basically in front of you in Nepal, and then are all shocked when the situation blows up and leads to us actually creating the bomb you're trying to stop from being..." She trails off and just froths for a moment. "That was in the field too. That was your chance to stop things. Because, shit, Felicity isn't going to do it. Because she goddamn sucks. Kayla is the goddamn best of you and she in all seriousness suggested holding a cage match of potential suitors so she could weed out weak seed. She showed me a location she had picked out for the bloody octagon. That is the *best* you have to offer. Remember that. Please. If you remember nothing else of me. Remember that. This stupid bloody rant, that is likely bouncing off your remarkably thick skull."

If I remember nothing else of her? I try to puzzle that out. Apparently not even the blood caked on my cheeks is enough to hide that. It just fuels Hannah's frustration.

"I am putting in for a bloody transfer. The paperwork will take a week or two. But I am out of here. Part of your team, Wallace? Fuck no."

I stare at her. Her bloody visage staring back at me.

"But," I say. "The Uhrwerkgerät. The end of the world." I can't believe... Except I can. Of course I can believe it. This has been as inevitable as everything else. And it doesn't matter. In a short-term world of course it doesn't matter but...

"If I'm going to stop the end of the world," Tabitha interrupts me, "I'm sure as hell not going to do it working with you wankers."

And that's it really. There is no arguing with that. If I even really wanted to argue. This, in many ways, is the desired result. But, Jesus, Felicity is going to kill me.

53

FELICITY'S OFFICE

"You're asking me to kill you, aren't you? This is some warped suicide attempt. That's it, right?"

There are not many times a man gets to use the word apoplectic in his life. This is one. Felicity is apoplectic.

She also seems set on getting an answer.

"No." I barely whisper the word.

"You're sure?" she barks. "Absolutely, one hundred percent certain that all this imminent death thing hasn't gotten to you and you want me to right here, right now rip your balls off and beat you to death with them?"

I nod, almost imperceptibly. "Yeah. I'm pretty sure."

We've had fights before, of course. We're like any other couple. And the nature of our jobs has put us through the fire on more than one occasion. But, usually after the event, I like to think that those are the sorts of fires that forge us into a stronger whole. This feels more like the flames of hell checking in to see how long it will take them to melt us to oblivion.

"So why in the name of all that is good and holy on this goddamn planet did you not say a goddamn word when she told you she was quitting?"

"She," I start, but I'm still at the barely audible level. And if I want to be able to ever meet Felicity's eye again after today that is not how to go forward from here. "She did not give the impression," I say, louder this time, "that she would be entirely amenable to a protracted plea for her to stay."

"Oh really? Rrrrrreally?" She rolls the word about, tasting it. I don't think she likes it very much. "And I wonder why that would be? Perhaps it would be that contrary to every piece of advice I've given you, contrary to every promise you have made to me, despite me spelling out to you the very high price that would be paid, you have continually and actively gone out of your way to antagonize and alienate her? Could that possibly be the goddamn fucking reason, Arthur?"

She punctuates this by flinging a folder at me. Papers explode out, littering the air around me. By the time it strikes much of its heft has gone.

I feel numb. Too beaten up and exhausted to deal with this. Because it doesn't matter. Nothing matters.

"It's not going to happen," I say. "You shouldn't worry."

For a moment I think Felicity's eyes are actually going to explode out of her head and rip through me like shells fired from a rather attractive cannon.

"Shouldn't..." she manages.

"It will take weeks," I say. "We don't have that long."

For a moment, nothing. Just a long, dead silence stretching out, out—

Another folder follows the first. Another. Another. Felicity is yelling something but I can't make it out. The room is full of flying paper. Analog static, filling the room. Manilla edges strike me again and again. I retreat down the office's narrow length.

"You stay goddamn there!" Felicty's bellow will be obeyed. My feet know that before my head even registers what she said. I stand there. A piece of paper is stuck to a patch of blood on my shirt that hasn't completely dried yet.

"It's pointless," I say to her. "Those were your words."

Felicity looks very tired then. She flings a final folder at me, but it's half-hearted. It doesn't even make it all the way to me—

skids to a halt an inch shy of my feet.

"It probably is," she says. She's closer to my volume now. "But doesn't that make this time even more important? Doesn't that mean that we should be striving even harder now than we ever have before? I mean this, this…" She stares at me. "This pathetic capitulation, Arthur. What the hell is that?"

I could tell her, I think. *Tell her everything that Hannah said.* But what good would it really do to tell her that she is really Hannah's biggest complaint? How would that make this situation any better?

"This was my life's work, Arthur," Felicity says. She sweeps an arm up and around, pointing to the ceiling, the walls, the whole damn edifice. "This place. This was everything I strived for. And we were so close to being something bigger, something better. It could still have happened, before the end. Whatever end that is. But now it can't. Because of you."

And OK, I'll admit that hurts. My eyes sting. She's done it. She's cut through all the apathy, and the shock, and the physical goddamn pain, and she's found a way to hurt me.

Because I love her. And I've hurt her so much.

"My first anniversary present." Felicity shakes her head. "Well done, Arthur. You've really outdone yourself."

There has to be something. There must be. Something I can do to try and take the hurt away from her.

"The only thing," I say, "I want to strive for, when everything is ending, is you."

Felicity's face cracks. Disappointment bursting its dams, spilling into sorrow, scorn, anger, and maybe worst of all, love.

"Well you fucked that up, didn't you?"

As bare and bald a statement as there can be.

"Didn't even try to move in with me. Didn't even pack your boxes."

The accusations mount one upon the other. I can't deny a single one.

"You know what, Arthur? I don't think I want you to move in anymore. I don't want to see you at my apartment even for a moment. Not this version of you."

"I—" I start, not really knowing what sentence follows from there.

"Get out, Arthur."

Felicity stands there. Implacable. Her words… inevitable. I get out.

54

FAR TOO MANY DRINKS LATER

Honestly I couldn't even tell you how I got to London.

Wait...

Is this London?

Jazz billows and blooms about me. A saxophone melody sidles through my consciousness. A lilting bass line insinuates itself between the glasses scattered on the table in front of me. Pint glasses rattle against whiskey tumblers, make an awkward syncopation.

Around me, couples lean together, whisper beneath the melody. Groups of students wear fedoras and try to look as if they invented the style. A few herds of businessmen, ties loosened, let their eyes rove. And then there's the odd lonely, useless bastard: a man with his eyes closed in rapture at the notes; another reading a book and sipping from the same whiskey glass he's been nursing all night.

So what stereotype does that make me? The lonely drunk, drowning his sorrows in alcohol? Jesus, I'm even a washed-up detective.

The cocktail menu slips from my hand, lands on the floor. I curse, bend to pick it up. The room heaves in front of my eyes. I decide against it.

As a teenager, I used to dream of coming to places like this. Now, almost twenty years later, here I am. Almost twenty years and in that time I have personally helped save the world from imminent destruction three times. Me. And what's it gotten me? An inability to enjoy this bloody music is what.

I go for another slug of booze but all the glasses are empty. I appear to have been rather enthusiastic in my consumption. I swirl a hand above my head. Eventually a waiter interprets the signal, comes over. There is a look of resignation on his face.

"Another one of…" I survey the empty glasses. "That one," I say pointing to a rather interesting looking glass.

"That one?" the waiter says. He sounds like he wants to say more. To hell with him. I am a young buck once more. Hell, thirties isn't old. It's a long downhill slope from here.

Well, it would be if the world wasn't utterly doomed…

I start to giggle at that. The waiter seems to take that as a cue to leave. Probably not a terrible idea on his part.

I close my eyes, try to sink into the music, to remember what it was that teenage version of myself wanted to do when he got here.

I seem to remember my younger self imagining friends being here. I think he imagined better jazz than this as well… Something less Latin and with sharper, harsher edges.

Maybe the problem is in the specificity of my dreams. They're twenty years out of date. All I really want is to recapture that moment when the future was bright and bold and too big to even hold. Before all the decisions closed it down to one stupid pinprick of obsolescence. Fuck all that.

I stand up, unsteady. My chair falls over, lands next to the cocktail menu. I attempt to rescue it from the floor, rethink the idea as my stomach sloshes. A waiter says he has it, hands me a drink and a bill.

"How bloody much?" I ask him

He tells me, and then points out that a gratuity is not included in the bill.

Jesus, no wonder I never came here as a teenager.

The cold of the London night bites. I check the time on my phone. There don't seem to be enough numbers. Well, piss on it. I hail a cab. By the time the third one stops, I've learned to sit down and strap in before I open my mouth.

"A club," I slur at the driver. "A night club. With dancing. And music." I think hard. "And booze. And young people."

It strikes me that calling them "young people," is probably not something young people call themselves. "Cool people," I correct myself. Yes. That sounds right.

The cabby says something incomprehensibly cockney. It sounds disparaging. I laugh. Show bloody him. What it'll show, I'm not completely sure.

Still we arrive. I can feel a dance beat shaking the pavement. Yes. This is more like it. I remember the Park End in Oxford. I enjoyed that. Yes. Dancing and drink and… fun.

The queue is short. The bouncer is dubious. Possibly more so when I tell him, "I'm a young buck," as defiantly as I am able.

"You going to be trouble?" he asks me.

"No," I tell him. "I'm going to be awesome."

This doesn't seem to entirely reassure him. Still he lets me in with a solid pat on the back and the words, "Go on, you plonker."

For a moment, on the cusp of the club, I question the wisdom of my decision-making. A sweaty, jumping beast of a crowd oscillates before me. I'm pretty sure I'm the oldest person here by a clear ten years. Even the bartenders look like I should card them.

And then, unbidden, I think of Felicity. No matter how deep I drown those thoughts they keep bubbling up. And I don't want to think of Felicity. I don't want to think at all. I want to be a young buck. Stuck in the eternal *now*. No future, no past, no goddamn worries. Just this, here, now.

I fling myself at the crowd.

In retrospect that phrase probably shouldn't be used literally. Still, I dust myself off, and stagger away before confusion can change to accusation.

The music batters at me. I have another drink, close my eyes, try to stop thinking. The music slowly morphs, becomes less of an assault, more of a channel, pushing me, pulling me. My body starts to find a way to move.

I fall off my bar stool. I'd forgotten I was on that.

More dusting off. I am distantly aware of pain in… pretty much everywhere actually. I order another drink, head to the dance floor.

I spin. The room spins. I abandon sense. I dance. I fucking dance. And screw the kids staring at me. I am a buck, maybe not young, but, but, but...

I think I'm going to throw up.

It turns out I'm right.

The bouncer comes to collect me from the dance floor.

"Not what I'd call awesome," I hear him tell me, but the world has gone sideways. I laugh at that but then I throw up again. The bouncer isn't so friendly after that. What's more it turns out he's terrible at bouncing. I land on the floor and just lie there.

Finally I manage to gather up enough dignity to stagger into an alleyway and heave out the last of the alcohol in privacy. My stomach clenches. An ugly mess of beer, regret, and defeat spills onto the floor and stains my shoes.

55

IN THE HORRIFIC LIGHT OF DAY

Oh God. Oh God why? What in the name of hell was I thinking? Acting half my age last night, and now I feel twice it this morning. I didn't arrest the forward march of time, I bloody accelerated it.

On the plus side, if the world decided to end today, I'm not sure I'd be all that sad.

My apartment feels as small and cramped as my skull. There is too much shit here. The contents of my fridge horrify me. The roiling in my stomach convinces me breakfast is something made for braver men on better days. I make coffee instead and swallow more ibuprofen than the packaging recommends. My stomach doesn't thank me for that.

When I reach the office the pounding in my skull has at least decreased from full-on siege bombardment with heavy artillery to more of a running battle. If I could just find a small corner to curl up in, that would probably be fine. I'll let Tabitha and Clyde find Friedrich today. With any luck he'll need another day or two to complete the Uhrwerkgerät. We'll have some time to...

To...

I should have stayed in bed.

The elevator rumbles down into the bowels of MI37. My

stomach rumbles right back. I take deep breaths before I step out into the corridor. Fluorescent lights flicker. Long corridors full of long empty offices stretch out on either side.

Soon, they'll all be empty, I suppose.

Will MI6 be so bad? Probably. I wonder if I'll go back to police work.

I catch myself. I'm still thinking about the future. Like it's a tick I can't quite shake.

But it's what I know. And nihilism hasn't exactly been working out for me. Maybe I've been playing this all wrong. I should be going full Dylan Thomas. Raging against the dying of the light.

Would anger be better?

I'm too hungover for this. And as that realization hits, Felicity's head appears from out of a door. Conference room B. At the sight, my stomach lurches yet again. It's not got much to do with last night's excesses this time.

"If you could step in, Arthur," she says, emotions in tight control, "we're having a full staff meeting."

She's formal. That's all I can get. Not hostile. But far from warm.

I should have stayed in bed.

We're all there, in the conference room. All as dysfunctional as ever. Tabitha and Clyde, Kayla and Hannah.

The only remaining seats are close to Felicity. I prop myself up against the back wall, between Clyde and Kayla. As far from her as it is possible to be.

She stands at the front of the room. She looks perfect of course. Not a strand of hair out of place. Not a single crease in her suit that isn't meant to be there. Immaculate.

There is no smile to acknowledge us. No nod of the head. She just starts.

"I'll keep this brief," she says. "There's not much to tell really. Two pieces of information. That's it. Firstly, I will not sugar coat this. MI37 as it currently exists is over. It's to be rolled into MI6. You will all still—"

But she doesn't get any further.

"What the feck?" Kayla is the loudest, the most outraged, on her feet. I half expect to see her drawing her sword.

"The fuck it is." Flat-out rejection from Tabitha.

"Wait... are you sure? I mean, not that I'm calling you into question. Well... I mean, I guess, by the whole effort of this vocalization I am. But very much routed in my own disbelief. My own issues involved here..." Clyde wanders into the conversational fray.

"Huh," is all Hannah can muster.

And as for me. Well, I knew, didn't I? I maybe didn't expect it to happen so soon. But... It was coming. Or perhaps it still is. Maybe the word isn't official yet and this is just fatalism on Felicity's part. Maybe this is a death she's made her peace with. The death of dreams, of ambition.

Felicity waits until the chaos quietens. Clyde's voice fading last of all.

"...anything I can do." He glances around. "Oh. Sorry."

Felicity surveys us. She still hasn't looked directly at me. I'm not sure I can really blame her.

"Secondly," Felicity says, "effective immediately I shall be taking a leave of absence. I need a damn vacation. Arthur will be in charge until my return."

And then she looks at me. Right then. Right there. Reap what you have sown. And before I even have a chance to respond, to even process, she's out the door. She's gone.

And yes, I really should have stayed in bed.

56

In different circumstances, I might take time to be surprised that so few people can make so much noise.

"What the feck?"

"The fuck he is."

"Wow, that is... well, I mean first off congratulations to Arthur. Sure he's ready for the responsibility. Never want to be seen to suggest otherwise, but that's quite the double whammy."

"Huh."

And me too. I find my voice.

"No." This can't be how things are playing out. This can't be the solution. This can't be Felicity Shaw giving up on me and her dreams. Even though it is, I still deny it. But I'm not loud enough to be heard over the general hubbub.

Kayla has kicked her chair back with enough violence that its legs crumple slightly as it hits the wall. She strides to the door after Felicity.

"No," I say again.

Maybe she hears me, misinterprets the negative. Maybe she just thinks better about where to direct her invective. But she stops shy of the door handle and wheels on me.

"You," she hisses at me. And suddenly I am the focus of attention in the room. "This is your feckin' fault."

This is how the rabbit feels when the headlights strike. Kayla and I have been at peace for a fair while now, but I get the distinct impression that someone just turned the friends switch to off.

"I…" I manage. "I didn't…" My eyes seek out Hannah. And this is her fault. She is the one who quit. She's the one who doomed us. She's the one who never understood us. Who never even tried. She's the one who—

But when I find her she's looking at me not with victory, not with malicious humor, not even with dull-eyed indifference. She looks at me, and it looks like sympathy.

So I look away.

"I didn't know," I protest. "I had no idea."

"You're fucking her!" Tabitha snaps. "How the fuck you expect us to buy that?"

"I was out last night," I protest. The thunder of my hangover is surely loud enough that they can hear it as proof as well. "Something must have happened."

Oh God. I know exactly what happened. But half truths might just save me from being kebabbed by Kayla.

"I'm sure it's going to be all right." Clyde is on his feet, moving around the table. Not toward me, but toward Tabitha. "I mean, not that I've suddenly gained any sort of prophetic powers. Though that would be incredibly handy and really help me prepare for events like this. Though, if myths are anything to go by, foresight isn't the most wonderful gift. All sorts of trade-offs. That poor Cassandra girl, for example. Very great pity, that. So, maybe better off all told. But I suppose that's what I'm talking about. I mean, we don't know for sure we'll be worse off with Arthur in charge." He puts a reassuring hand on Tabitha's shoulder.

"Get the fuck off me," she snaps, and pulls away.

"You don't know what you're feckin' talking about," Kayla says to Clyde.

"I don't think we need to assume that I'm happy about this situation," I point out. "My girlfriend just went on a vacation she'd never mentioned to me."

I don't think anyone is willing to buy the sympathy angle.

"Great." Tabitha throws up her hands. "The future. Just hand it to Friedrich. Might as well set off the Uhrwerkgerät now. Nice knowing you all." She looks directly at Clyde. "Well, not all of you."

Ouch.

"Oh come on," I say.

"It's not as bleak as that, Tabby," Clyde protests. "You know. Chin up. Think of England. Sun never setting, all that. And we've found ways before. Quite a successful team, you and I."

"Oh give it a fucking rest." Tabitha is out of her chair now too. "Just give it a fucking rest."

For a moment an unfamiliar emotion seems to ripple across Clyde's face. Exasperation? Anger even? It's so unexpected I can't quite pick it out.

"I was going back to MI6 so I could avoid all this crap." Hannah is the only one left in her chair.

"—this a permanent deal?" Kayla is asking no one in particular. "He in charge for the long term? At MI6?" She points at me. "Is she out?" She thumbs off in the direction Felicity went.

"We just need to rally together." Clyde tries again. He even reaches out for Tabitha one more time. She pulls away.

"Clyde's right," I say. "We've surely got through worse things than my temporary leadership." Actually, I'm not sure that's true...

"Got through worse things with Felicity in charge," Tabitha points out.

"Sure, let's argue about this," says Hannah. "This is more important than trying to stop the Uhrwerkmänner."

"Oh shut up, you fucking quitter," Tabitha spits at her.

"Oh be quiet," I snap at Tabitha. "For once she's bloody right." There, that's payment for the sympathetic look. Now we can go back to mutual animosity.

"Look, Arthur," Clyde says, leaping to Tabitha's defense. "I don't think that tone is maybe the most helpful—"

"Will you give it a fucking rest!" Tabitha wheels on Clyde. "I don't need you. Don't want your help. Your defense. You. Are. Unwanted."

And for a moment silence actually fills the room.

And there it is again. That look. And it really is something close to anger. Frustration maybe? Hurt?

But this time it doesn't flicker away. This time it explodes.

57

"Dear God, I've fucking had it!"

Clyde stands at the end of the conference table, clenches his fists, and loses his shit. And that shuts us up. That makes us all take a collective step back. Because the uncomfortable truth is that, while he is a very decent affable chap, Clyde has the power to drop this whole building on us if he wants to.

He looks away. "I'm s—" he starts, then cuts himself off. "No, you know what, I'm not actually sorry. You know. I probably should be, but I'm not." He looks directly at Tabitha. The rest of us might as well not even exist.

"I try, Tabby," he says. "I try, and I try, and I try. And I understand that you are upset, and hurt, and though you would never admit it, you are very afraid. The future is a terrifying place, and you carry it in your stomach, and it is precious to you, and it scares you, and you do not want to be scared, and you do not feel ready, and you blame me for every conflicted emotion, for every moment of dread that this thing has brought to you. I truly do understand, Tabby. I understand all of it. Because, as I have stated many times before... and actually maybe that's the problem. Maybe I say it too much so that it no longer registers. It's just some tic, and I have devalued the words. I don't know. If so, then that is most definitely and squarely on me. But this is all to say, in fact I was saying it, the exact words. I understand. And I try to make allowances because I do understand. And I love you."

Then he puts his hand to his head. "But Jesus fucking Christ. Could you give it a rest for a moment. Could you at least attempt to show that under the layers of hurt and blame there is a spark of compassion in you? And I know you display your affection differently. I know you. Intimately. In fact so intimately that one might consider that perhaps some degree of allowance might be allowed on your part rather than this total, cataclysmic shut down of affection. Because that is *inappropriate*."

The way he says the last word makes it sound as if it is the word one should use to describe the act of smearing excrement on church walls.

"And I have made allowances. And maybe that's a terribly patronizing thing to say. Maybe you want no allowances. Maybe if you hurt, you feel you should be allowed to express yourself in any which way you please. And maybe screaming 'shut up' was controlling and rude of me. But simply know that if your chosen form of expression is repeatedly shitting on me from as great a height as possible then that act is not without consequences. Your acts exist in a social context. Or more specifically, to be more concrete about the example, it is getting righteously on my tits. I am upset. I am angry. I am at the end of my fucking tether."

He sweeps his arm around the room. "All this. Everything that happened in the last ten minutes. And my world is destroyed. Everything I thought I fought for is gone. And I reach out to you. Not unselfishly. I will admit that. It would be a dishonest moment to say that I wasn't hoping for some comfort in return for trying to provide it. And again, it's perhaps wrong to expect anything from someone. It's not a right. But maybe it's common social courtesy. Part of that whole social contract. The bit where we aren't total selfish arses to each other. The bit that you seem to want to flagrantly ignore vis-à-vis me and everything that involves me.

"I tried, Tabby. I tried." He is almost imploring. Even in his anger I think he's looking for something, some forgiveness. But either Tabitha is too caught off guard, or too backed into a corner to give it to him. "But I can't fucking take it any more. I just can't.

I'm swearing even. It's all falling apart. I am. And I can't take it. I can't. I can't. I can't."

His argument is falling apart. His words collapsing in on each other. And it feels like this is it. The moment where the storm will pass, or whirl into a tornado and rip us all apart.

I search Clyde's fingers for batteries. Thank God he's not holding any.

Maybe he feels the moment too, and is neither willing to let the moment simply blow out, but nor does he want to inflict any more damage than he already has.

"I can't take it," he says one more time, then bolts for the door, and the path out that Felicity has forged.

58

We all stew in that one for a moment. Tabitha somehow is the first to speak.

"Prick," she says. But there is no feeling to it, no heart.

Hannah is shaking her head. "Bringing all this to MI6," she says. "Whoop-dee-bloody-doo."

"Hannah," Kayla says, her voice very low, "I love you like the sister I never feckin' had, but now is not a good time to for you to keep talking."

Hannah looks over her shoulder at Kayla, still standing by the door. Her expression is incredulous. "Really?" She gives brief voice to her patented bitter laugh. "I mean, you're a smart sensible woman. You don't look at this and think, we put *these* bloody people in charge of saving the world?"

Kayla steps toward her. "This is my feckin' family," she says. Her voice is still low. Not the good, tender sort of low either. The sort of low that creeps around with a silent blade and an attitude problem.

"This is a military bloody organization!" Hannah looks aghast at Kayla, as if she's been betrayed.

"No." Kayla shakes her head. "This is different. That's why you've never feckin' liked this, because you haven't figured that out. We are messy, and stupid, and we feck it up a whole feck of a lot. But we work. We feckin' do. You told me that first day how feckin' excited you were when you read our case files. We do good feckin' work."

Hannah shakes her head. "And I honestly have no bloody clue how."

"My whole feckin' point!" Kayla shouts. She sounds as exasperated as any of us now. "If you had a feckin' clue then you wouldn't be such a feckin' quitter."

"A quitter?" Hannah weighs that one. "A quitter." She tastes it. Nods. "And you look around and see no possible place for improvement."

Kayla snorts. "That's all I feckin' see," she says, which seems like a poor sort of way to defend us. "But," Kayla says, "when you fix something, you get it back to how it's meant to work. You don't go about making it into something new." She gives Hannah a sad look. "There's good here if only you'd see it."

Hannah doesn't bend for a moment. "Well, I don't see it," she says. "Probably had too much shit thrown at me to see clearly."

There's a lovely image.

And how long do we have before Hannah walks out too? Or Kayla? Or both? We're spiraling out of control. We've even managed to piss off Clyde. Which is pretty bloody difficult. And now I am the one who has to stop it. Because Felicity's gone.

Jesus. Felicity's gone.

How the hell do I deal with that? I mean, are we over? She and I? Is she thinking our over-ness over?

I close my eyes for a moment. Shut out the world. Kayla's right. There was a good time here once. Something to preserve. To get back to. I just need a little hope to ground me. Something. Anything.

The idea that I can make Felicity smile one more time before the end. That has to be enough.

"This has to wait," I say.

"—people win the lottery three times in a row," Hannah is saying. "Some people write reports in such a way as to make themselves—"

"This *has to wait*," I say again. Louder, with some actual force this time.

"You call Felicity Shaw a feckin' liar?" Kayla takes a step forward.

"Grow up, Kayla." This from Tabitha.

"Shut up!" I yell. "All of you!" I rub my head. Everyone needs to start doing this in whispers. Even me. Especially me.

"This is obviously," I say, "a bad time. The worst time maybe. This is shit creek. And we just had our oars confiscated, but I'm not going to watch you guys saw a fucking hole in the bottom of the boat."

Three women full of antipathy look at me. I'm glad my back is literally up against the wall. It limits my ability to bail on this.

"Let me be clear," I say. "We're fucked. The world is fucked. We are out of options. The opportunity for victory is basically nonexistent."

I survey my limited audience. Even I have to admit, for pep talks, this is not an auspicious opening.

I do my best to crack a smile.

"Come on," I say, "this is our comfort zone. This is where we come through. Let's do this."

59

There is a moment of underwhelmed silence. "Let's do this?" Tabitha says. "That's your big moment?"

"Well," I say, "I thought there was an outside chance that would be more productive than just discussing how shit we are."

"Prick." Still, there's more warmth to that word than there has been to many of the others Tabitha has said this morning.

"Look," I say, gambling on honesty, "I'm not going to say I don't think this is futile. I do. But my head is not in a good place right now. It hasn't been for a while. I don't think any of ours are. We just have to do our jobs. Keep pushing, feeling the place where this case breaks."

I risk looking them in their eyes. And Tabitha is at least willing to put her hurt and rage into the fight. Kayla... well, she's pretty much always willing to murder someone. And Hannah. Hannah is a soldier in the end. A professional. And even if she's put in for her transfer, she'll do the work.

"All right then," I say, "so where the hell are we?"

"Shite creek," Kayla says immediately. "You feckin' mentioned."

"Anybody else?" I ask. It's hard not to feel the time pressure on this one.

Hannah shrugs.

"What about the Uhrwerkgerät?" I ask. "That looked...

incomplete last night. Like they still had work to do. That's got to buy us some kind of window."

Tabitha shuffles her feet in a decidedly un-Tabitha-like way. "Maybe not so much of one. Or, well…" She grimaces. She normally lets Clyde do the uncertainty part of discussions. Already she's struggling in his absence. She tries to rally. "First thing. Don't know how big the Uhrwerkgerät has to be. So, completion could be very close. Or may have the resources to complete it already. Maybe just use their own people for it." She shrugs. Another echo of Clyde. But I let it pass.

"And second?" I ask her. I have a distinct impression I'm going to like second even less than I liked first.

"A theory. Rough edges. Holes. Wanted to talk to Clyde about it." She looks to the closed door. And I notice her hand moves unconsciously to her stomach when she does it. "To do with the Uhrwerkgerät. With future echoes. They seem to come when we're interacting with it. But… need to work it out. Going to be slow. One person doing the work of two." She looks to the door again. "Prick."

"To do with us interacting with it?" This sounds interesting. It sounds like an angle to work. Maybe there's a way to sabotage it. Not that sabotaging a magical bomb sounds like the sort of thing you get to walk away from with all your fingers intact, but given the array of options, I'll take a few lost digits. "Care to elaborate?" I ask.

"No."

"What if I asked really nicely?" I suggest.

"What if I'd already told you, need more time?"

Potentially, negotiating with the brick wall would have gone better.

"Fine then," I say. There's only so much time remaining to us and I don't want to waste it in pointless arguments with Tabitha. "Do what you need to do. See if you can find us an angle. We'll look for others."

"Whatever." Tabitha leaves the room in a billow of black fabric and bad attitude. Still, at least she's not heading for the office exit at speed.

OK, that's one thing down. "What else?" I stare at Kayla and Hannah. They give me nothing.

What would Felicity do?

Walk away? Give up? Is that what she's done? Is this cowardice? Capitulation?

Was Hannah right?

I don't have time for that. I need to focus. Keep track of the right questions. How do I stop this? How the hell do I get Clyde back?

What would Felicity do?

And then a thought, a memory. I point to Kayla. "Remember what Felicity said," I say.

"I'm not doing feckin' relationship counselling," Kayla says.

"Yeah, but if you did," Hannah says, "you should film that stuff and put it on TV."

Kayla points at her, without looking. "Still having feckin' issues with you."

"This is not a relationship moment," I say. "I have neither the time nor the mental capacity for those. This," I say, "is about reality magic. That's the basis of this bomb, right? And Felicity said it. We have an in with someone who knows reality magic far more intimately than anyone else."

"Oh feck no," says Kayla.

Hannah actually looks interested. "Who?" she asks.

"I'm sorry, Kayla," I say.

"I'm not feckin' doing it." Kayla shakes her head violently. "She won't come anyway. It's a waste of feckin' time. She's a shite."

"Who?" Hannah asks again.

I ignore Hannah, keep focused on Kayla. "You'll ask her," I say, "because you know we have to. Because we're out of options."

"Feck." Kayla shakes her head.

"Who the bloody hell are we talking about?" Hannah is finally out of her chair, has finally shaken off her lethargy.

"Ephie," I say, finally addressing Hannah. "Kayla's daughter."

Hannah's eyebrows shoot up. "Her daughter?" She takes a moment to digest that. To digest Kayla's pent-up fury. To assess the phrase, "She's a shite."

Hannah sits back. "So," she says, "the world's still fucked then."

60

Kayla looks at me, face tight with suppressed emotion. She is trying so hard to make sadness and fear look like anger she almost manages it. But the despair is there at the corners of her eyes.

"She won't come," Kayla says. But she knows that line of defense will be about as useful as it was last time. She still has to call. That's what we're down to. Last hopes and long shots.

I do my best to smile with sympathy. "Have you ever considered," I say, "that she might be more predisposed to come if you stopped calling her a shite "

"Have you ever considered how far I might shove my sword up your arse if you keep on giving me unsolicited parenting advice?"

I nod. I actually have. "She might come," I say. "It might work."

Kayla snorts derision. But only silence follows. She shakes her head, closes her eyes, breathes deeply.

She's delaying, but if my teenage step-daughter had the power to turn me into protozoic green sludge, I might be nervous too.

"Ephie," Kayla calls out, all preamble done. "Hey, Ephie, I'd like a word." It's as if she's calling to someone on the other side of a street.

For a moment, nothing. And then for a moment longer still.

"See," Kayla says. "I feckin'—"

And then, as if simply to spite her mother, Ephie appears.

There is no puff of smoke, no ripple, no sweeping wave of ether. She simply isn't in the room, and then she is. Like two strips of film spliced awkwardly together.

She looks much the same as when we last saw her. An unseasonably flimsy looking black tanktop. Big hoop earrings. An unreasonably short skirt. Her skinny legs stick out, very pale.

But... oh, goddamn it... there is one change. Though maybe, just maybe, Kayla will recognize this moment for what it is. Maybe she will control herself.

"Is that a feckin' tattoo?" Kayla screeches.

Oh crap.

It obviously is a tattoo. An anarchists' "A" in a circle scrawled jaggedly on her bare left shoulder.

"Oh Jesus." Ephie rolls her eyes. "Now you bloody care."

"The feck were you thinking?" Kayla's voice stays in the upper registers.

"Oh come on," I say. A little prayer to the gods of absurdity. "Can't we just once..."

"Oh," Ephie rolls her eyes, "I was totally thinking about you and your reaction, because my every decision revolves around you and how it will affect you."

"Oh good," Hannah mutters to herself. "So this plan is going about as well as I would have thought."

Kayla is still spluttering. Ephie turns to Hannah, a look of mild curiosity on her face. "Who are you?" she asks.

"Oh," Hannah flaps a hand. "Don't worry about me. I'm barely here. I quit."

Ephie smiles. A perfect teenage know-it-all smirk. "So you're the smart one?"

Kayla finds her voice. "Do you even know what that symbol means?" she says. "You're stuck with that for life."

The ink on Ephie's shoulder wriggles, twists, reforms, becomes a clenched fist that slowly extends its middle finger to wave solemnly in the air.

It's a small, casual display of power, but it's almost more effective for that. Young though she may be, Ephie handles authority like a pro.

Kayla, however, has never been entirely comfortable with authority. "Oh, threats is it?" she says, nonchalant. "What are you going to do? Rearrange the limbs of the woman who raised you? Who rescued you? Who gave you care and shelter?"

"You dragged us around half of England so you could kill monsters!" Ephie yells. "That's not a fucking childhood."

Kayla's sword is out again. She advances on Ephie. That really is a terrible instinct to bring to parenting.

"Of course." Ephie throws up her hands. "I can't threaten you, but you can threaten me."

"Oh piss off," says Kayla. "Like this could really feckin' hurt you."

Ephie shrugs. "You're right."

Kayla's sword abruptly droops, the metal becoming plastic soft. Then she holds a bunch of flowers. Then a giant rubber tentacle. Then a flapping, gasping herring. The images slam together. The same film-splice abruptness of Ephie's appearance. Next Kayla is holding a feather duster. Ephie seems to like that reality. She freezes the flow of images.

Kayla looks up. There's a fire in her eyes. "Oh, you think because you took my sword away I'm less likely to give you a thrashing."

She flicks out with the duster, lightning fast. There's a crack as its plastic spine lands on Ephie's arm.

"Ow!" she yells.

Suddenly Kayla isn't holding a duster but something small, furry, and rabid. It spits and scrabbles at Kayla, back legs clawing against her arm. Kayla flings it away toward the wall and a sudden death.

Before it gets the chance to become a bloody stain, it's a sword again, burying itself in plasterboard up to the hilt.

"You know," Hannah says to no one in particular, "smart one isn't really that much of a compliment in this place."

And, goddamn it, that's it. "Stop it!" I yell. "Just bloody stop it. God! This bickering bullshit is why we're in this goddamn mess in the first place!"

Shock tactics seem to have bought me a second or two. Even Hannah seems to be paying attention. I shove forward, away from the wall, past Ephie, jamming myself between her and her adoptive mother.

"There's a bomb," I say. "A great big bloody reality-destroying bomb. And I don't know how much of reality you control, but this could take out more than you might want to lose. You and all of your tribe. Your dominion diminished. Maybe gone entirely. Nowhere left for you to exist. This affects *you*. So we need your help. We desperately need your help. To figure this out. To stop this.

"Look," I implore Ephie. "If you don't help us, people here will die. I will die, Ephie. Me. Felicity. Tabitha. Clyde. Your mom. Hannah here. All of us. The people you grew up with. Please. You can help us. You can save us, maybe. Save so many people. We just need some information."

Ephie looks at me. And it's not the good sort of looking. Scorn fills her eyes.

"Save you?" she asks. "Because that's what I am? Some handy personal deity? Kayla looked after me for a bit so now whenever reality doesn't go your way I'm meant to bend everything to help you all. Bend *everything*. I mean screw the collateral damage. Not that you even really know what you're asking.

"I'm a Dreamer," she snaps. "My responsibilities extend so far beyond what you perceive it's laughable. Everything in this room. You, and you, and you." She points. She makes it clear this is not a general "you." "You are so petty," she finishes.

"You try and replace me," she points at Kayla. "And you can't even ask for my help. If I was like you, I'd bend you out of existence. Stick you in some backwater reality where you can wallow in your own spite. But I don't do that, because I have priorities and responsibilities. And you're too small to register on either list."

"You," she points at me, "so paralyzed by your fear of death you're unwilling to do anything more than cravenly beg for some sort of second chance." At my confusion she rolls her eyes. "Yeah, I bloody watch. I pay attention. Because you were all there. You were family. Were. Past tense. So now all of you, even you," she smiles at Hannah, "can go fuck yourselves."

And with that, she's gone.

61

It is like the aftermath of a storm. Standing, waiting. Wondering if some tree has been shaken loose of its roots, will topple and fall, crushing all in its path.

Mostly I stare at Kayla. If looks could kill, they'd have dropped her on Hiroshima. Then she slowly lets the muscles slacken.

"Feckin' told you," she says.

I claw gently at my cheeks, and bite my tongue. Because it's done now. We fired the long shot and missed the target. That's all there is to it. Further recriminations will only get me turned into an Arthur Wallace-shaped kebab.

And, honestly, I think I have a little sympathy for Kayla's position after all that. Bloody teenagers.

"All right. All right," I say, trying to swallow my disappointment and move on. Trying to bring some semblance of clear-headed plan to the surface.

But in the end, we don't have leads so much as we have a tattered pile of frayed ends. "We're in the same place," I say. "We still need to know more about the Uhrwerkmänner. About Friedrich. The devil is in the details." I think aloud in the hopes someone else will jump in when they're good and ready. "Tabitha is looking at the papers we got from Nepal. So that leaves two sources. Whatever we didn't have time to look at in Lang's underground hidey-hole in London and the Uhrwerkmänner themselves."

"Don't think they're feeling overly chatty right now," Hannah points out.

"Which is why," I say, the next steps clicking their heels in my head to show they're ready now, "you are going to take your winning personality to London to retrieve anything you think might be interesting from Lang's papers."

"Messenger duty?" She sounds incredulous.

"While Kayla and myself go to the Uhrwerkmänner in Sheffield and charm and cajole them in equal parts until they tell us something useful." I nod. "They know more than they're sharing." I say it like it's a fact and not a prayer.

Hannah purses her lips.

"Come on," I say, "let's hear the better plan. You've only got a little while to get these off your chest."

There's cynicism in Hannah's eyes. "When you say a little time, are you saying it because of my transfer, or because your fuck-ups are going to end the world?"

"You're one of us too, right now," I say. "These are your fuck-ups as much as mine."

Hannah stares at me for a moment. I expect hostility, but it's something more subtle than that. I wish I knew what.

"London then," she says after a moment.

"London," I say.

"Whatever." A moment later Kayla and I are alone in the room.

TEN MINUTES LATER. KAYLA'S CAR

"You drive." Kayla tosses her keys to me as we approach her car. I manage to get a hand up before they break my nose.

To describe the silence as tense would be a little like describing the Uhrwerkmänner as giant mechanical robots designed by the German, Joseph Lang. It would be describing it perfectly.

As we pull out into traffic I feel I need to break the silence before it breaks me. "We have to do something about Clyde," I say. "Talk him back down. I can—"

"Shh," Kayla hisses at me.

I glance over. She has her mobile held to her ear. "Yes," she says, her voice far softer than I've ever heard it before, the harsh edges of her accent become gentle curves. "Doctor Merrigold please." A pause. "Yes, I'll hold."

God, is Kayla going to make a booty call while I'm in the car with her? Though some old-fashioned part of me is impressed that she's hooking up with a doctor at least.

The traffic nudges forward, disgorging us into a faster moving road—cars eager to escape Oxford's maze of streets.

"Hello," Kayla says, pauses. "Yes, I've thought it over and I looked at the files you've given me." Another pause. "Yes, I found a candidate I like. A very impressive selection. Thank you." Another pause. Then a laugh. Soft and sweet. And genuine, which is what really blows me away. "Yes. Next week sometime? Tuesday sounds fantastic." She hangs up. After a moment she catches me looking.

"Feckin' what?"

"Who—" I start.

"Feckin' personal business," she snaps.

I shrug, still mindful that my pre-emptive death could trigger a whole end-of-the-world type of scenario. We escape the gravity of Oxford's roads.

"Sperm bank," Kayla says suddenly. I almost crash into an oncoming Vauxhall.

"What?" I manage.

"On the phone earlier," she says. "It were the sperm bank. I've picked one to baste my belly."

Well there's a lovely turn of phrase. I try to avoid the image it wants to summon. "Oh," I say. I think I even manage to keep my voice level. Then an additional concern hits me. "Not the guy from the restaurant?" I say. My voice is less steady this time.

Kayla snorts. "No, not that wee one. Pretty, but far too feckin' interested in organic composting for me to want to carry on his feckin' seed for another generation."

Personally, I think organic composting sounds like a noble goal, but maybe it's not a good opening gambit on a first date. There again, given the state of my love life maybe I'm not one to give advice.

I try to think of more substantive commentary, mindful of Kayla's threat regarding her sword and my posterior.

I settle for a good, meaningful, "You're sure about this?"

"I just rang the fecker and made the appointment."

I nod. There is that, but…

"And you saw her," Kayla says more quietly, maybe sensing my unspoken objection. "She's not interested in me any more. She's off to bigger, better things. I'm wee, and mortal, and… old. She's a Dreamer. What can I offer her that infinite possibilities can't?" She suddenly sounds very defeated. But then she rallies. "I'm going to start over. My child. Something I have a stake in. That has a stake in me. I'm taking charge of my future. Some bullshit like that anyway." She looks at me, and the belligerent fire is back in her eye. "Feck this preordained destiny bullshit, I feckin' say. I'm captain of my own feckin' ship. And it's a pirate ship, and we drink rum every night, and piss on our enemies. And anyone who wants to steer the feckin' tiller is going to have to go through feckin' me." There is a swagger in these last words, a tricky thing to pull off in a car passenger seat, but she pulls it off.

"Aye captain." I even throw her a salute.

"You making feckin' fun of me, Agent feckin' Wallace?"

"Not for a moment." And it's the truth too.

"But you're still going to be a miserable bastard about all this? This going-to-die shite?"

I shrug. "I'm here, aren't I?" I say. "I'm still fighting."

"That because you still have a spark of feckin' hope in you, or just because you don't know what the feck else to do with yourself?"

Kayla's words are as sharp as her sword sometimes.

"Can it be both?" I ask.

She shrugs. "I don't feckin' know. I don't watch that morning television shite. I just pick something and feckin' do it. All this waffle bullshit isn't worth the time."

I smile. I should spend more time hanging out with Kayla, I think. Even if it might require body armor for me to feel totally safe.

"Amen to that," I say, and we drive on.

62

A RATHER SHITTY LOOKING INDUSTRIAL WASTELAND ON THE EDGE OF SHEFFIELD

The abandoned factory is much as I remember it. Kind of shitty. Kayla and I traipse through. She has her sword drawn and tosses it from hand to hand, watching the blade catch the light.

"No offense," I say, "but I do wish Clyde hadn't run off so he could be here still."

"Feckin' supportive," Kayla says.

"You know what I mean," I say. "He's good for when we go up against people twice our size."

Kayla sniffs, still mock-offended. I chew my lip. Reassuring chats with Kayla are never particularly reassuring.

"He'll calm down," I say, so at least one of us is doing the inspiring-confidence thing. "He'll come back."

"Before or after this apocalypse shite you're so busy crapping your pants over?"

I am saved from needing to explain the difference between the apocalypse and reality popping like a wayward soap bubble by an unexpected sight. Unfortunately it's not a good unexpected sight. Rather, it's the vast chunk of rusting machinery that hid the entrance to the Uhrwerkmänner's tunnels flung aside like a child's plaything.

The massive hulk of machinery lies on its side, looking more deflated than steel ever should look. I am reminded of a horseshoe crab turned on its back, the sense that somehow all this is beneath its dignity.

The gash in the floor lies exposed.

My eyebrows furrow in concern. "Is it just me," I ask, "or did they seem quite particular about keeping that hidden last time we were here?"

"Like grannies fussing over wee porcelain feckin' figures, they were." Kayla unsheathes her sword.

I hold up my hand. For a moment we just stand, still and silent.

"Is someone doing construction work down there?" I ask.

"Well," Kayla shrugs, "it's either that, or you know, having feckin' discussed at length how Friedrich needs to use his kin for spare feckin' parts to build this giant feckin' bomb that has you knotting your panties into a bunch the size of Westminster Cathedral, it could be him kicking the ever-living shite out of the folk we've come to see." She shrugs. "One or the other."

"I was really hoping you were going to say construction work." But I'm already moving.

"Hold up," says Kayla behind me. "You bring a sword?"

I shake my head. Kayla looks exasperated.

"You're better with a sword," she points out.

This is actually true. Except, "I get to be a lot further away from the giant murderous machines with a gun," I say.

"You get to do shite all feckin' damage with a wee pop shooter. You got anything less than a feckin' rocket launcher in your pocket then it's a waste of feckin' time."

Sadly that is true.

Kayla sees me hesitate, and paces toward the hulk of rusting machinery so fast she blurs slightly. She reaches into the tangled mess of it, rips out something, tosses it to me. I catch it on reflex. A heavy steel rod, about an inch in diameter and three feet long. It's been sheared off something and the last foot of the metal spends its time becoming a wicked point.

"Try that," she says. "Actually be feckin' effective for a bit."

"You fuss like my mum," I tell her.

Kayla nods. "Then your mum's a feckin' badass. Let's go."

63

My feet slap on hard unrelenting rock. Kayla's are a distant thrum. The sound of combat rises like a storm racing across a plain toward me. Assuming it's raining autowrecks at least.

I plunge into the tunnel leading down to the Uhrwerkmänner's shanty-cave. My feet skid down the steps. Somewhere at the back of my head my sense of self-preservation gives up yelling, puts up its feet, and goes on a coffee break.

The stairs open up onto utter chaos. Machine pounds machine. There is no delicacy, no holding back. They simply fling themselves at each other. They fling each other at each other. This is the no-holds-barred UFC championship version of anarchy. Gobs of flaming oil fly back and forth across the room. There is the rattle of something that must be incredibly similar to heavy artillery. The buzz of a saw screaming through steel. The baritone crunch of steel on steel. Sparks flying like rain before a hurricane. Screams and howls that I cannot be sure don't come from unhinged minds.

An Uhrwerkmänn advances through the crowd. It's marching straight forward while its torso blurs in three hundred and sixty degree arcs. Its arms are extended and in its fists it clenches bundles of jagged rebar that jut between bronze knuckles. A robot wanders within range and loses a substantial portion of its torso in a spray of oil and sparks. Flame licks the room like a lover.

Some sort of shot passes through another Uhrwerkmänn's head, shredding gears. One robot puts its fist through the weakened armor plating of another and it lodges there. The Uhrwerkmänn limps around using its spasming opponent as a makeshift battering ram, dealing titanic damage to anyone and everyone around it.

It's too much to take in. A vast bricolage of deranged violence. The sort of ecstasy of destruction that would make Hieronymous Bosch all hot beneath the collar.

I fling myself at it. For a moment I just give into the madness, the fear, the frustration. For a moment I just don't care. It's almost impossible to tell one side from the other, so I pick one that looks better cared for than the others and spear it in the calf.

Something has punctured the metal. My sharpened steel rod finds the nick like a key slotting into a lock and then violently fucking with it. I wrench left, right, swirl the rod about, feel things giving way. The Uhrwerkmänn staggers a step, drags me with it. I gain my feet for a second, rip the rod free. As the Uhrwerkmänn stumbles to the floor two more leap on it, start pounding away.

I whirl. Adrenaline calls to me, corrals me. I leap up onto another shiny-looking robot, hands clamping onto the back of its thigh. I brace my feet against the knee joint, find something important-looking jutting from its lower back, and proceed to level it off in a shower of sparks. The Uhrwerkmänn jerks, almost throws me clear. To stabilize myself, I go ahead and stab it in its exposed spine. That seems to suffice.

I jump free as it falls. I even twirl the rod around my fingers as I land. Kayla is right. I am better with a sword. There is a tactile quality to this violence that gets something dull and barbaric chanting in my gut.

I lunge at another machine, jab-jab-jabbing with the blade of my makeshift sword. I slam it against armor until I feel something give. I lever sideways. Flame gouts out of the hole I tear. I stumble back as the Uhrwerkmänn stomps away bleeding fire.

Another of the crazed bastards registers my presence, comes crashing after me. Its feet rise, fall, make the ground shake as it tries to pound me into the dirt. My steel rod suddenly feels a little more toothpick-like than I'd really like it to.

Still, one of the nice things about being half the size of every other combatant on a crowded battlefield is that it does mean there's a lot of cover. Admittedly most of that cover is involved in a life-or-death struggle and has a tendency to thrash about a lot, but I'll take what I can get right now.

I duck between the legs of one of the Uhrwerkmänner and hear my pursuer go crashing into it. I keep moving before one or both of them take it into their head to collapse on top of me.

I take a moment, try to get my bearings. The effort is truncated by an Uhrwerkmänn's head landing next to my feet. Kayla follows shortly after it.

"What are you waiting for?" she asks me. She's not even out of breath. She flicks her fringe from obscuring one eye to obscuring the other. "Let's go get that one."

She points at the largest of the visible Uhrwerkmänner, a beast about two-thirds the height of Friedrich. Fighting near one wall he gleams silver among all the muck and rust.

"That one?" I check. "He's huge."

"That's why it's the most fun." She darts toward him.

Fun. Not exactly the word I would have gone for. Suicidal seems a more suitable replacement.

And yet, I'm following in Kayla's wake. Adrenaline screams its battle cry into my veins. The heft of the steel rod feels good in my hand.

I see Kayla, already fifty yards ahead of me, launch herself into the air, a sword-pointed arrow flying toward the Uhrwerkmänn's torso. It catches sight of her almost too late, twists. She scores a hit on its shoulder, glances off, up and away, but she bends at the waist, like she's hinged there, and her feet slam into its head. The angle of her flight abruptly changes by ninety degrees. She whips around its head, curling her body, her sword completing a circle of torso, leg, and steel that spins around its head scoring deep gashes in the armor plates.

The Uhrwerkmänn claws at her with a hand. She twists but he snags her, flings her away.

She's back on her feet when I get there, ready to launch.

She goes high and I go low. I hear her blade strike steel but then my own dance of death distracts me. My rod wedges in a knee joint and I'm dragged along as it stumbles back under Kayla's ferocious onslaught.

It stops and I slam into the leg. Still I hang on, dragging, pivoting, searching for leverage. I brace my feet against what passes for its shin, heave. Something gives beneath my body weight. A spray of black fluid. A stumbling step. The knee gives, and my feet hit the ground.

I wrench my rod free as the Uhrwerkmänn comes down. The point glistens in the flickering firelight of the battle. I upend it, shove it up with all my might.

The point snags in a crack in the tumbling torso. Whether it's a natural seam or one Kayla hacked into its body I don't know. I don't have time to find out. I dance back, out of the reach of descending death, and watch as the thing's bulk drives the rod to the floor and then deep into its chest cavity like a nail coming home. The Uhrwerkmänn twitches once, twice, lies still.

Kayla slides off its back, lands, follows my gaze to where the tip of the rod is still visible poking from a crack in its chest.

"Fine," she says. "We'll call that one feckin' fifty-fifty all right. You were lucky."

"This is a competition?" Kayla's enthusiasm for violence never quite sits right with me.

A roar cuts off her answer. The felled Uhrwerkmänn spasms once more. It lurches up onto its hands and knees, scrabbling toward us. A flailing arm swats at us, close enough that even as I jump back I feel the wind of it sweep across my face. I land awkwardly, half-sprawl.

Kayla lands like a cat, looks down at me. "Not feckin' dead yet. Game's still on." And then she's off, bounding toward it, sword held high.

It swipes at her once; she rolls; a second time; she leaps, lands on its elbow for a fraction of a second, hits its back. Her sword spears down. She buries it to the hilt in the Uhrwerkmänn's back.

She's adopting my tactic, I realize, trying to spear its inner workings. I'll take some time to be proud of that later. Right now, I decide to worry about the way my weapon is stuck in its midriff with no way for me to retrieve it.

Around us, Uhrwerkmänner roar and bellow. Something massive crashes to the floor not far behind me. Rogue shots boom overhead, stitch a series of craters in the cavern's wall. Cracks spider out around them.

What is this place? What is it buried under? And how bloody sturdy is it?

Kayla stabs into the Uhrwerkmänn's back again. It roars out a howl of grating metal, flings itself upwards. Kayla scrabbles for purchase, fails to find it and goes down. I scrabble for my pistol. With Kayla out of the firing line I open up at the hole I've punched in its chest. The armor is weak there, I know. And I get more than ricochets. I see ragged holes open up.

Bellowing, almost screaming, the Uhrwerkmänn stands. In defiance of my onslaught, in defiance of its knee, which buckles sickeningly under its weight, but which does not give.

I keep firing, empty my magazine, reload and keep on.

Behind it I see Kayla stand. In the shadow of the curving cavern wall, the Uhrwerkmänner have dumped their trash. Mashed cardboard and wood chips are matted in her hair. She flicks something greasy and sodden from the blade of her sword.

Another magazine down. The Uhrwerkmänn lunges toward me.

Fire arcs overhead. Another crater, high above us this time. Dust and concrete chips rain down on us.

I reload.

Kayla lunges, slashing at the back of the Uhrwerkmänn's legs. It screams again.

Adrenaline makes my hands shake. Screw grouping my shots at any particular weak point. Bullet holes pepper the chest of the Uhrwerkmänn. If Kayla was sensible she'd duck. But, hell, if she was sensible she'd never have been recruited to MI37. Maybe that's the problem with Hannah. She's just too sane for this job.

Time would cure her of that. If we had any.

God, what am I doing here? Risking my life here? When I know what that means?

But it's too late. I can feel the end of my clip coming. Five shots left. Four. Three.

A bullet hole opens up in the Uhrwerkmänn's head.

Its roar abruptly shuts off. It gapes, soundlessly. I swear I can even hear Kayla grunting as she hacks at the legs, somehow audible over the scream of battle around me.

The Uhrwerkmänn steps backwards. Kayla dances out of the way. It takes another stumbling step. The last sporadic jerks of life as gravity takes hold. It slams into the cavern wall. The largest crater so far. Collapses. Dead.

I stand beside Kayla. We watch it sag. Finally she nods. "Feckin' fine then. Sixty-forty yours."

Flame explodes overhead. We both duck, heat roiling over us. A ceiling of flame.

Something massive and flaming lands in the lap of the Uhrwerkmänn we just killed. Maybe one of his kin. It's so ruined I can't tell. Flames obscure our kill.

I think of the bullet holes, the ruined knee, the vast quantity of oil leaking from that bastard.

I am throwing myself at Kayla, screaming "DOWN!" as it detonates.

Too slow again.

The shockwave punches me. Like being slapped by God. We fly through the air. A tangle of legs, and arms, and yells of "Get the feck off me."

My landing is bony, but softer than expected. Probably because it's on top of Kayla. It saves me a number of broken ribs, but earns me a backhand that'll leave me a bruise I'll still be seeing next month.

"Ow," I say to her when I sit up, as pointedly as I can manage.

"Not over yet." She points.

There is a charred ruin where the Uhrwerkmänn used to be. Behind it a black circle, blast marks radiating out like a sun shown in negative.

And cracks.

Great big, spreading cracks. Wider, and wider, and wider. Joining the craters of the guns like some catastrophic dot-to-dot puzzle, the solution to which is several tons of concrete pouring down on my head.

"Run!" I yell just in case Kayla has become completely brain dead in the half second since she pointed out the collapse to me, and then I get on with following my own advice.

I get further with this than I did with avoiding the exploding Uhrwerkmänn, though admittedly, it's not very far.

I have a good three paces between me and my starting place when the walls start to roar. A deep bass grunt of collapsing rock. Sound that becomes the world, that becomes physical substance I am running through, the air vibrating so much it fights my passage.

Rocks and boulders bounce past me. I'm screaming something I can't hear or understand. Waiting for the rocky rearrangement of my body from 3D idiot to 2D bloody smear.

A fist of concrete zooms past me with enough speed to punch through one robot's chest cavity. He dies in a glistening burst of gears and bronze spindles. To my right a boulder the size of Felicity's minivan casually crushes a pair of Uhrwerkmänner still locked in combat, oblivious to the oncoming death. It carries on unimpeded, takes out a crawling Uhrwerkmänn that's missing everything from the waist down, comes to rest as the gravemarker for another group of three. Around it, other boulders provide variations on the theme.

After the rocks comes the cloud. Thick, gray, boiling, slowing me as I hack and cough. It rises, fills the cavern. I can't see more than a few yards, a yard, I just plain can't see. I am running in total blackness. A blackness I can feel, gritty and cloying, staining my skin and lungs. I cough harder, but I keep running. Keep pushing myself, until I hit my limit like a wall. My knees buckle, my arms flail, no strength left in them. The floor comes up to meet me.

64

Deep underground, something like dawn comes. It is gradual at first, nothing more than a realization that pitch black has become dark gray. Then the gray lightens. Shadows begin to move, size and distance still only vague suggestions, and then suddenly I am in defined known space. The lizard brain rejoices; another night survived.

Except this space is in complete chaos. Uhrwerkmänner stumble looking for... friends, limbs, purpose? I never really understood these robots and I still don't.

I sit up, the last dregs of adrenaline still swilling in my system. I feel exhausted and stupid. And yet, beneath that some fundamental tension has unknotted slightly. We came, we saw, we kicked something's arse at last. I'll take that, I suppose.

I cough, spit out a wadge of brown phlegm.

"Tasty." Kayla slaps me on the back, knocks another spray of brown out of me. "Gonna be tasting that for a feckin' week." For some reason she smiles when she says this. Her teeth are white in her gray-stained face.

"Now, why did we even feckin' come here again?" Kayla asks. "I honestly don't remember." She's grinning.

She's right. We're here for a reason. And it wasn't to beat on anyone. It wasn't to work through my ridiculous issues. "We came for answers," I say.

"Right." Kayla nods, sheathes her sword. "So who do—"

"You!"

The single word cuts in. A lightning strike of accusation, rage, and humorless German inflection.

"We talk to Hermann," I say to Kayla.

And then he is upon us.

"This... This..." He spits the word out, as if trying to clear it from the cloying mess of the air. One of his arms is still mangled from our last encounter with Friedrich here. He sweeps his good one around the space, trying to convey the enormity of the destruction. "You did this," he manages through his sputtering rage.

"Yeah," Kayla nods. "We were forty-nine heavily feckin' armed Uhrwerkmänner who came in here and attacked you and set off a whole bunch of high-explosive bullshit. That was totally us."

Wait, Kayla actually counted the number of combatants on one side? Or did she make that number up?

"We walked into the middle of this," I try to say, while Hermann is still busy dealing with his rage issues. "We couldn't abandon you. Of course we helped."

I have no real idea if we helped or not, but it seems a good idea to suggest we did.

"I told you never to come back. Never."

A crowd of Uhrwerkmänner are gathering about us now. I may have underestimated how unwelcome we'd be. Why did Lang have to build the bastards so big?

Kayla beckons to Hermann. "I've taken down bigger fecks than you. Want a feckin' turn?"

Well that's not helping...

I step between Kayla and Hermann. Wait until his attention is on me. All their attention.

I sweep my arm around, echo his movement. "This is why we're here."

"I—" Hermann starts, but I cut him off.

"Not to cause it. Because this is just the beginning. Friedrich needs to build the Uhrwerkgerät bigger. And he's going to use you to do it. He's not going to use his own people. He's going to use you. He's going to kill you. Before your minds can rot away. He's

going to come in and take you and make you part of his bomb.
And he can call that living forever, or he can call it evolution, but
you and I both know it by its real name: murder."

I turn. A performer in the round, trying to address them all.
"Look," I say, "I know MI37 fucked up. I get that. But we were
fighting for you when we did. And we haven't stopped. We're still
going. Except we need your help. If we're going to finish this fight,
we're going to need someone on our side. Friedrich's forces are too
big, and too much for us. We can't even find them."

This doesn't exactly sound like me selling our expertise, I
realize. Time to change tack.

"But you can," I say. "It's within your power. With us. Together.
A whole that's greater than the sum of its parts. A gestalt. That's
a German concept, right? You get that. We could be that. Together
we find him. Together we stop him."

Hermann hulks before me. And I almost think he's going to
pulp me right there and then.

"So we can do what?" It's another of the Uhrwerkmänner, not
Hermann. Someone in the ring surrounding him and us. "Risk our
lives so we can go mad and die?"

It's a fair question, I suppose. Bit defeatist for my tastes.

"You were built to conquer this world," I say. "To be the
ultimate army. But you saw the hand that guided you was evil.
And you stood up and refused to do simply as you were told. You
chose to fight evil. You chose to matter."

"We ran away," says another voice. "We were hunted until we
found a hiding spot they could not."

Man, these guys really aren't into the whole optimism thing at all.

"Look around you," I say. Giant metallic corpses litter the
room. "You fought back today. You won some of these fights."

I decide not to push that point too hard. The ring of
Uhrwerkmänner looks decidedly thinner than last time we were
here. "You can beat these bastards. You can fulfill the promise of
your rebellion against Lang."

For a mercy, nobody takes the opportunity to tell me how
useless they all are. I seize the moment, march toward one corpse,
swing myself up to stand on its chest.

"You started this fight seventy years ago," I say. "You thought it was over, but Friedrich's here for round two." I survey them all. "But you can finish him. You can end Lang's poisonous legacy. You can prove you are... Hey, wait a minute, what's that?"

OK, not my most rabble-rousing finish. Except maybe I just saw something more important than an army. Maybe I just saw the answer I came here for.

I stare closer. The way the Uhrwerkmänn is designed... It's not exactly a utility belt, more a string of boxes and compartments at its waist. But jutting from one small metal box—it looks exactly like the desk ornament we rescued from Lang's office in Summertown. A dull black oblong with a staggered grooves running down its side.

I bend, pluck it from the Uhrwerkmänn, oblivious to my audience. I stare at it. More than a desk ornament. A reality key. It unlocked a pocket universe. And is this the same as the one we found? It looks the same...

I jump down off the Uhrwerkmänn, hustle toward another corpse.

"Where are you going?" I hear Hermann spit from behind me. "Come back here."

Funny, I could have sworn he was trying to get rid of me a moment ago. Anyway, I have bigger concerns than Hermann right now. What the hell is one of Friedrich's men doing with a reality key? Is that how they're getting about? Or hiding? Is that his secret?

I reach the next Uhrwerkmänn. There's nothing at its waist. No compartments at all. Then I remember Hermann stowing Lang's notebooks in his leg. Their storage compartments aren't always in plain sight. I start banging panels while Hermann harangues me from a distance. He seems unsure if he should chase me out or demand I come back to him. A panel pops open. I reach into the compartment.

"So," Kayla walks up to me, "is this the part where I realize you've lost your feckin' mind, club you over the back of the head, and drag you off for the straight jacket and the little padded cell?"

I pull out a second reality key from the Uhrwerkmänn's storage compartment.

"No," I tell her, "this is the part where we start worrying."

65

"To be totally feckin' honest with you, Arthur," Kayla says, "I'm a wee bit feckin' far past starting to worry. It's more a way of feckin' life, truth be told and all."

"Worry more," I tell her.

"You keep this sort of encouragement up," she tells me, "I might start to agree with Hannah about what a feckin' shite field lead you are."

Oh God… Hannah… Oh no.

"You will listen to me!" Hermann screams across the room. He stamps toward me. "You will—"

"No," I cut him off. "You will listen to me. Friedrich just came here and raided you for spare parts. He stole your family from you. Because he's going to use them to make his bomb." I wave the reality keys at him. "And no thanks to you, I think I finally know where."

"Wait," Kayla says. "You do?"

And deep underground, in the cloying smoke, massive robotic figures hazed by still-billowing dirt ringed around me, I do suddenly see very clearly.

"London," I say. "Lang's pocket reality. Because they're all carrying the keys to get in."

Kayla gets to the next step quicker than I did.

"You feckin' sent Hannah there."

"I know."

Hermann seems nonplussed by all of this. He stares back and forth between the pair of us. "You…" he starts, less certain this time.

"No, you." I'm sick of Hermann and his bickering. "This is it," I say. "Unless this is an especially great day for porcine aviation fanatics, Friedrich just finished up amassing all the pieces he needs for his apocalyptic jigsaw puzzle. And now he's hiding in a pocket reality in London sorting the corners from the edge pieces."

I sometimes wonder if metaphors are not my strong point…

"I'm going there now. To save my team. To try and save the goddamn world. To do anything and everything I can, no matter how small and meaningless it may end up being. If you are even an echo of the people you used to be, the people you were trying to preserve, then you will come with me. Or you can sit on your hands and diddle yourselves. Quite frankly, I no longer care."

And with that I turn on my heel and march away.

A moment later Kayla is at my elbow. "Not exactly General feckin' Patton, are you?"

I shrug. "General Patton probably didn't ever head into a fight that the universe had promised him he was pre-destined to die in."

Because there's no doubt in my mind now. These are the moments the future echoes foretold. This is the day. This shitty, hungover day. Today I die.

On the plus side, Kayla doesn't have a pithy comeback to that one.

66

I let Kayla drive. Her reflexes are better suited for the speeds we're going to need to hit. And I need to make phone calls.

First up is Hannah. I need her to get the hell away from the London Underground. If I'm right, I just sent her wandering into a death trap, and while she's not exactly my BFF, we're still several notches of antipathy away from me wanting robots to tear her limb from limb.

She doesn't answer. Which, to be fair, is a reasonable reaction given our working relationship. Still, frustration has me flinging my cellphone into the footwell. "You call her," I tell Kayla. "She might actually talk to you."

It's a mark of Kayla's concern that I get no back-chat. But she gets no more of a response than I do. Which probably means that Hannah is underground already.

Shit.

I retrieve my phone, leave a message. It is slightly panicky and mostly consists of the phrase, "Get the hell out of there before something turns you into a person patty!" Hopefully it makes up in urgency what it lacks in eloquence.

"An ear bud," says Kayla, apropos of nothing.

"Is this an artificial insemination thing?" I ask. "Because now may not be the time."

"The feckin' things we use in the feckin' field to talk to each other, you dumb feck." I think it's a good thing I had Kayla drive. It hampers her ability to skewer me.

"Oh right."

I speed-dial Tabitha.

"What?" she says as she picks up.

I think, if the world survives I should talk to Felicity about MI37 getting a slightly better receptionist. Then I remember that Felicity has stormed off and MI37 is destined to die even if the world chooses not to do an impersonation of a wet tissue meeting a bullet today. So maybe a receptionist isn't our top priority.

"Has Hannah got an earbud?" I ask. Then for clarity, "Something she can put in her ear. Something you can talk to her through." And then for good measure, "Nothing to do with artificial insemination."

There's a chance I need to calm down a little.

"Jesus," I hear Tabitha say. And then something like, "Need to include an instruction manual with them." Then she says more clearly, "No. Range is only a few miles. She's in London. Me: Oxford. So, pointless."

I curse. "Can you try her mobile?"

"Oh sure. Was doing important work to determine fate of the universe. But a secretary. Yeah, can totally be that."

I almost check to see if the venom coming through the phone has damaged the touchscreen.

I try to remember what I'm interrupting. Tabitha had an idea, was doing research. About… About… About the damned bomb.

"What did you find out?" I ask.

"Oh," Tabitha switches from acidic to petulant with the ease of a teenager. "Now you want to know?"

"I know where the bomb is," I say. There is a satisfying pause after that.

"For sure?" she asks.

I need Clyde to answer that exactly. But I'm building my way up to Clyde, maximizing the time he has to cool off. I imagine Clyde loses his shit about as often as Halley's comet passes the earth, so it might take him a while to put the pieces back together. I will have time for just one shot to get him back on board with us, and I don't want to waste it. Still, Tabitha won't benefit from any of that information, so I go with, "I'm certain enough."

"OK," Tabitha says. "So… what I have. Theoretical. Not as rigorous as I'd like it to be. Needs confirmation." Despite the staccato rhythm she's waffling as much as Clyde.

"Just hit me with it," I tell her.

"This is weird." Weird enough that she's still hedging. Which is worrying.

Still, "I've dealt with weird before," I point out.

"OK." Tabitha takes a deep breath. "Bomb goes off. Massive damage. Damage so monumental it causes echoes in reality."

"Intimately aware of that," I point out. My sinuses are still stinging from my last encounter.

"Except the bomb never goes off."

"Say what now?"

"Manipulating realities. Playing with them. Lang's whole thing. The Uhrwerkgerät—his biggest plaything. See, the echoes get larger and larger closer we get to the big boom. Eventually it causes one so large, it destroys the Uhrwerkgerät itself." She pauses for effect. Because despite herself, Tabitha, loves a little drama. "Destroys it before it goes off."

OK, I concede the point. That's weird.

"A future echo of the Uhrwerkgerät going off destroys the Uhrwerkgerät *before* it goes off," I say, just to make sure I'm still playing along at home. From the driver's seat, Kayla gives me an odd look.

"Yes."

"But that's—" I start.

"A paradox," Tabitha finishes. "Fucking huge one."

And that does seem a fair assessment of the situation.

"Nature hates a vacuum," Tabitha states. "Reality hates a paradox. Same thing. Making an analogy. But our reality is actually a composite reality. Made of many realities. We perceive the most likely realities. But have spare ones. So to fix the paradox the composite brings less likely realities forward to plug the hole."

"OK," I nod. "So no problem." But even I can't deny that sounds like wishful thinking.

"Right," Tabitha agrees with me for about half a second. "Except paradox is too big." Another deep breath. "The Uhrwerkgerät—Lang designed it to be highly reality permeable. Exists in many, many realities. So it causes paradoxes throughout all of them. So finding an undamaged reality in the composite to fix things is hard. Means the solution is a really unlikely reality. Means bringing it forward ends up being worse than the original problem. Causes more paradoxes. And the composite tries to fix them. Brings forward more realities. Even more unlikely ones. But just makes more paradoxes. And more. And more. Keeps trying to fix them, keeps making it worse."

I picture it like a tear in cloth. The Uhrwerkgerät ripping through the weave and weft, leaving a ragged hole in its wake. So you try to patch the hole, but the cloth is too weak to hold the thread. And the rip gets worse. So you bring in more patches, more thread. But everything keeps ripping, and ripping, tearing itself to shreds. Except it's not cloth. It's reality. It's everything I live and breathe. Tearing itself to shreds.

"How bad does it get?" I ask.

Kayla looks over at me again. Considering she's going in excess of a hundred and twenty miles per hour, I wish she'd keep her eye on the road more.

"Everything ends," Tabitha says. "Everything. Just gets worse and never gets better. Until there's nothing."

Shit. Shit and balls. "Lang designed this thing?" I check. "Designed it to do exactly that?" The mentality behind that decision is beyond me.

"Total Nazi fucker with a hard-on for mass destruction. Saw humanity as tainted. This was the ultimate purge."

I've actually tried time travel before, and I know how awful and dangerous it is, and how, in the long run, it would probably cause the same sort of damage as Lang's bomb. But still, I would so sorely like to go back in time and neuter Lang's father with a handsaw.

Not a helpful thought, unfortunately. I reach for something more relevant. "How do we stop it?" I ask.

"Actually," Tabitha says. "Opposite problem. You have to make sure it goes off. Only way to stop the paradox."

"The huge bomb that causes a detonation so large it ripples backwards and forwards in time? The bomb that is going to kill me? I have to ensure it goes off?"

And for a moment I really do think Kayla is going to take us off the road.

"Echoes have already happened. Means it's gone off. Only way to stop the paradox is have that happen." There is no give in Tabitha's tone. Ugly little truths handled with professional dispassion.

And… Shit, she's right. That is the only way. Sacrifice this… what? City? Country? Continent? But save something. Maybe not all the world, but at least part of it.

Just not my part.

"Brilliant," I say. "Just brilliant."

Kayla keeps driving, but part of me wishes she'd take us to our destination just a little slower.

67

I try Hannah again, though I don't even know what to tell her now. Head to the southern hemisphere for a while? She doesn't answer anyway, so I don't have to work it out.

Clyde is next. He lets it go to voicemail. Unless he's underground—or being beaten to a pulp by a World War II-era robot—as well. I almost fling my phone out the window at that point, but I give him one more shot.

He picks up on the sixth ring.

"I really don't want to talk about it, Arthur," he says before I can even say hello. "I know that's probably very rude, but I really am very upset about the whole thing. About my own behavior as much as anything else. Really an unforgivable way to act. Not to say that I am the only guilty party. See, I don't want to get caught in that trap. You see, I know myself, Arthur. I know what happens when I get to talking. I'll end up talking myself into coming back and making apologies that really I'm not sure I'm ready to give, or really should give. But if we get engaged in this whole thing, well that's what will happen. And sometimes a man just needs to let himself stew for a bit, get it out of his system. Well, I say man, but really it could be anyone of any gender. Or of indeterminate gender. Though I don't think that's the term. My upbringing was rather conservative, and sometimes it means my terminology is a little south of the politically correct term. But hopefully you catch my intent."

"I—" I try to break in and fail.

"No, Arthur. I'm sorry. I really don't like being firm. Firm things in general are generally not my personal favorite. Foodstuffs, mattresses, even book covers. Always go for the soft version. Cheese being the exception, actually. Always been a fan of those super-hard Italian cheeses. A bit of Asiago. Oh my. Actually that was something Tabitha and I really connected on. Both big Asiago fans. Wouldn't think it to look at her. I had her pegged as a Brie girl myself. A lot of people really do like Brie a lot, but I just don't understand the appeal. And don't get me started on cottage cheese. Thoroughly revolting. Got excellent taste in cheese, Tabitha. Makes her own smoked Gouda as well, which you have to respect."

"I—" I start again, but apparently I have lost all control of this conversation.

"Oh God, it's already started," Clyde blunders on. "See this is why I didn't want to answer the phone. But that always seems terribly rude in this day and age. We're always expected to be accessible twenty-four hours a day. Which isn't really a reasonable expectation, if you ask me. This whole social media thing. It's the death of alone time. And I mean, I know that one can disengage if one chooses. It's not like they've got a gun to your head, though sometimes I think it's only a matter of time before that becomes the advertising campaign. But there is so much social pressure to conform and engage. And I do like to be polite, Arthur. Today's little outburst standing as a notable exception of course. But as mentioned, I do feel very bad about that. Not to mention embarrassed. And I do really understand the pressure Tabitha is under. I tried to explain that. Did you think I explained that?"

I open my mouth, but before sound manages to escape he's off again.

"Well of course you do. You've always been a very reasonable person. And very supportive. Really the best of friends. And an excellent field lead. Though, I suppose... gosh, I hadn't even given it much thought, but you're more than field lead right now. Felicity left you in charge. And what's the first thing I do? Storm off in a cloud of my own self-importance. And I know I was just railing against social media, but that shouldn't be taken as me wanting to deny that humans are social creatures. Terribly important. It's just the pressure with the media thing that bugs me. The idea that our social nature is being commodified. But being part of a close-knit social group is important to me. And I betrayed that impulse today. Not that we don't all need moments of selfishness. Everything is a balance, of course. But there's a time and a place. And maybe this morning wasn't my time or my place, and really I could have dealt with it a lot better. But I didn't. I really left you in the lurch at the worst possible time."

"Look—" I try to say.

"Well that's very kind of you to be understanding. But then that is your nature. To be a good and kind human being. Except I really must say that you're being *too* kind. It was pretty shitty of me, Arthur. Not to beat around the bush. Honestly, I'm almost too ashamed to show my face. But that would just be compounding the problem, not solving it. No, that's not the course of action at all."

There is a genuine pause then. Except I am too disoriented by the swirls and eddies of conversation to work out which way is downstream.

"I really should thank you for calling me," Clyde says into my confusion. "I was very caught up in myself, but you really helped me sort it all out. As you always do. And I must apologize. Ready to throw myself back into the fray. I'll meet you back at the office, shall I? I really do apologize for the inconvenience."

"Erm…" I manage. "Actually Lang's pocket reality in the London Underground would be the best place to meet right now."

"Oh all right then." Clyde's voice is as bright as the summer sun. "See you there then. ASAP and all that. Love acronyms. Wonderful things. One of the whole reasons I was so tempted by military intelligence in the first place actually. But I won't chew your ear off about it now. Do it in person. Good gosh, I have been wasting time. OK, on the move now. Moving even as we speak. Joy of the cellphone. Totally mobile. The clue is in the title, I suppose.

All right. Totally off. Except I'm talking. Going to stop that. And hang up. Both at once. Not something to brag about really. Hardly a complex maneuver. But I'm going to do it. Wait, how do I… Is it this button? Bear with me for a second. Barely ever use this thing. Maybe if I—"

The line goes dead.

I sit for a moment trying to work out what just happened. Then I decide I don't need to know right now. Clyde is coming to London. And with him comes the sliver of a chance to succeed.

68

LONDON. IN THE SHATTERED REMAINS OF BROKEN SPEED LIMITS

I cannot claim to be exactly sure how Kayla parks the car. It seems to involve rotating through seven hundred and twenty degrees and using the curb as a brake. The car rocks up on two wheels for a moment, then settles. My stomach takes slightly longer.

We're beside a brown brick building with a sign that announces in crisp white letters that this is Hammersmith Station. Clyde or Tabitha are nowhere to be seen on the street outside.

We bundle through to the station, shove tourists aside, and hurdle the gates. Several yells pursue us. I bat the objections away with wild waves of my badge.

Clyde and Tabitha aren't on the station either. There again, if Kayla had driven a handful of miles per hour faster and pointed us against the spin of the earth I think we would have traveled back through time, so perhaps the fact that we got here first is not that surprising.

I grab my phone from my pocket.

"Just feckin' text," Kayla says, already heading for the tunnel. "Hannah is already down there."

I tap keys on my phone, send "Going down," to the rest of

MI37, and hurry after Kayla's rapidly retreating form.

Just before the tunnel swallows me, the phone buzzes again. Tabitha has replied. "No time for sex talk."

Well, at least we're going into this with a professional attitude...

IN THE TUNNEL

One plus of racing to save the world is that it leaves you less time to worry about the dangers of oncoming trains. Plus there's much less wrestling with the rusty door leading down to the service tunnel now that Kayla has kicked it open a second time. Still, I will admit to blanching when my foot hits the sixth step and a train's passage slams the door shut behind me. It's about now that some situational awareness might come in handy.

Time to slow down. Kayla is still well ahead of me, but I stop taking the steps two at a time. Lang's pocket reality is about a hundred yards to my right once I'm through the door.

And if Friedrich has guards posted? He didn't last time. Unless the mad machine we found last time was a guard who had slipped a few gears. But we saw no evidence of Friedrich last time... Wouldn't he have stopped us raiding the place? Except, what if I have picked the wrong place? What if Friedrich is, right now, in a totally different pocket reality putting the finishing touches on his plan?

And about then I realize that I've stopped, paralyzed by indecision, and I'll never know if I'm in the wrong place or not if I don't make it to the bottom of these stairs.

I take another ten steps. The light of the workmen's lamps in the tunnel beyond outlines the door before me.

If there are sentries, was there cover? I seem to remember a few piles of wood, and maybe one of electrical equipment.

Who the hell was doing work down here anyway? God, I wonder if Friedrich's forces killed them. Jesus.

There weren't sentries last time. It'll be fine.

"Just so you know," says Kayla's voice from nowhere, "you breathe much louder and you'll have the whole bloody lot of them down on us."

So much for situational bloody awareness. I scan the darkness of the stairs, but can't pick out her shadow from any of the others. I decide to forgive myself a little. Kayla is as close to a real life ninja as I've ever met.

"Crap," I say quietly. "He left sentries, didn't he? How many?"

"About ten."

"Double crap." I look around for silver linings. "At least we know we found the right place."

"Or it's a great big feckin' trap."

"Or that." I close my eyes. It makes no real noticeable difference to my surroundings. "Any sign of Hannah?"

"No." There's an edge to her voice. I can't tell if it's fear or anger.

"Any sign of any large blood stains?" I probably could have phrased that better.

Kayla snorts. "Hannah is like a feckin' black belt at stealth infiltrations of enemy-held facilities. Kind of her whole feckin' thing. You read her file, right?"

I decide to skip right over that. "Think we might have similar luck?" I ask instead.

"I'm generally a wee bit feckin' louder than that."

It's unsettling talking to Kayla in the dark. The black humor of her violence is more menacing without a wiry red-headed frame to fit it to.

"I wish I'd held onto that steel pipe," I say.

There is the sound of steel being unsheathed.

"Ach, feck it," Kayla says in the darkness. "You take this."

It takes me a moment to work out what she's trying to give to me. I mean, it's obvious what it is. But... but...

"Your sword?" I say, complete in my incredulity. It's like Kayla is offering me her arm, or her leg. *Here, just use this body part for a while. I don't need it.*

I expect sarcasm, but instead there's just a pause. Just long enough for me to feel how insubstantial everything seems in this much darkness.

"You know where I got this sword?" Kayla says finally.

I have no clue. I've never imagined her without it. "Is it a family thing?" I ask. It seems like something where the sentimental value would be high. The way she treats it I can imagine it being handed down from generation to generation. Some ancient MacDoyle heirloom won at a great price by some long-ago ancestor on a long sea voyage to Japan. Five hundred folds of steel and all that sort of thing.

Kayla chuckles, low and brief. "No. It was a feckin' renaissance fair. I was sixteen. Trying to hunt down some lass with an alien in her head."

I am forcibly reminded that Kayla's teenage years were rather different than mine.

"I had this kitchen knife stuffed down the back of my shirt, and then I passed this good-looking chap, soot all over his arms. And he was bashing at some feckin' bit of metal, and had a rack of all this medieval shite. And then there was a bucket with a bunch of samurai feckin' swords sticking out of it. Should be feckin' mentioned that the wanker hadn't actually made any of the shite he was selling. Imported it all from Taiwan and then set up the wee forge to make himself like a big man. Feckin' stupid. But I was feckin' stupid too. I was sixteen. Comes with the feckin' territory." Another low chuckle. Something mocking in it, though I don't think I'm the one being mocked. "Set me back ten feckin' quid that sword did. Worth it though. Much easier to kill someone with that than with a feckin' kitchen knife."

I have to admit, it's not quite the legend I expected. And yet the sword seems almost more personal for the telling.

"Why are you giving it to me?" I ask. I feel like I missed something.

"Because I stand a chance against those feckers without it. Not sure I can say the same for a skinny wee shite like yourself. And according to the plan you need to live long enough to get blown up by a feckin' bomb."

She's a practical girl, is our Kayla.

Our Kayla.

I'll miss her. The full impact of that thought takes a moment to hit me. And maybe she'll miss me. Maybe that's what that story is about. Letting me past her guard a little is a farewell gift.

I reach out gingerly, worried about cutting myself, but Kayla has the handle held unerringly close to my hand.

"Way I figure it," Kayla says as I take the sword, "time might be best spent with me kicking these arseholes' arses. You try and sneak past them, get to Hannah. Try to do something feckin' right by her. It's about feckin' time you did."

Kayla just gave me her sword, so I don't object to that. There's likely some truth to it.

"Ready to go on your feckin' say so and everything," Kayla says. "You being all acting head of MI-feckin'-37 and all that shite."

"You want to take on ten Uhrwerkmänner unarmed?" I say. Just because there's homicidal and then there's suicidal.

"Feck, yes." Kayla's voice is a blade in the night.

"Well all right then." I put a hand on the door. "Let's go fuck some people up then."

69

It's not like subtlety has ever been MI37's strong point.

Kayla's foot crashes against the door, the impact tearing it off its hinges, and sending it flying across the tunnel outside. It smashes against an Uhrwerkmänn's leg, folds around the limb.

By the time it's figured out what's going on, Kayla is on the leg as well.

She attacks with a fluid ferocity that is staggering to behold. I have always thought of Kayla's sword as a natural extension of her body. I never considered that it might actually be getting in her way.

The Uhrwerkmänn flails at her, its fist raising dull echoes as it smacks at its own skin. But Kayla is like mist, or some particularly violent Highland monkey. She swarms over it, flinging herself out of the way of its fists. Her slender hand plunges into exposed joints, comes back stained black, ragged cogs and pipes clutched in her fist. First one arm is disabled, then the other.

The others start to converge, but Kayla is beginning to enjoy herself now. With no arms to defend itself the Uhrwerkmänn is largely at her mercy. It thrashes about, trying to dislodge her, but Kayla could teach bull-riders a few lessons on tenacity. Before the others reach her, she's already managed to rip her way into the thing's neck, and some fairly vital looking gears are finding their way to the floor.

I remember I'm meant to be sneaking, that Kayla is raising a distraction for my benefit. There is something hypnotic about her expertise at this, but now is not the time to succumb. I turn away, stay close to the wall.

"Hands off, you cheeky metal feck," echoes after me. The noise of tearing steel follows.

I feel like things should be easier for me. I have the lesser task. But considering I'm in a tunnel buried deep below ground, there's a distinct lack of shadows for me to sneak through. The damn workmen's lamps cast zebra stripes of light every twenty yards or so. I'm safe for a moment then horribly exposed. All it's going to need is for one Uhrwerkmänn to have decided to hold back.

Like that bastard.

I freeze, letting the breath tremble in and out of me. It's standing in one of the dark patches, almost hidden because the lamps keep destroying my night vision. I'm only thirty feet away. If the German robot wasn't so intent on the fight with Kayla, I would already be only so much meat paste. But apparently watching Kayla go a few rounds with six Uhrwerkmänner all at least twice her height is pretty entertaining stuff.

I shuffle one foot forward, then the other. I feel like I've barely moved. *This is just giving it more time to look around and see me.* And it didn't notice me when I was moving fast a second ago. Maybe Lang designed their eyes differently from ours. Less sensitive to movement, but more to... Something else, I guess.

I just need to keep bloody moving.

I accelerate. Just a little.

Its head snaps round.

Shit and balls.

Before the Uhrwerkmänn has time to fully register what it's seeing, I launch myself at the thing. Kayla's sword feels right clenched in my clammy fists.

I bring the blade down on the upper thigh, and it skids off the metal. Just like I was expecting it to. As the Uhrwerkmänn lunges left to swipe at me, I go with the momentum of the rebounding blade and jam the point into the ankle joint of the opposite leg.

I duck, roll past the swatting hand, between the legs, rip the blade free.

The Uhrwerkmänn goes to turn to chase after me, feels its ankle giving way, tries to correct, and goes down on one knee.

I scramble to my feet. I'd been hoping the bastard would go fully down, and give me a good angle on its neck. As it is, I'll have to make do with the one I've got on its waist line.

My sword hacks into the seam between gut and hips while the Uhrwerkmänn pistons its arm trying to regain its balance. I tug sideways, enjoying the satisfying feel of resistance giving way.

This is so much better than fighting people. I can't imagine I'll have half so many bad dreams afterwards.

Then the blade sticks. Because the one problem with fighting giant robots is that they have giant chunks of metal inside them.

Damnit. I heave on the blade. And superhuman strength would really come in handy right now. Kayla makes this sort of thing look so easy.

The Uhrwerkmänn growls. A low, slightly slurred noise. It's hurting, but it is decidedly not dead.

I heave again. Nothing.

"Stupid renaissance fair piece of shit!" I yell. Hopefully Kayla can't hear me over the sound of six Uhrwerkmänner trying to stomp on her head.

A fist comes at me. I abandon the sword, roll. It swipes over my head. I get my bearings just in time to see the other fist coming down, palm flat, looking to crush my chest. I roll back the way I came.

With a roar the Uhrwerkmänn brings down both hands, a vast plain of steel, too big to roll away from.

I do a backwards tumble instead, feel the wind of its fingers graze down my back.

I scramble to my feet as it recovers its balance. For a moment we just stare at each other. It's still on its knees and we are almost eye-to-eye. This is an impasse. It can't pursue me, but I really need to get Kayla's sword back.

It cocks a fist.

God, I'm going to have to get the timing really right on this.

I dart forward, seize the handle of the blade.

The first flies toward me, too fast to dodge.

I push myself sideways as fast and as hard as I can, still hanging onto the handle of the sword.

The fist hits me. A great heaving impact that makes my whole body ring with pain, barely mitigated by my attempt to roll with the blow.

Pain shoots down my arm, flares into my fingers, and for a moment I fear I'm going to lose my grip on the sword, but I hang on. And it comes free. The momentum of the blow sends me and the embedded blade skidding sideways. There is an ugly ripping sound, and whether it comes from the Uhrwerkmänn's guts or my shoulder is unclear for a moment.

I lie on the ground and ache, trying to bite back a scream. Doing stealthy ninja shit definitely does not involve screaming.

After a while I become aware that I am still not dead yet. At great personal expense, I lever my head up and look around.

The Uhrwerkmänn is lying on the ground. One leg spasms slightly. A gentle kick repeated over and over. Some gears lie in a pool by its side. The gash in its gut appears almost insubstantial. Still, it seems to have done the job.

I glance over to the other gaggle of machines. Waiting for one to look my way, to start shouting. But Kayla is doing a very good job of capturing their attention. Apparently, constantly punching people in their vital parts tends to really focus them.

Using the sword, I lever myself to a standing position. After a moment's contemplation, I decide to transition from careful stealth to a more sort of desperate hobbling.

It strikes me that there's been no sight of Hannah yet. Did she get past the sentries? Did she turn around as soon as she saw them? It would be pretty typical of this entire endeavor if she showed up on MI37's doorstep just as we plunged into the hornet's nest.

The alternatives are, I suppose, that she was taken prisoner for some reason I can't quite fathom, or the slightly more likely dead-as-your-favorite-type-of-nail theory.

Slowly I approach the place where the door should be. The makeshift office we set up with all of Lang's papers is nowhere in evidence. Does that mean it's been cleaned up, or that the reality key isn't turned? That Hannah is trapped somewhere and I can't get close?

I paw my way along the wall. Behind me I hear a sharp cry. Not a mechanical shout. Something very human.

Kayla.

The texture of the wall changes beneath my hand. A slight indentation. Rough concrete giving way to battered metal. The loose crackle of rust beneath thick layers of paint.

I glance back. The Uhrwerkmänner are in a tight knot now. I see fists rise and fall. I can see no sign of Kayla. She must be in the thick of it.

I have her sword. I'm using it as a damned walking stick.

Forward or back. Save or sacrifice.

Except I'm committed. And Uhrwerkmänner or bomb, it's almost certain Kayla will die today. She may not have had the time to think that through. She may still be stuck on hope. But basically the only choice is whether her death will be meaningful or not.

God, I fucking hate saving the world. It sucks every goddamn time.

My hand finds the door handle. I push, and I'm through.

70

I brace for an angry roar, for impact, for the inversion of the curves of my face.

But nothing. Nothing at all. The room is not stuffed full of Uhrwerkmänner. It is, instead, pretty much exactly as I remember it—an elongated egg shape, walls lined with books and papers, floor littered with the detritus of academic obsession. I step past a box of curling brown sheets of paper, squeeze between a moldering blackboard and a stack of textbooks five feet tall.

It's empty. The whole place is bloody empty.

"Hannah?" I hiss as loud as I dare. Approximately as loud as a mouse with a mild anxiety disorder.

There is no answer.

"Hannah?" I hiss again, this time perhaps hitting the volume of a slow puncture in a bike tire.

No answer.

I feel suddenly ridiculous, whispering inaudibly in a self-evidently empty room.

"Hannah?" I say a third time. This time actually putting a little lung power into the word.

And still no answer. Where in the name of all the hells—and from what I now know of the world there are probably many of them—is she?

I kick in irritation at a stack of paperback books. It topples. It turns out not to be a fabulous idea. I watch as it topples, collides with a bunch of poorly stacked picture frames. The stack slews sideways, old wood clacking together. The topmost frame spins to the floor. It's enough to bring an end to the long-standing fight between a freestanding chalk board that leant against them and gravity. I watch in horror as the board topples.

"No," I whisper, a small useless sound. "No, no, no."

The board pays no attention. It slams into a small plaster statue of a cherub. The statue's shards rocket like shrapnel into a crate of rolled sheets of paper, send it skidding across the floor.

At a certain point you just have to give up and facepalm.

The crate slams into another stack of books. They fall. Take another one with them.

Slowly, piece by piece, it all comes down. It's as if I stand in the center of some giant godawful Rube-Goldberg device. And one domino push was all it took. The delicate equilibrium of the room collapsing. A small wheeled table loaded with books careens across the room, crashes into a seven-foot-tall mirror that shatters, spilling shards of glass as it tumbles backwards, slamming into the far wall.

A shelf gives way. And then another, and another, and another, and another, and another. Shelf after shelf, reaching up to the distant ceiling. They each give way. Books fall like dead birds. An avalanche of arcane knowledge. Dust fills the room, obscures everything. I hack, and splutter, and stare in horror.

Finally it is over. About a sixth of the shelves on the wall have collapsed. Books make a small hill against one side of the room.

I stare. Jesus.

"Hannah?" I venture one final time.

And nothing. Of course nothing.

And then not nothing. Something... an ugly twisting sensation in the region of my central cortex. Some violation of reality snapping at the heart of my brain.

Oh shit. Shit and balls. A reality key. Someone is using a reality key.

I spin around, trying to blink away sinus pain. What just changed? It must have been out in the corridor, outside this room.

Some Uhrwerkmänner finally breaking from Kayla's onslaught long enough to think about cutting this reality from the main one. They heard the goddamn noise and they trapped me here.

But, no. There is the door. There is my way out.

So if that didn't change...

A noise. From behind me. A harsh mechanical sound.

Grinding gears.

But I am still alone here.

"*Vas?*" A word. A German word. From...? From...? I scan the room again.

From behind the goddamn pile of books.

Oh shit and—

The mountain of books bulges. Explodes.

A shape bursts from the pile of books. It flings them aside. Leather-bound grenades, shedding white shrapnel as they detonate against wall and floor.

I stagger backwards, the back of my knees colliding with drawers protruding from a writing desk.

The Uhrwerkmänn tears out of the spilled books. Like some great piston-powered knight of old. It has something vast and steel clutched above its head. "*Schänder!*" it bellows. I get the impression that's not a good thing to be called.

Behind it, I can now see an archway has appeared from nowhere. The reality key unlocked it. The books hid it. And I gently positioned my paddle-less canoe directly for shit creek.

Part of my panicking mind, trying to step away from the moment, is happily going, *a pocket reality inside a pocket reality!* over and over.

However the larger, more sensible part of my mind is running along lines that more closely resemble, *oh shit. Oh balls.*

The Uhrwerkmänn looms over me. It brings down... whatever the hell it is that it's wielding in a massive, two-handed arc. I lunge awkwardly sideways, caught flatfooted.

It's a girder, I realize. A steel girder that plows through the desk, less than eight inches from my skull. Shards of wood send me sprawling. I land on my arse, sit there stupidly, looking up at the towering machine.

"*Heide*!" it screams. The girder goes up again.

Oh God, it's happening again. I'm sitting on the fucking ground and something's going to cave my head in. It's the moment when this all started all over again. That fucking Scottish bar. I am bathed in sweat. My limbs suddenly drenched in sweat. And my muscles feel like they're made of water. And Clyde isn't here to save me. Clyde's not even in the same reality as me.

It seems apropos to say, "*Scheisse*" as the girder starts to descend.

A blur of motion to my right. Glimpsed from the corner of my eye. I start to twitch my head toward it, a futile end to a futile fight.

Someone crashes into me with considerable speed and force. I slam back across the floor. Something… someone… is on top of me, barreling over me. A spinning fury of legs and limbs.

The girder cracks the flooring of the room, a thunderclap that rips through me dropping the bottom out of my stomach.

My stomach that has not just had my head caved into it.

And someone just saved my life.

Who the hell just saved my life?

I blink my vision back into focus. They're off me now. Standing, arms outstretched. Firing a gun.

Wait… Hannah?

She empties her magazine at the Uhrwerkmänn's head. It's the shape of a ship's prow, tall and sharply angled. Iron gridwork gives the slightest impression of eyes lurking deep in the skull. Bullets ping and whine between them, raising a fleeting patina of white sparks.

The Uhrwerkmänn growls again, unintelligible this time. It swings its girder in a flat horizontal arc.

If I had the breath I'd yell out a warning. She's leaving it too late. She's going to get hit. I am going to lie here and watch as Hannah Bearings' midriff is put on the extreme crushed-to-a-narrow-pulp diet.

Where did she come from? What the hell is going on?

The air screams as the girder whips around. The Uhrwerkmänn pivots back on its heels to compensate for the momentum.

Hannah flings herself backwards, her whole body collapsing

back above the knee. She fires as she goes. The same tight pattern of sparks around its eyes.

The girder whistles over her, over me. A deadly blur that fills my world for a fraction of a second, leaving nothing but sheer terror in its wake.

Hannah is lying next to me, flat on her back. Still firing.

The Uhrwerkmänn grunts in frustration, abandons its girder, raises a foot to stomp down.

Well, it was a noble effort, and I suppose this means I won't have to die alone.

And then... Maybe it's the shift in weight that does it. Tilts the head back at just the right angle. Maybe it's just a random fluke. Maybe it's the universe saying, "Not yet, I've got plans for you."

Hannah's bullet finds its home.

71

There is a noise not entirely dissimilar to a pebble rattling in an empty paint can. The Uhrwerkmänn freezes. Hannah lies flat, the robot's foot poised above her.

Its shadow looms. The moment hangs.

I lie there, breath coming in short sharp gasps, waiting for the foot to fall, for Hannah to be reduced to nothing more than an abstract stain on the floor beside me.

Another breath wheezes in. I reach out, push at her shoulder, but my hand is too weak to move her. She doesn't even look at me, just at the Uhrwerkmänn tottering above her.

And then, slowly, the Uhrwerkmänn reaches the tipping point. It crashes back into the books, posters, papers, and shit that litter the room around us. Dust blooms, forms a dry dirty fog.

We lie there, both of us staring at the empty space the Uhrwerkmänn used to occupy. I haven't a clue what to say.

"Holy fuck balls." Hannah breaks the silence.

Breath manages to make its way back into my lungs. It comes back out in something that sounds a little like a chuckle.

"Jesus," I manage. And then, "What…? Where did…?"

I look at her. She turns, looks at me.

"*Thank you.*" That's where I should have started. Because I really, genuinely mean it. Honestly, in this moment, I could not be more grateful to see Hannah Bearings. "Thank you," I say again. "Holy shit. I... I thought it was going to... just... going..."

"It's OK," Hannah says. "That's..." And then she stops. There are words for this moment, but not for us in this moment.

So I abandon words and pick myself up so I can reach down, help her up too. It seems the best fit for the moment that I can manage.

"I was calling out to you," I say, still trying to make sense of events. "You weren't answering. You weren't... You couldn't hear me?"

Hannah shakes her head. She looks as confused as I feel. "I came here, trying to check things out like, you know, you asked. And there were Uhrwerkmänner in the corridor but they're not the most observant bloody lot. Not that hard to sneak past."

Given my experience I'm going to give some credence to Kayla's insistence that Hannah is an infiltrations expert.

"So I get in here, and I can't take any of this shit out with the tunnel guarded and all. So I figure I'll just photo stuff. But where the hell to start? And I'm working that out when there's this weird feeling in my head. Like when we set off that reality key that first time. And then there's that archway over there appearing out of bloody nowhere." She points to the wall, the pile of books, the recently arrived archway. "And then—" she pauses, twisting her head to the side, trying to recapture the memory. "And then there was noise, someone coming, so I hid. And there were bloody Uhrwerkmänner everywhere. Coming in and out, dragging things through here. Construction materials, bits of... themselves. Other Uhrwerkmänner. And I was hiding for-bloody-ever. And then I felt that feeling again, that twist in my head. And suddenly books were on the floor, and you were there, and that thing was coming at you. And I just..." She shrugs awkwardly.

"Went and saved my life," I say. "That's what you just did."

She shrugs again.

And God, we are not good at this. I don't know how to express gratitude to her. She doesn't know how to receive it.

We stand in awkward silence.

"Erm," I say. Down to business perhaps. "Any idea what's going on through there?" I point to the archway.

She shakes her head. "I haven't been through there yet," she says, "but we should. There's a ton of them back there. We should figure it out."

The view through the archway itself is less than revealing. All I can see is a short passageway. Large stones making a wall that defines a corridor angling sharply to the right. Nothing visible beyond that. A few dull clanking sounds emanate from it.

But we were just screaming. Yelling. There were gunshots. We must have garnered something's attention. We won't be alone for long. But how do we close that hole? We have no reality key.

I turn to the Uhrwerkmänner's corpse, lying massively across the room. It must have a key on it somewhere. To get in here it must have one. So there must be a way to turn it back. But can I use it without magic?

"The rest of MI37 is coming," I tell her. "We should wait for them." I get down on my hands and knees, search the corpse, looking for the key. Maybe I could use it, close the archway, keep us safe 'til Clyde, and Kayla, and Tabitha all arrive.

Hannah walks slowly toward the arch. "But if we just do some recon...?" she says.

I find the key, reach out, take it. It is cold and flat, sharp edged in my hand. It is made of something that feels halfway between stone and metal. I run my fingers down the grooves in its sides. It has no obvious give.

"The Uhrwerkgerät is through there," I say distractedly. I'd forgotten how out of the loop Hannah was. "They're building it."

I hear the scuff of Hannah's feet and she whips around. "It's the what?"

I push and pull at the reality key. Clyde made it look so simple. Something grates, something deep and internal, but there is no change in its external appearance.

"Yeah," I say without looking up. "Just found out. Didn't know that when I sent you here. Obviously. Well... hopefully obviously, anyway. I tried to call and warn you. But I think you were already underground."

Silence. I don't really mind. It lets me concentrate on this damn key. I need to close that door, buy us some time. At least until Kayla or Clyde arrives. Preferably both.

"I ignored your call," Hannah says quietly. Almost as if it's not really a statement for me.

I answer anyway. "Understandable," I say. There's no ire in my voice for once. It's hard to be mad at someone who just risked their life to save yours.

"Not very professional of me," she says. Something between embarrassment and humor.

And what the hell is up with this damn key? Does it have a child safety lock on it or something?

"Best that could have been expected under the circumstances," I say. This really isn't the time.

Another long silence. Electricity, I realize. The reality key is magical. It'll need electricity to work. And I doubt Lang fitted this place with outlets.

"Yeah," Hannah says. Her feet scuff again, turning away.

My cellphone battery? Do I just jam that in my mouth the same way Clyde does with a nine volt? That's not very appealing.

"But—" Hannah continues. Then doesn't.

I yank on the key again. Still nothing.

The silence from Hannah is still going on. It feels wrong. I glance up.

Hannah is frozen. Staring.

At the giant bloody Uhrwerkmänn that fills the archway.

Oh goddamn it.

It has its arm outstretched. A barrel protrudes from its arm, extends over its fist. A thick, greasy black pipe, swelling at the end. Like an enormous version of Hermann's flamethrower.

Oh shit.

I stumble to my feet. The reality key is still in my hands. Some part of my brain that hasn't quite caught up yet, still fumbling with it.

I plow a shoulder into Hannah as the barrel starts to hiss. Blue light shines through the exposed gears of the monster's arm.

Hannah sprawls. I stare at the barrel.

Giant sparks crack down the Uhrwerkmänn's arm. The blue light swells, bursts out down the barrel. Not a flamethrower then. But I don't think it's going to shower me with rose-petals and rainbows.

Shit and balls.

Sparks race to the barrel's tip, seem to cluster there. And then one arches out, strikes me like a whip. I scream, feeling every muscle in my body tense.

The key suddenly gives in my hands. A grinding jerking movement that feels deeply and profoundly wrong. Planes of movement that shouldn't be possible. Stone intersecting with stone, passing through stone. And light flashes bright, blinding me from everything, from the flame racing down the barrel about to turn me into part of a nutritious breakfast.

Something wrenches at the inside of my head.

And then back. Back in the same room. Still waiting to die.

But the archway is gone. The archway that the Uhrwerkmänn was standing in.

And so is half of the robot.

We have shifted realities. And the Uhrwerkmänn stood on the threshold. Half in. Half out. When the wall of broken bookshelves reappeared it cut the creature in two, neatly bisecting it from brow to heel, making it less of a threat and more of a Damien Hirst artwork.

And then it starts to fall. But not away this time. There is no away now. There's a great bloody wall in the way. It falls forward. Toward me. Toward Hannah, lying where I knocked her.

I dive on top of her. No real thoughts in my head. Just some dull stupid version of anger, that after having gone to the trouble of actually saving us, I've managed to just put us in more danger. I have no real illusions that my body will stop a ton or more of metal from crushing Hannah to death—hell, the annihilation of reality subsequent to my death will do for her regardless—but it just seems like the right thing to do.

The front half of the Uhrwerkmänn lands. The floor quakes beneath us.

But we do not die.

After a moment, I become aware that I am lying directly on top of Hannah, and holding her very tight. If Felicity walked in right now, I'd likely have some explaining to do.

As it is, I think I have some explaining to do.

"Erm," I say, which seems as good a way to start as any. "Just, you know…" I push myself off her as quickly as I can. "Well…" I finish.

Hannah looks at me, then to the side. The Uhrwerkmänn's splayed arm has landed perhaps six inches from where we landed.

She looks back at me. "Little bit bloody close that," she says. Her eyes are very wide.

"Well," I try again, "you know. You'd just saved my life. Wanted to, erm… well, just repay the, err…"

"Yeah," Hannah says quickly, mercifully cutting me off. "I mean, erm, thank you. Like a shit ton."

"Not a problem." I reach out as if to shake her hand, realize what I'm doing and turn it into an awkward pointing gesture. "Fellow team members." I point back at myself. What the hell am I doing?

Hannah looks awkward. "Yeah, but I quit," she says. Then, just for a moment, she looks as if she wishes she hadn't.

"Well," I say, "papers probably haven't been processed yet. Once they are, you're on your own. But up until then…" I shrug.

"Yeah," Hannah nods. "Until then." And is that a smile at the corners of both our mouths?

Maybe this whole shit show would have all gone so much more smoothly if Hannah and I had had our lives mutually threatened earlier on. Though that might have been a slightly more contentious team building exercise than the night-club trip.

There is a sound from behind us. A door being opened. We spin. Hannah points her pistol. I point the reality key. I'm honestly not sure why.

Kayla looks at us both. She has a black eye, is missing one shirt sleeve and is dripping blood onto the carpet.

"Put that down, you silly feck," she says, "feckin' cavalry's arrived already."

72

"Oh thank Christ for that." I collapse down onto what's left of a desk. It wobbles ominously.

"Shit," Hannah says, looking at Kayla. "What the bloody hell happened to you?"

Kayla shrugs. "Other way around. I feckin' happened to about ten of those mechanical bastards out there."

That seems to take Hannah back a step. Though it's possibly a lesser blow than the one I land when I clap Hannah on the shoulder and say, "Don't worry, eventually you get used to her saying things like that."

Kayla's eyes flick back and forth, suspicious. "What's with the feckin' camaraderie bullshit? If I have to fight feckin' doppelgangers today," she says, "well, that's feckin' it. Big German bomb or no big German bomb, I'm going home after that. Feck with your head, doppelgangers do. They're my feckin' limit."

"Oooh!" says a voice from behind Kayla. "Doppelgangers? Really? I've read all about them, but never actually met one. Should be fascinating. Though watch out for the poisonous spit."

Clyde pushes his way into a field of crumpled brows.

"Hello," he says. "Sorry it took so long to get… oh wait, are you the doppelgangers? Well I must say that really is quite impressive. Really took me in at first. I never thought it would be that—"

"I am bloody Arthur," I say to Clyde. "This *is* Hannah." We don't have time for this now. There is the bisected half of an Uhrwerkmänn lying unguarded in a reality not too far from here.

Clyde nods, then slows. "Wait," he says, "you would say that if you were a doppelganger…"

"Clyde," I say, "there are no doppelgangers here. Kayla was making a joke."

Clyde's eyes narrow. "If you were the real Arthur, you would know that Kayla doesn't make jokes."

Kayla wheels on him. "What? I'm funny as feck." It is possibly fortunate for Clyde that I still have Kayla's sword.

Clyde, pressed up against the wall, flicks his eyes from me and Hannah to Kayla. "You're all doppelgangers!" he gasps.

This job makes too many implausible things seem possible.

"Clear the damn doorway already. A pissing queue out here." Tabitha shoves her way into the room. "No damn doppelgangers in here," she snaps at Clyde. "Goddamn idiot."

For some reason Clyde smiles at this.

"Good," I say, "everyone's here. Now we can—"

But the influx of irate people doesn't stop there. Stooping through the tight corridor of shelves into the room, comes Hermann.

"Wait…"

And then another Uhrwerkmänn. And another. Four of them. Five. We are rapidly running out of space.

"What the hell?" I'm knee deep in the pile of books I dislodged from the far wall. "What's going on?"

"Bumped into them on the way down," Clyde says as if this is the most perfectly natural thing to do on any given day.

But I fix my eyes on Hermann. Fresh plates of metal are welded to his body. The seams still shine fresh. His ruined arm has been straightened, splints of steel bracing the joint. "You didn't want anything to do with us," I say. "You told us to go away."

Hermann snorts. "This is not help. This is not trusting you to do things correctly." It's hard to tell but I don't think he quite meets my eye as he says that.

"*Machen Sie Platz,*" calls a voice from back through the doorway.

"How many of you are there?" I ask.

Hermann shrugs. "All of us."

Holy crap. It may be small, but I think MI37 suddenly has an army at its disposal.

"Just out of interest," Clyde pipes up, "but just before this becomes one of those tricks involving clowns and small cars. Like a Mini for example. Pretty quintessential small car, though I do think they use VW Beetles from time to time. And probably some less well known, cheaper vehicles, I imagine. Not that the type of vehicle matters I imagine. Imagine it's all done with trapdoors really. Unless clowns are all part of some underground magical fraternity, I suppose. Not entirely out of the realm of possibility. Take Morris men for example. Seem totally harmless, then you deflate one's pig bladder, and good lord, you better be on the move fast. Which is a useful life tip, I suppose, but not what I was aiming to say. Actually more interested in the sort of why and wherefore of the aforementioned cramming. At least I think I mentioned cramming. Us that is. Cramming in here. Still not understanding why we're doing it. Lovely room as this is, of course. Didn't mean to cast aspersions on Lang's decorating aesthetic. Totally fine with aspersions on his political point of view. Total shit of a man. But I do sort of dig this room."

Finally he takes a breath.

"Nested realities," I say into the gap before he can get going again. Clyde's mouth opens but no sound comes out. He twists his head, looks at me.

"An archway," Hannah puts in. "It opens up right in that wall. Great big bloody thing. Goes to some place full of Uhrwerkmänner. Kept on coming in here and trying to off us, they did."

"Sort of put paid to them, didn't we?" I say.

"We did that." Hannah grins.

Clyde looks at the mutual grins, gasps again. "Doppelgangers!"

"Oh shut up," I manage.

"It's not... No." Hannah is infringing on my ineloquence copyright. "I still quit. It's just..." She shakes her head. "Look, are we going to put an end to these arse-wipes or not?"

"I should probably mention," I say, "they're building the Uhrwerkgerät in there."

Clyde's jaw drops.

An exasperated snort bursts out of Hermann. "This is why I do not trust you," he says. "You take too long."

"Got a point," Tabitha says. "The giant metallic arsehole does."

"Would you mind ever so much just giving me the reality key?" Clyde asks. "I mean, if it's not too much bother. And presuming you don't—"

I shove the key into his hands. "Do what you need to do. I don't understand the bloody thing."

Clyde turns and twists the key this way and that, a puzzled look on his face. Then suddenly he grins. "Oh," he says. "You clever bastard." He twists hard, light blooms, and somewhere deep in my skull reality takes a punch in the nadgers again.

73

The Uhrwerkmänner stream past me through the archway. Watching them, I realize MI37's army is a little less than might be hoped for. They're in a bad way. Some limp. Others drag dead limbs after themselves. Some manage to limit themselves to just jerking and twitching, little spastic movements rippling through their bodies. And yet others mutter to themselves, grumbling and grinding as they move.

They're breaking down. And that's how we ended up in this whole mess. Volk and Hermann's desire to save their people from decline.

Maybe the Uhrwerkmänner aren't so different from me after all.

Kayla, Clyde, and Tabitha have gone ahead. Hannah and I form the rear-guard. We wait until the last Uhrwerkmänn has passed then turn and step through the archway. The column of robots jerks and shudders its way forward.

"What do you think?" I say to Hannah.

"Me?" She shakes her head. "I think we're proper fucked."

I decide that some witty pre-combat banter is perhaps not what I'm looking for after all, at least not here.

I follow the Uhrwerkmänner in silence. We are far from quiet, though. The robots' combined shuddering and shaking fills the cold stone space with a mechanical sussuration. The sound seems to echo in the enclosed stone space. I wait for a cry from the front, for discovery. But none comes.

The corridor is shorter than I expected. Barely thirty yards from the archway it comes to an abrupt halt, overlooking a large, light-filled space. Sound echoes up. A growing industrial murmur—metal clanging against metal. And maybe it is enough to drown out any noise we might make.

The back of the column no longer seeming like the best place to be, I push forward between massive legs. The smells of oil and grease are thick in the air.

"What's going on?" I whisper, as I approach Kayla.

"Hush," she whispers. "Get down."

I crouch, crawl forward. We're on a ledge overlooking an enormous cylindrical hall, reaching down fifty, maybe sixty yards into the ground. The corridor we're in breaks to the right, becomes an open stairway, spiraling down the wall to the ground below.

The space is full of Uhrwerkmänner. They are the source of the sound.

They are building.

They are building the Uhrwerkgerät.

And it is vast.

I can still make out Volk at the heart of it. A blunt coffin shape glowing with dull blue light. But he seems small now, an almost insignificant part of the whole. Other Uhrwerkmänner have been arranged around him. Their inner workings exposed. Pistons and gears laid bare. Bodies fusing. Amputated limbs reattached in a sickening mockery of form. A massive interconnected network of broken anatomy.

It is a horror show for the clockwork robot crowd. A vast depravity. It is a bomb made of corpses. The ultimate expression of Lang's disregard for his creations.

"Holy shit," I whisper. "It's fucking enormous." I'm never at my most eloquent when faced with imminent death. At least I'm accurate though. The Uhrwerkgerät would dwarf the average four-bedroom family abode. You could walk around in it, climb up its beams, and parade along boardwalks of mechanical corpses.

And there is Friedrich. The architect of this travesty. He stands clear of the bomb near the foot of the curving stairs, pointing and shouting instructions I cannot understand. *Uhrwerkmänner* scurry to obey him, clambering over the corpses of their brethren. They fix vast girders in place, scaffolding to prop up the sheer bulk of it.

"It is too big." Hermann's voice is a dull whisper. "It is too much. There are too many."

We are outnumbered to the most egregious extent. Five to one? More perhaps? And Friedrich's Uhrwerkmänner, while they may be beaten and scraped, appear significantly healthier than the ones behind me right now. He has so many in fact, not all of them are working on the Uhrwerkgerät. He's managed to post a ring of sentries around the bomb.

This is not going to be exactly easy.

What's going on inside those Uhrwerkmänners' heads? Is it horror? Do they see what they're doing? Do they think it's too late to fix it? Or are they sold on this? Are they zealots like Friedrich?

I don't know. I don't even know if it matters. They are between us and the machine. We're going to have to find a way through.

"We cannot do this." Hermann is hardly hitting the high notes of optimism right now.

"There's a way," I say. "There has to be."

"No." Hermann shakes his head. "To get to it... they will destroy us."

It's true. Most likely they will. But survival was never really an option coming into this fight. Hell, we're here to ensure a bomb blows up. It's not like we'll be heading out for a picnic and a quick game of footie afterwards. But I forget how long I've been living with the certainty of my own death. The others still have to disentangle themselves from their own hopes. It can be a painful process.

"I'm sorry," I say to Hermann. "I wish I could offer you more. But today is going to be a shitty day." I smile a sad smile. "But what's the alternative?" I look back down the corridor. And what do I have back that way? A girlfriend on the brink of leaving me. The collapse of MI37. "It's not going to get any better back there," I say. "As crappy as this is, it is the best of the bad alternatives."

Hermann looks back at me. His mechanical face is impossible to read. No emotions are truly capable of making their way through the thick metal of his face. And yet… there is something there, in the dull glint of his eyes. Some pathos? Some empathy.

"We will die today," he says. A great sadness resonates in his chest. "All of us. We have searched for salvation, but instead we have found this."

It's not exactly a positive spin, but on the other hand I'm not sure this is really the time for an inspirational quote about life, and balance, and the importance of mimicking a meditative mongoose climbing an ice cliff.

"We will die today," Hermann says again, looking back at his thirty or so warriors, his friends, the last of his kin. "But it will not be meaningless. It will not be a slow collapse into dotage and madness. We will die stopping Friedrich. We will die stopping the monster he has become. We will die defeating Lang's legacy. We will stop it all." His gaze levels on me. "And you will help us."

74

Kayla, always sensitive to the timbre of a dramatic moment, nods to Hermann. "All feckin' right then."

Hermann chooses not to bother acknowledging her.

"You know," says Hannah from the other side of me. "Can't say I'm totally sold on the whole suicidal charge thing here. No chance we have the slightest bit of a plan this time around, is there?"

I nod, but only slightly. They are not going to like this part.

"So... erm..." I start, filling them with the usual levels of confidence that I inspire. "Yeah, the thing about that is... well..."

"We will destroy the bomb," says Hermann decisively. "You and you." He points to the two Uhrwerkmänner who seem to be twitching the least. "You will lead the charge down the stairs. We will follow behind you, forming a spear head to crush the machine."

The two Uhrwerkmänner take a step forward in unison.

"No! Stop!" I hiss. "We can't destroy it."

This proves an unpopular suggestion. Hermann lets out a derisive snort.

"Maybe you cannot destroy it, little man," he says, "but you do not have the might of German engineering on your side."

"No!" I splutter. "This is not about German engineering. Or English engineering for that matter." A moment of national pride makes its misplaced way into the conversation. "Listen," I say, and slowly I start to lay out the issues I am having with the destruction of the Uhrwerkgerät.

"If it's destroyed," I conclude, "before it goes off, then those future echoes become paradoxes. It doesn't matter if we destroy it or it destroys itself. We have to prevent any paradoxes. If it's not going to tear all of reality apart, we have to let it go off."

I still do not seem to have brought anyone around to my way of thinking.

"You are insane, little man," says Hermann. "We must destroy it. It is the only way."

"Actually," Clyde interjects. "Sorry to disagree. Well... I mean I'm not sorry about what I'm saying. Well... I am sorry about what I'm saying to the extent that it does not agree with what you're saying. Erm... making a hash of this. Look, I agree with what I'm going to say. And I disagree with what you said. That's true. Got to be clear about that. Wish I didn't. But, you know, the facts being what they are and all... The thing is if we do destroy it, well, Arthur is right. And therefore, really, following on from that, you know, ergo, et cetera, you're not. Sounds terrible when I say it out loud, but, well, if we listen to you then we will all be completely annihilated along with the rest of reality. Not what we want at all. And so, I think what we maybe should do is go with Arthur's plan of not destroying the bomb and instead keeping it very safe indeed. Sort of like a puppy or small child. And not with your plan at all in any way, shape or form. Basically."

Hermann stares into the wake of this speech. "But..." he starts, more hesitantly than he's managed so far, "this bomb. It will destroy this city, this country. It could... We don't know what it could do."

"Yes," Clyde concedes. "Potential world destruction is the detrimental aspect of the plan." The way he says it, it doesn't seem to bother him perhaps as much as it should. "But, you know, bigger picture, the rest of reality survives. Probably some nice blue-green planet out there somewhere raising sustainable life. I mean, we haven't found it yet despite the Hubble telescope poking around. Very nosy device is the Hubble telescope, I always thought. Voyeuristic even. Never understood what all the fuss was about. But, well, even if we haven't found the alien folk, they're probably out there somewhere. Hopefully hiding behind some sort of intergalactic curtain so we can't catch them with their pants down. But, you know, yes, they'll survive. And it's an admirable thing, I think, for us to save those unknown strangers. They may not really get to appreciate it, but morally, I think we're getting to take the high ground."

Hermann shakes his head. "So you want us to lay down our lives for a plan that saves no one, that preserves nothing?"

Hannah grimaces. "To the German fella's point—" she nods at Hermann, "—this does seem to be a bit of an exercise in futility. I mean what exactly are we hoping to achieve here?"

Kurt Russell never had to work this hard to sell saving the world to people…

"The little blue-green planet," Clyde puts in. "The terribly modest people living upon it."

"Fuck those people." Tabitha rather succinctly sums up the feelings of the group.

I spread my hands. "Look, I'm open to suggestions. But the future echoes… This stuff is pretty much predestined."

"Wait!" The urgency in Hermann's voice brings us up short. "The paradoxes. The echoes." There is an edge of excitement to his voice. "Describe them to me."

He's insistent enough that I go ahead and comply. I tell them everything. The appearance. The agonizing pain in my head. The blood.

"The bomb hurts you," Hermann says. "It may even kill you. But the detonation—that is not part of it, correct? Not explicitly?" He leans down to put his head close to mine. I feel small in the shadow of his mass.

"I… I guess not explicitly," I say. "But it's a bomb. How else is it going to kill me?"

Hermann's mouth twists as much as it is able. An ugly approximation of a smile. "That," he says, "is exactly what we need to figure out."

75

"Wait, what?"

Maybe it's the imminent death thing, but I'm really not tracking.

"Oh, I get it," says Clyde.

It's an uncharitable thought, but I think I might have preferred if Clyde didn't. The explanation would likely have been quicker.

"See the future echoes aren't paradoxes *yet*," he continues. "That's what Hermann's getting at with this whole specificity issue. The echoes set up a certain set of conditions. But they don't dictate the situation fully. And so we are left with a certain set of parameters that have to be fulfilled. But the detonation of the bomb isn't the only potential way to fulfill them. If we can provide an alternate explanation, a sort of logical path of least resistance, then we can avoid both the detonation and the paradox."

"You know," says Hermann, "you are not so stupid as you often appear."

"Why thank you." Clyde bows slightly.

A logical path of least resistance. At least it doesn't sound stupid to someone. Still, I like the bit where the bomb doesn't go off and reality isn't destroyed.

"The echoes," I say, applying my gray matter's pedal to the topic's metal, "they always happened around the bomb. Around either injury to me or to it."

"Yes," Clyde nods.

"Anything else?" I ask.

"Well," Clyde hums, "I mean there are a lot of variables to consider—

"Nope," Tabitha supplies the answer. "You getting fucked. By a bomb. Pretty much it."

"Your nose bleeds a feck of a lot," Kayla points out.

"Head trauma," Tabitha says, apparently eager to be helpful all of a sudden.

I nod. "OK then." I bite my lip, stare at the massive structure of the Uhrwerkgerät. "How the hell do we bring that down?"

An Uhrwerkmänn standing a few paces away stumbles forward, nudges Hermann. He looks down at the Uhrwerkgerät, nods.

"A structural weak point," he says. "Near Volk. The intersection of those beams." He points.

I see it. Just left of the center of the thing. Two beams crossing each other. They don't seem special though. Just… two beams. "You're sure?" I ask.

"Mechanical being," says the Uhrwerkmänn in a low, almost embarrassed voice. "You get to know stress points pretty well." He ducks back into the crowd before I can question him further.

I shoot a quizzical look at Hermann. He nods. Fair enough then.

"So," I say. "Clyde, you send some great big spell, hit the stress point. The structure collapses. Destroy the bomb before it goes off. And I get in the way so I get my head injured."

And in the back of my skull, a small golden-winged bird called hope starts to flutter.

There is a very palpable pause.

"Well," Clyde hedges, then seems to want to go no further.

Oh crap.

"You see," Clyde starts, then stalls again.

"Injury," Tabitha says, like a blow from a blunt object, "may not exactly cut it."

Clyde won't meet my eye. And at the last even Tabitha looks away. Only Kayla will meet my gaze head on.

Actually if Kayla turned out to be the grim reaper then I wouldn't be too shocked…

I guess I'll get to find out in a minute.

Jesus.

"We will die alongside one another," Hermann intones. "We will share in each other's glory." He is rapidly becoming a little too enthusiastic about the certain death thing for my personal taste.

"So," I say. My voice sounds flat to me. *Dead* might be another way to describe it, but I'm not capable of really going there yet. "So we destroy the bomb and it falls on me, and it crushes me, and kills me. That's about it, right?"

Another pause.

"Right?" I ask, my voice rising. And it's not fair to be impatient, but goddamn it. The world suddenly seems full of things I haven't done.

"Well…" It's Hannah. The little golden-winged bird of hope takes one look at her face and decides to hibernate until everything blows over. "I mean, what if it doesn't?"

I can't work out what she's talking about. I need plain talk. Or no talk. Or silence. Or another fucking plan where I don't die. Jesus. Shit.

"What if it doesn't kill you?" Hannah continues. She at least has the decency to look unhappy as she talks. "I mean what if… I'm sorry, but what if you just shatter your pelvis or something. I mean you could end up pretty fucked up but also nominally alive. Human vegetable or something."

God, we're trying to make sure I don't end up drooling on myself and pissing into a catheter but for all the wrong reasons.

"I mean," Hannah says, staring at her hands, "it's not that I want you to die. You just saved my life, like, five minutes back, and to be honest that goes a pretty long way, even if we did have some disagreements. But there's this whole predestined by the universe thing."

"Yeah," I say. It feels like the out of body experience is coming on a little early. "Yeah, we totally need to figure out a way to guarantee my death."

Laughter is bubbling at the back of my throat. The mad dog of fear is starting to bark in the back of my skull.

"Oh God," says Clyde and he suddenly wraps me in a tight hug. "This is awful."

"Yeah." I push the laughter down, try to keep my voice flat.

"She's got a point," says Tabitha, still not looking directly at me.

"So someone needs to be killing me at the same time the collapsing bomb is killing me?" I check.

"I'll feckin' stab you," says Kayla with a shrug. "Done it before. It weren't that hard."

I think I'm going to be sick.

"No," Hannah shakes her head. "You'd get crushed too. There's no need for you to die as well."

Oh, so it's fine for *Kayla* to survive...

Which of course it is. I mean the whole point of the noble sacrifice move is to save people's lives. If I wasn't saving anyone then why the hell would I be sacrificing myself?

The noble sacrifice move...

Jesus. That's meant to be something you decide in the heat of the moment. The flush of adrenaline sweeping you up into a moment of glory. This cold dispassionate discussion of how best to ensure my death... I think the only reason I'm holding it together right now is because nausea, hysterics, and madness can't decide who gets to go first.

"So how we going to feckin' do it?" Kayla asks.

"I can't. I can't. I just can't." Clyde is shaking his head. "I'm sorry. I really just can't do it. I'm not that person."

And that's a little more like it. I reach out, touch his arm. Try to reassure him.

"You don't have to," I say. "You'll be hitting the weak point so the bomb drops on my head."

Clyde sobs harder. And who am I kidding? Nothing is going to make this OK.

And so, even as I pat his arm, I look over at Hannah.

"You do it," I say.

Her eyebrows make for the ceiling.

"You're the best shot here," I say. "You won't have to be close. Just close enough to hit me. We take out the bomb, and as it all comes down you plug me right between the eyes." I tap the spot. "Head trauma. Do it right."

Hannah's eyes flick left then right. Looking for an escape? This morning I think she might have leapt at this chance.

Or is that unfair? I guess I'll never have time to find out now.

Finally Hannah looks back. Looks me right in the eye. "All right then," she says. "That's the plan. Let's do it."

76

I take another look over the lip of the stairs. Another look at my fate. Below me, Friedrich's Uhrwerkmänner still scurry industriously, piecing together their personal doomsday device.

Shit.

"I wish Felicity were here," I say, mostly to myself.

"She's going to be so pissed at us." Tabitha peers over the ledge to my left.

Clyde appears to my right. "I don't know what to say." He seems on the edge of tears. "I wish somehow, that maybe... Well, can't be totally dishonest and say that I wish it was me. I don't wish it was me. But I wish it wasn't you either. Not sure if I'd wish it upon anyone really. I guess that's what I'm trying to say. Terribly sorry that anyone has to die. And even more so that the person in particular has to be you. Don't want it to seem like this is some general regret that doesn't really affect me personally." He sniffs loudly. "Obviously it is. Very keen on you actually, Arthur. Totally platonic of course. Wouldn't care for any, 'Kiss me, Hardy,' confusion here at what is ostensibly presenting itself as the end." Another sniff. "Just, you know, very good friends, and..." He descends into further sniffles and snuffs.

"Bit fucked," says Tabitha, nodding at Clyde with what might be significantly more affection than she has given him in a while. "What he's trying to say."

"Yes," I manage. "Yeah, that had occurred to me."

"So," says Kayla from behind the three of us. "Any bright ideas on how to get to that feckin' weak point then? Once more into the feckin' breach and all that shite?"

Is there something like emotion in her voice? It's very hard to tell.

I look down again, try to see the space as a tactical problem rather than a meat grinder I am about to throw myself into.

"Erm," I say. This has never been my strong point, despite the fact that it's at least fifty percent of my job description. Cat-herding, that's really what I can do.

And now I'm going to leave them all behind. MI37. The dysfunctional bastards. Some MI6 wanker will be in charge of them next, I suppose. Jesus.

Unfinished business…

I really do wish Felicity were here. Then I could apologize. I could try and set things right.

I look over at Hermann. There is a man at peace with his future. At least that is how he appears, readying his troops, going through the ranks, talking to them one-by-one, making sure that they too are ready for the sacrifice.

I'm bloody not. Not at all.

I should have said something to Felicity. Explained myself. I could have done so much differently.

That's a sad thought to have just before… this.

God, I really fucked up the past few days. Trapped in my own head instead of thinking about all the things going on outside of it.

This was always coming. That's the sad little revelation I have at the end. This moment was always inevitable. I didn't perhaps expect it to be as startlingly apparent as it is now, but there may be some good in that too. A moment of clarity before it's all over.

I got too caught up in the dying. Not in all the bits that happened on the way, that's the problem.

And now… Felicity. She's never going to have… I don't know… what I could have offered. Who knows if that really would have been that good, but for a while she seemed to enjoy my particular brand of boyfriend-ing.

God, I fucked it all up at the end.

I look down at the stairs. Feel the eyes on me, waiting expectantly. The plan…

What goddamn plan? We'll get down the stairs and the Uhrwerkmänner will meet us like a metal fist connecting with a soft fleshy jaw.

I glance to Hannah. "You're meant to be good at this, right?" I say. "You got any ideas?"

She looks at me for a moment, suspicious.

"No," she says. "Honestly. I've got nothing right now."

And that's something else I've screwed up, I see now. Felicity was right all along. Hannah is a resource I could have used, rather than someone for me to butt my head against.

Ah well, better late than never.

Hannah waits until it's clear that really no one is about to make a sarcastic comment, and then creeps forward to the ledge.

"Well," she says, "point of ingress is obviously the stairs. Don't have any rappeling gear. Bit under-prepared, but I think we can manage. But it means we're going to need a pretty hardcore tip of the spear and then some fairly withering support fire from up here."

Support fire. I look around. "Clyde," I say, "that's you."

"Yeah," Hannah agrees. "I'd say me too, but you and I need to leg it down there and get in position."

I nod, and try to avoid dealing with the reality of that statement. "So we're helping lead the charge."

"What? No! Are you bloody mental?" Her eyebrows pop up.

Maybe there was a reason why I didn't consult Hannah on this stuff more frequently.

"It's *vital*," Hannah points out, "that you stay alive right up until the point where, well, you know, you need to…" She whistles, looks upward, closes her eyes, and crosses her hands over her heart. I think that might be meant to pass for sensitive. "Any premature rigor mortis on your part," she continues, "and that bomb's going to be as pissed as any girl who's been cheated of the main event. She's going to blow up all over the place."

I probably could have gone to my grave without having seen the poetry that lurks in Hannah's soul.

"Nah," Hannah continues. "I think, actually, we send the Uhrwerkmänner down first. Hermann and his boys. They're outnumbered like crazy, but their goal is pretty specific—open a path. You and me, we let them pile down there. Help Tabitha and Clyde out a bit. Then, once the path is open, we head down and see how much shit we can fuck up."

That last bit sounds a lot like one of my plans.

"What the feck am I supposed to be doing?" Kayla asks. "Sitting here twiddling my feckin' thumbs?"

"Well, you're fucking up shit already, aren't you?" Hannah doesn't even bat an eyelid. "That's your whole thing. Didn't think I'd have to hold you back."

"Actually," Kayla says with a nod, "I think I feckin' like it when you plan."

And seriously? The moment of disloyalty couldn't have waited until after I'm too dead to hear it?

Footsteps behind us, heavy and clanking. I turn. Hermann, it seems, is done getting his forces on board. "We are ready," he announces.

Everyone just looks at me. Apparently I have to condemn myself. As if I'd have the opportunity to hold it against them for longer than five minutes.

I nod. "Same here. More or less."

"Buck up," says Clyde, "blaze of glory and all that." His voice breaks at the end, and he turns away, eyes glistening.

I worry that if we hold on any longer we're going to slide away from more and toward less.

"The Uhrwerkmänner have to lead the charge," I say to Hermann. "Hannah and I will head to the Uhrwerkgerät as soon as you open a path."

Hermann nods. "Then the honor will be all ours," he says. "It is as it should be."

I decide not to be offended, and just take his agreement as a victory.

"Feckin' wanker." Kayla is less charitable.

Fortunately Hermann is too wrapped up in his moment of glory to pay even the slightest attention to Kayla. He turns to the gathered Uhrwerkmänner.

"For our past!" he shouts. "For the future that lies beyond us! For honor! For victory!"

And then, before I can really get a handle on the fact that this is actually finally happening, he's moving. The charge is on. The end begins.

77

It is, I have to say, an impressive sight. As battered, dented, and outnumbered as they are, Hermann's troops do put on a pretty good show at the end.

They move with all the mechanical precision they have been endowed with. Their feet fall with one motion. The ground shakes at the combined impact. Their arms swing—thirty pairs of synchronous pendulums. The glowing blue light that suffuses the Uhrwerkgerät reflects off the sharp edges of the gashes in their metal skin. Their battle-scarring becomes their glory in this moment.

They are going to die. They know that. And they charge into the moment with their heads held high.

Personally I'm more concerned with not shitting myself. Nobody wants soiled trousers to be part of their legacy.

Clyde is muttering to himself. I can hear the battery clacking around behind his teeth. "Hold," I say. "Hold."

The Uhrwerkmänner are only a quarter of the way down the stairs before they're spotted. A cry rises from below. Another. Robots turn and stare.

I can see Kayla among the descending Uhrwerkmänner. She rides first on one robot's shoulders, then another's. She dances over them, making her way forward, blade gleaming.

The dull boom of Friedrich's voice joins the chorus rising up to meet them. The sentries start to move, to bunch at the bottom of the stairs.

Hermann, Kayla, and the others are halfway down now.

Friedrich keeps yelling. The Uhrwerkmänner start to form ranks. Row upon row of them. Weapons begin to bristle.

On the ledge, Clyde has his battery in his mouth. It click-click-clicks against his teeth. Hannah has her gun drawn. Tabitha's laptop is open.

"Hold," I say.

Three-quarters of the way down the stairs now. Clyde begins to mutter.

"Hold."

Closing the distance. Clyde's voice starting to rise.

"Now!"

Clyde flings out his arms. "*Maldor!*" he bellows. And then he is flying backwards through the air, as if yanked by an enormous bungee cord, up and away, slamming against the ceiling of the stone corridor before collapsing like a rag doll to the floor.

Below us, the front ranks of Friedrich's Uhrwerkmänner come apart. Something massive detonates in the heart of them. They fly like steel leaves caught in an autumn tempest.

Hermann's forces hit the bottom of the stairs, pile into the suddenly tattered ranks. Fists fly. Flame arches and leaps. Harsh Germanic cries fill the air, like seagulls without a sense of humor. I see Kayla fly from the shoulders of the Uhrwerkmänn she was riding, arc up over Friedrich's forces. She comes down blade first.

Hermann buries a fist into the face of one of his opponents, crushes metal, turns the skull inside out. Cogs and gears fly, but his opponent keeps on swinging. Wild, uncoordinated limbs crash against Hermann's sides, denting the bronze panels. Hermann brings a fist down on the truncated skull, exposing the stump of the neck. His fist opens, closes, rips. Gears spill like silver rain. The body collapses to the floor, still kicking spastically.

Around him, further chaos reigns. Uhrwerkmänner stomp and kick. I see one of Friedrich's robots bury its foot in the knee of one of Hermann's men. The joint is crushed, the leg splays out sideways. The Uhrwerkmänn goes down and within moments he is trampled to death.

Kayla appears for a moment, flitting from shoulder to shoulder. Her sword snicker-snacks in and out of Uhrwerkmänner joints, introducing limps, stutters, and jerks. Her blade is black with oil. Hermann's forces take full advantage.

Friedrich himself wanders into the fray. He is like a giant among children. He backhands one Uhrwerkmänn out of his way. Whether it was on his side or Hermann's I'm not sure. I don't think Friedrich cares. The Uhrwerkmänn goes flying, cracks against one wall, lies still. Friedrich sends another after that one. His fist floors another. He piles toward Hermann as the fighting swirls around him.

I turn to Tabitha. "We *need* to take Friedrich down."

Behind us, Clyde is lying on the floor, blood dripping from one ear. Tabitha runs to him.

"Shit," she says. "Get up. Get up, you stupid shit." She slaps him about the head and neck.

It's not the most tender expression of affection I've ever seen, but there is a chance—

"Get up, you dumb fuck."

OK. Possibly not affection after all.

Beside me, at the ledge, Hannah has her gun up, is firing down into the crowd. Whether she's hitting our Uhrwerkmänner or Friedrich's, I have no idea. I doubt she's doing much to any of them at this range. But it's better than nothing. Neither time nor numbers are on our side.

I try to assess the situation. Can we descend yet? But the path to the Uhrwerkgerät is still clogged with mechanical bodies fighting and flailing.

I glance back at Clyde.

"What the hell happened to him?" I ask.

"Recoil," is all the explanation Tabitha is willing to give. She slaps Clyde again. His head snaps sideways.

"Come on," she mutters. "Stupid lack of team redundancy." She grabs him by the lapels, heaves him into a sitting position, and proceeds to vigorously shake him.

"Maybe," I suggest, "that's not the best way to—"

"Have to agree!" Clyde blurts, his eyes flying open. "Could we perhaps, possibly, please…"

Tabitha stops her shaking, releases his lapels, drops him. Clyde sags, only just catching himself on one elbow.

"Oh," he moans, raising the other to his bruised temple. "Going to feel that tomorrow." He looks about. "Did it help at least? One does like to feel that one is being helpful. Sort of validates oneself. Especially when significant personal injury is involved."

"Get back there," is all the encouragement Tabitha gives him.

"Fair enough." Clyde stumbles to his feet, manages to scamper two steps forward, lands on all fours, regains his feet, and makes it the rest of the way leaning heavily against the wall of the corridor.

I glance at Tabitha. She shrugs. "Best we've got," she says.

Best we've got. God, that's actually a pretty accurate assessment of the entire situation.

I meet Clyde at the ledge. "We've got to take down Friedrich," I tell him. "Something substantial."

Clyde turns. "Tabby, what have you got?" He starts rooting through his pockets, pulls out a large oblong battery about the size of his fist. "Preferably something that involves this." He licks both his thumbs, presses one to one contact on the battery, leaves the other hovering over the second.

"All right," Tabitha mutters. "Try this." She flips around the screen of her laptop so Clyde can see.

"Oooh." His eyes light up. "I always wanted to try that one. Possibly not very sporting of us. But then it doesn't seem to me like the chap aiming to end all of reality as we know it is particularly sporting either. So let's see what sort of damage we can do, shall we?"

He grins at Tabitha. Her utterly blank expression meets the smile and absorbs it without a ripple. Clyde appears oblivious. He starts to mutter.

"*Calthor mal maltor cal talto.*" The gibberish of magic. "*Caltem kel talnor.*" He presses his spare thumb to the battery's second contact. "*Feltor!*" he yells. And as he does, something begins to emerge from his mouth.

A black cloud explodes out of his mouth. Smoke exhaled with a speed and ferocity that makes it seem as if it possesses a will of its own.

Clyde reels back, gasping.

The cloud streaks across the room. The smell of sulfur and soot clogs the space around us. I cough, back away, still trying to keep track of what's happening even as my eyes start to stream.

The smoke smashes into Friedrich, seems to cling to him, cloying. He is enveloped in seconds. Jagged plumes spin out from the maelstrom, strike those around him. I see raw gashes of pitted metal left on those it hits.

"What the hell?" I manage.

"Invention of a Slovenian man, I believe," Clyde says. His throat sounds raw. "Little caustic on the lungs unfortunately. Think I'm going to have to rest for a bit after that." He coughs. Redness stains his lips. "Maybe longer than a moment."

Friedrich flails. He is almost more deadly now than he was before. One hand catches an Uhrwerkmänn full in the face. The head lifts from the shoulders, flies across the room, smashes into another robot, sends it sprawling to the ground. Friedrich slams into one wall, spins around.

"Shit," Hannah breathes. "If he blunders into the bloody Uhrwerkgerät…"

But the smoke is starting to dissipate now, the bulk of Friedrich emerging. He is still standing, but the surface of him is ruined. The once shining metal is pitted and scarred. In parts it's worn away completely—the gearwork beneath exposed. The thick bulk of his head is ruined on one side, the steel skull showing through horribly.

"Ooph. Fucking right," Hannah says. "Score one for the home team."

Beside me, Clyde coughs again, more blood dribbling down his chin. "Might have to sit down in truth," he manages, sagging downward.

I cast a look at him, concerned. "You OK?" I ask.

"Erm," Clyde hedges, and hacks again.

"Shit," Tabitha says, but she hasn't looked over once at Clyde, she's looking down into the pit.

I follow her gaze. Friedrich, the ruin of him, is standing at the heart of the frothing fight. He is staring directly at us. And I think Clyde's spell just gave our position away.

Still at least there's a considerable number of Uhrwerkmänner he'd have to wade through even to make it to the stairs. Maybe now he's injured he'll have a hard time making it all the way.

That thought seems to cross Friedrich's mind too. He plunges a massive fist into the crowd, comes up clutching a smaller Uhrwerkmänn by the metallic scruff of its neck. It kicks and spits furiously. An angry dervish. Friedrich braces.

I realize what is about to happen the moment before it does.

"Oh shit." Tabitha echoes my thoughts.

Then Friedrich's arm sails forward. With a mighty heave he flings the Uhrwerkmänn through space toward us.

78

The Uhrwerkmänn lances through the air, a shrieking whirlwind of bronze and unfettered rage.

Tabitha shrieks, genuflects away. I dive for cover, though the chances of me making it to any sort of safety are so slim they make fashion models everywhere jealous. Whether Friedrich is aiming to land his acolyte among us, or just looking to use him as a vehicle-sized grenade, I don't know, and I don't think it matters.

Hannah stays on her feet, keeps firing. But those shots that do hit their target achieve nothing in impeding the course of our assailant.

Clyde staggers to his feet. Blood is running freely down his chin now. He jams a battery into his mouth. His jaw starts to work.

"No!" Tabitha yells.

The oncoming Uhrwerkmänn is yards away. Less than a fraction of a second.

Clyde's arm comes up. He bellows a word. Blood sprays from his mouth in a great gout.

The flying Uhrwerkmänn detonates. Less than a yard from us it makes impact against a vast invisible wall. Limbs, and gears, and bronze sheet metal, and copper rods, and ball bearings fly through the air, bursting around us.

Clyde flies back as if struck. Blood sprays from his mouth and nose. He lands heavily on his back, not moving.

Pieces of the Uhrwerkmänn rain down on the Uhrwerkgerät and the fight below.

"Shit!" Tabitha rushes to Clyde, seizes his shoulder, stares. "Shit. Shit. Shit."

I join her. Blood leaks from Clyde's mouth, a slow but steady stream. It is starting to pool around his head. His breath is shallow and wet. Tabitha has an eyelid pulled back. His pupil is buried somewhere in the confines of his skull, staring at nothing.

"What did he do?" I ask. I feel helpless.

"Don't know," Tabitha says, not looking at me. "Too much." She is not slapping or shaking him now. Her fingers are soft as they explore his skin.

"Arthur!" Hannah yells from behind me. "Now!"

At first I don't understand the words. I am too caught up in the disaster before me. This is not how this was supposed to go down. I am the one who is supposed to die. Not Clyde. This is the time for my noble sacrifice, not his. I am meant to die to save him. That's the whole point. To save my friends. Now is the time for my sacrifice. Not his.

Now.

Now.

"Now!" Hannah yells again. "We have to move!"

Oh God. She means… this is it. This is the moment. And I am not ready. But I have to be ready. I have to…

I stumble away from Clyde, not quite able to take my eyes off him. The pool of blood around his head is too big. Is too much.

I hit the stairs, stumble, try to right myself. I can see down into the pit below.

Hermann has driven himself at Friedrich. The hand of his splinted arm has torn through the devastated armor plating covering the giant Uhrwerkmänn's stomach, and his fist is buried among the cogs beneath. Friedrich is smashing great blows down on Hermann's shoulder, like a blacksmith at the forge. With each blow Friedrich's damaged fist flakes great shards of metal, but still he crushes Hermann's joint out of recognition.

With his remaining good hand Hermann delivers a pile driver of a blow to Friedrich's exposed chin. The ragged metal gives way.

The jaw unhinges, tears away. Gears and oil gush out. Friedrich gives an inarticulate roar. His blows redouble. But Hermann drives his feet forward, pushes the giant back.

We are halfway down now. I look back, search for Clyde, but he has disappeared behind the lip of the stairs. I stumble over one step, another. He has to survive. He has to pull through. He has to be alive so I can save him. I have to save all of them.

That thought gives me the strength to keep my feet steady beneath me. Hannah reaches out, grabs my wrist, helps pull me forward, onward, down.

An Uhrwerkmänn sees us coming, steps to block the bottom of the stairs. But then Kayla is there. She swipes her sword across the back of its knee. It topples.

Then we are on it. Hannah and I leap together. My feet strike the Uhrwerkmänn's toppling back, and then I am scrambling and slipping down, jumping over its tangling legs.

Then we are in the thick of it. Running pell-mell across the battlefield. Hannah's hand helps propel me. We run parallel. Then I am ahead. Then I am leaving her behind. There is a moment of panic. With two of us, this seemed more manageable. But navigating the field of smashing limbs alone… But then I remember: she has to drop back. She has to be ready to take the shot. This is on me.

I skid beneath a flailing limb, hurdle a rogue leg. I twist between two clashing bodies, pull up short as two Uhrwerkmänner crash through my path, then dive forward as flaming oil arcs through the air toward me.

I set my sights on my goal. Volk's blunt corpse in the heart of the Uhrwerkgerät. The structural weak point beside him.

Wait.

The structural weak point.

That Clyde is meant to destroy. Clyde who is unconscious and bleeding out above me.

How the hell am I meant to take down the Uhrwerkgerät? It's massive. A welded monstrosity of steel girders and titanic bronze bodies. And I am not equipped with explosives, a grenade. What the hell do I do?

I want to slow down, to call a timeout so we can all think this through rationally. But the momentum of the moment has me, is pulling me forward. There is no stopping this now.

Shit. Shit. And shit. And balls.

A final Uhrwerkmänn lunges in front of me. It aims a claw-like hand at me, swipes. I skid to a halt, tottering on the tips of my toes. The claws whisper past my stomach. I am less than an inch from having to carry my bowels with me as I run.

The Uhrwerkmänn steps forward, ensures the range is more disembowelment-friendly.

And as if in response to the invitation, Kayla is there, disemboweling the machine.

I am struck by how similar the moment is to a human death. An oil slick chain slips from the wound, drags larger clots of gearwork with it. The Uhrwerkmänn stands staring for a moment.

I stare at Kayla. "Where did you...?" is all I can gasp.

"Get the feck on with you!" Kayla shoves me forward. I fly a few additional feet closer to the Uhrwerkgerät.

"I can't," I say.

"Can't?" She stares at me as if assessing me for signs of a serious mental defect. "The thing's about to feckin' go. Can't you feel it?"

This is as desperate as I've ever seen Kayla. And it's that alone that makes me pause, take stock. And she's right. I can feel something. An ugly pressure in my sinuses, behind my eyes. The first quaking warnings of a headache that will split my skull. Oh shit.

"The weak point," I say. "The structural weak point. We can't..." I am too out of breath to get it all out.

"Clyde," Kayla snaps. And he was indeed the plan.

"Down," I pant back.

Kayla rolls her eyes. "Want something done..." she says. And starts to accelerate toward me. I brace for impact.

Somehow another Uhrwerkmänn manages to insert itself into the space between us. Kayla's blade whips out fast enough to make the air crack. Then the Uhrwerkmänn is no longer between us.

She is beside me. "Come on." And then we are running together. Her grip is like a metal band around my arm. My feet fly over the ground, barely making contact.

And then we're there. In the heart of it. I am staring up at Volk. At what is left of Volk. Bathed in the cold blue light of him.

The pressure is greater here. The pain in my sinuses has sharp edges. There is a buzzing in my ears and the edges of my vision are blurred. I grit my teeth. The sounds of the fight beyond seem distant, muffled. As if they're happening elsewhere. Or not everywhere that I am. *Highly reality permeable.* That was how Tabitha described this bomb. And the blurring at the edges of my vision. It comes clear for a second. Other realities lying over this one. Other fights. Other forces. Robot fighting man. Man fighting man. Other, more exotic encounters. And a blank room. And no room at all; just rock; everything buried in rock.

I clutch my head.

"No feckin' time for that shite." Kayla's voice is more present, more insistent than the fight. She's close to the core with me. Everywhere and everywhen that I am.

She grabs a hold of one girder, flips her body horizontal, suspended above the ground, braces her feet against a cross-beam and starts to heave.

I can't understand what she's doing at first. Because it's absurd. Impossible. And then I see the welds. Fat and fresh, holding the beams together. And it's still absurd, still impossible. She is trying to force the girders apart, through sheer force of muscle. And even for her...

There is an ungodly popping noise. A crack like the sky splitting. The ground shakes beneath me.

There is a crack in the weld.

Kayla's entire body is taut. Her skin is a red that puts her hair to shame. Muscles bulge. She makes an anatomical model of herself. A dull moan of effort slips between clenched teeth, adds itself to the background rumble of distorting realities.

And that crack got the Uhrwerkmänner's attention. I can see them turning, staring.

Another earth-shattering crack. The split in the weld is larger now. The pain in my head spikes sharper, the pitch of the buzzing in my ears is higher. The flickering of other nows almost blinds me.

Overlaid over it all, Kayla drops to the ground in front of me.

"Come on," she says. "Feckin' help already."

"I…" I stare at the beams. I shrug at the impossibility of it. "I'm not like you."

"You have to be the one, right?" Kayla says, voice urgent. I can see Uhrwerkmänner starting to move toward us through the tangle of the bomb's infrastructure. "That was the whole point of your talk up there, wasn't it? You have to bring it down?"

"I…" I say. "I don't know." I can't remember now. There's too much chaos within and without.

"Well it's a bit feckin' late to gamble." Kayla reaches over her shoulder, pulls out her sword. "Jam this in the gap. Use it like a lever."

It's a ridiculous thing to ask. Like I could contribute anything that wasn't utterly insignificant. But maybe insignificant is enough. It will be a contribution. I don't know the rules I'm playing with here. But I do know that the Uhrwerkmänner are closing in on us.

I jam the blade into the crack. One inch of the sword's tip finds its way in. I push to no avail. Kayla takes up position on the far side of the girder. She strains.

I heave. I feel like a fool. What can I expect to do?

The Uhrwerkmänner are closer now. They are too large for the going to be easy or half as fast as our entrance, but they will still get here and get here soon.

Another crack. The fabric of reality seems to shimmer in front of me.

Not yet. Not another future echo yet. This was meant to be quick. A single strike. This is giving reality too much time to drop a brick in its pants.

"Come on!" I urge no one in particular. Thankfully Kayla is too busy grunting with exertion to take it personally. "Come on!"

Another crack. The blade sinks six inches into the seam. I heave, even as reality roils. I can feel the blade flex. But… is there something else too?

Kayla is screaming now, barely audible over the whine of the *Uhrwerkgerät* as it starts to go critical. Another sound. Less of a crack and more of a crunching, ripping sound. The blade jerks beneath my arms, I stagger back.

The girder has given way. A great bend in it. Above us metal starts to buckle. The Uhrwerkmänner slow in their approach, suddenly wary.

Kayla drops to the floor. Sweat has soaked every inch of her. Her hair is matted to her scalp and shoulder.

"All you now," she pants. "One last heave."

I yank on the blade. It's as ridiculous as it ever was. I feel the blade flex dangerously.

"Not feckin' yet!" Kayla snaps. "Wait 'til I'm feckin' clear."

"I can't," I say, trying to wipe intruding realities from the corners of my eyes. Kayla is a blur. "The blade will break," I try to explain.

"So let it feckin' break." She shrugs. "Renny fair piece of shite. And anyway, what am I going to do? Kill you?"

Oh God. This is it. This is genuinely it. My stomach drops and keeps on going. There is no bottom for it to hit. Just the endless maw of eternity opening up before me.

Kayla turns away. I grab her shoulder. "Tell Felicity," I say. "Tell her…" I don't have the words. There's too much to tell. "Tell her everything."

"Aye." There's surprising softness in Kayla's voice. "I'll do that."

I smile, grateful. "Hell," I say, "if there's any way you can patch things up with Ephie in the next eight seconds and have her save my ass, that would be great too."

"Feck off." And then Kayla is gone, speeding away, a blur of motion of shimmering realities.

I am on my own, surrounded by Uhrwerkmänner. They restart their approach. And this is it. This is the end of the end.

79

I take a breath. I grab the sword. I heave.

Why the hell didn't I move in with Felicity? What sort of jackass am I?

The blade starts to bow. Above me metal cracks and crunches, welds popping, girders buckling.

I got so caught up in dying. God, I really screwed MI37 over. They're going to be rolled into MI6. Because of me. That's my goddamn legacy. Jesus.

I heave harder on the blade. I reach the maximum pressure I can exert. I swing my legs up, mimicking Kayla, legs braced against the cross-beam, hanging almost upside down, heaving on the sword handle, punching metal with my legs.

Give. Give way, you bastard beam.

Hannah. I should have been better to Hannah. If I'd just listened to Felicity I could have left something so much better behind.

The blade bows further. The feel of something shifting beneath me.

Shit. Hannah. She has to shoot me. She has to... God, she has to kill me. I've lost track of her in the chaos. I search the crowd but it's out of focus, the Uhrwerkgerät screaming too loudly in my head to let me see.

Can she see me? Can she take the shot? God, this could be an awful mess.

One last heave. And something gives. Something breaks. I feel it the instant before the consequences hit me. Time is warping, becoming strange and sluggish. The blade breaks. A clear ringing sound, a beautiful counterpoint to the static of the Uhrwerkgerät.

The beam beneath my feet gives way. With a noise to end the world.

I smash to the ground. Pieces of Kayla's sword spatter the metal plates around me.

And above...

I see the first girder give way. It looks like it's falling in slow motion. Clanging against another, knocking it free. Turning end over end. Another then another. All of the Uhrwerkgerät coming down on me.

And then, beyond that. A flicker of motion, up on the ledge of the stairs. Back where I left Clyde and Tabitha. But not a scruffy collegiate man. Not an angry Pakistani goth with her short hair molded into devil horns.

A beam hits the ground beside me. Plunges through an Uhrwerkmänn, unseaming it. Another strikes, crushes two of the robots.

I barely pay attention. I am trying to see. It's someone else up there. A girl perhaps. Flowing hair. A bright yellow and pink summer dress billowing about her.

I pick myself up on one elbow, raise myself even as everything else collapses.

A girder eclipses my vision. A yard away. It is the face of oblivion.

And then Hannah's bullet smashes against my temple and buries itself in my brain.

80

AFTER?

God, oblivion blows.

I mean, for starters it can be really goddamn painful. It arrives, it drifts—the pain—swirling over me. And I am buried by it in the dark. And then it fades, melting away, some warmth flooding my veins. Only the darkness remaining. And then time passes in its own vague meaningless way. And then it all starts again.

Yes, oblivion is excruciatingly repetitive. That's another thing I dislike.

It strikes me that I had a lot of regrets when I died. That I had made a lot of poor decisions. So perhaps this is hell. It seems a little low budget compared to what was advertised, but I can imagine an eternity of this really starting to grate.

The next time the pain comes it brings other things with it. A dull beeping, which does little to improve the atmosphere. And an uncomfortable pressure all over my body. It strikes me that the pain is gaining specificity. My head, my legs, one arm. The pain is sharper there, duller elsewhere.

At least it's a change.

Time passes. The pain comes again. But this time, instead of burying me it brings light. A sharp crack of it that I try to shy away from. But it pursues me. There is the beeping, but other noises too. I get the impression of being surrounded by enormous amounts of activity. And I don't want any part of it. It is too much. I think of the falling girders.

Oblivion, I think, is taking a turn for the worse.

CONSCIOUSNESS

"He's awake!"

Whoever is shouting is doing it too loudly.

I blink. The room is a smear of too-bright color and sound. Beeping, and chairs scraping, and voices, and feet slapping on a vinyl floor.

"He's awake!" The same voice again. The same volume. But I know that voice.

I blink more, try to bring things into focus. I feel like I have been too confused for too long.

Aren't I meant to be dead? Wasn't that part of the deal? I seem to remember being sure about that.

Didn't I get shot in the head?

I try to raise my hand, to feel for the spot where pain bloomed. It comes again, sharp and hard, leaving me gasping. My arm flops to the bed. It feels weak.

The bed.

I am in a bed.

More blinking.

"Arthur? Arthur, can you hear me?"

A shape. An oval. A silhouette. And then a face. And then a face I know.

"Felicity?"

"Oh thank God."

And it is her. And with that recognition everything else starts to snap into focus. Details of the room. Details of everything that happened before coming together at once.

A hospital bed. A hospital room. No, a ward. And more than

just Felicity here. Others too. And windows and light. It is day, and I am alive.

"I'm alive," I say. I don't understand it. This should be impossible. If I'm alive reality should be dead. So either way... Well, I should be dead.

"But you're not." Felicity kisses my forehead. Her lips feel sweet and cool, tamping down the fire of the pain there.

I'm not.

I'm not and Felicity is kissing me. After everything I did. After everything I failed to do. I do not deserve this.

I try to twist away, but my body feels sluggish and it makes my head hurt. Still she pulls away. There is concern in her eyes.

"Are you—?" she starts.

"I'm sorry," I say. It needs to be said. "I'm so sorry. I screwed everything up. I got... I got everything twisted. I made everything worse. MI37... Moving in..."

She shakes her head. "There's nothing to worry about. We'll talk about that later. When you're feeling better."

Nurses and doctors are entering the room. Other people are leaving. I should be paying attention to who they are, but I only have eyes for Felicity.

I jerk my hand about, find hers, squeeze.

"I don't know why I didn't move in with you," I say. "I can't think of the reason why."

She smiles. "Well, you took a blow to the head."

"Please," I ask. "Please, if I haven't screwed up too much, can I move in with you?"

And she smiles. But, "We'll talk," is all she says.

AFTER THE REMOVAL OF SEVERAL RATHER INTIMATE TUBES

Just before the nurses leave, they prop me up, and pull the curtains back from around my bed so I can get a proper look at the room. It has four beds in total. Two are empty. One is not.

Clyde lies in the bed opposite mine. He has an oxygen mask pulled down around his neck. He waves.

"Hello, Arthur, terribly good to see you." His voice sounds husky. "They tell me I'm not supposed to speak for another few days but that's rather an exercise in futility, I'm afraid. Just keep jibber-jabbing on to people about how I'm not meant to talk to them, and then I keep on going until all of a sudden I'm coughing up blood again, and then the nurses come in and tell me how I'm not meant to talk to anyone. So then I start trying to explain it to them. And that just makes everything worse, but it turns out I have an almost pathological tendency to tell people not to make a fuss. So, to make a long story short, they tend to tranquilize me quite a lot. Not entirely unpleasant, though one does worry about developing a dependency. The last thing I—"

"You. Shut it." A strident voice from the door. And Tabitha, it seems, has a different tactic from the nurses.

"Oh, sorry," Clyde says. "I was just—"

"Shut it." Tabitha crosses to his bed, eyes aflame.

Clyde hesitates, mouth still open.

"It. Shut. Now."

Clyde shuts it.

Tabitha sits on the edge of the bed, reaches out, messes his hair. "Fucking idiot," she says. Clyde grins hugely.

I narrow my eyes. "Wait…" I say. "Are you two…?"

Clyde opens his mouth.

"You say a word," Tabitha tells him, "and I will throttle you with your own tongue. See if they can fix that."

Clyde satisfies himself with grinning hugely.

"Yes," Tabitha says. "Easier to have a discussion with him when he can't talk. Freaked out a bit. I did. First pregnancy. Then the whole near death thing. His. Mine. All that. Latter put the former in perspective."

"Oh," I say. "So…" And how to broach this exactly. "The…" I look at her stomach.

Tabitha grimaces. "Gone," is all she says. Then, as if sensing that maybe even from her this isn't enough. "In the fight. Nothing permanent done."

"Another time," Clyde says in his scratched voice. "I mean not to suggest necessarily that it would be me, or you, well obviously it would be you, I suppose, but—"

"Shut the goddamn fuck up." And then to make sure he does, Tabitha kisses him.

I turn away. That moment is not mine to watch. Instead I try to process the news. I can't tell if it's good or bad. But the kiss is still going on, so maybe that is all the answer I really need.

Another face appears at the door. Not Felicity's. That's all I care about at first. Just some young girl. And then I realize that I know who it is.

"Ephie?" I say.

Clyde and Tabitha break their clinch. Clyde has the decency to look embarrassed. Tabitha doesn't.

Ephie looks at Clyde as she steps into the room and rolls her eyes. "Like that's the worst a pan-dimensional demigod has seen you two do," she says.

"Ach, I'm right here. There's stuff you have no need to feckin' share." Kayla follows her step-daughter into the room.

Ephie it seems has decided to modify her wardrobe slightly. Her hair is not scraped back in a ponytail, but instead hangs loose. She's dyed the tips light pink. They match her sun dress, unseasonable in the November chill, but good for showing off the tattoos that cover her shoulders and upper arms. Dense floral patterns in green and red and yellow.

Kayla catches my look. "We're negotiating," she says, looking grim.

From Ephie's smile, it looks like she's winning the negotiations.

I try to work out why the Dreamer is here. There's only one reason I can think of.

"You're why I'm alive," I say, "aren't you?"

Ephie's smile dissolves like so much mist. She nods, serious now.

"You said you wouldn't," I say. "That it would violate too many other realities."

"Yes," she says. "I said that."

It takes me a moment to realize it, but she looks embarrassed.

"So it didn't."

She shrugs, awkward, looking for a moment like the thirteen-year-old she is. "Think I'm probably going to get in some trouble," she says. "But, well, you twisted a lot of things to help me out. Collapsing the device, getting injured. There was a lot less I needed to do to make sure the future echoes were only promising you injury, not death. Not to say there wasn't collateral damage…" She trails off, but it seems like she's leaving out the most important part.

"Collateral damage?" I prompt. Possibly with slightly too much alarm in my voice. A machine pings.

"Like," she shrugs, "who do you think killed JFK?"

I stare at her for a moment. "Lee Harvey Oswald," I say. "With the grassy knoll, second-gunman theory knocking about."

"Yeah," Ephie says, "so that's changed."

Wait… "I used to think it was someone different?"

Ephie shrugs. "I wouldn't worry about it. Just give yourself a headache."

Kayla grimaces. "I did."

I can't help but notice that Kayla hasn't threatened her daughter with a sword any time in the past few minutes.

"You two seem on better terms," seems like the more tactful way to say it.

"Well," Kayla shrugs. "She did good. Even with tattoos." She reaches out and ruffles her daughter's hair.

"Mum!" Ephie pulls away, tugs at her hair, then shrugs. Reality ripples and suddenly her hair is piled upon her head in a giddy heap of tangles. The pink hints have become blue.

Kayla rolls her eyes. "Feckin' kids."

Ephie smirks. "Had enough of them, have you?"

"I've feckin' apologized!" Kayla throws up her hands. "God, more of you feckers. Don't know what I was thinking."

Which makes it sound like the artificial insemination plan is off the table. Or off whatever it was on. I don't want to think about that too closely. Still, this seems like a more unmitigated positive for me to get behind.

"There you bloody are," a voice says from the door. It's Hannah. She's looking at Kayla. "I thought you said we were going to go down the pub now we know he's awake."

"Ephie wanted to see him," Kayla says without any hint of apology in her tone.

"She finished?"

"Good to see you too," I say.

Hannah looks at me. "You know you've ruined my perfect record of kill shots, don't you?" She grins.

I point weakly at Ephie. "Technically that was her not me." I swear I can still remember the bullet striking my skull. I can remember dying. A shiver runs through me.

"Come on then," says Ephie, "we shouldn't tire him out."

"I'm fine," I protest, but truth be told I am tired now. Kayla and Ephie cross the room. Tabitha though seems to show no sign of leaving, settling her head on Clyde's shoulder.

"Maybe you'll end up permanently mute," she says to him, a smile on her lips. He kisses the top of her head. I don't think I'll ever understand them.

Halfway across the room, Kayla pauses. "Hey," she says to Hannah, still waiting in the doorway, "did you tell him yet?"

"How the hell would I have bloody told him? He's been conscious for about twenty minutes and you've been here the whole time I have."

Kayla shrugs. "Telepathy?" Off Hannah's expression, "This job has shown me weirder shite than that."

"Tell me what?" I say before the moment spirals away from me.

Hannah grimaces slightly. "MI6 turned down my transfer request," she says. "Looks like I'm stuck with you bunch of dysfunctional bastards."

And then she's turning away, and she's gone, Kayla and Ephie eclipsing her exit, and before I can even process that news they're all gone.

"How are you feeling?"

I start at the sudden interruption into my thoughts. And it's Felicity. The one person I was waiting for and I almost didn't notice here because—

"MI6 turned down Hannah's transfer request," I say.

Felicity nods.

"So she's not going to MI6," I say.

Another nod.

"She's staying with MI37."

Felicity nods a third time, but I know her patience isn't legendary.

Hannah's staying. Which means…

"MI6 isn't taking over MI37," I say. "They turned Hannah away."

And Felicity smiles. "Yes," she says. "I knew that."

"So I didn't…" I try to come to terms with this new reality. "I didn't screw it all up. I didn't steal your legacy."

Felicity nods. "Not for lack of trying maybe."

Oh fuck. Oh Jesus. And how to put it into words. "I am so… I can't even express…" I look at her, helpless before the limits of my vocabulary. "I fucked up," I tell her. "So much. And I couldn't see it. Not until it was too late." I bite my lip. Realization hits me. "It's too late, isn't it?"

Felicity sits down heavily on the bed next to me. "Well," her smile is a little tight, "you were under a fair amount of pressure at the time."

"Not enough to excuse what I did," I say. "I was an ass."

Felicity's smile is broader this time. "Not much of a defense attorney, are you?"

"I will make it up to you," I say. "Even if you don't take me back. Even if it takes the rest of—"

"Well," Felicity cuts me off, "you did save the world." Another smile. "Again."

I shrug. "I suppose so, yeah."

"That's why they denied her transfer request, you know? Because of you."

I need a moment with that.

Because of me.

"You saved MI37, Arthur," Felicity says quietly. "You're the one who put it in danger, but you saved it in pretty spectacular style, I do have to say." Her fingers curl around mine. She leans in close. "You almost died," she says. Her voice is a fist of emotion.

"I thought I had to," I say. "I couldn't see another way out."

There are tears in the corners of Felicity's eyes. They are in mine. "I don't want to live without you," she says.

"I didn't even want to die without you," I tell her.

She holds me then, pulls my weak body up out of the bed and

clutches it to her. We kiss. Long enough that I think it may make Tabitha regret hanging out with Clyde.

When we break, her hair is messed. I push it out of her eyes.

"Can I ask you a question?" I ask.

"Yes."

"Can I please move in with you?"

"Yes."

It is like light inside of me. A bubble of joy filling me as we kiss again. Longer. Deeper.

Eventually she pulls away. We're still smiling.

"To new beginnings," she says.

I smile and nod. "To new beginnings."

ABOUT THE AUTHOR

Jonathan Wood is an Englishman in New York. There's a story in there involving falling in love and flunking out of med school, but in the end it all worked out all right, and, quite frankly, the medical community is far better off without him, so we won't go into it here. His debut novel, *No Hero* was described by *Publishers Weekly* as "a funny, dark, rip-roaring adventure with a lot of heart, highly recommended for urban fantasy and light science fiction readers alike." Barnesandnoble.com listed it has one of the twenty best paranormal fantasies of the past decade, and Charlaine Harris, author of the Sookie Stackhouse novels described it as "so funny I laughed out loud." He has continued the Arthur Wallace novels with *Yesterday's Hero*, *Anti-Hero* and *Broken Hero*, all available from Titan Books. He can be found online at

www. jonathanwoodauthor.com.

YESTERDAY'S HERO

BY JONATHAN WOOD

Another day. Another zombie T-Rex to put down.
All part of the routine for Arthur Wallace and MI37—
the government department devoted to battling
threats magical, supernatural, extra-terrestrial, and
generally odd. Except a zombie T-Rex is only the first
of his problems... Before he can say, "But didn't I
save the world yesterday?" a new co-director at MI37
is threatening his job, middle-aged Russian cyborg
wizards are threatening his life, and his co-workers are
threatening his sanity.

"Give **Yesterday's Hero** a well-deserved read, and think
about what you would do when faced with a slavering
dinosaur that figures your skull would make a tasty
treat." **THE EXAMINER.COM**

TITANBOOKS.COM